Praise for Juliet E. McKenna

"If your appetite is for fantasy in the epic tradition, with compelling narratives, authentic combat and characters you care about, Juliet E. McKenna is definitely the author for you."
- Stan Nicholas, author of *Orcs*

"The book is a feast of intriguing plot and well-drawn characters, set in a splendidly realized world. High magic, treachery and revenge keep the reader turning the pages."
- Katherine Kerr, author of *License to Ensorcell*

"Juliet McKenna writes classic epic fantasy at its best: with swords, sorcery, fights, and intrigue a-plenty, wrapped around compelling characters struggling to stay alive in an exceptionally well-drawn world whose order has been disrupted by violence, betrayal, and greed. McKenna's got all the things in her books that I read epic fantasy for."
- Kate Elliott, author of *Cold Magic*

"Juliet E. McKenna invariably delivers an epic fantasy world of real people, sympathetic motivations and delicious consequences. I never know what's going to happen next and I always want to find out!"
- C.E. Murphy, author of *The Walker Papers* series

"Inventive magic, devious intrigue and appealing characters make for an exciting tale, well-told."
- Gail Z. Martin, author of *The Sworn*

"Juliet McKenna's latest mixes magic and politics in a fully realized fantasy world. A rewarding new fantasy from a master of the craft."
- Patrice Sarath, author of *Gordath Wood*

Book 1 of THE HADRUMAL CRISIS

DANGEROUS WATERS

Juliet E. McKenna

SOLARIS

First published 2011 by Solaris
an imprint of Rebellion Publishing Ltd,
Riverside House, Osney Mead,
Oxford, OX2 0ES, UK

www.solarisbooks.com

US ISBN: 978 1 907519 96 3

10 9 8 7 6 5 4 3 2 1

A CIP catalogue record for this book is available from the
British Library.

Designed & typeset by Rebellion Publishing

Printed in the US

For Ernie
much loved and much missed

— CHAPTER ONE —

The Barony of Halferan, Western Caladhria
12th of Aft-Spring
In the 8th Year of Tadriol the Provident of Tormalin

SHE STOOD AT a crossroads. The lodestone twisted on the pewter chain looped around her fingers. She frowned. Until now the metallic black crystal had led her unerringly in this direction. Now it wavered between two roads.

Jilseth disliked imprecision. Furthermore, she had refined this magic herself, blending an untried combination of spells. If there was some flaw in her understanding, she must find it. She had hoped to submit her discovery to the Council of Wizards on her return to Hadrumal. Not now she wouldn't, if there was some inherent ambiguity in the magic for other mages to seize on.

She could ignore those who'd merely seek to draw out her embarrassment, but she wouldn't risk the possibility that someone might find a solution, claiming a decisive share in the credit for her work.

Jilseth focused on the lodestone, on the power flowing around it. Expanding her wizardly senses, she felt its connection to the damp earth beneath her feet, to the rock below the muddy track, to the elemental iron so far beneath that.

In some remote corner of her mind, she still marvelled that so few could see those lines of power. Even a pigeon could feel their tug. But no, for the mundane majority, the way in which pins were drawn to a shiny black rock was a trivial curiosity, perhaps of use to tailors but no more than that. To Jilseth's wizard sight, the unseen forces flowed through the lodestone unhindered. All was as it should be.

What of the magical use she had made of the crystal? Expanding its affinity to sense any magics manipulating earth and stone. This was an old sorcery, honed by generations of wizards and well practised by Jilseth herself. She found no error there.

The next step. To sense the elemental air, fire and water that combined with the essence of earth to make up the world around her. Magebirth only conveyed a single affinity in most cases; an innate understanding and the ability to influence one of the four elements. It took an apprentice wizard several years of dedicated study to master other magics in addition to those of their birthright, and only then when guided by more experienced mages with a talent for explaining their own instinctive perceptions of the elements.

Now Jilseth's awareness encompassed the breezes ruffling the new leaves on the ill-kempt hedges. She sensed the warmth of the sun lending vigour to those leaves. She felt the water drawn up through the roots spreading vitality throughout the buckthorn.

Jilseth had been a diligent pupil. She had been equally quick to move beyond the magics of each individual element to the next step in her education; to the quadrate wizardry that blended all four into more complex magecraft. That had only been the start.

Along the way she had also learned caution and control. She kept a tight hold of her wizardly instincts lest she be overwhelmed by the intoxicating sensations of the magic. Now her concern must be the second spell that had attuned this lodestone to search for elements beyond her own mageborn, intuitive grasp. This was a new magic not yet recorded in Hadrumal's libraries, never credited to some long dead mage.

Jilseth tempered her pride. She couldn't claim all the credit. Archmage Planir had summoned her along with three other wizards whose talents he'd noted. He had suggested that they share their understanding of their individual affinities to see what they could learn together of quintessential magic. Where quadrate magic stemmed from one wizard combining the four elements into a single spell, quintessential sorceries required four mages to work together, each drawing the element of their affinity into a union that offered wizardry with a scope far beyond anything that a mage working alone could hope to attain. Like the others, Jilseth had relished the challenge.

Standing on the muddy track, she was soon reassured. They had indeed succeeded in attuning this lodestone to find magic borne of any combination of the elements. Better yet, quintessential magic wasn't subject to the vagaries of wizardry still inextricably tied to the vacillating elements. Quintessential sorcery was as robust as the diamond that was its symbol.

Which only left her individual contribution to this artefact. Only Planir knew of that. Only the Archmage could sanction studies in the esoteric discipline she had chosen.

This was the most compelling of the reasons that kept Jilseth in Hadrumal when erstwhile friends and fellow apprentices had quit the wizard island's strictures.

Peddling magecraft on the mainland was a far less demanding life.

Though some, it was murmured by pupil wizards in Hadrumal's wine shops, some went to Suthyfer now. Mageborn had lived among those merchants and hired swords engaged in trade across the distant ocean for this past handful of years. The rewards for wizardly aid in defying the deadly storms and tides included liberty for mages to explore their talents however they saw fit. Ideally on some suitably remote reef among the scattered islands that were such vital stepping stones to the empty lands the Tormalin Emperor's men had discovered on the far side of the ocean.

Jilseth couldn't deny such freedom was a tempting thought. But she was an earth mage and Planir the Black was not merely the Archmage. He was the Stone Master of Hadrumal and the finest mage of that affinity in ten generations. Even his critics on the Council of Wizards couldn't deny that. There was no one better to teach her.

Besides, she wasn't some mainland mageborn already uprooted from hearth and home when an adolescent elemental affinity had caused chaos and alarm. Some of her fellow apprentices had been shipped off so swiftly that they arrived on Hadrumal's dockside with only the clothes that they stood up in. Starting a new life a second time, on terms of their own choosing, that wasn't such an overwhelming prospect.

Jilseth was the latest daughter of a line of mageborn five generations long. Her roots in Hadrumal went deep. Perhaps that's why Planir had chosen her for this quest. The Hadrumal mageborn would feel most deeply wronged if Minelas's treachery ever came to light.

She had summoned up the elemental echo of blood spilled and bones broken by the foul renegade's magic at the foot of the cliff where his ship had docked. She had bound this lodestone to every resonance of the rare earths and minerals in those dead men's bodies. The unique reverberation of his spells would lead her to the wizard who had so betrayed his birth and his oaths to Hadrumal.

Focusing all her mage-sense on the conflicted stone, she understood. Her spell was working perfectly well. The lodestone indicated a choice of routes. Either way, she'd find a place where Minelas had worked magic.

The question remained. Which road to take? Jilseth looked around. No one worked in these empty fields. Not a cow nor a sheep cropped the first growth of weedy grass. Even though this sodden coastal region lay as flat as rush matting, no roof or chimney stack rose above the horizon.

Had the Caladhrians already abandoned these coastal regions for fear of corsairs' summer depredations? The raiders coming up from the south had been plaguing this coast and the sea lanes offshore for a handful of years now and the spring equinox usually marked the start of the sailing season.

She closed her eyes, the better to sense any infinitesimal variation in the magical resonance. Now that she knew what she was looking for, the difference soon became clear. Minelas had worked magic in two places. He had only killed in one and that had been his most recent magecraft. She must follow the road to the shore.

Jilseth began walking. Twenty or so paces on, the tug of the lodestone drew stronger. The shining grey crystal swung upwards to pull its chain out straight ahead, true as a mariner's compass needle. This was definitely the right path, even if she must measure every pace of it with her own feet.

Not for the first time on this quest, she cursed one limitation of magic. Not only of her magic. All wizards were similarly bound, whatever the tavern tales might say of their uncanny ability to step across hundreds of leagues in a blinding flash of light.

While almost every wizard worthy of the name could use magic to travel from place to place, they could only revisit somewhere they had already been. If not, like Jilseth on this journey, mages were subject like everyone else to the inconveniences of ill-sprung coaches, lame or recalcitrant horses, rutted and mud-choked roads.

Since the best the last village could offer had been a plodding ox cart, Jilseth had opted to walk. At least she could use a sling of woven air to relieve the burden of the battered leather sack she carried, its drawstring over her shoulder.

In the event that she encountered some peasants, or even trailblazing corsairs, she didn't anticipate trouble. Her modest gown was the soft shade of a pigeon's wing, the better to travel unnoticed. There was little else in her appearance to prompt unwelcome interest, even if this spring sunshine found some auburn glints in her long brown hair. Only her luminous hazel eyes might prompt a second glance.

In any event, she could wrap herself in elemental air and simply disappear, leaving the Caladhrian bog-trotters to entertain their mud-stained friends with a tavern tale of encountering a magewoman. Corsairs could flee trembling at the thought of their narrow escape from a wizard's wrath.

She followed the lodestone's continuing pull as the buckthorn hedged fields gave way to open pasture, still with no sign of livestock.

So Minelas had killed a second time. That was an unwelcome revelation, if not entirely unexpected. Jilseth scowled as she trudged along the muddy track. She'd been unpleasantly surprised by tavern tales on this journey, as she sat unnoticed in some corner with a bowl of unremarkable pottage. These mainlanders were far too eager to dwell on magecraft's potential for violence.

There'd been no such stories told in her childhood. Even islanders on Hadrumal with no elemental affinity knew the reality of wizardry. There was no need for wizards to kill. There were countless other ways in which Minelas could have evaded pursuit, when his arrival on Caladhria's shore had been threatened by mounted assailants. Villains they might have been, Jilseth allowed, but Minelas had killed them merely to show off his powers to the awestruck Caladhrians who hoped to hire him to defend them from the corsairs.

As her leather half-boots squelched, another gloss of magic kept them and her stockinged feet within safe from insidious dampness. The ground underfoot was growing markedly wetter, the air dank with the scent of decay. Not the death she was seeking; merely the slow rot of sedge and rushes into the brackish water.

Before she had gone half a league further, glistening shallows stretched away to either side. Only the track rose high enough above the salt marsh for a traveller to pass dry-shod. Two horses might ride abreast, if anyone wealthy enough to travel mounted had business in this backwater.

Jilseth studied the moist ground. A whole troop of horsemen had ridden this way. Hoof prints clustered thick in the mud, crossing and overlapping. She sank down to pass a hand over a waterlogged crescent. A handful of days ago.

She sighed. Then again, not so very long ago, she'd been ten whole days behind Minelas. She was closing in on him. Standing up, she continued, glancing back and forth from the hovering lodestone to the water-blurred path ahead.

It took no magic to mark her destination. Vegetation lay broken on either side of the track. Mud was churned up all around, darkened with lingering bloodstains. Jilseth shoved the lodestone into a pocket in the folds of her skirt and her touch quelled its sorcery. She didn't want any distractions.

Now she could use her chosen expertise. The magic which only those born with an earth affinity could even attempt to master. Nearly all chose to shun it, repelled by its very name without even attempting to understand its fascinations. Necromancy.

Where were the bodies? Jilseth frowned once again. Finding them should have been simplicity. She added a touch of fire to her mage-sense. The mainland custom was always to burn bodies on funeral pyres. That said, if anyone had tried building a pyre here, from sodden wood and green leaves, she wished them luck. They'd need a wizard to raise even a spark and Minelas would have no interest in reducing his victims to ash for a funeral urn.

There! Her wizard sight glimpsed a sunken body deep in the fen. The corpse itself was a horse but Jilseth's necromantic perception could see the dead man trapped beneath it.

Green magelight spread around her feet; the emerald hue of water magic. With her own affinity so focused, she had scant attention to spare for concealing her other workings. It hardly mattered. There was no one here to see but some frogs.

Once off the path, her wizardry ensured her firm footing a handspan above the muddy water. She walked over to the dead horse. Reed lizards had gnawed its ears and nose while some larger scavenger had ripped into its underbelly, releasing bloated entrails into the bog.

A sparkling sapphire veil of air defended Jilseth from the stench. She carefully balanced that spell with the contrary force of the water magic beneath her. By comparison, heaving the horse's dead weight aside demanded a trifle of her inborn affinity with the earth, an amber haze barely colouring the air.

As the dead horse sprawled with a noisome splash she saw the man's corpse. Jilseth locked her anger in that remote corner of her mind where she was accustomed to shove such distractions. Unbridled emotion threw wizardry into confusion, from highest to lowest, and she couldn't afford that here.

The dead man wore a woollen shirt beneath a scuffed leather tunic and buff breeches. A base metal brooch fastened the coarse cloak wrapped around his shoulders. He'd had greying hair but beyond that, no one would ever know him again. Worms and crabs had eaten their fill from his discoloured hands and face.

Jilseth wondered what twist of fortune had left this Caladhrian rotting faceless in the marshes. Well, she could soon find out and those mindless scavengers had made her task a little easier. A necromantic touch plucked a finger from his ravaged hand. She only needed the smallest of bones.

Walking back to solid ground, she unslung the leather sack from her shoulder. The black cloak she had stuffed in the top could protect her skirts from the damp ground. She needed all her energies for other magecraft now.

Folding the heavy cloth, she sat cross legged upon it. The dead man's finger hovered beside her as she took her things from the leather sack. A silver bowl. A small, securely stoppered bottle. She uncorked it to pour clear oil into the bowl. It trickled slow as honey. As she passed her hand over the liquid, amber radiance glowed.

Her gesture sent the dead man's finger into the bowl. The oil seethed, amber magic darkening. Jilseth swept her hands through the steam and thickening smoke, deftly shaping a latticed orb threaded with golden magelight.

A vision formed at its heart. The dead man's last moments. He'd been riding into battle with the troop whose horses had left these hoof prints. Jilseth could see the resolve in their faces.

The dead man turned in his saddle to rebut some comment behind him. 'He's no milksop. He couldn't handle that stallion if he was.'

His nod told Jilseth who he meant. Blue-cloaked, some way ahead, Minelas was riding beside that poor fool of a baron.

As soon as Jilseth learned his name, that noble lord would be answering to the Archmage and the Council of Hadrumal alongside the renegade mage. The edict was absolute. Wizards did not engage in warfare. No matter how grievously these coastal regions had suffered at the hands of the raiders, Minelas had no business taking Caladhrian gold in return for unsanctioned magic killing the corsairs.

So what exactly had happened? Jilseth concentrated on her spell. Once she knew the extent of his guilt, Minelas would learn the true meaning of the Archmage's wrath.

'This is salt marsh.' The dead man was pointing something out to the man riding beside him. The captain of the troop, judging by his finer linen and padded green tunic. 'See, samphire and spearweed.'

As the man nodded at the saw-edged plants, blue magelight flickered. Minelas's magelight. His affinity was with the air. Lightning flashed across Jilseth's spell. Another burst of radiance followed. Water and mud exploded all around.

The dead man yelped with pain as an arrow bit deep into the back of his shoulder. The Caladhrian troopers were shouting and drawing their swords. Their mounts plunged and snorted, obedience sorely tested by their terror.

More arrows struck men and beasts alike. A cry went up to dismount but the dead man was desperately clinging on as his horse reared up. It lashed out with iron shod hooves as black clad raiders emerged from the marshes.

Jilseth's contempt for Minelas deepened. He had led these men straight into an ambush. So much for his wizardry giving them an edge against the corsair raiders.

Worse, his lurid magecraft was doing far more harm than good. One Caladhrian's swinging sword cut through a floating ball of lightning. The magic killed him in an instant.

The wounded man's horse reared again and this time he lost his grip. He screamed as he hit the ground. Blood gushed from the ragged wound and he couldn't reach to staunch it.

Corsairs clubbed the surviving Caladhrians into submission on all sides. Jilseth leaned forward, brow furrowed, her careful hands never slowing. The black-clad raiders were carrying chains.

'What do they want?' a boy with a bloodied face quavered.

'We want slaves,' a swarthy rogue grinned.

'No!' The boy raised defiant fists.

The Caladhrian trooper beside him sent the youth sprawling into the mud. 'Don't be a fool.'

'Listen to him,' the raider advised as he chained the older man's unresisting wrists and claimed his weapons. 'You might live to see tomorrow.'

The necromantic spell flickered horribly. The wounded man wouldn't see another day.

Jilseth gasped, shocked. The Caladhrian baron lay face down in the mud, his captor's boot on his neck. A heavy-set corsair strode towards Minelas with his welcoming hand outstretched. The wizard brushed fragments of azure light from his gloves and nodded a greeting.

The spell-crafted vision was cut short as the dead man's head was wrenched backwards. The Caladhrian's last sight was the cloudless spring sky as a corsair cut his throat. Abrupt as a slamming door, the necromancy died.

Had she truly understood what she had seen? Jilseth licked dry lips as she reshaped the mingled magelight and smoke. The illusion of the dead man returned and the same events unfolded. Fighting a growing tremor in her hands, Jilseth strained her ears to pick every word from the confusion. She searched the fading edges of the vision for Minelas to see what he was doing.

She would have done so a third time but weariness defeated her. Her hands sank into her lap and the amber radiance in the oil faded. She closed her eyes for a moment. Only a moment.

A sweep of her hand sent the oil back to its bottle, leaving the silver bowl spotless. A flick of sapphire air magic tossed the dead man's finger into the reeds. As long as she kept weaving the spell, she could watch the men die time and again. Once she let the magic unravel, there was no recalling their fate, not from that bone anyway. Necromantic visions could only be summoned once from any mortal remains.

Though the faint scent of cooked meat lingered, that wasn't what made Jilseth nauseous. She took a brass mirror from her leather sack and kindled a stub of candle with a crimson spark springing from the snap of her fingers. Ruby reflections swirled around the polished metal.

'Jilseth?' A distant voice floated through the circling magic.

'It's worse than we thought.' She wasted no time on courtesies. 'Minelas took the Caladhrian baron's gold but then he betrayed him. He led the whole troop into a trap so the corsairs could take them as slaves. The raiders' captain hailed him as a friend.'

'A friend who will doubtless reward him.' The Archmage's anger rang across the countless leagues bridged by the spell. 'Minelas is out to make money from the Caladhrians' fight without redeeming his pledge to use magic.'

'His spells foiled all their attempts to fight back.' Jilseth was still appalled by Minelas's treachery. She'd long known he was greedy and lazy, but it had been a shock to realise that he had no hint of a conscience.

‚'That breaks the edict as surely as using his own magic to kill,' The Archmage said grimly. 'What of the noble baron?'

'He's dead.' Jilseth had seen him murdered by the raiders' leader as she revisited the vision.

'Then he's beyond our chastising.' Planir sighed. 'I see no reason to add to his widow's grief by accusing him, not when that could see this whole disgrace dragged into the daylight.'

Jilseth looked around the ravaged marsh. Her necromantic sight indicated more corpses. 'Should I do anything more here?'

'Find his body, you mean?' The Archmage's intuition wasn't hampered by the distance between them. 'No, regrettably. The less anyone knows of your presence there, the better. There'll soon be a search, when the baron and his troop don't return home. Follow Minelas. Our business is with him now.'

'Of course.' Jilseth was already wondering what penalties the renegade would face, accused before the Council of Wizards.

'Be careful.' The Archmage's warning ended the bespeaking spell.

Putting candle and mirror in the bag, Jilseth stood up to shake the wet mud from her cloak. A feeble crackle of grey magelight carried the dirt away. Folding the pristine cloth, she stowed it away and pulled the drawstring tight.

As she took the ensorcelled lodestone out of her pocket, her innate affinity reawakened the spells within it. The darkly glistening gem led her onwards until scant moments later it dangled, limp and useless.

Jilseth didn't need to examine her magic. She had felt the snap of the spell in her bones, a thread broken beyond mending. Minelas's air-born wizardry had carried him away, directly in opposition to the earth magic underpinning her own sorcery.

Did he know that he was pursued? But Planir had only shared his suspicions with her. Minelas could have no reason to suspect he'd attracted the Archmage's attentions.

On the other hand, he'd know the Caladhrians would be out for his blood once they knew his promises of magical aid were lies, worse than lies, if they ever learned the true depth of his betrayal. If they didn't have magic to find him, they had scent hounds and experienced huntsmen, well able to track him through this wilderness.

Jilseth glared at the spreading salt marsh. If she sought any other mage, it would be the work of moments to ensorcel some water with ink or oil and scry out the renegade's hidey-hole. But Minelas had studied all the ways to hide himself from scrying and devised new ones of his own. Such diligence in an otherwise indifferent student had been one of the first things to catch Planir's interest.

She would have to return to Hadrumal and wait for the Archmage's discreet allies ashore to send fresh word of the treacherous mage. Every one of Planir's enquiry agents would be seeking him now.

As soon as Jilseth could stand where he had once stood, the lodestone would find him again. Sooner or later she would catch up with Minelas. As long as herons and toads were the only witnesses to this depravity, Hadrumal's reputation would remain unsullied.

In the next breath, she was gone.

— CHAPTER TWO —

In the domain of Nahik Jagai
23rd of For-Summer
In the 8th Year of Tadriol the Provident of Tormalin

CORRAIN LOOKED UP. The whip master was striding along the walkway that cut the deck of the galley in two. The raised width of planking ran from the stern platform to the prow, a solid barrier between these rowers and those on their benches on the other half of the deck. Shouting in his southern barbarian tongue, to someone on the prow platform which the rowers couldn't see as they sat facing the rear of the ship, the whip master sounded like a cat choking on a hairball.

The brute took his orders from the galley master; Corrain had worked that much out. The galley master relaxed in a comfortable chair up there on the stern platform beside the steersman who wrestled the single vast oar that did duty instead of a tiller.

Two slaves scurried to do the whip master's bidding. Trusted slaves; not chained like the rest even if they remained marked out by their ragged heads and beards. Only the galley crew enjoyed the luxury of razors and shears, some going so far as to shave themselves bare as a newborn babe.

Corrain didn't blame them. He'd have done the same given half the chance. Lice were a constant torment for the rowers, especially for the mainland captives who had far more body hair than the darker skinned Archipelagans. With everyone stripped to the waist that was painfully apparent.

The piping flute which he'd come to loathe slowed and stopped with a trill. Though Corrain couldn't understand the Aldabreshin language, he'd learned those signals soon enough. Along with the rest of the fettered rowers sitting at this oar, he raised its blade free of the water and drew it inboard to rest on the bulwark running along the side of the ship.

Corrain seized the respite to reckon up his count of everything that had happened since the corsairs had enslaved him. Sixteen days after that and he'd been sold like some fattened hog on an auction block, on a nameless beach in the Archipelago. That was when he'd lost sight of half of those to survive the wizard's treachery back in Caladhria.

Eight days after that and he'd arrived at the anchorage where, forced to fight for the corsairs' entertainment, more of his comrades had died. Were they the lucky ones, or those like himself, who'd won their fights and been shared out among the galley captains to be chained to these oars?

The dead weren't going to be whipped into helping the very raiders who plagued Caladhria. It had taken Corrain some while to realise it, but the anchorage was home to yet more of those accursed corsairs.

A contingent of warriors had embarked on the galley for this voyage. They wore no chains, and though none were clean shaven like the mariners, they kept their hair and beards cropped short, offering no hand hold to a foe in a fight. These were free men, as far as Corrain could tell, even if they lived in little more comfort than the rowers, bedding down on the decking at prow and stern.

They all looked to a man who could only be their captain. Corrain had spent his adult life as a trooper in his lord's service. He knew fighting men when he saw them. Raiders, every last one of the scum.

How long before they were forced to row north so these savages could pillage and rape? The sailing season was well advanced now, even if in the fifty one days since they'd arrived at the corsair anchorage, the galley had only rowed from island to island within the Archipelago. Fifty one days? Fifty two? Uncertainty gnawed at his gut as cruelly as hunger.

What was happening now? Every few days they were released from their oars to haul water from the sea and to wash down the decks but they'd done that just this morning.

Corrain watched the trusted slaves open one of the lockers beneath the walkway. One dragged out a basket while the other uncapped a battered leather flagon, tall as a top-boot and doubtless plundered from some mainland tavern.

The man chained beside him on the inboard side of their shared oar sat up straighter. So did most of the rest of the rowers as the whip master's trusted slaves began walking alongside the benches.

The one with the basket was dipping torn hunks of what passed for bread in these nightmare islands into the flagon. The rowers were passing the dripping sops along to those sat by the bulwark pierced with oar ports, the chains fettering their feet jingling.

It was some while before the slaves handing out the soaked bread reached Corrain's bench, twelfth of the twenty five on this side of the galley. He was the middle of the five men forced to sit there, their feet shackled together and secured by a heavier chain running through the loop between each man's ankles, secured at both ends with formidable locks.

As the slaves with the basket and flagon reached them, Corrain held out his hand. His stomach growled with desperate anticipation. The man sat on his bulwark side laughed. Corrain paused before handing him the first sop, meeting his eyes with a warning stare.

He couldn't guess where this man had come from, paler of skin than the islanders though darker than the captured Caladhrians. Was that the touch of the sun or a natural burnish in his blood? Corrain had tried asking but if they shared some common tongue, the man was keeping that to himself. He didn't talk to anyone, not that Corrain had seen.

One of the trusted slaves said something and the man shrugged. He passed the sodden bread on to the youth sitting at the outermost end of their oar. Hosh stuffed it into his mouth, whimpering with gratitude.

Corrain breathed a little more easily. While he reckoned he was stronger than the silent man, he didn't relish the thought of fighting in the cramped space between the benches some dark night, in order to teach the silent man that Hosh was under his protection.

He passed the silent man the next sop and then ate his own. He nearly choked. The bread had been dipped in wine harsh enough to clean old pots and liberally mixed with white brandy.

But Corrain had always heard that the Aldabreshi scorned strong drink. That was what everyone said. They didn't have the head for it, so Caladhria's tavern warriors insisted with scornful amusement. So much for that homespun wisdom.

The two slaves on his inboard hand exchanged a few words as the whip master's lackeys moved on. Both were Archipelagans or of mixed blood, dark of hair and eye. Corrain couldn't understand a word they spoke and they knew nothing of his own Caladhrian dialect or of formal Tormalin, used right across the mainland by merchants and traders, legacy of that long vanished Empire's hegemony.

Regardless, Corrain treated the inboard rowers with wary respect. It was self-evident that the strongest men were set to hauling the innermost ends of the oars. When the heavy chain at their feet was unlocked, releasing them from the oar to sleep, they were the ones who enjoyed the comparative comfort of the bench padded with flock-stuffed sackcloth and crudely cured goat hide.

Corrain swallowed his pride and slept as best he could down on the planks with the others. That way he could keep an eye on Hosh. The stronger slaves would prey on the weakest, given half a chance.

'Corrain,' Hosh quavered. 'What's going on?'

'Shut up and eat your bread,' Corrain growled.

He looked to make sure that Hosh was eating his sop. The lad needed every scrap of food to sustain him, to maintain the pace which the whip master's flute player demanded. Corrain had earned his muscles through years of sword play whereas Hosh had only joined Lord Halferan's guard at the turn of the New Year gone. Corrain had served nineteen years and risen to a captaincy before his own folly saw him thrust back down the ladder to serve as a trooper and be grateful for that leniency.

Corrain's heart pounded painfully in his chest. Of all those enslaved when that foul mage betrayed Lord Halferan, only Hosh remained of the handful purchased by this galley master.

Greff's leg had been accidentally gashed when they had first been fettered. The wound had ulcerated in the moist heat, leaving Greff weak and feverish. As it festered, the whip master had sent one of his two underlings to unchain him. Were they going to tend him? Corrain hadn't shared Hosh's hope. He had been right. Greff was stabbed in the back of the neck and his corpse thrown to the sharks that constantly shadowed the ship.

Someone had strangled Orlon quietly one night, his body discovered the following morning. Hauled up onto the walkway, one by one his bench-mates were tied to the upthrust stern post. None would say what had happened, despite being brutally flogged by the overseers.

As for Kessle and Lamath? Corrain only knew that replies no longer came from the far benches, unseen beyond the walkway dividing the deck, when he risked shouting their names in the darkness.

'Corrain?' Hosh begged for reassurance.

The whip master's overseers had hauled a rower up from an oar some way ahead. His bound hands were tied to the stern post and the crack of the whip sent a shiver through the rowers from stern to prow. Somewhere behind, some corsair raider laughed callously.

'You've done nothing wrong. You've nothing to fear.' Corrain only hoped that was true. A flogging would most likely be the death of either of them.

Beaten senseless, violent or recalcitrant slaves might be briefly revived by the agony of having vinegar and salt rubbed into their wounds to keep the flies away. Then they were thrown down the stern hatch into the hold, into the narrow space between the galley master's cabin at the rear and the locked compartments for looted cargo.

By Corrain's count, fewer than one man in five emerged. The rest were hauled out lifeless, already gnawed by rats, and tossed overboard to delight the sharks. Corrain had taken his turn at that grisly task, as had Hosh. Corrain reckoned the whip master wanted the new slaves to see what fate awaited anyone contemplating disobedience.

How long could Hosh endure this torment? A sword pommel clubbing him into submission when they had been captured had left a visible dent beside the boy's broken nose. While his bruises had faded, he was now plagued with a constantly weeping eye and an oozing nostril.

'Remember your oath, boy. Our allegiance to Halferan holds.' Corrain had made the lad swear to return and see that treacherous wizard hanged. If Hosh died—

No, he wouldn't contemplate that possibility. They had come this far together. They would get back home. They would have their vengeance. The sour wine and liquor warmed his blood and limbs.

The overseer finished flogging the man. To Corrain's surprise, he was returned to his oar, still conscious albeit with blood coursing down his back. The other overseer shouted a warning, the tone unmistakeable even if the words were meaningless. The inboard rowers on their oar exchanged a cowed look.

Corrain hastily swallowed the last of the sodden bread as the whip master blew his silver whistle. The flute-player replied with a piercing note. Like everyone else, the five of them hastily readied their oar before either overseer cracked a lash over some laggard's head.

The whip master set the pace, swift and merciless. The flute-player took up the rhythm and the oars dug deep into the waves. The galley surged forward.

If he couldn't see where they were headed, Corrain strove to see what was going on aboard the galley. Raiders were hurrying back and forth from prow to stern and back again. Leather-wrapped bundles were being hauled up from the hold below. Armour and weapons, he soon realised. They didn't have to row all the way to the mainland to find themselves going into battle.

As his hauling arms slackened at the thought, the others were taken unawares. Their oar briefly faltered. An overseer's warning was backed up with a lick of his whip to raise a welt on their innermost rower's shoulder. The man beside Corrain growled a fierce rebuke.

'Sorry,' Corrain muttered. He concentrated on keeping a steady rhythm, using all the might in his shoulders, his back, his belly and legs, bare feet wedged against the board that jutted up from the deck.

He had seen enough. Those Archipelagan raiders, nearly as numerous as the rowers, were armouring themselves in stiff leather cuirasses. Some carried swords, others shouldered quivers with short bows in hand.

The whip master's whistle mercilessly increased the pace. The strongest rowers strained to keep up with the piper. A couple of armoured Aldabreshi ran along the top of the narrow bulwark on the outboard side of the ship. A single slip and they would fall to a brutal death among the scything oars.

The Aldabreshi didn't fall. Instead they hauled on ropes to spread out a great expanse of cloth. It was suspended somehow from the galley's single mast which Corrain had begun to think was only there for hanging signal flags.

Was the awning to shield the rowers from the punishing sun? As Corrain looked up, he saw the cloth twitch. Dark silhouettes of arrows lay snagged overhead. An excruciating itch burned between his shoulder blades. If some lucky shaft tore a hole, an arrow could bury itself in his back and he wouldn't even see it coming.

A taste of smoke drove that fear away with worse. Corrain snatched a desperate glance over his shoulder to see if something had set the awning alight. If the galley caught fire, chained as they were to their oars, they would sit there burning alive until the waves overwhelmed the sinking vessel to drown any who'd survived that long.

'Corrain? Are we dead men?'

As the silent man's mocking laugh drowned out Hosh's terrified plea, Corrain caught a glimpse of what was happening up on the crowded prow. He shouted what little reassurance he could.

'It's only charcoal, Hosh. They've lit a brazier.'

As he wondered why, as Hosh appealed for more answers, Corrain saw two Archipelagans hauling a barrel up from the hold and dragging it towards the prow. He risked twisting around a second time, ignoring the inboard man's furious snarl.

An Archipelagan reached into the barrel and took out something roughly the size and shape of a pomegranate. He reached for a wooden-handled copper spike thrust deep into the bright heart of the charcoal. Touching the glowing metal to a thick thread trailing from the pomegranate, he waited a moment to be sure it was alight. Then he hurled the thing high and hard, right over the galley's prow towards whatever lay ahead of them.

Sticky fire. Corrain had heard of that Archipelagan abomination, though he'd never seen it for himself.

Before he could speculate further, the overseers' screaming reached a new frenzy. The whip master blew rapid trills on his whistle. Before Corrain could guess what any of this meant, he was struck hard in the chest by their own oar.

The galley had come to a complete stop amid a horrendous cacophony of splintering wood and screaming voices. The armoured men waiting in the stern charged up the walkway. From the sounds of clashing swords and agonised yells, those who'd been in the prow had already joined battle.

Were he and Hosh unwilling partners in a corsair attack on some Caladhrian trading vessel? Even with the raiders prowling the sea lanes, trade between the mainland and Archipelago was too lucrative and too widespread to be significantly interrupted.

Were they attacking some other Aldabreshin ship? Everyone said that southern barbarians fought each other like packs of wild dogs. If it was an Archipelagan ship, did it carry better swordsmen than their own?

If it did, Corrain could hope that their own galley master, the whip master and his overseers would find themselves captured and burdened with chains, some token of natural justice. But if the rowers were sold on again like brute beasts brought to market, there was no knowing where he and Hosh might end up. Worse, they might be separated.

Corrain closed his eyes amid the incomprehensible shouting. He was still alive. Hosh was still alive. As long as they were alive, they could hold fast to their oath. They could cling to the hope of one day seeing Minelas punished for his treachery.

Wherever the wizard had gone, whatever he had done in the meantime, once he got back to the mainland, Corrain promised himself that he would hack the bastard's head from his shoulders and piss down the bleeding stump of his neck.

Aye, and he'd tell everyone from the eastern ocean to the western forests, from the southern shore to the northern mountains, why he'd done it. Those wizards of Hadrumal had been so virtuous and upright, swearing on the sanctity of their precious edict.

Corrain would see them all shamed for the perfidious liars that they were.

— CHAPTER THREE —

'LADY ZURENNE.' MINELAS strode through the door to her private chamber without the courtesy of the most perfunctory knock. 'I have business in Relshaz that may well occupy me to the turn of the season. While I am away, you will obey Master Starrid's words as my own.'

His casual gesture indicated the smirking man at his side.

'Of course.' Zurenne pulled her thread through her embroidery, careful not to let it tangle.

This was an unlooked for respite. She would cherish every day without Minelas's loathsome presence. Except that his return would be all the harder to bear. Stabbing the linen, she wished that the fine needle skewered the vile man's eye.

'Have any letters come for me?' she asked offhand.

On the far side of the table, both her daughters looked up hopefully from their own sewing. Zurenne's sharp glance warned them to stay silent. She hid her relief as they both obediently returned to their needlework.

'No, my lady, alas.' Minelas's regret was as insincere as always.

Zurenne set another methodical stitch in the cloth. Still no letters, not since the end of Aft-Summer and she'd only been given those with their seals already broken, every word doubtless already read.

No letters and, so, no news of anything beyond the manor house's enclosing wall. The cities of Trebin and Ferl could have burned to the ground. Kevil could have been washed away by the sea and she would know nothing of it.

Come to that, the village beyond the brook where the Halferan demesne labourers and the manor's servants lived could have burned to the ground. She wouldn't know about it unless she smelled the smoke on somebody's clothes. Minelas had forbidden her to go beyond the gatehouse, after learning that she'd asked one of her husband's pensioned-off troopers to carry a letter to her sister. She still didn't know what the poor man's fate had been.

'Master Starrid will bring you any correspondence in my absence,' Minelas continued briskly.

'Indeed.' Zurenne didn't believe that for an instant. Minelas wouldn't risk her writing some reply with an appeal hidden amid her words. He had dictated every syllable from her pen in reply to those Aft-Summer letters.

She refused to despair. Her wits were sharper than Starrid's and if Minelas was truly to be gone for twenty days or more, there might be some chance of her sending word to her distant family. Her brothers by marriage would see this usurper justly punished when they knew the truth of what he'd done, and worse, what he'd threatened. Zurenne would go and watch him hanged and she'd ignore any disapproving whispers at such unseemly behaviour in a wife and mother.

She steeled herself to look up at Minelas, all innocent enquiry. 'May I ask what your business in Relshaz is?'

'Your business is your children and household, my lady.' His pale blue eyes hardened with voiceless threat. 'Nothing else need concern you.'

'Of course.' Zurenne looked down at her embroidery again.

He didn't look like a villain, this stranger who'd turned the manor she'd come to as a bride into a prison for her widowhood. He was slender and handsome with golden hair, seldom seen in these regions. But those fine features were a mask for depravity that Zurenne hadn't imagined possible.

What wickedness had he wrought elsewhere? Who else was hunting him, intent on bloody vengeance? That was the explanation, Zurenne had concluded, for him hiding out here in this remote barony on Caladhria's western coast. Since that darkest day when he'd come to tell her that her life was ruined, that her beloved husband was dead, he'd only left to attend the Summer Solstice Parliament. He'd had to do that to secure his false claim on the Halferan estates and to present affidavits from the neighbouring lords of Tallat and Karpis that they had no objection to his grant of guardianship.

Zurenne focused fiercely on her stitches. Halferan had been the truest love of her life, save only for their daughters. He had sworn to protect and to cherish her when they wed and she'd never had cause to doubt him. In every crisis, she had turned to him. Whatever challenges arose, he met them.

That didn't lessen her rage at him for dying. For dying after he'd brought this man among them. Who was this

Minelas of Grynth, with his promises and deceits? As sly and destructive as a fox in a henhouse.

Halferan had only said the mysterious newcomer knew how to defeat the corsairs. Zurenne need no longer worry about the raids on their coast each summer, the plundering of helpless villages, their tenants left homeless and hungry even if they managed to escape the slavers' chains.

She need not concern herself with the details. It was a lord's duty to protect his family, his home and his people while it was her wifely duty to ensure his comfort, to manage his household, to nurture and educate his children.

So Zurenne had done as she had always been taught. Now that unquestioning loyalty saw her a prisoner in her own home, subject to the whims of a stranger and insulted by insolent servants whom she couldn't dismiss.

She looked over at Starrid, as if struck by a sudden thought. 'You must give Master Minelas a cage of courier doves. So he can send us any urgent word. So he can give you a day's warning to make ready for his return.'

The stocky man's fleshy face coloured unattractively. 'I, that is to say, Master Minelas—' His apology foundered in confusion.

Minelas waved that away. 'I have no need of courier doves.'

Zurenne sighed and gazed at Starrid as though saddened and disappointed.

'Courier doves are none of your concern,' the steward said brusquely.

'Indeed.' She returned her attention meekly to her sewing.

Looking up through her eyelashes, she saw Starrid was looking uneasily after Minelas as the blond man prowled the room, picking up music from the clavichord, closing the marquetry lid on its honeywood and ebony keys. Now he was rearranging the dried flowers on the mantel shelf. He did this every time he came, uninvited, to her apartments, to underline his mastery of every aspect of her life.

How did Starrid stifle his conscience, knowing he'd betrayed his dead lord so foully? After all the chances which Halferan had given him, to make good on his persistent failures. Inability to manage the courier bird loft up above the manor steward's dwelling was merely one of the man's inadequacies. Was he worrying now, lest Master Minelas prove less merciful?

Zurenne contemplated her embroidery. If she sought to remind Starrid of his guilt, she didn't spare herself. She bore her own share of blame. She hadn't thought to question Minelas, on that first appalling day when he'd brought her husband's body home.

Racked with weeping, she couldn't compose a single rational thought. Even after all this time, she couldn't comprehend the disaster that had befallen them.

Halferan had ridden out such a short time before with a full troop of his household guards, well armed and armoured. Whenever the manor gates had opened, all that day and the next, she expected to see him ride in, anxious to explain away this foolish misunderstanding.

But the sun had set and risen again and still he didn't come. Finally Zurenne had struggled to explain his absence to their daughters. Saying it aloud, that their adored father was dead, it had felt like a lie. She even prepared her apologies for distressing them so, when it proved to be nonsense.

But it was very far from nonsense, with his body laid on a funeral pyre outside the manor's wall by the brook. With the widows and orphans of the dead troopers lamenting beside her, even those who had no body to burn. At least Zurenne could hope for the consolation of Saedrin's mercy, as the greatest of the gods opened the door to the Otherworld to allow her beloved husband rebirth in that unknown realm.

'Show me your work, girls,' Minelas ordered.

Zurenne set another precise stitch, her lips pressed together. Though it burned like acid, she must keep her wrath hidden for fear of making their parlous situation worse.

Looking up, she saw him standing between her daughters, his elegant hands hovering as if about to caress their shoulders. Zurenne stiffened with fear.

'Mama?' On the far side of the sewing table, Ilysh held up a cambric kerchief, its central design steadily gaining a border of maidenstars. An entirely suitable flower for a girl on the threshold of womanhood.

'That's lovely, my darling.' Zurenne forced genuine warmth into her words. Maiden and mother bless them, her girls had little enough to brighten their days.

'And mine?' Esnina anxiously held up a grubby square adorned with half a yellow butterfly.

Zurenne hardened her heart. 'You must be more gentle, my darling. See how you're pulling the thread so tight that it puckers the cloth?'

Maiden and mother help them, her daughters had to learn a good wife's skills, if they were ever to make a marriage to escape this incarceration. If Minelas would ever allow it and risk whatever he sought to hide here somehow coming to light. If he hadn't already made good on those threats that curdled Zurenne with terror.

'That's very pretty, Neeny.' The monster smiled down at the little girl, all solicitude.

He had been just as kind and attentive, steadying Zurenne's shaking hand when she carried the burning brand to set Halferan's oil-drenched pyre alight. Choking on her tears, she had silently blessed this stranger for his generous tributes to her lost beloved, his words carried by the wind to the assembled household. She could not have spoken, incoherent with regret for loving words unsaid, for misunderstandings never to be resolved, for their shared future now lost.

Zurenne's only duty, Minelas had declared, was comforting her bereaved daughters and honouring her husband's memory. He would see to the manor's continued good governance, to the needs of the demesne and the broad swath of the barony beyond with its tenants and farms. When the barons gathered for the Summer Solstice Parliament, he would speak up for their interests. These were a man's burdens to shoulder.

She had been so relieved. How grievously her lifetime's instincts betrayed her. She'd never dreamed he would claim formal guardianship. But Minelas had done just that. After all, he had the late Baron Halferan's own signature on that last testament of his wishes in the event of his death.

Zurenne knew that parchment for a forgery without even having to see it. Halferan would never have set his signature and seal to such a thing. But she had no way to prove it. She couldn't even see the document to challenge her husband's supposed penmanship. A mere woman had no right to petition the parliament of barons; no standing to challenge

Minelas's standing as arbiter of her fate and that of Halferan's orphaned daughters.

No right to inspect the ledgers detailing the revenues and commerce of the barony. No chance to see how much of her daughters' inheritance the scoundrel was squandering on finery like today's cobalt blue jerkin of finest velvet, sapphire-studded links in the cuffs of his shirt.

How much had Minelas paid for Lord Karpis's sanction for those false documents, to stop Baron Tallat challenging him? Or had he shared whatever secret he had to defend them from the corsairs? If he had such a secret.

Summer had come and gone and with it, presumably, the annual plague of raiders from the sea. Without any news from outside, Zurenne had no way of knowing how bad their depredations had been. The manor itself was ten leagues from the coast, too far to be threatened directly.

She spoke up to draw Minelas's attention away from her children. 'I wish you a safe and comfortable journey, particularly at this season.'

They weren't long into Aft-Autumn but the roads would already be deteriorating along with the weather and they would only get worse by For-Winter.

'Thank you, and indeed, I must set off if I'm to make the most of the day on the road.' He rubbed his hands together, betraying some secret amusement.

'Good speed to you.' Zurenne smiled to hide her growing curiosity. Why was Minelas going to Relshaz? To spend his ill-gotten gains on whatever vices he cherished behind that handsome, trustworthy face? He couldn't indulge them here without everyone knowing him for the fiend he was.

He walked towards the door, pausing on the threshold for one last smile at her daughters. 'Be good girls for your mother and for Master Starrid, and perhaps I'll bring you some presents.'

'Thank your kind guardian,' Starrid immediately ordered them.

'Thank you,' they chorused obediently.

Zurenne contemplated her embroidery scissors and imagined ripping the points down Starrid's florid cheek.

As the two men left the room, Zurenne smiled at her daughters with all the reassurance she could feign. 'Let's see how much more we can get done before the noon bell rings.'

'Oh, Neeny!' Ilysh plucked the calico square from her little sister's unsuspecting hands.

'Lysha—' Zurenne braced herself for Esnina's wails of outrage. Then she'd have to rebuke Ilysh and both girls would be in tears. A featherweight more on the scales of her misery and Zurenne knew she would be weeping too.

'Let me smooth it for you.' Audibly curbing her irritation, Ilysh edged away, turning a shoulder to stop Neeny reclaiming her work.

Seeing her sister painstakingly using a pin to tease the thread backwards through her stitches, Esnina folded her hands in her lap, biting her lip to stop its quivering.

Lysha was very much her father's daughter; decisive, inquisitive, assertive. She resembled him so strongly, with her light brown hair and hazel eyes. Her long limbs already promised height above the common for girls while her strong features would be judged handsome more than beautiful.

Neeny would be the pretty one. As slightly built as Zurenne, she had been blessed with the same delicate nose and rose petal lips, wide dark eyes and an abundance of glossy chestnut tresses.

Who would find Ilysh a husband to value her as she deserved? A man of good character and willing to set aside his own name and family to become Baron Halferan in his turn. Someone to warn off the adventurers and fools sure to be lured by Esnina's beauty and to see her safely wed.

Ilysh looked up and Zurenne saw her eyes were shadowed with awareness too old for her years. The older girl had realised some while ago how powerless her mother was. How truly helpless any widow was, deprived of the husband who should love and protect her once she left her father's guardianship.

Zurenne closed her eyes to deny the treacherous thought she couldn't stifle. If only she had borne Halferan a son. How foolish they had been, telling each other there was time enough for Drianon to bless them with an heir. The girls had proved her husband's manhood and Zurenne hadn't suffered her mother's childbed misfortunes.

No, she could not blame this calamity on that circumstance. If Halferan had neither brothers nor uncles, there were more remote cousins to whom he would have consigned the care of his family. Zurenne's sisters had husbands who would do their duty if called upon. The law allowed for such cases, in the absence of close male kin.

So why had none of them come forward in her time of need? Tears finally escaped Zurenne's closed eyelids. Two halves of spring. Both halves of summer. For-Autumn and now the aft-season would soon turn to For-Winter. So long without her beloved husband and

Halferan's loss still ached beneath her breastbone like a freshly struck bruise.

But she could not weep without distressing the children and her poor daughters didn't deserve that. She swallowed hard and forced her thoughts towards more practical questions. What might yet come to their aid?

The promise of their birth runes? Both girls were embroidering around the sigil formed from the three runes cast at their birth. As was Caladhrian custom, one of the three-sided sticks had been drawn at random from the set of nine by Lord Halferan, one by Zurenne and the honour of drawing the third had been given to the husbands of Zurenne's two eldest sisters. Nine runes, three sides to each, twenty-seven symbols in all.

Halferan, Zurenne and her sisters' husbands had thrown the chosen rune sticks onto the shrine table, each one shaped like the crystal prism which Halferan used to split candle light into rainbows to amuse the girls. With one of the three faces hidden, the other two showed their runes, one upright and one reversed. Earth, Fire and the Harp had been the runes in their positive aspect for Ilysh.

Born at mid-morning, she enjoyed the Sun's blessing too. That symbol was set in the downward pointing heart of the sigil customarily drawn by arranging the first two birth runes side by side and then topped by the third to form a larger triangle. The Earth indicated that her life would be honoured with rank beyond her birth, so Halferan had said, as befitted the confidence and skills that the Fire foretold, along with the Harp's beauty and perseverance.

Zurenne could only pray that he had been right. Of late, she had come to fear that Neeny's runes had merely indicated her younger daughter's character. The Oak and the Mountain were certainly apt symbols of Esnina's stubbornness and defiance. Though the Eagle promised freedom and overcoming difficulties and as another day-born baby, she too could hope for the Sun's promise of justice. Perhaps the Oak and the Mountain promised the strength of character which Neeny would need, to endure and overcome these troubles.

But Zurenne found it increasingly hard to believe that the runes could truly have seen their current plight in Esnina's future and even if they had she refused to feel guilty for not having had the wit to see their warning.

Neeny was a For-Winter baby. Once again, tears threatened Zurenne. Five years ago, and eight long years since Ilysh's arrival in the second Aft-Spring after their wedding, Zurenne and Halferan had celebrated the anniversary of their marriage with their new daughter's first birth festival. What a wonderful Solstice that had been.

What a miserable festival lay ahead for them this year, with Master Starrid ruling the roost. He delighted in denying them the most trifling sweetness in their miserable lives.

'Can we play a game of runes Mama?'

Zurenne opened her eyes instantly at Ilysh's question, anger burning through her grief. 'No,' she snapped.

So slight compared to the other insults that this man had offered her, it infuriated her nevertheless. How dare he introduce her daughters to the games of chance that stable hands and common troopers played? Not that Zurenne ever dared to object when Minelas imposed his company on them, uninvited of an evening, rattling bag of rune bones in hand. But she need not allow such unseemly behaviour while he was away.

She relished the thought of his absence once again and wondered what else could improve their lot. Divine intervention? Zurenne contemplated the panel she was embroidering. She would hang it in the manor shrine where she honoured her husband's ashes daily with her prayers to Saedrin and to Raeponin, god of justice.

Before her life had been cast into this disarray, she'd made only occasional visits to the shrine. For the seasonal festivals and sometimes, if she succumbed to idle dread, when Halferan was travelling to whichever Caladhrian town was hosting the quarterly parliament. Mishaps on the road, some unforeseen malady; everyone knew that such things could cut short even the strongest men's lives.

A visit to the shrine soothed such fears. Zurenne would arrange some boon for the demesne folk, perhaps for indigents tramping the roads. She would pray to draw the gods' attention to her charity so that they would reward her family with the favour they deserved.

Now she prayed to Talagrin daily, along with Saedrin and Raeponin. Halferan had a particular fondness for the god of the martial skills that were the truest mark of a man. Talagrin was also the god of the hunt and of wild places. Halferan always said he'd look fondly on their rough-hewn lands, so far from the tidy fields and neat coppices approved by Ostrin, the farmers' god.

Once she'd sought the hunter god's vengeance on Halferan's killers, Zurenne turned to Halcarion. She prayed that the moon maiden's favour would bring love and luck to her innocent daughters. She asked Drianon, goddess of hearth and harvest, for the strength to be a good mother amid the troubles that beset her.

Finally each day, Zurenne made her devotions to Maewelin, the aged goddess of winter and of widows. This hanging she was currently working depicted the goddess cloaked and stooping, leaning on her stick. With For-Winter ahead sacred to the crone, what could be a more decorous choice for her needle?

But these men who kept her so confined and frightened, they knew nothing of the goddess's secret role, confided by mothers to daughters across untold generations. The Winter Hag was the avenger of mistreated women, bringing down their curses on the guilty men.

Zurenne had promised the ancient goddess this new shrine decoration in return for some sign of hope. She would see her honoured with a costly new statue if someone would rescue her children. By all that was holy and profane, she and her daughters deserved redress.

Maewelin send that Minelas's unexpected absence would offer some opportunity for her to summon help.

— CHAPTER FOUR —

The Wizards' Physic Garden, in the Island City of Hadrumal
Spring Equinox Festival, First Day, Noon
In the 9th Year of Tadriol the Provident

KNEELING BY A freshly dug herb bed, the Archmage crumbled dark soil between his lean fingers. Pale bone markers indicated which plants the apothecaries had sown to flourish through Aft-Spring and For-Summer before their potent leaves, seeds or roots were crushed, steeped or dried.

'Is she dead?' He squashed the rich loam and tossed the clod away.

'No.' Jilseth replied. 'I believe she will recover entirely.'

'A blessing for them both.' A savage edge undercut Planir's words.

'You don't propose to discipline him?' Jilseth's query held the merest hint of rebuke.

Planir rose swiftly to his feet, no hint of stiffness despite the silver frosting his close-cropped black hair and beard. 'You think I should punish him for using his magic to save the life of the woman he loves?' he chided.

She didn't yield. 'I think you have an obligation to uphold the precepts of Hadrumal. To uphold the edicts of your predecessors who wore that ring. The foremost has always been that wizards do not involve themselves in warfare.'

51

'Indeed.' As the Archmage turned his hand, sunlight splintered around the great diamond that symbolised his rank. Shards struck the facets of the sapphire and amber, the ruby and emerald that framed it. It was the only manifestation of his rank. Planir was wearing dusty boots, faded breeches and a balding velvet jerkin over a shirt which his laundresses must despair of.

'You don't think I know the costs of sending mages into some petty fight beyond our shores?' He held up his hand. An ugly scar circled his finger beside the ageless splendour of his ring. 'You don't think that salutary tale deters any prentice-wizard tempted to defy the Council? I make certain that every hesitant mageborn hears every gory detail,' he added with some bitterness.

'Not every detail,' Jilseth ventured. 'Just the story that best serves your purpose.'

'Thus I fulfil my duty to my office,' he retorted, grey eyes steely.

'You couldn't have saved Larissa.' Jilseth's voice wavered despite herself. 'You didn't send her into peril either. She chose to go.'

'It's all one.' The Archmage grimaced. 'She still died.'

And every mage in Hadrumal knew it, Jilseth reflected, even if only the Element Masters and Mistress knew the full story of that conflict far away in the eastern ocean, when wizardry had saved the Tormalin Empire from an insidious threat.

After which, some wizards had chosen to settle in Suthyfer, that chain of scattered islands in the middle of those wild seas. Beyond that, Jilseth had no clear idea what exactly had happened.

She had heard plenty of other wizards speculate, from

Council members down. Not on what had happened but what the outcome meant for Hadrumal.

How had the loss of his lover affected their Archmage? Which of his decisions during this past handful of years might have been different without that personal tragedy? How far did lingering emotion undermine his reasoning in the service of wizardry?

She suspected that blunter questions were asked behind closed doors in Hadrumal's tallest towers. Did romantic dalliance leave a wizard unfit for high office? Especially the highest office responsible for disciplining those mages who defied Hadrumal's edicts. Most particularly when it proved necessary to assert wizardry's eminence among the princes and nobles who ruled the mainland.

Was Planir going to ignore what had happened in Lescar this past half-year? Jilseth chose her words carefully.

'Now that the Duchess of Triolle is not likely to die, she has more to answer for than merely benefiting from the gallantry of a half-trained wizard like Sorgrad. If you wish to overlook his infatuation with her, that is your privilege. Granted, he did no more than get her to a surgeon to staunch her wounds, though it is arguable he should never have been present in the first place, or involved in negotiations with the Duke of Marlier. But Archmage, Litasse of Triolle hired Minelas to use his magic to help her husband's armies prevail!' Jilseth couldn't hide her outrage at that heinous offence.

'Which came to nothing, thanks to you and, let us not forget, thanks to Sorgrad.' Planir more than met her challenge with his own. 'How do we punish Litasse of Triolle for suborning sorcery in Lescar's wars, imposing sufficient penalty to deter other nobles tempted to similar folly, without letting all and sundry know that renegade wizards such as Minelas are out there?'

He gestured beyond the modest houses enclosing the garden, beyond the whole island itself. 'What happens when the mainland's mundane populace learns that Hadrumal does not merely shelter and educate the mageborn, saving their families from the inconveniences of overflowing wells or chimney fires when some adolescent's elemental affinity manifests? When they realise that despite all our efforts, some mages prove corrupt? That some are willing to trade the powers afforded by their affinity for the opportunity to indulge their basest lusts? Won't such knowledge do far more harm to Hadrumal than keeping one desperate duchess's folly a secret?'

'You don't think wizards tempted to turn renegade should learn of Minelas's fate?' Jilseth countered. 'To convince them that playing that particular game is never worth the cost of the candles?'

'Perhaps.' The Archmage's sudden smile deepened the fine wrinkles around his eyes. 'I don't have all the answers. I can only follow the safest path I see.'

He shrugged. 'In the event, Minelas's magic didn't affect the outcome of any battles and the duchess had truly repented of her monstrous bargain before you had to threaten her with my wrath.'

He raised a hand before Jilseth could respond. 'On the other side of these scales, I cannot believe that Sorgrad will stand idly by and let me chastise Litasse, even if I could devise a suitable punishment. What then? The authority of my office will hardly be enhanced by a squabble with a rebellious mage over an ignorant girl.

I certainly couldn't let such defiance go unpunished, so would you have me impose my authority by killing him?'

'It wouldn't come to that!' But even as she protested, Jilseth recalled Sorgrad's unyielding will.

'How could it not?' Planir demanded. 'If my authority is undermined by Sorgrad's defiance, my authority over all wizards is weakened, in the eyes of mageborn and mundane alike.

'What follows from that?' he challenged her. 'Some baron or prince claiming authority over a wizard who's settled in his lands? Those who rule on the mainland only accept that Hadrumal alone has the right to discipline wizards as long as Hadrumal is deemed capable of keeping renegades in check.'

'No mage would submit to such authority,' Jilseth said slowly. 'No noble could imagine they would. Hadrumal alone governs wizards because Hadrumal alone has the power to.'

'I wish I shared your confidence that good sense would prevail,' Planir said drily. 'I find it all too easy to imagine some bumptious lordling clashing with a barely trained mage who lets his temper get the better of him. What then? If I must see that foolish wizard hanged for some inadvertent murder, I might just as well have killed Sorgrad in the first place.'

He shook his head. 'Never mind how ill either death would sit with the other mages of Hadrumal. Consider what the mainland populace would make of an Archmage striking down one of his own. They wouldn't be reassured. They'd be terrified. Those generations when mages were feared, the mageborn shunned, even murdered for fear of magical tyranny, those days may be long past but they're not forgotten. Chimney corner tales and tavern songs still recall the fiery death of Lady Shress and the foolish ambition of Frelt of Algeral that laid waste to the Hecksen demesne.'

Jilseth wished she could protest but in good conscience, she couldn't. All Hadrumal's apprentices learned the litany of the dead, disgraced and mad from the days before Trydek's decrees. They fervently agreed they would never become so arrogant, so deluded, that their names would become such a byword for wizardly folly.

Planir gestured to the trees planted along the garden's enclosing walls. Stirring from their winter torpor, the barren twigs were budding.

'Who would sell us apples, pears and quinces if Hadrumal was feared and loathed? Archmage Trydek found us this sanctuary where we can grow life's necessities but I prefer to enjoy those luxuries which trade with our neighbours brings. So let's be content that this Lescari upheaval is subsiding without tangling Hadrumal in its coils.'

Jilseth's lips narrowed. 'Sorgrad will think he's got away with his insolence.' She wondered why Planir had sent her hunting for him, Minelas, and any other mage even slightly involved in Lescar's revolution, if he wasn't going to act on what she discovered.

'Does that matter,' the Archmage asked lightly, 'if we're the only ones who know? If there's one thing that Sorgrad can do, it's keep a secret.'

Jilseth shook her head in silent disagreement before trying another line of attack. 'What of Minelas's previous treachery in Caladhria? Hiring himself out to fight the corsairs and then taking the enemy's coin too?'

'Once again, I ask where's the profit in poking that sleeping snake with a stick?' Planir shook his head. 'Baron Halferan paid for that recklessness with his life, so there's no penalty I could impose on him. If there was any sign that his neighbours were tempted to follow in his footsteps, then we would assuredly revisit the matter. Until then?' The Archmage shrugged. 'What's done is done.'

The five bells of midday sounded from the towers some distance away in the heart of Hadrumal. As the peals subsided, the Archmage followed the gravelled path between the low hedges separating the plots. 'We should get back before we're missed.'

Jilseth followed, silently exasperated. In her firmly considered opinion, the mageborn of Hadrumal should know of Minelas's crimes, and know that such crimes didn't escape the Archmage's notice.

As they reached the gate that forbade the ignorant access to the garden and its perilous plants, Planir turned. 'I know that some of your peers saw fit to mock you, when your lodestone magic was unable to find Minelas last summer, until we picked up his scent in Relshaz. Do you want them to know what happened in Lescar to restore your reputation?'

Jilseth swallowed hard. 'I don't believe so, Archmage.'

Was that really true? She hoped it was. All the same, now that Planir had challenged her, Jilseth was forced to admit that she would like to see some of her contemporaries choke on their insincere commiserations for the failure of her magecraft.

The Archmage grinned at her. 'Never fear. You'll have plenty of opportunities to show Ely and Galen that they'd be fools to underestimate you. For the moment, let's be glad that neither Minelas nor Sorgrad has mired Hadrumal in scandal and enjoy the festival. Will you be dancing this evening? At Hiwan's Hall or Wellery's?' The Archmage gestured and metal whispered across metal as the gate unlocked.

'At the Terrene Hall, Archmage.' Once through, Jilseth relocked it with a touch of her own earth magic before following Planir through the shadowed alley.

The Spring Equinox festival had yet to get underway in this artisans' quarter. Housewives were busy in their kitchens preparing the first of the five days' feasts. Carpenters and joiners, weavers and shoemakers were tidying away their tools and any half-finished commissions. Children stayed prudently quiet, for fear of provoking parental wrath before the holiday's treats appeared.

Planir and Jilseth left the warren of workshops and humble dwellings that lay between the wizard city itself and the quays and boatyards that framed the modest river's estuary. They walked towards the lofty towers on the flagstone path alongside the masterfully crafted road. Hadrumal's labourers took no less pride in their endeavours than the island's scholars.

As the high road followed the gentle slope of the land, imposing buildings soon obscured the view of the green hills at the heart of the island. That was where the stone to make them had been quarried, so Jilseth had learned from her mageborn grandmother.

Scudding clouds obscured the sun and the commanding façades faded from gold to grey before brightening again as the shadows passed. No two buildings were alike; some were stern with narrow, angular windows squinting defiance at the weather, others were flattered

by arches softening their doors and stone tracery
decorating their windows. Some long-dead wizards
had even been seduced by the florid excesses of High
Tormalin style, bequeathing edifices embellished with
frivolous carved swags and cornices. Together, Jilseth's
grandmother said, Hadrumal's halls offered the finest
history of architecture through the twenty generations
since the first Archmage, Trydek, sought sanctuary on
the island.

That sanctuary was now truly a city. Orderly
quadrangles accommodated those apprenticed to
master mages and magewomen. Towers offered more
eminent wizards a refuge from their pupils' chatter and,
so it was always claimed, a clearer perspective on the
mysteries of magic through their unobstructed views of
the island and the sky and sea beyond.

Along the high road, merchants and tradesmen had
long since claimed whatever space originally separated
those havens of wizardly learning. Today the wine shops
and bakeries were crowded with prentices and pupils
enjoying the festival respite from their studies. Accents
and fashions from every mainland realm mingled with
the subtly different dress and dialect that marked out
the Hadrumal-born.

A wine seller stepped out of his doorway to hail the
Archmage. 'Master Planir!'

'Master Noak.' The Archmage inclined his head in
amiable greeting.

'I have some cases of that Trokain vintage,' the wine
merchant confided.

'Excellent.'

'Archmage?' A stout man emerged from a pie shop.
His festival finery was fresh from the tailor, in sharp

contrast to Planir's shabbiness. 'Madam Jilseth.' He seemed less than pleased to see her.

'Hearth Master Kalion.' She greeted him politely before acknowledging his slender companion with a cool nod of her head. 'Ely. What a pleasant surprise.'

The elegant magewoman in sage-green draperies scowled. Before she could find some reply to Jilseth's veiled sarcasm, the Hearth Master spoke.

'Archmage, forgive me,' he said curtly. 'I know it is festival time but we must discuss this latest news from the mainland.'

'By all means.' Planir sat on the wine shop's window ledge, tucking his hands into his breeches' pockets. 'What news in particular?'

Kalion narrowed his eyes, exasperated. 'Not here in the high road.'

'As you wish.' Planir stood up and smiled at the wine seller. 'I'll call back later, Noak. Fair festival to you and yours, and don't sell all the Trokain.'

'Trokain vintages?' Kalion was momentarily distracted. 'Of which Emperor?'

'Bezaemar the Generous,' the wine seller said promptly.

Planir grinned. 'Why don't we discuss these urgent matters over a glass, Kalion?'

'It will be my honour to serve you,' the wine seller offered at once. 'In the rear parlour?'

Jilseth could see this was far from what Kalion wanted but the Archmage had already entered the wine shop, following Master Noak towards the rear door. She glimpsed men and women already in there sat on either side of white raven boards, playing the strategy game that so many found enthralling.

She had never seen the appeal of either challenge; capturing the solitary white bird with an assortment of other forest fowl, or escaping those painted figurines shifted turn by turn by the player seeking to trap the fugitive raven amid wooden trees and thickets. Jilseth would rather read a book offering some insight into her wizardry.

The flame-embroidered hem of Kalion's red velvet mantle thrashed eloquently around his polished boots as he followed the Archmage.

'You don't need to wait.' Spurning Jilseth with a shrug of her shoulder Ely hurried inside. She quickly took a stool at the counter where Master Noak's daughters were serving dishes of wafer cakes.

Jilseth wasn't about to be dismissed so easily. She followed and took the next seat. 'It's been a good while since breakfast and it's longer till dinner. I'll have two of those and a glass of Ferl River red, if you please.' She nodded at the coarser wafers, spiced with caraway and topped with slices of mutton boiled in verjuice and wine.

Ely had already opted for sweet wafers with honey and almonds, spread with fresh curd cheese. She looked sideways at Jilseth, finely plucked brows drawn into a disapproving line. 'You're spending a great deal of time with the Archmage.' Her insinuation was clear.

'He's not ploughing my furrow, if that's what you're asking.' Jilseth already suspected it was Ely spreading such gossip. 'Any more than you're quenching the Hearth Master's poker.'

Let Ely reflect on that; she wasn't the only one who could loose a rumour in Hadrumal. Not that Jilseth had any interest in such tittle-tattle. Nor was she interested in luring any bed mate, man or woman, from the Archmage down. Jilseth's abiding fascination with her element left no time for such trifling. Why couldn't people believe that?

Ely coloured with indignation. 'No one would ever suspect me of playing Galen false.'

'Of course not.' Jilseth sipped her wine. That was true, and was also why any ribald speculation about Ely was entirely centred on why such a lissom and lovely magewoman remained so devoted to a stolid bore like Galen.

Entertaining as it was to repay Ely for her spite, Jilseth was more interested in what the Hearth Master might be saying to Planir. With the door to the rear parlour half-open, she could see them sitting with their heads close together, their expressions serious.

Unfortunately all she could hear was two newly arrived apprentice wizards, each one trying to explain their imperfect understanding of their own affinity to the other. The girl had caused chaos in a village bake house when the oven fire had roared in sympathy with her anger at a schoolmate's treachery in kissing a boy whom they both adored. The youth had found his temper summoning up a coil of air to throw his brother so hard against their bedroom wall that his ribs had cracked along with the plaster. Both were equally desperate to learn how to turn their unsuspected magebirth into proper magecraft, and then to learn the more complex wizardry enabling them to command the other elements.

'Do you know what particular news from the mainland concerns the Hearth Master?' Jilseth chewed a mouthful of mutton and spiced wafer.

Ely took a swallow of straw-coloured wine. 'I know a good many mages think it's well past time for Planir to give up the office of Stone Master. The office of Archmage was always intended to stand apart from the Masters and Mistresses of Element.'

Jilseth wondered if Ely was deliberately changing the subject or if she didn't know what Kalion sought with Planir. For the present, she had no objection to discussing this recurrent topic of conversation around Hadrumal.

'When Planir finds a mage with an earth affinity strong enough, and the strength of character to meet the office's challenges, I've no doubt he'll propose a candidate to the Council.'

And that won't be Galen, she thought silently. Ely's lover might have substantial talents, Jilseth readily acknowledged that, but he had no imagination when it came to exploring earth magic and scant feeling for other people's sensibilities. That alone would make him a disaster in high office. If Ely was hoping for influence through his advancement instead of her own, she was doomed to disappointment.

Jilseth might as well have said so. Ely looked as affronted as if she had spoken aloud. 'The Council will never advance a necromancer as Stone Mistress.'

Jilseth laughed. 'Is that what you think I'm seeking? Truly, my only interest is honing my magecraft.' She shifted in her seat to look straight at Ely. 'Why don't you spend more time with Flood Mistress Troanna? Master Kalion is the finest Hearth Master we could have but with your own affinity in direct opposition to his, he can only guide your studies so far.'

Ely's lusciously painted lips thinned. 'You look to your own wizardry and I will look to mine.'

'As you wish.' Jilseth shrugged and ate another mouthful of mutton.

Ely bit into one of her wafer cakes. Jilseth drank some more wine and finished eating her meal. She was soon rewarded. Ely could no more sit in silence than a brook could flow without chattering.

'You've been in Lescar a great deal this past half year, haven't you?'

'On the Archmage's business.' Jilseth raised a hand to summon one of Master Noak's daughters: 'A white syllabub, please.'

'The Duke of Marlier has abdicated,' Ely observed. 'With the other dukes dead or fled, Master Kalion says Lescar is entirely ungoverned.'

'Lescar is no longer governed by dukes,' Jilseth corrected her. 'Since those six noble houses have always paid more heed to their squabbles and rivalries than the welfare of the common folk, the ordinary Lescari consider this a considerable improvement.'

'Until anarchy overwhelms them.' Ely was clearly echoing Kalion. 'Until the Emperor of Tormalin sends in his legions to secure peace along his border or Caladhria's merchants demand the same of their barons and the parliament.'

Jilseth shook her head. 'I see no reason to fear anarchy. Those ordinary Lescari raised militias to rid themselves of their tiresome dukes and now their guildsmen and priests and noble scholars are spending this very festival debating how to rule themselves.'

Ely dismissed that with a scornful gesture. 'That will end in chaos unless wiser counsel guides them. Master Kalion is sure of it.'

'Master Kalion is offering himself as that wise counsellor?' That seemed entirely likely. Jilseth could see the Hearth Master gesturing emphatically at Planir. She frowned. 'But what if Hadrumal's very involvement prompts Tadriol the Provident to send Imperial legions across the river, or Caladhria's parliament sends armed baronial envoys to safeguard their interests for fear of wizardly interference? Kalion could end up enmeshed in far more than the Lescari settlement.'

Ely smiled, complacent. 'The Hearth Master is equal to any challenge. He has considerable influence with the Caladhrian parliament and many friends among Tormalin's noble houses. He has spent many seasons persuading the Empire's great princes that wizards would make valuable advisors and trustworthy partners in their trading endeavours, rather seeing us as mere hirelings to be summoned when a harbour needs dredging or heath fires threaten their timber.'

Jilseth heard her echoing Kalion's words again. She decided to remind Ely of Planir's oft-stated position. 'The Archmage has always been in favour of magecraft offering every possible assistance to the mainlanders, from humblest to highest. That has no bearing on Trydek's decree that mainland governance is none of Hadrumal's concern.'

'Is that so?' Ely's sarcasm was biting. 'Then why have you been travelling the length and breadth of Lescar's dukedoms, and visiting Tormalin, Caladhria and Relshaz besides? If the Archmage truly has no interest in influencing any settlement in Lescar?'

Belatedly Jilseth remembered Ely's superlative scrying skills. Planir often spoke of her potential, if she would only bring that same talent to bear on the magics born of other elements.

She spread innocent hands. 'We cannot ignore mainland affairs. The Hearth Master is quite correct, just as Planir honours the Council's wishes by not involving Hadrumal directly. Who better to discover exactly what transpired on a battlefield than a necromancer?'

Jilseth smiled sweetly as Ely recoiled from the notion. Let that put paid to her questions.

Instead the magewoman surprised her with another abrupt change of subject. 'There are rumours of magic other than wizardry influencing Lescar's wars.' Ely sipped her pale wine.

'Artifice.' Jilseth wondered where this turn of their conversation might lead.

'Is it true?' Ely asked with sudden anger. 'These ragtag rebels were using some purloined lore to send messages to one another, as easily as you and I sit talking here? While the dukes were left to make do with courier doves and despatch riders?'

Jilseth's glass of syllabub arrived. She was glad of the interruption giving her time to consider her reply. Whatever she said to Ely would go straight to Master Kalion's ear and then into the gossip swirling around Hadrumal.

'Artifice, that's to say, aetheric magic, is hardly purloined lore,' she said carefully. 'This magic of the mind was well understood in the Old Tormalin Empire and our own archivists have been helping those mainland scholars who are trying to piece it back together.'

Since, as Jilseth had heard Planir say more than once, as long as Hadrumal was helping the curious academics in the universities of Vanam and Col, then the wizards would know exactly how studies of this entirely separate magic progressed. Of late, he was pleased to say, the scholars' understanding of the ways in which Artifice might enable one adept to speak to another's mind or to see or hear through another's eyes was advancing imperfectly and very slowly.

The more advanced enchantments continued to elude them; where aetheric magic could supposedly influence the physical world through the concentration of thought achieved through the recitation of arcane rhymes. If only they could fathom the underlying principles which the ancient adepts had followed when devising those resonant phrases, the scholars lamented.

'Our fellow mages in Suthyfer are also working with aetheric adepts,' Jilseth pointed out, 'comparing and contrasting their respective magics.'

'Entirely typical of those ingrates and malcontents, sharing our secrets with would-be Artificers who owe our traditions no allegiance.' Ely looked through the open door at the Element Master and Archmage still deep in conversation. 'That's hardly the worst of it. The Hearth Master says that the Emperor of Tormalin has his lackeys searching every noble house's archive for any hint of such lore. He talks of granting a new university its charter to draw every scrap of such learning together. We cannot ignore such an affront to Hadrumal's standing!'

She seemed genuinely offended, not merely reflecting the Hearth Master's ire.

'As I understand it, Emperor Tadriol has talked of founding this new university for the last five years,' Jilseth observed. 'No stone's yet been set atop another. Can you think of a city which would welcome a congress of Aetheric adepts, any more than their forefathers welcomed Archmage Trydek when he sought a refuge for the mageborn?'

'That could change in a heartbeat,' Ely snapped, 'when these so-called adepts of Artifice woo the mainland's lords and princes with offers of magical assistance that owes no allegiance to the Archmage and is not subject to his authority. Who knows what other underhand means they might use? Sending suggestions into a sleeper's dreams or strengthening a mere inclination into absolute conviction. You said yourself this is a magic of the mind.'

Jilseth was beginning to think she'd spent too much time away from Hadrumal of late. Was this fear and suspicion of Artifice gaining a foothold on the island? She had only thought it an oddity dredged up by the Lescari rebels. Any real understanding of aetheric magic had been lost in the collapse of the Old Tormalin Empire. Without its arcane enchantments, those noble houses had never been able to regain their dominion over Lescar, Caladhria and Dalasor. Nor would they, now that wizardry had arisen to its present eminence, untrammelled by the fealty which the Artificers had sworn to their princes.

'You don't think that the longer we hold ourselves aloof, the more influence these adepts of Artifice will gain?' Ely demanded. 'Don't forget, it's a magic that anyone can learn.' Her lip curled with graceful contempt. 'Anyone but the mageborn, that is.'

Jilseth knew that was the aspect of Artifice that most intrigued Planir; his principle reason for sanctioning Suthyfer's co-operation with the few truly proficient adepts, which had the added benefit of keeping them safely adrift in the far eastern ocean.

Why was this alternate magic so inimical to elemental affinity? All but the feeblest mageborn could eventually learn some skill, even with the element antagonistic to their own; fire opposed to water, air challenging earth. Not even the most skilled and erudite wizard had yet mastered a single aetheric enchantment of the most elementary kind.

Once again, she chose her words with care. 'As I understand it, Aetheric magic requires years of study to master. Scholars prepared to devote themselves to it remain few and far between. Those that have done so encounter unforeseen problems at every turn. These would-be adepts among Lescar's rebels found establishing a link with another's mind is far easier than cutting that tie. Their dreams were invaded by each other's nightmares.'

Ely was startled. 'Do these scholars tell their would-be adepts so?'

'I believe so.' Jilseth decided not to tell her that Planir had made very sure that this unsettling knowledge reached the mentors and students of Vanam's university and Col's. It was fortunate that so many scholars travelled to Hadrumal to gain wizardry's insights into their alchemical or botanical studies.

'That's all very well but—' Ely broke off and slid from her stool in a flurry of muted green silk.

Planir and Kalion emerged from the rear parlour. Every head in the wine shop turned, discreetly eager to read the Archmage's mood, to catch any hint of what the Hearth Master might have said.

'Fair festival, Madam Jilseth, and good day to you.' Kalion swept past, barely inclining his head to her.

'You can be on your way, Ely.' Planir looked unsmilingly at the slender woman. 'Why not join the dancing in the Seaward Hall tonight? I'm sure that

Flood Mistress Troanna would be agreeably surprised to see you.'

'Archmage.' Ely bowed deep to hide the unbecoming blush staining her fine cheekbones and hurried after Kalion.

Jilseth looked warily at Planir. 'Archmage?'

He frowned at her, not crossly but as if he had no idea why she was there. What had Kalion being saying to him?

He smiled suddenly. 'Is the mutton good today? I'll try it for myself, but don't let me keep you now you've eaten. Go and enjoy the festival. Perhaps I'll see you at the Terrene Hall tonight.'

'I look forward to it, Archmage.' With every eye in the wine shop on her, Jilseth wasn't going to betray any discomfiture at this polite but unmistakeable dismissal.

Leaving the wine shop, she made her way through the crowded side alleys towards her own room in the Terrene Hall's rearmost ivy-clad courtyard.

She could bide her time until the evening and tell Planir what Ely had said. It looked as though the Archmage was right. Hadrumal had far more immediate concerns than Minelas and his crimes. As Planir had told her, the renegade's scheming had come to nothing and besides, no one beyond Hadrumal knew the truth of it.

— CHAPTER FIVE —

CORRAIN LOOKED UP at the sky, through the ragged leaves of the ugly tree he was leaning against. Back home, this was the height of the spring festival. There'd be feasting and drinking and relishing the punishments meted out in Raeponin's name.

Petty thieves would be pilloried outside the manor's gatehouse, to be pelted with garbage by their wrathful victims. The worst offenders would be trying to excuse their misdeeds at the baronial court held in the manor's great hall. Lord Halferan was a compassionate lord, inclined to justice tempered with mercy and restitution wherever possible. Nevertheless, every year or so, there'd be a body hanging from the baron's gibbet before the day was out.

The manor's guardsmen would draw lots to see who would whip drunkards and disturbers of the peace from the manor's shrine to Saedrin's statue in the village, to remind them they'd answer for their selfishness when death finally brought them to the mightiest god's threshold. The priests said only true repentance would persuade Saedrin to unlock the door to the Otherworld.

What was going on without him, was Master Minelas sitting at Lord Halferan's high table? A year and more and Corrain still couldn't believe the murdering scum's villainy in forging that grant of guardianship to steal the barony's revenues. Corrain still felt the urge to crush the blond wizard's throat with his bare hands.

But Captain Gefren had tried that when they'd been taken prisoner in the marsh, when the bastard had gloated over his plans, taunting their helplessly pinioned lord with an ensorcelled parchment. A bolt of wizardly lightning had struck Gefren down before he could get within ten strides of Minelas. If Corrain was going to kill the treacherous mage, he'd have to find some way to attack him unseen.

He stared up at the empty sky, struggling with insidious despair. He had to get back to the mainland before he could avenge his murdered lord. Meantime, he was here, hungry and filthy, surrounded by carousing corsairs. These scum didn't fear Raeponin's justice or Saedrin's judgement. They didn't fear Poldrion's demons, their talons and teeth waiting to rend those whom the Keyholder turned away.

So Corrain didn't believe in the gods either, not anymore. Not since they had abandoned him to this fate.

At least the weather was turning warmer. The nights through both halves of winter had been as cold as any Corrain remembered at home. Here he had no roof, no blanket and any slave lighting a fire risked being thrust face down into the flames.

He glowered at the grey beach mottled with debris. Caladhrian tales of the Aldabreshin Archipelago praised the gleaming white sands of these lushly forested isles where a man might pluck all the ripe fruit he could eat, idling in endless sunshine.

No tavern songs mentioned the relentless rains of Aft-Summer and For-Autumn when the clothes on your back turned mouldy. When anyone foolish enough to wear boots would soon find his feet rotting inside them. Nor of the winter storms that hurled seaweed, driftwood and drowned corpses onto these rock-strewn shores.

But now it was spring and that meant open water voyaging, not merely prowling the backwaters of this maze of reefs and islands. Corrain contemplated the ships beyond the beach, gently rocking in this sheltered anchorage between two thrusting headlands.

That ochre pennant with a tangled black design signified the *Reef Eagle*, the galley they had been sold to. When would their galley master order a venture north across the seas dividing the Archipelago from the mainland, for the richer pickings of the coast?

Would there be any chance of escape? There hadn't been even the sniff of such an opportunity on the *Reef Eagle's* handful of raids the year before. They'd only made landfall twice, encountering merchant ships in the sea lanes on their other voyages. When they had drawn into the coast, Corrain hadn't been able to see anything he recognised. He was used to seeing the shore from horseback, a Halferan trooper. Everything looked utterly different when he was chained to an oar bench.

Where was Hosh? Corrain hauled himself to his feet. He could wish him a fair festival for what little that was worth. The fool boy was sure to be moping and thinking of his mother so far away.

They could not afford despair. They were oath-bound not to give in. They were Caladhrians, not cowards like those slaves who had killed themselves over the winter; eating berries which they knew to be poison, wading into the surf to let the currents take them, grinding a shell shard into a blade to open a vein.

Corrain looked across the grassy expanse between the ragged and twisted trees fringing the shore and the long low houses built from the island's coarse black rock. There was Hosh, lurking in a side doorway beneath the jutting eaves that shaded every side of the spacious dwelling.

Ever since they'd first been brought here Corrain had wondered who'd built those houses. Craftsmen who knew this island, that was clear. The ruddy oiled wood staunchly resisted the nameless insects gnawing at the more recently built driftwood huts.

He guessed the builders had fallen victim to the corsairs, their corpses slung into the brushwood now tattered by hacking blades greedy for firewood. Corrain had found bones and skulls when he'd been searching there for food, for shelter, for whatever might keep him alive until they were chained aboard the galley once more.

He had to stay alive. If he died, or was injured, and injured was as good as dead here, Hosh would have no one to defend him. Then none of Lord Halferan's men would survive to see that bastard Minelas pay for his treachery.

Hosh raised a discreet hand and walked down the steps. All the houses had been built on raised platforms, to entice any passing breeze into their wide, slatted windows. He strolled casually towards a solitary nut palm.

Corrain joined him a few moments later. He didn't go near the house, not after that first beating to warn him that the galley master didn't allow any slave rower within arm's length. Not one as well-muscled as him. Hosh was clearly far less of a threat and had other uses besides.

'I have a festival gift for you.' With a twisted smile, Hosh offered Corrain a crude cup.

It had been shaped from a nut palm husk. Such woody shells were harvested once the rains had come and gone, packed with nuts shaped like citrus segments. Naturally slaves only got the hardest, bitterest nuts or those softened with mould. These husk cups were sought after and prized.

'Thank you, and fair festival.' Corrain swallowed his irritation. How did the fool boy imagine he'd be able to find a festival gift for him?

'The *Red Heron* has anchored.' Hosh spoke quickly, in the coastal Caladhrian dialect. There was no one left alive on the island to share it with them.

'How far did it sail?' Corrain demanded.

'To Relshaz and back,' Hosh assured him.

Who would have thought it? This lad, never travelling more than twenty leagues from the village of his birth, had discovered a ready ear and a swifter tongue for unknown languages. Hosh gave thanks to Trimon, god of travellers, the divine harpist whose music transcended all tongues. Corrain would have done the same, if he still believed in the gods.

'They've landed a fresh cargo of slaves.' Hosh's face tightened with misery. 'They're to be put to the test and the survivors shared out to crew the galleys. They're planning the first raids of the season.'

The first attacks on helpless Caladhrians. Coastal hamlets looted for whatever coin or treasures the early spring trading had already secured, in return for wares and ornaments painstakingly crafted through winter's enforced idleness. Whatever stores had outlasted the winter would be stolen away and those too slow or foolishly unwilling to flee risked murder, rape or enslavement.

'Have you heard when the *Reef Eagle* will haul anchor?' Corrain demanded.

Then they'd be burdened with chains again. The only good thing about being ashore was being unshackled. After all, where could a slave run on this island?

Hosh shook his head. 'Not yet. Now, come on, you know we have to witness the test. And don't raise anyone's hackles by curling your lip,' he added anxiously.

Corrain swallowed his anger. Hosh had a point. Too often, Corrain's height and heft prompted challenges from a slave out to beat down someone taller and stronger to deter other predators.

Corrain had to fight back and win. Shirking a challenge or being defeated would bring greedy hands to steal his food, jostling shoulders to deny him shelter, until hunger or disease killed him.

Not that Hosh was much safer. Bullies were drawn to weakness here like anywhere else. Always skinny, now cruelly undernourished, Hosh looked pathetic. Over the winter, half the teeth in his upper jaw had followed those knocked out by the blow that had broken his nose. It was a wonder the lad's spirit was unbroken.

Well, Corrain hoped it was. In depths of winter, some rheum in Hosh's damaged nose had turned to corruption, swelling the whole side of his face. In agony and delirium, Hosh had begged for death's release.

Corrain had cursed the boy for a coward. He'd pinned him bodily to the ground to strip him and sluice him with rags soaked in sea water to curb his burning fever. He'd traded his food for days for herbs that an Aldabreshin whore promised would cool Hosh's blood.

Mercifully the boy had recovered with no apparent recollection of that piteous plea. Regardless, Corrain stayed alert for any hint he was losing hope. Lose Hosh and how could he sustain his own resolve?

As he followed the lad through the driftwood huts built between the galley masters' houses, Corrain scraped a hand through his matted hair, dragging dirty locks out of his eyes. Yet again, he wished fruitlessly for shears, for a razor to be rid of this straggling beard.

The brushwood soon yielded to taller trees, thrusting straight up, their wood as hard as iron, unlike the twisted spongy trees of the shoreline. Spice plants bruised underfoot sweetened the air. So valuable on the mainland, they grew wild here, disregarded. In days gone by, Corrain had paid good silver to perfume his linen with their essence. Never again, he vowed. When he got home, he'd buy orris root instead.

Men were gathering from all over the island. Slave or raider, no one ignored such a summons. Only the few women whom the corsairs kept for themselves stayed secluded in the houses and huts. The galley master's favourites would be preening and adorning themselves while those who traded their cooking skills for some control over the abuse of their bodies would be cooking a sumptuous feast, to celebrate the *Red Heron's* return with a cargo of slaves.

Corrain's mouth watered despite himself. Once the galley master, the whip master and their fellow brigands had stuffed their bellies, they'd retire behind the window shutters and drink themselves senseless on stolen liquor. Then the slaves could have their masters' leavings and there would be plenty to go around. This Aldabreshin custom was another degradation that Corrain had to swallow if he ever wanted to sleep with a full stomach.

He was forced to admit that the Archipelagan food was tasty, especially the fish and goat meat stews spiced with unknown potherbs. As long as he avoided those little red pods floating in the broth. Biting one of those was like chewing a wasp.

Corrain and Hosh obediently followed the crowd to a hollow some distance from the camp. Far enough for the stench of dead bodies to be carried away on the breeze. Not too far for the ship masters to stagger back to their stolen homes after swilling plundered liquor and laying wagers on men forced to slaughter each other.

Archipelagans would lay bets on anything. Except, to Corrain's bemusement, on throws of the runes. He'd not seen a single set of the three-sided bones, as they were named whatever substance they might have been carved from.

Corrain had spent endless evenings in Halferan's guard hall, casting three triangular bones drawn at random from a cloth or leather pouch. Throw them onto the table and the bottommost side was hidden as they landed, leaving two runes showing on the sloping faces, one upright and one reversed. With twenty seven symbols for chance to favour, the permutations were endless. So fat purses were won or lost on wagers over who might throw the combination of the strongest upright runes. Would the Water quench the Fire or the Wolf consume the Deer? Would the Drum drown out the Chime or the cold Mountain Wind overwhelm the warm Sea Breeze?

Hosh's voice broke into his thoughts. 'This is good enough.'

They sat down on the grassy slope. Oar slaves couldn't hope for shade. Further down, beneath the leafiest trees, trusted slaves were settling earthenware bowls beside heaps of cushions. Bottles of searing liquor stood in water cool from the island's jealously guarded wells. The ship masters were arriving.

Corrain was still thinking about runes. He'd have thought the Archipelagans would have relished the game and with so many Aldabreshi merchants trading with the mainland, they must surely have come across it. Come to that, not all these thieves and murderers were even Archipelagans.

He had come to realise that tawny heads and clean-shaven chins indicated mainlanders here and there, even if the sun and wind had tanned their skins like old leather. That had been merely one of the winter's unpleasant revelations, as a double handful of galleys had returned to wait out the season's storms among allies.

Corrain watched the oldest and most feared of the corsairs being guided to a seat by a faithful slave. A black silk scarf around the corsair's eyes hid whatever ruin lay beneath. His loose tunic and trews were scarlet silk and he wore sapphire studded gold bracelets as fine as any warlord's adornments.

What manner of man must this blind corsair be? Not merely to survive being blinded by Aldabreshin cruelty but to remain in unquestioned command of his ferocious trireme, as well as the raiding galleys that followed him for the sake of the warship's protection?

'No women.' Hosh's voice cracked with relief. 'Nor children.'

The *Red Heron's* miserable cargo was being herded towards a hollow in the ground, an arena of sorts, around which gathered the corsairs. Corrain watched armed raiders separate the bemused and bedraggled men. One by one they were shoved towards the twelve stones set around the ditch that ringed the floor of the hollow. Each stone was carved with a symbol.

Hosh had explained these indicated the constellations that the Aldabreshin followed around the heavens. Their movements conveyed potent omens, as did the wandering courses of the individual coloured stars, so bright and solitary in the night sky. Archipelagans named each of those for a gem while the Greater Moon was called the Opal and the Lesser Moon the Pearl.

Over the course of the winter, they had learned how completely the Aldabreshi allowed happenstance to govern their lives. The circle of the compass was divided into twelve arcs and each one conveyed special significance to any signs seen within it. Anything could be taken for a portent; a bird's flight, a sea serpent in the distance, even some unusual cloud. Or bloodier signs like sharks devouring a half-dead rower thrown overboard.

Contempt burned Corrain's throat as the blind corsair drew a white shell token from a gourd. His faithful slave held it up and a hush fell over the hollow.

None of the captives realised what lay ahead. They still wore the clothes of the mainland; linen shirts and woollen breeches, torn and stained. Some were watching the armed corsairs guarding the outer rim of the ditch. Others looked beyond their captors to the men sitting on the grassy slopes. A few tried ingratiating smiles, others squared belligerent shoulders. Most stood dazed and wretched in their soiled rags. The scented breeze of the island wilted beneath the stink of their despair.

'The Sailfish.' Hosh translated the Archipelagan's shout.

Halcarion's Crown, according to the old sergeant-at-arms who'd taught Corrain his stars on night watches as a young trooper.

A sword landed in the dust in front of the Sailfish stone, tossed by one of the men guarding the ditch. The newly arrived slaves looked at it before nervously eyeing each other.

'The Spear.'

Consternation stirred by that marker as a pole arm with the curved blade and recurved barbs of the islands was thrown down before the slaves.

'Pick it up,' Hosh murmured under his breath.

Corrain's stomach curdled with sour anticipation. Ducah had stepped over the ditch.

Where everyone else ashore, slave or raider, wore the loose tunic and trews of the islands, Ducah invariably went bare-chested, however brutal the wind or rain. That left the vicious scourge scars criss-crossing his broad back plain for all to see, along with the shackle marks at wrist and ankle.

Corrain didn't know what had earned the man such scars or how he had survived, still less how had he escaped the oars to become *Reef Eagle's* overseer ashore, guarding the galley captain's house and the loot stowed in its capacious cellars. He'd warned Hosh off asking any stupid questions. Rouse the big man's anger and he'd kill the lad without a second thought.

Half a head taller and more heavily muscled than any of the dull-eyed slaves, Ducah scooped up the sword lying by the Sailfish stone. He hacked the nearest man's head from his shoulders with a single murderous stroke.

Spattered with the dead man's blood, the closest captive fell to his knees, pleading for his life. Ducah grabbed him by his collar, hauled him to his feet and forced the bloodied sword into his hand. Kicking the corpse and its severed head into the ditch, the brute shoved the unwilling swordsman towards the Spear stone.

All around the circle, Corrain could see men belatedly recognising the dark stains in the earth. Blood. This was a killing ground.

Two men went for the pole arm. One yielded that dubious honour, a copper-haired lanky youth with sun-seared skin. Forest blood bequeathed such hair and a pale complexion.

Corrain wondered what malign fate could bring a man so far. Travel the whole length of Caladhria, three hundred and fifty leagues from Attar on the southernmost rocky tip to the trading city of Peorle at the White River's mouth, and a man would have the same distance to walk again across Ensaimin's self-governing cities and fiefdoms to reach the Great Forest's endless woodlands.

The man who picked up the pole arm was the usual mongrel found in Caladhrian harbour towns. Did he know how to fight? What of the hapless swordsman?

'Don't fight the weapon. Fight the man,' Corrain snarled under his breath.

The swordsman couldn't drag his eyes away from the pole arm's lethal blade. He hacked vainly in hopes of splintering its wooden shaft. The mongrel made a few hesitant thrusts and then the shining steel darted forward, biting deep into the swordsman's belly. Blood gushed onto the dusty ground as his intestines bulged from the wound. The spearman's next wild swipe ripped out the swordsman's throat but Corrain reckoned he was already dead before he hit the ground.

Hosh watched the blind corsair's slave hold up another token 'He's going to the *Knot Serpent*.'

A corsair whip master muscled through the crowd and jumped across the ditch to drag the victorious spearman away.

'That's not the best of omens,' Hosh said seriously. 'The Sailfish stands in the heavenly arc of health. The Spear stands with home and family and these slaves are so far from either. The swordsman should have won.'

How could Hosh cling to his faith in the uncaring gods and take these Aldabreshin superstitions to heart as well? It exasperated Corrain. But the lad's credulity had its uses. Corrain valued Hosh's warnings, when those imaginary patterns in the skies put Ducah in a fouler temper than usual.

He sighed as the blind corsair drew a new token, the Vizail Blossom. A brawny youth with Tormalin features swiftly killed a luckless man thrown forward from the Winged Snake.

'Pearl for calm and Opal for loyalty and both in the arc of fellowship with the Blossom. Nothing but the Topaz with the Winged Snake and that's always an ambiguous gem,' Hosh observed.

'The *Bloody Claw* look pleased to have him.' Corrain wanted to see who'd end up on the *Reef Eagle*.

He needed allies who could handle a sword, whose outrage at being enslaved burned as hot as his own. He couldn't escape with only Hosh to back him.

The blind corsair drew the Sailfish again and this time that red-headed lad snatched up the pole arm. Perhaps he believed that longer reach could defeat the older man stepping forward from the Net. Or he just sought a quick death.

Corrain noted raiders around the hollow offering each other wagers. These Archipelagans would gamble on anything but they liked life and death most of all.

'The Diamond and the Amethyst stand with the Net in the arc of Life,' Hosh murmured. 'They think it's a foregone conclusion.'

Diamond for strength of purpose and Amethyst for calm. Corrain had learned that much of Aldabreshin superstition.

The grim faced man advanced on the Forest-born youth. He thrust hard, straight at the younger man's face. The Forest youth stepped back, knocking the blade aside with the pole arm. The grim faced man ducked below the pole arm's back stroke with a low cut that could have shattered the Forest youth's knee. The copper-headed lad blocked the blow, quickly stepping back once again.

The grim faced man attacked, stepping in much closer. This time his free hand reached for the pole arm's shaft, to deny the Forest lad his weapon as the sword swept towards his head.

Quick as thought, the Forest youth slid the pole arm's shaft back through his hands. Gripping right below the blade and half way along, he smacked the solid length of wood into the swordsman's forearm. The crack of snapping bone echoed around the hollow.

As the man dropped to his knees, the blade falling from his nerveless fingers, the Forest youth brought the pole arm's razor sharp blade up, over and down to bite deep into the back of the swordsman's neck. As the man collapsed, his life blood soaking the ground, the Forest youth walked back to the Sailfish stone, his face betraying no reaction.

Hosh nudged Corrain in the ribs. 'Look, over there!'

The *Reef Eagle's* whip master was coming forward to claim the red-head as the blind corsair's slave waved a token.

If Corrain believed in these Aldabreshin portents any more than he believed in his own gods, he could take that for a good omen. The red-head would have news from the mainland. Something that could help them plan an escape?

— CHAPTER SIX —

Halferan Manor, Caladhria
Spring Equinox, Fifth Day, Afternoon

STARRID THREW OPEN the withdrawing room's door. 'You have a visitor.'

Zurenne longed to challenge his impudent intrusion but that would be folly. As foolish as hurling her book of pious meditations at his head. She'd have liked to do that too. Instead she set the leather-bound volume on the table beside her upholstered settle.

'Who is it, if you please?'

'Lord Licanin.' Starrid scowled. 'Without a word of warning.'

No wonder the rogue didn't dare deny him. 'He is naturally most welcome.'

As welcome as he was unexpected. What could have prompted her eldest sister's stolid, scholarly husband to come here? Abrupt apprehension tightened around Zurenne's heart. Had some evil befallen Beresa? A six day journey wasn't lightly undertaken even with spring breezes drying out the roads.

'Zurenne?' Licanin's outrage echoed up the stairs leading from the great hall to the upper storey of the baronial tower. He didn't sound like a man bereaved.

Two sets of heavy footfalls followed him. Starrid's men, unless Lord Licanin had brought sufficient force to rescue her and her children. But how could he know she needed help?

'Ilysh. Esnina. Be ready to greet your aunt's husband.

The girls quickly put their pens away in their boxes. Ilysh screwed the inkwell's cap tight while Esnina sanded her sheet of carefully copied letters. Zurenne spared a moment to regret the worn nap of her blue velvet gown. But there had been no reason to don any finery, festival or not. They hadn't been allowed beyond the door leading to the stairs for eight days now.

The girls' russet wool dresses were shamefully short, their petticoats showing at the ankle and far too tight in the sleeve and the bodice. Zurenne had asked Starrid for a seamstress only days before. She'd even said she would sew their clothes herself, if he allowed her cloth and shears. He delighted in denying her, saying such matters must wait until their master returned.

Licanin appeared in the hallway, flushed with annoyance. 'I have no need of your assistance.'

To Zurenne's bitter disappointment, the armed men who accompanied him looked to Starrid for instruction. When the steward nodded, they went silently back down the stairs.

'You may leave us.' Licanin shrugged off his riding cloak and held it out.

Zurenne recalled he always preferred the saddle to a carriage. If he had left his youth behind, he wasn't yet in his dotage.

Starrid made no move to take the heavy garment, offering only an insolent shrug. 'Master Minelas left me to stand guardian to Lady Zurenne and her daughters while he's away.'

'I look forward to you rendering account of your

service,' Licanin said sternly. 'Meantime you will see that I am provided with refreshment. This is scarcely a festival welcome!'

For a moment, Zurenne truly thought that Starrid would refuse. The man's impertinence broke new ground with the turn of every season, just as his tunics and breeches grew more costly.

'Of course, my lord.'

As Starrid took Licanin's cloak, Zurenne saw the glint in his eye. He left the withdrawing room door open, walked the length of the hallway, opened the door to the stairs and shouted down to the great hall. 'Cakes and wine for the baron. Hop to it, one of you!'

Shutting the door, he leaned against it smiling smugly. No, he had no intention of letting them speak in private.

Then to Zurenne's surprise, Licanin raised a gloved finger to his lips before turning to address the steward.

'Has your master gone all the way to Duryea for the Spring Parliament? I would not travel so far, not with unrest from Lescar spilling across the Rel,' he remarked to Zurenne.

She saw Starrid's grip tightened on the baron's cloak. 'My master — that's to say, my lord, we haven't had word.'

Licanin tugged each fingertip of his gloves loose. 'I was hoping to discuss that unhappy realm's prospects with Master Minelas,' he explained to Zurenne. 'Saedrin only knows what will come of this conclave of theirs. Landowners, townsfolk and peasants debating how to harness themselves together to agree on their laws and taxes.' He shook his head dubiously. 'When we face those cursed corsairs returning on the Aft-Spring tides.'

'When will your master return?' He looked at Starrid, expectant, as he tossed his gloves down on the table. 'I have written three times since Aft-Winter turned to For-Spring and have had no courtesy of a reply. Have you sent my letters onwards?' Licanin demanded.

'No, that's to say—'

Zurenne couldn't decide which delighted her more: Starrid's impertinence sagging so utterly in the stocky baron's presence or realising the steward had no notion where Minelas might be. She'd thought he refused to tell her purely out of malice. Now she saw that he truly didn't know.

'Hush!' Licanin crossed to the window, mud-spattered top-boots noisy on the floorboards. He looked down and exclaimed, affronted. 'Halferan offers insults instead of welcome, and at festival time? Get your household in order, steward!'

Zurenne heard shouts rising up from the courtyard.

'My lord—' Starrid hesitated, threw the cloak to the hall floor and disappeared down the stairs.

'Stay here,' Licanin ordered Zurenne. 'Can you lock that door behind me?'

'I—' She wanted to ask him a score of questions. She thrust them aside. 'No, he took all my keys.'

That was when she had known Minelas was no friend to Halferan. When he'd returned from the Summer Parliament and ripped the chain girdle from her waist, stealing the keys that were every wife's honour and ornament, from the humblest cottage to the most opulent manor.

The sound of strife below was mounting. Esnina began to grizzle, frightened. Ilysh put an arm round her sister's shoulders. 'Mama?'

Zurenne saw a fearless spark in her elder daughter's eye.

'Who are these ruffians disgracing Halferan's livery?' Licanin demanded. 'Where are your husband's men?'

'Dismissed, disgraced.' Zurenne fluttered helpless hands. 'Minelas replaced them with hirelings from the wharves of Attar, Claithe and worse.'

'None too doughty then, with luck,' Licanin said grimly. 'Stay here, all of you, and bar the door with the table.'

As he strode from the room, Zurenne hurried after him. 'How did you know of our plight?

Halting at the door to the stairs, Licanin shook his greying head. 'I didn't until last night. Then some of your tenants sought an audience at the village where we halted on the road. They said no one was allowed to see you!' He was outraged. 'Talagrin be thanked, my escort includes the finest warriors of my household troop for fear of Lescari bandits on the road.'

'Ostrin bless our loyal vassals.' Zurenne felt a pang of guilt for misjudging them.

'How—?' Licanin broke off. 'Stay here.'

As he hurried down the stairs, Zurenne ran back to the withdrawing room. 'Neeny, clear the table. Lysha, help me move it.'

Between them they dragged the polished oak to bar the door. Esnina managed to spill the blotting sand over the floorboards and she began to wail loudly.

'Never mind that.' Zurenne picked her up and sat her on the table. 'You must be quiet and listen. Shout if you hear anyone coming up from the hall. Lysha!' Zurenne nodded to the room's second doorway, leading to her own bedchamber. 'Tell me if you hear anyone on the secret stair.'

Had Starrid betrayed that to those louts? The narrow stairway hidden behind the panelling to ensure no lady of Halferan could be trapped up here by fire or malice. Zurenne glanced at Esnina. Both girls had sworn before Saedrin's statue that they'd tell no one of it but was it fair to ask that of such a little girl?

In the darkness after midnight, Zurenne had wondered more than once about trying to escape that way. But Starrid had her keys and both of those hidden doors were locked. Even if she managed to force them open somehow, she couldn't imagine they could sneak through the manor's guarded outer gates unnoticed by Minelas's brutes. The thought of his retribution once they were recaptured was too terrifying to contemplate.

Ilysh yelped. 'Mama!'

Zurenne saw she was obeying, in that she had gone into her mother's bedchamber. Only Ilysh was looking down into the courtyard instead of standing by the secret door.

'Step back from the window,' Zurenne ordered. But someone had to know what was going on. She steeled herself and went to see.

The Licanin barony's men were easily recognised by their livery. Forewarned, they had ridden through the gatehouse, alert, armed and armoured. Starrid's hirelings were hurrying out of the manor's guard hall, some still in their shirtsleeves.

Even the mangiest cur barks on his own doorstep, Zurenne recalled her husband saying more than once. One thug ripped his blade into a Licanin man's leg. The trooper collapsed, writhing in agony.

The thug lunged at the man beside him. The Licanin trooper brought up his sword and the two hilts ground together. So deftly that Zurenne barely saw it, the Licanin swordsman let one hand slip free from his grip and seized the thug's elbow.

With a move more suited to the dance floor than to combat, he shoved hard enough to spin the unwary thug around. With the startled thug's back exposed, the Licanin trooper smashed his sword's pommel on the back of his neck. The thug collapsed.

Stunned or dead? Zurenne found she didn't care. She heard her elder daughter cheer. 'Lysha!'

'Mama, they're winning!' Ilysh crowed, unrepentant.

'I can see that. No, Neeny, stay where you are!' Zurenne could save one of her daughters from these horrors. Dead and wounded men sprawled on the cobbles. Amid her distress, Zurenne allowed herself a thrill of satisfaction at seeing most were her erstwhile captors.

Half of the Licanin men had dismounted, swiftly cutting down those hirelings caught unawares in the guard hall. Now Zurenne could see some of the rest throwing down their swords in surrender.

Of those Licanins still horsed, one mounted contingent was blocking the gateway so none of the villains could flee. The rest were riding down stragglers trying to find some refuge among the buildings enclosed by the manor's wall.

Zurenne saw some of them scurrying around the back of the guard hall, behind the stable block standing between that wooden-walled and shingled building and the brick and plaster gatehouse. Others had fled the other way, heading past the steward's dwelling towards the kitchen and the bake house, to hide in the storehouses that lay beyond.

She couldn't see who might be cowering beneath the baronial tower's walls, or by the great hall's steps. Were any of the scoundrels claiming sanctuary at the manor's shrine, abutting the other end of the lofty building?

'Mama! Can you see?' Ilysh exulted.

Those usurpers not dead or beaten senseless were throwing up their hands. The brief, vicious battle was over.

'Mama!' Esnina screamed. 'Someone's coming!'

'Go to your sister!' Zurenne snatched her up from the table and threw her bodily through the bedchamber door. She braced herself against the table, ready to fight against any intruder. 'Ilysh—'

'Zurenne?'

Recognising Lord Licanin's voice, she almost wept with relief. 'We're safe,' she managed to say.

'Open the door,' he ordered.

Zurenne's legs felt weak as water and her hands were shaking. She could barely shift the heavy table until Ilysh came to her aid. Even Esnina tried to help, plump face wretched with fright.

Two men with gory swords forced their way inside while the door was barely ajar. The table juddered across the floor. Esnina was knocked off her feet.

'It's all right, Neeny.' Zurenne scooped the little girl up. 'They're our friends.'

'Is he here? Lord Licanin demanded while his men went to check Zurenne's bedchamber. 'That villain of a steward? Have you seen him?'

'No,' Zurenne cried. 'How could I?'

Glancing at the children, Licanin hastily swallowed an oath. 'He seems to have given us the slip.' He was hoarse with emotion and exertion.

'You two may go. Send someone to the village and summon the headman.' He sheathed his sword which, for her daughters' sake, Zurenne was relieved to see was bloodless. 'Since that villain's not here to answer for his crimes, you'll have to tell me what you know.' He shook his head, exasperated. 'Who is this Master Minelas? Where is he?'

'I don't know.' Zurenne protested. 'He left here mid-way through Aft-Autumn. I've heard nothing of him since.'

'Aft-Autumn?' Licanin looked momentarily surprised, before nodding, more reflective. 'That would explain it.'

Zurenne could have shrieked like Neeny, she was so frustrated. 'Explain what?'

'He was nowhere to be seen at Winter Solstice.' Licanin scowled. 'I saw him at the Summer Solstice Parliament, all courtesy and charm, though we barely spoke. Come the Autumn Equinox Lord Karpis and Lord Tallat said that all was well here.' He looked at Zurenne, reproving.

'I believe stolen Halferan gold bought our noble neighbours' lies,' she hissed.

'Is that truly how it stands?' Licanin glanced at Ilysh and Esnina.

Zurenne took the hint. 'Lysha, take Neeny into my bedchamber and find a quiet game to play.'

For one dreadful moment, she thought Ilysh would refuse. Seeing Lord Licanin's glowering face, the girl thought better of it and led her sister away.

Licanin barely let the door close before he accused Zurenne. 'Your own letter confirmed Halferan's grant of guardianship, when my lords of Karpis and

Tallat presented Master Minelas to last summer's parliament.'

'I never saw that hateful grant before Minelas returned with my husband's body.' Zurenne's voice cracked with anguish. 'I wrote that cursed letter at his bidding. Else I—' She couldn't go on.

Licanin gestured towards the closed door. 'He threatened the children?'

'He said that he would wed Ilysh,' Zurenne's hatred spilled like pus from a boil, 'and bed her too.'

'Surely not!' Licanin was appalled.

'Believe it.' Zurenne couldn't repeat what else Minelas had said. The details which had convinced her that despoiling little girls was nothing new to him.

'If he wed her, the Halferan lands would be his lifelong by right of marriage. If I yielded—' Self-loathing thickened her voice. 'If I yielded, he said he would assuredly tire of playing the lord of this manor some day. When that day came, he promised he would draw up a grant of guardianship in favour of whomever I wished.'

Not that Zurenne believed a word on his poisonous tongue. But what else could she do? She'd had no one to help her. Did she now?

'Did you find it so easy to believe,' she demanded, 'that my husband should treat me so shoddily?'

'We were taken so unawares by Halferan's death and then by this supposed guardianship.' Licanin looked sorely troubled as he paced from door to window and back again. 'But one does not interfere in another man's affairs without compelling reason. Noble witnesses endorsed Master Minelas along with your own words, supposedly. You wrote regularly to your sisters through summer and For-Autumn,' he reproached her.

Tears blurred Zurenne's vision. 'Every word from my pen was a lie.'

Why hadn't they seen that? Beresa and Celle and Danlie? But why should they doubt what they read? It wasn't as if the sisters knew each other's hearts.

Eight years and five infant brothers' deaths separated Zurenne from Danlie and they were the closest in age. Licanin had cut Beresa's wedding plait and laid it on Drianon's altar nearly twenty-five years ago. That was a full generation by any almanac's reckoning and Zurenne had been a year younger than Neeny was now.

Licanin cleared his throat. 'Beresa grew concerned when you replied to none of her winter letters. So I wrote to my lords of Fandail and Brason and we learned that neither Celle nor Danlie had received any letters. Baron Fandail, Baron Brason and I discussed how to proceed and concluded this Master Minelas could hardly object to a festival visit.'

All these letters going back and forth the length and breadth of Caladhria, when winter weather meant an ox-cart struggled to cover four leagues a day. No wonder it had taken her brothers by marriage until now to act.

'I've received no letters since Winter Solstice.' Zurenne had imagined herself utterly forgotten through those cold, dark days.

'We can assume that villainous steward withheld them.' Licanin's indignation swelled afresh. 'Raeponin rot the man. Is this how he repays his liege-lord's memory?'

'He was given his position for his dead father's sake, a man of very different character,' Zurenne said wearily.

'My husband had already threatened to dismiss him more than once.'

Then Minelas had returned with Halferan's body and Starrid had wormed his way into the scoundrel's good graces quicker than a maggot into an apple.

'We'll lay this whole vileness before the next parliament with a petition to make me your guardian,' Licanin said abruptly. 'Pack what you need for the road and I will take you and your daughters under my own roof. This Master Minelas can try to reclaim you if he dares.' Grey haired or not, he looked more than ready to make a fight of it.

'No, please,' Zurenne begged. 'That's to say, I will willingly submit to your guardianship but we have to stay in Halferan. Otherwise my daughters will be left with nothing. Lord Karpis and Lord Tallatt will send troopers from north and south to divide the manor's lands between them.'

'No—' But Licanin broke off.

'Who will gainsay them with Minelas gone? If Halferan's hall is abandoned, Lord Karpis and Lord Tallat will claim whatever they wish of our lands.' Zurenne folded her hands at her waist to stop them trembling. It was hardly seemly for a woman to argue such issues of property but she was desperate. 'Irrespective of that false grant of guardianship, three-fifths of the parliament's barons will agree that the populace must be protected, come what may.'

To her relief, Licanin couldn't deny it. 'They may even have hoped for such an outcome, when they agreed to support this Minelas. But who is this blackguard?' he demanded with fresh anger. 'Why by all that's holy did Halferan bring him here?'

'I don't know!' Zurenne was nearly screaming with vexation. 'My husband had long sought some means to defeat the corsairs. You know how long and hard he argued the coastal cause before parliament, to no avail. The inland lords are only ever concerned with unrest spilling across the Rel from Lescar.'

She saw that Licanin was outraged to learn that Halferan had told her about the parliament's debates. She didn't care.

'Then Minelas came and Halferan said they had a plan. They left that same day with nearly all the household's troopers. Only Minelas came back escorting my husband's body and my whole life was cast into ruin!'

Zurenne's nerve failed her and so did her knees. She sank into a chair.

'I have been left wholly friendless, my daughters' virtue at that man's mercy. Not even mistress in my own household, my children dressed in rags. No one—'

Licanin cut her short with a sharp gesture. Zurenne's heart missed a beat. Was he so insulted, so appalled, that he simply would wash his hands of her? Unshed tears burned her eyes.

After a seemingly interminable pause, he nodded. 'I understand your fears for your daughters' inheritance. All their hopes of honourable marriage rest on Halferan's continued prosperity.'

Zurenne felt faint with relief.

'But there are graver dangers on the horizon,' Licanin continued grimly. 'The corsairs grow ever bolder. Their raids have reached as far as Lescar. They sailed up the river Dyal barely thirty days ago, burning and thieving as they went.'

'But the dukes—' Zurenne protested weakly.

'Don't you know—?' Licanin clicked his tongue, annoyed. 'No, you won't have heard. Well, if you can credit it, the Lescari populace have overthrown their dukes.' Disbelief warred with his indignation. 'We can only be thankful that the Duke of Marlier's militias remained loyal and drove the corsairs back to the sea.' He sighed. 'We fear they will soon return to this coast, looking for easier pickings. As soon as they sail north of the cliffs around Attar, these saltings are indefensible.'

For an instant Zurenne was viciously pleased to think of Lord Karpis and Lord Tallat's baronies being plundered. But no, only the innocent would suffer, along with Halferan's tenants.

'Can we expect no help from the inland barons?' she asked, desolate.

'If the summer's raids prove truly vicious, there will be voices raised—' Licanin shook his head. His next words surprised Zurenne.

'Much good that will do. Some of us have a different course in mind. Indeed, your own husband was the first to propose it. I did not think it wise at the time but given the corsairs' new boldness in Lescar—' He hesitated. 'I came to consult with Master Minelas as well as the other coastal lords who had supported Halferan's original proposal.'

Now Zurenne understood Lord Licanin's concern. If corsairs had sailed up the river Dyal, that surely meant they could sail up the river Tantel in Caladhria just as easily. Distance from the sea was no longer the safeguard it had been for Licanin's own barony.

'What did my husband propose?' she demanded.

Licanin took a breath before deciding to tell her. 'Halferan asked for help from the wizards of Hadrumal.

We must renew our appeal and this time we will not be denied.'

'What?' Zurenne was astounded.

'We have always agreed that mages should hold themselves aloof from warfare between mainland dominions.' Licanin's belligerence sounded rehearsed for the Archmage already. 'We can imagine how much blood would have been shed this past year in Lescar if wizards had joined the battle. But these corsairs are dogs of another colour entirely—'

He broke off. 'Never mind. This is hardly talk for a lady's ears. If you are to stay here, you need a new steward, to serve until I send my own representative. I will secure the parliament's grant at Summer Solstice to take formal charge of your household.'

'Some of my husband's former guardsmen live pensioned off near the village. They will be loyal.' Hope surged in Zurenne's heart. She had been so long without it she scarcely recognised the sensation. 'Can I rid myself of the other servants who've betrayed me? Can I write to summon merchants to supply us with what we need?' She gestured at her shabby gown.

Licanin looked uneasy. 'We will have to break into the strong room, to see what coin remains.'

Zurenne looked downwards, as if she could see through the floorboards. The ground floor of this square baronial tower, as broad as it was tall, was given over to lordly business. A large antechamber accommodated those waiting to be admitted to Halferan's audience room. Leading off from that, the muniment room held generations of archived grants and writs. A locked and barred door and iron grilles on the stairs defended the basement strong room below from thieves. Unless those thieves had stolen the keys, as Starrid and his new master surely had done.

She looked up at Licanin. 'Is there any way we can hunt down this man Minelas? To reclaim what he has taken? To see him hang?'

Licanin looked thoughtful. 'I believe that there may be.'

— CHAPTER SEVEN —

Trydek's Hall, Hadrumal
15th of Aft-Spring

'MY LORDS, IF you please?' As Jilseth's sweeping hand urged the barons through the door, they barely acknowledged her.

She had to admit this wasn't the male arrogance seemingly bred in Caladhrian bone. They were overawed by the prospect of meeting the Archmage. Their haughtiness had been steadily declining since the fogs had swirled around their ship; dense, unnatural and stirred only by the magelit winds. Out in the distance, they could hear waves crashing on mist-shrouded reefs. Accompanying them on their voyage, Jilseth had seen them wondering what else lay in wait for anyone voyaging to Hadrumal.

Their unease subsided somewhat when they saw Hadrumal's commonplace docks. This wasn't so different from Claithe or Pinerin, they had said to each other. Until they looked up at the milky sky and realised that the veil of cloud hid the sun completely. No sailor, however diligent with sextant and compass, would ever find his way back here without the Archmage's permission.

Their disquiet returned and redoubled on the carriage ride to the city. Deposited amid the looming halls and towers, they were further unnerved to realise that, whatever rank they might boast of at home, Caladhrian barons didn't warrant a second glance from Hadrumal folk.

Jilseth by contrast had been greeted by several of her acquaintances, interested to know where she had returned from. Now two of the barons were sneaking sideways looks at her, belatedly wondering if the Archmage's envoy was more than a mere letter carrier, despite her petticoats.

'Good day to you, my lords.' Planir sat in a high backed chair in the centre of the lofty dais at the far end of the hall.

There were no seats for anyone else. The long tables and benches that usually accommodated prentice and pupil mages at mealtimes had been cleared away. The Archmage's courteous words echoed in the emptiness, floating up to the dark beams above. His stern predecessors stared down from portraits along the whitewashed walls. Their garb ranged from archaic robes to sober mantles not so different to the Caladhrians' own.

Planir wore a high-collared black doublet over breeches of the same velvet. The creamy linen of his shirt showed through slashes in the sleeves, each one caught together with a silver-mounted pearl. Light from a high window struck a dull gleam from black silk stockings and a brighter glint from silver buckles on his shoes. With his greying hair and beard, the gems of his ring of office offered the only hint of colour.

Even Kalion would approve such elegance. Jilseth had wondered what other passing wizards had made of their Archmage's unaccustomed finery this afternoon.

'My lords?' Planir prompted as the noblemen drew closer together, exchanging uncertain murmurs.

Jilseth walked on to stand by the steps leading up to the dais. She would have quite liked to sit down after her journey but she could wait, the better to accommodate Planir's stratagem, whatever it might be.

Baron Saldiray cleared his throat. 'We were most surprised by your invitation.'

'As was I by your letter,' Planir observed.

'Most honoured,' Baron Myrist said hastily. 'To meet you in person.'

'Quite so.' Planir's tone offered him no encouragement.

Lord Saldiray tried again. 'You wish to discuss our appeal for wizardly aid against the corsairs.'

'You wish to renew your appeal,' Planir corrected him. 'I'm curious to know what you think will change my mind. I'm also interested to learn why you don't appeal to your own parliament, for Caladhrian ships and troopers to rid your shores of this menace. Weren't your fellow barons assembled in Duryea, not twenty days ago?'

'The most recent parliament naturally turned its attentions to Lescar.' Baron Taine wasn't so easily intimidated, even if he had spent the first day and night of their voyage here puking over their ship's stern rail. It had taken Jilseth that long to convince him that a simple quadrate cantrip would calm his stomach's rebellion.

'My lord Archmage.' Lord Saldiray paused before continuing. 'When Baron Halferan appealed to you before, you explained that wizards do not involve themselves in mainland affairs. But now we know that is not precisely true.'

Despite herself Jilseth stiffened. She only hoped none of the barons noticed.

'You accuse me of lying?' Planir arched curious brows. 'Forgive me, my lords. Please sit.'

He snapped his fingers and a half circle of chairs appeared behind the Caladhrians' huddle. A stool appeared at Jilseth's side. She took it as the barons sank into their seats, subdued.

All save Baron Taine. He remained on his feet. 'We mean no such insult.' He looked annoyed. 'But you sanctioned magic to resolve this war in Lescar. We learned that at our Spring Parliament.'

Now Jilseth regretted sitting. She couldn't see Planir's expression.

'Do explain,' The Archmage invited, faintly sceptical.

Baron Taine swept his mantle back, clasping his hands behind his back. 'Emperor Tadriol of Tormalin was granted a wizard's assistance to determine who truly murdered Duke Orlin of Parnilesse and his family.'

So that's what he meant. Relieved, Jilseth supposed it was inevitable that such a startling story had flown across those lands once under Tormalin's dominion which remained linked by tradition and commerce.

She wondered how the barons might react if they knew she had been that very necromancer, drawing images of tortured death from Parnilesse's murdered duchess's head, stolen from its gatehouse spike. She winced inwardly at the memory.

'In the interests of justice, yes, I agreed to that wizardry,' Planir agreed with deceptive mildness. 'The last thing the benighted Lescari needed was Tormalin legions crossing their borders. Once Emperor Tadriol knew that the rebellion's leaders were innocent of that appalling crime, the Lescari were free to punish the guilty men themselves.'

Braced, Taine stood facing Planir. 'We seek freedom for Caladhrian innocents and punishment for the guilty.'

Planir shook his head, regretful. 'As I explained when Baron Halferan first sought our aid, sinking corsair ships breaks those very edicts against magical interference in mainland affairs which your parliament values so highly. You could not have wished to see wizardry double and redouble the recent bloodshed in Lescar?'

Jilseth was pleased to see the seated barons grimace at that prospect.

'Surely your magic could drive them off course with a storm?' Baron Myrist asked hopefully.

'So some other coast can suffer?' enquired Planir. 'Where do you propose we send them?'

'Then stop them sailing north to begin with.' Taine betrayed some irritation.

'Imprison these raiders in their Archipelagan lair, and we would need to go scrying to find them first.' Planir considered this. 'Madam Jilseth, would that fall foul of Aldabreshin strictures against using magic in their domains?'

'Arguably not the scrying, Archmage, if that was worked from Hadrumal. However—' she raised her voice as Taine opened his mouth to speak, '—wizardry confining ships to Archipelagan waters would be considered a gross violation of the natural order that delivers omens and portents. From highest to lowest, my Lord Archmage, the Aldabreshi would be outraged.'

Planir looked unblinking at the barons below the dais. 'Which would you prefer to face, my lords? Raids by these corsairs or the wrath of uncounted Aldabreshin warlords?'

Lord Blancass spoke for the first time, sneering. 'Archipelagan superstitions—'

'Their beliefs are as sincere as your own.' Planir didn't grant him the courtesy of his title. 'Since no one can know the absolute truth of whatever lies beyond this life, I suggest you refrain from mockery.'

'There are merchants from Relshaz to Col who would have an interest in your proposal,' Jilseth remarked. 'If the Aldabreshi suspect northern magic at work in their islands, they will close their waters to northern traders.'

'I don't doubt it,' Planir agreed.

Taine's jaw jutted belligerently. 'You invited us to come all this way merely to say once again that you will not help us?'

Planir looked steadily at him. 'I invite you to consider every possible consequence so that you understand my decision. Do you know that wizardry is a capital offence among the Aldabreshi? A warlord must flay a mage alive to purify a domain polluted by sorcery. Which of my pupils or apprentices must suffer that fate for your sake, if they encounter outraged Archipelagans in Relshaz or Col who would knock them senseless and load them with chains?'

'They would not dare!' Baron Blancass was outraged. 'Barbarians!'

'Really?' Planir mused. 'No Aldabreshin would hang a starving man for stealing from a household with plenty to spare yet you would sanction that punishment, my lords, and the Archipelagans would call you barbarians for doing so.'

As the other barons gaped, Saldiray rose to his feet. 'What of the consequences of doing nothing? Their first raids have already ravaged three villages between

Attar and Claithe not a handful of days after the equinox.'

'And the villagers?' queried Planir. 'Haven't they found sanctuary inland?'

Jilseth didn't need to see Saldiray and Taine exchange a sheepish glance. Flood Mistress Troanna had been scrying the Caladhrian coast since Cloud Master Rafrid first told Planir that the sailing season had begun.

'If our people retreat from the coast, we risk ceding a permanent foothold to these vermin.' Baron Taine glared at the Archmage. 'We had to burn out one such nest in the Linney estuary last winter.'

'Successfully?' Planir nodded. 'As I have always said, I have every confidence in Caladhrian strength of arms.'

'So this has been a long journey and a tiresome voyage for no worthwhile return.' Blancass rose to his feet, not bothering to conceal his anger. 'Shall we catch the next tide, my lords?'

Jilseth had to curb a frown. She hadn't expected such an open lack of respect even when the lords realised that Planir would not yield.

'A moment more if you please, my lords, my lord Archmage.' The only baron who'd remained silent thus far stood up.

'Baron Licanin.' Planir smiled. 'I confess I'm curious to know why you're here. Granted, the River Tantel is navigable for thirty leagues or so inland but your estates must be twice that distance from the sea, up by the headwaters.'

Jilseth was pleased to see the Archmage's omniscience gave Saldiray and Blancass pause for thought. Then Licanin's reply drove such thoughts from her mind.

'I am concerned with the Halferan estates. My own wife is sister to the baron's widow.'

Planir nodded. 'My sympathies on her loss.'

'Baron Halferan wasn't lost,' hissed Baron Blancass. 'He was murdered by corsairs.'

Licanin shook his grey head. 'My wife's sister has lost far more than her husband.'

To Jilseth's growing bemusement the barons looked horribly embarrassed.

Planir leaned forward in his chair. 'Please explain.'

'Baron Halferan was killed by corsairs a year and a season ago.' Licanin cleared his throat. 'A grant of guardianship was presented to the following Summer Solstice Parliament, according to custom. A mere formality to ensure the care of Halferan's widow and children. The document was supposedly signed by Halferan himself and his neighbours attested to the fitness of his designate.'

He hesitated before continuing with visible effort. 'But I have recently learned this supposed guardian was a stranger to Halferan's wife. The grant of guardianship was a forgery. Worse, this man robbed the barony and has now disappeared.'

Now Jilseth understood. No wonder the barons looked so mortified, if their parliament had been so thoroughly duped.

'A vile crime,' agreed Planir, 'though what—'

'Wizards have long sought out the lost.' Licanin looked up. 'People and property. I have already asked a mage in Claithe for assistance. He was unable to find the man so suggested I seek help in Hadrumal.'

Planir nodded slowly. 'It's not always an easy task, for any wizard to find someone unknown to them. What is his name?'

'Minelas Estadin,' said Licanin.

Planir raised a hand to clarify his question. 'The man you seek, not the mage.'

Licanin shook his head impatiently. 'That is the man's name, the thief's.'

'Forgive me, I misunderstood.' Planir apologised swiftly. 'What can you tell me about him?'

Jilseth sat, stony faced. This must be some different Minelas. If uncommon, the name wasn't unknown in Caladhria and she'd never known him claim Estadin as his family.

Licanin's expression lightened at the Archmage's encouragement. 'Zurenne tells me, my wife's sister, that his accent was of Ensaimin. He mentioned a childhood home in Grynth.'

That did away with Jilseth's hope of some harmless coincidence. Now she was desperate to learn what else this baron knew about Minelas.

'He lingered through the summer seasons and into For-Autumn last year.' Guilt clouded Licanin's face. 'He installed his own henchmen in the household and threatened Lady Zurenne and her children. It wasn't till after he left that we learned of these deceits.'

So that's where Minelas had hidden while she'd been searching. She had been so close!

'When did he leave?' Jilseth couldn't help asking.

'You've heard nothing since For-Autumn?' Planir reclaimed Lord Licanin's attention at once.

'Not a word all winter,' the grey-haired baron admitted. 'But Lady Zurenne is tormented by the thought that he may yet return. She is distraught, my lord Archmage.'

It took all Jilseth's strength of will to sit still, as expressionless as a statue. If Licanin knew of Minelas's wizardry, he would say something, if only to lay these debts of dishonour at the Archmage's feet.

'Then the scent is cold.' Planir shook his head dubiously. 'But if this man spent some seasons in Halferan there may yet be something there tied to him. That could anchor a scrying spell. We can certainly try,' he agreed with every appearance of goodwill. 'Madam Jilseth, please see these lords and their ship safely back to Claithe with the next tide. Then you should travel to Halferan with Lord Licanin.'

'I will be glad to help, if I can.' Jilseth strove to match the Archmage's calm and the sincerity of his deceptive assurances.

'This – lady wizard?' If Blancass was the only one who spoke, the rest were looking askance.

'I have every faith in her considerable skills, as should you, my lords.' Planir rose to his feet. 'Please, until your ship sails, take your ease in the Boar and Elder tavern. Tell Master Sasper that you're my guests. Madam Jilseth will join you once she and I have discussed how best to search for your thief.'

Planir clapped his hands and one half of the hall's double door opened. A burly man in a midnight blue tunic looked through. 'Archmage?'

'Tornauld, kindly escort our noble guests to the Boar and Elder. See that they get a private parlour,' Planir added.

'Of course, Archmage.' Tornauld bowed respectfully to the Caladhrians who were getting to their feet, surprised at the Archmage's unexpected affability.

Jilseth breathed more easily. Tornauld's wits were as sharp as a winter wind. He would realise Planir didn't want these visitors adding anything to the potent mix of Hadrumal's gossip.

As the door closed behind the noble lords, she gave way to her frustration. 'I could have put a stop to Minelas's plundering! If only I had followed the lodestone to Halferan's manor instead of into the marsh,' she castigated herself.

'Only mainlanders think wizards are infallible.' Planir surprised her with a grin before looking deadly serious. 'You would have discovered this petty deceit but not his graver crimes in betraying Lord Halferan to the corsairs and taking their coin in return for his magic. Do you think he would have allowed you to search out the truth in the marshes, once you had discovered him installing himself as lord of that manor?'

Jilseth was faintly insulted. 'No mage with an air affinity could disrupt my necromancy.'

Planir shook his head. 'He wouldn't have attacked your spells. He'd have tried to murder you too, with magecraft or a knife in the back, if the alternative was being unmasked as Lord Halferan's killer and a renegade mage. Would you have been ready for that?'

Jilseth wished that she could say so. Honestly? She instinctively recoiled at the thought of one mage killing another. That wasn't something she ever wanted to contemplate.

'But they don't seem to know anything of his magic.' That was one consolation she could cling to. She looked at Planir, at a loss. 'Why should I go to Halferan and act out some masquerade? What do you want me to do there?'

'I've had enough of these chance discoveries of new twists to Minelas's treachery,' Planir said grimly. 'Let's learn everything we can from Halferan's lady and from whatever bodies still lie out in the marsh. Let's find out if anyone there has the slightest suspicion that wizardry has been so vilely misused.'

'If I do discover someone who knew of Minelas's magic?' What did Planir expect her to do then?

'We'll spread that straw when we fear a stumble.' Planir smiled once again, at Jilseth's surprise hearing this homely wisdom. 'I don't know. What we'll do will depend on who it is and exactly what they know. Kalion may imagine I spend my days plotting and planning for every possible twist of events and their outcome but I see no reason to waste my time as he does.'

Jilseth wasn't overly reassured. 'Shall I tell Halferan's widow that she need not fear? That Minelas is dead?'

'Not yet.' Planir was adamant. 'That's an arrow we'll keep in our quiver.'

'But we will tell her?' Jilseth appalled by her error. If only she had gone to the manor, this woman and her children would have been spared whatever grief Minelas had caused them.

After a barely perceptible delay, Planir nodded. 'When we're certain there's no scandal smouldering. If there is, we may need exactly that news to snuff out the flames.'

Jilseth nodded reluctantly. 'Let's hope it doesn't come to that.' If it did, some rumour would surely find its way to Kalion's ear and the Hearth Master wouldn't hesitate to use this fresh failing against the Archmage.

He had already challenged Planir before the Council of Wizards over Minelas's crimes in Lescar, even though Sorgrad's brother had killed the renegade before he could make good on his boasts to win the war for Triolle. Jilseth closed her eyes with a shudder at unbidden recollection of that bloody scene.

'It's unlikely you'll find any cause for concern,' Planir

said sombrely. 'If Minelas had worked any magecraft through the summer, your lodestone would have found him hiding in Halferan. I don't doubt that wizardry's efficacy and you shouldn't doubt your talents.'

The Archmage sighed. 'From what you discovered last year, he only used his magic to kill Lord Halferan in order to steal his barony and to enslave those men for corsair gold. Who could have witnessed such an outrage, who wouldn't have already stepped forward to shout it from the rooftops?'

— CHAPTER EIGHT —

CORRAIN WAS BIDING his time. He ignored the stench of sweat and piss, of vomit from the newcomers. Despite his own nausea in the heavy seas, he was grateful for every wave sluicing through the oar ports in the bulwark. That washed away some of the sloshing vileness. He hauled steadily on the oar polished smooth by countless dead men's hands.

'Where did we land?' Hosh wasn't expecting Corrain to know. He just wanted someone to share his desolation. So near and yet so far from a coast that might have once been home.

Corrain answered him nevertheless, albeit with a curt rebuke. 'Quiet.' The last thing he wanted was the whip master's brutal attention drawn this way. If either of them were flogged, it could be the death of them.

The skies were darkening and the overseers were lighting lamps at the galley's prow and stern. The galley master had decreed the *Reef Eagle* would row on into the night for some reason. Corrain looked up to see the Greater Moon at its full, though the Lesser was dark. The last time, both moons had been at their opposite phase as the corsairs had come pillaging on the first raids of the season.

Now Corrain understood. Five days out from their Archipelagan anchorage and once again, the raiders were making good use of the highest tides prompted by the partner-dance of the moons. He vaguely recalled Captain Gefren mentioning such a pattern, not that corsair raids were ever certain and anyway, the Caladhrians ashore had no way of knowing where the bastards would strike.

Had anyone expected the *Reef Eagle*, when the galley rode the surging waters inshore the previous day? As chance would have it, dawn was breaking over the muddy bay. The raiders, Aldabreshi, mainlander and mongrel, had slid down ropes slung from the prow, striding through the shallow waters. Too soon, as the gusting wind wheeled, Corrain and Hosh heard their hapless victims shrieking.

Who were these people, roused from sleep to find a curved sword at their throats? Chained to their oars, the rowers would never know. The *Reef Eagle's* raiders hadn't brought any slaves back to throw in the hold. Corrain was relieved, much as he would have liked some notion of where they had landed.

He braced his feet against the board jutting from the deck and pulled along with his bench mates and wondered where they were going now. Heading back to the Archipelago, he'd have expected them to ride the powerful ebb sweeping the boat laden with booty back out to the open seas. But now he could smell salt marsh and hear night birds' cries achingly evocative of home.

The whip master called out something to his overseers. To Corrain's surprise, the galley master came forward from his seat in the stern, heading for the prow. One of the galley's crew hurried after him carrying a coil of rope with a heavy weight at the end and regular knots along its length.

The whip master's whistle signalled the flute player to lessen the pace of the oars. Soon they were barely making headway. Now those raiders skilled with the short, simple wooden bows which the Aldabreshi favoured in battles at sea were keeping watch at prow and stern. A night raid? Corrain had heard of such abominations when he'd served in Halferan's guard, but he'd never been an unwilling participant on the *Reef Eagle*.

The corsairs were calling out to each other, their words short and precise. Hosh spoke quickly under cover of sudden commotion in the prow. 'We're going ashore to take on water. They're taking soundings with that lead to find the channel.'

Hosh was soon proved right. The rustle of reeds grew louder and Corrain realised they were rowing into a shallow estuary. The thrum of the planking beneath his feet told him when the galley grounded, even before the whip master's muted shouts saw their anchors thrown overboard.

Not that Corrain would have called them anchors; great slabs of stone pierced to hold crude barbs of oiled wood, rope knotted around a central groove. That was a puzzle, when Aldabreshin smiths made the finest swords he'd ever seen. Why was there so little everyday metalwork in the Archipelago?

Or armour, come to that. Corrain pursued that thought as he hauled on his oar. Granted, some of the corsairs wore astonishingly finely wrought chain mail, the riveted links smaller than the curve of his smallest finger nail. But he'd rarely seen any raider wearing a decent cuirass or breast plate and never one that was Aldabreshin-made rather than stolen from the mainland.

Corrain looked down at his feet. The Aldabreshi must use up every pennyweight of ore making slave chains. Those were certainly made with as much skill as their swords. Careful to remain unobserved, Corrain had tested every link, lock and hinge of his shackles, chains and manacles. He hadn't found a single weakness.

He watched one of the overseer slaves unlocking the end of the long, heavy chain that secured their fettered ankles. At the man's nod, Hosh began dragging it along, through the smaller loops of chain that hobbled the rowers. Corrain watched the overseer hang the ring of keys back around his neck.

Getting hold of those was about as likely as getting his hands on the Tormalin Emperor's crown. Corrain watched the overseer unlock the next chain. Even if he had the keys, Corrain had calculated that he couldn't possibly unlock enough slaves fast enough for them to stand any chance of fighting back against the armed corsairs.

The whip master shouted again and the silent slave who sat between Hosh and Corrain shoved his way past to climb up onto the central walkway.

'We're to take the water barrels ashore,' Hosh explained, unnecessarily.

Corrain nodded. Taking the little barrels ashore to a spring, slinging them on poles to carry them back, this was a practised routine. Though so far, they'd always done that on some empty Archipelagan isle.

Hosh was listening as the overseers and the whip master talked. One of the overseers didn't seem too happy. The whip master rebuked him soundly.

'We drank too much water,' Hosh murmured, 'because so many rowers were sick.'

He broke off as the closest overseer clapped his hands sharply together. Slow and careful with his feet shackled, Corrain climbed up onto the walkway. As Hosh followed, the overseer grabbed his arm, snapping harsh orders.

Hosh nodded and addressed the rest of the rowers. 'We must take these smaller barrels ashore and fill them with water, to refill the big casks in the hold. Otherwise we might run short before we get home.'

It wasn't the first time the boy had been ordered to translate for the Archipelagans, since they'd realised he'd mastered their tongue. The whip master had finally been forced to accept that however hard he lashed the newly enslaved mainlanders, no amount of bleeding would induce them to understand Aldabreshin.

Corrain didn't necessarily like it. On the other hand, if Hosh was considered useful, surely that offered him some added protection amid the brutalities of this life.

Shouts at prow and stern indicated the anchors were secure. Corrain watched the red-headed Forest youth scramble awkwardly onto the central walkway. The chain between his ankles was painfully short for his naturally long stride.

Corrain had been watching him. Ashore, the youth had kept himself to himself, shunning both conversation and conflict. Disappearing into the ragged trees, he'd found somewhere safe to sleep that Corrain hadn't discovered.

Afloat, the red-head had concentrated on mastering his oar's demands. Corrain had watched him gauge how to husband his energies without risking the whip for slacking. Too many of the other newcomers wrenched their oars back and forth in a panic, only to exhaust themselves and suffer the very lashing they had feared.

As Corrain reached the galley's stern platform, he looked down into the lamp-lit hold, through the open hatch. Slaves were shifting the bundles of dried fish, the barrels of salted meat and sacks of unmilled grain that had been stolen earlier that day. An Archipelagan tossed aside a haunch of freshly killed mutton. The bloody muslin wrappings smelled repellently rank.

Hosh had said this raid was to steal supplies to fuel the summer's assaults. The old blind corsair said the omens promised a season of unequalled plunder.

They weren't just stealing food. Corrain also saw a heap of tanned cattle hides. That made sense now that he'd seen how most of the corsairs' armour was made from thick leather. Those hides would be boiled in oil or, more noxious still, in urine demanded at sword-point from the slaves. Wet and steaming, the leather could be shaped around a man's thickly greased body before it cooled and hardened. Corrain had seen how the corsairs liked to prove their valour to each other, not flinching from the ordeal.

'Why are they so wary?' He ducked his head to hide a sneer, seeing Archipelagan archers vigilant in all directions. What did they expect to attack them out here? Marsh eels?

Hosh was looking out to sea. 'A lot of the galleys take on water here before they head south. Fall foul of the wrong ship coming here tonight and we could lose all this booty to them, never mind finding ourselves sold on to a new master at another slave market.'

That was an unwelcome prospect, given the very real possibility that he and the boy would get separated. Beyond that, Corrain couldn't see why corsair losses would be any concern of his. He shuffled towards the stern ladders fixed on both sides of the upthrust stern post. He climbed carefully down, wary of tripping over the chain linking his shackles. The water was cold and reached to his waist. Mud squelched between his toes. The river was brackish enough to sting the raw galls around his ankles.

Slaves on board handed down the empty water barrels, each one small enough for a man to circle his arms around. Corrain shouldered one, no great burden empty, and waded towards the shore, to find a stretch of firmer land lurking amid the reeds.

What a fresh torment this was, when he'd thought life as a corsair slave could no longer surprise him. To stand on Caladhrian soil and know he'd be leaving before the first hint of dawn.

Hosh had gone on ahead, already telling the newly-enslaved they would eat once their labours were over. Corrain followed the red-headed youth as one of the overseers led the way along the solid ground. The man stopped and nodded to the first slave in line. Corrain guessed this stream threading through the reeds must be sweet enough to drink. The red-headed slave was looking around, contemplating the marshes.

Corrain caught his eye. 'Do you reckon we'll get some of the bread they stole or the usual steamed grain and grit?' He dumped his barrel on the squelching ground and held out a hand. 'I'm Corrain.'

After a moment's consideration, the Forest youth set down his barrel and offered his own empty hand. 'I'm Kusint.'

Corrain felt sword calluses on the youth's palm. 'Is that an Ensaimin name?'

When the parliament had last met in Trebin, Corrain had still been a captain in Lord Halferan's guard. A good many traders from Ensaimin made the journey across the White River to mingle with Caladhria's barons. He heard something of that accent in the younger man's voice.

'Ensaimin?' Kusint's lips twitched in a half smile. 'No. I'm Soluran.'

'Saedrin's stones! How did you end up here?'

Corrain had never met anyone from that distant kingdom, so far beyond even the Great Forest that once marked the limit of the Old Tormalin Empire.

'Why should I tell you?' Kusint withdrew his hand.

Corrain shrugged. 'In return for a jug of ale, if we find ourselves a tavern?'

'I've yet to see one of those among the Aldabreshi,' Kusint remarked.

Corrain held his gaze. 'Shall we look elsewhere?'

Kusint's green eyes hardened. 'In these marshes?'

Corrain could see he'd already assessed the idiocy of fleeing into the trackless saltings, exhausted and hampered by chains. Did the realisation pain him as much as it did Corrain?

'And be dead before dawn?' Corrain shook his head. 'No— Shit!'

A whip bit deep into his shoulder. One of the overseers hissed incomprehensible abuse. Kusint swiftly picked up his barrel, ducking his head, apologetic, before making haste to fill it.

Curbing an urge to strangle the Archipelagan swine with his own lash, Corrain did the same. Hosh hurried towards him, bringing a pole and a rope sling to carry the barrel.

'It's a lick.' Corrain knocked the lad's hand away from the oozing gash. 'My own fault.'

Hosh would have said something but the other overseer summoned him with an irate yell. Corrain quickly set his barrel down and went over to Kusint who was struggling to untangle a sling.

'Let me help.'

The Forest youth took a step back. 'I can manage.'

Corrain saw his eyes following Hosh, hooded with suspicion.

'Hosh is a friend,' Corrain assured him.

'He's lackey to the slavers,' the red-head snarled.

Corrain shook his head. 'He only grovels to the scum to keep his hide whole,'

'You expect me to believe he killed a man in that cursed circle?' Kusint was glaring at Hosh.

'I'll swear it to any god you wish.' There would time enough to explain how Hosh had been thrown into combat against a half-dead simpleton for their captors' vile amusement. He took the tangle of rope from Kusint's hand. 'So where did you do your soldiering?'

'Who says I've been soldiering?' Kusint slapped viciously at one of the night's biting insects.

'I know a soldier's skills when I see them, with sword or pole arm,' Corrain assured him, 'even if Solurans learn different drills to Caladhrians.'

Kusint cocked his head. 'How do you know so much?'

'Me and Hosh were troopers in Lord Halferan's guard, a barony somewhere along this very coast.' Corrain slung the rope around the heavy barrel and laid it on its side to thread the pole through the loops. He looked up. 'Care to share your allegiance?'

Kusint paused for so long that Corrain didn't think he was going to answer. Then he shrugged, stooping to lift one end of the pole up onto his shoulder.

'I signed on the muster with Captain General Evord Fal Breven. We won the war in Lescar, or so I hear, but not before my company was ambushed by brigands. We were sold down the river to Relshaz's slavers.'

Corrain silently rejoiced to hear bitterness to equal his own. Kusint would never be reconciled to this life, any more than he would. This news was unexpected all the same. He shouldered the back end of the pole and they began walking back towards the galley. 'Which duke did your captain-general serve?'

Lescar's dukes tore at each other like cats in a sack, Corrain knew, for sake of a high king's crown that no one had ever worn in all the generations since the Old Empire fell. When they ran short of vassals to send to pointless deaths, they hired mercenary companies with coin squeezed from their tenants. He remembered hearing rumours that peasants unable to pay the levy were sold to those Relshazri who'd long accommodated the Aldabreshin lust for slaves. One way or another, the dukes would get their money.

As Kusint answered, although Corrain couldn't see his face, he could hear an unexpected grin in the Soluran's words. 'No duke. An alliance of exiles from across Ensaimin joined forces with malcontents within Lescar. They hired Captain-general Evord to raise an army to throw down all the dukes. I enlisted as they marched through the Forest. I had a fancy to see somewhere new.' He sighed. 'Be careful what you wish for, isn't that what they say?'

Corrain was too astonished to answer. He had long known that any Lescari with a handful of wits fled their homeland, especially when the dukes' bloody skirmishing erupted into full scale warfare. Such vagabonds would drift along the coast or traipse the high roads into Caladhria. The parliament disapproved of vagrants, so barons' troopers with dogs and staves kept them moving onwards. Corrain had done his share of telling such unfortunates to seek better luck elsewhere. From what he'd heard in Trebin, most ended up in Ensaimin, amid that patchwork of fiefdoms and city states.

Where it seemed that some had prospered sufficiently to raise themselves an army. Corrain wondered what the barons' parliament had made of that.

'So what about you?' Kusint prompted. 'How did you end up in these chains?'

Corrain looked warily around. While he'd seen no sign that the whip master or overseers understood any Tormalin, there were enough mainlander slaves who would. None of them were too close. He lowered his voice all the same.

'We were betrayed, me and Hosh, our comrades in arms and our liege-lord, Halferan. A man called Minelas led us straight into a band of corsairs' clutches.' Hatred all but choked him. 'After taking our lord's gold and promising to defeat them.'

Kusint halted at the edge of the water, twisting to look back at Corrain, disbelieving. 'How could one man promise to defeat a whole band of raiders?'

Corrain could see the hope in his face nonetheless. Kusint sought some way out of these chains as fervently as he did.

Corrain hesitated. Though Lord Halferan was a year and more dead, he was still loath to reveal their baron's secret. 'Not a man. A mage.'

'Oh.' Kusint turned away, disappointed, hefting the pole again. 'So it was just lies.'

They began wading out towards the galley, arms braced to lift the pole high to keep the barrel clear of the water. When they reached the stern ladders, slaves at the top tossed down the net used to haul the heavy barrels up. With one last effort, Hosh and Corrain hefted their burden into the mesh, rope sling, pole and all.

As it slid upwards, Corrain stooped to wash the whip cut on his shoulder. Gritting his teeth against the sting of the saltier water, he scrubbed harder. He couldn't risk it festering.

'He wasn't lying,' he said distantly. 'He really was a wizard. I saw his magic for myself. He killed a handful of my friends with it, so the corsair leader could murder my lord.'

Corrain wondered if he would ever see that giant corsair again, with those gold chains plaited into his beard. On some Caladhrian beach or trading island, not merely in his dreams. Corrain had woken so many times after ripping a sword through the villain's throat or spilling his entrails with a dagger.

The Forest lad was frowning. 'I thought your wizards were forbidden to kill. When there was rumour of magic at work in Lescar, everyone said that it was impossible.'

'So Planir of Hadrumal told us.' Corrain's throat tightened as he recalled Lord Halferan's anguish at the Archmage's dismissal. 'But this Minelas, he said that he would help us for the sake of natural justice.'

And they had all been deceived, even their wise and noble lord. Because Halferan was desperate. Because Minelas was so poisonously plausible, with his open and courteous manner.

Corrain should have thought it through. Mage or not, any man betraying a lifetime's oath should never be truly trusted.

He looked around the moonlit estuary. It had been so long since he'd spoken of any of this. He'd thought he'd become accustomed to that ever-present pain; the ache of knowing how utterly he'd failed his oath and his allegiance. Putting it into words prompted more anguish than he could bear.

If he tried to flee, was there any chance he could escape? Would the Aldabreshin arrows miss him in the dimness? Could he outstrip the searching raiders, burdened with these fetters? Could he hide somewhere in the reeds until they were forced to quit the hunt, the galley drawn away by the tides?

'Corrain?' It was Hosh, floundering in the sucking mud.

No. He couldn't try to flee now, not with the fool boy in tow, and he couldn't leave Hosh to suffer whatever revenge the whip master would inflict on him.

But that didn't mean they couldn't escape. They'd been talking of nothing else, the two of them, when they could find some peace and privacy. They had finally come up with a plan which would work as well, if not better, with three. If it worked at all.

Corrain seized Kusint's elbow to stop him climbing back aboard just yet. 'Can you handle a small boat? Can you swim?' He couldn't and neither could Hosh but they'd agreed that couldn't deter them.

'I can swim,' Kusint said slowly, 'and I know something of boats. I was raised beside a river that makes your Rel look like a rain-fed stream.'

Corrain looked steadily at him. 'We have a plan to escape these slavers. It's not without risk.'

'Life without risk is like meat without salt.' Kusint grinned with a recklessness born of unforeseen hope.

A belligerent shout from up on the galley startled Hosh so badly that he nearly lost his footing. 'We have to get back aboard!'

He scrambled for the ladder. Corrain and Kusint followed with every appearance of cowed obedience.

As Kusint grasped the rungs, he nodded at Corrain. 'Till later, then.'

— CHAPTER NINE —

Halferan Manor, Caladhria
21st of Aft-Spring

'YOU WON'T DELAY your departure?' Zurenne swallowed. She didn't want her voice to tremble. 'The skies do look ominous.'

As Baron Licanin looked from the groom leading his horse from the stable to the scudding clouds above, the lady wizard spoke up.

'It won't rain today, my lord, not before sunset. You'll have no trouble on the road.'

Zurenne could have slapped the woman. She had, in those reveries she allowed herself in the manor's silent shrine. The lady wizard showed no shred of piety and never followed her there.

'I must go home to mind my own mutton,' Licanin said briskly. 'There will be matters arising across my barony which only I can resolve.'

Zurenne could hardly deny that and she knew she should be grateful that he'd spent so much time on Halferan's affairs. But the prospect of being left alone with this unlooked-for guest, this lady wizard, made her nervous, though she was hard put to know why. The woman looked so unassuming, unremarkable to the point of plainness in her dove-grey dress.

Perhaps it was the intensity in Jilseth's hazel eyes, as she asked for every detail of Master Minelas's time here.

Or was Zurenne imagining things, her emotions still churning with her hatred of the man?

Granted, Zurenne was desperate to know that the scoundrel was captured, that her daughters' inheritance was restored. All the same, the question remained. Why had Licanin gone to Hadrumal to seek wizardly assistance? Why was he so loath to discuss that visit with her?

Zurenne was beginning to suspect that Licanin was keeping secrets from her. She had accepted such behaviour from her husband without question. From her brother-by-marriage, it was as constant and as tiresome an irritant as a blistered finger.

'I scryed over your demesne this morning.' Jilseth was reassuring Licanin. 'All seems well with your manor and tenants.'

'My thanks for that.' Licanin beckoned to the groom and mounted his placid steed. He paused to look around the courtyard.

Whatever Zurenne's other tribulations, it was such a comfort to see her home restored from Starrid's callous neglect. The cobbles were swept with no fugitive wisp of straw escaping the stable block. The steps up to the great hall opposite had been scoured clean. The windows of the baronial tower gleamed, newly washed. The oaken door of the shrine at the other end of the great hall gleamed with new coins nailed there as token of fervent vows, in gratitude for the barony's restoration.

Licanin grunted, apparently satisfied. 'I will write from the road tomorrow,' he promised Zurenne. 'Send my messenger back to let me know how everything goes on here. Send one of your own men whenever you need my guidance. As soon as I reach home, I will send a cage of our own courier doves and one of my own loft men to start raising birds here.'

'My thanks indeed.' Zurenne was sincerely grateful for that. Whether through Starrid's malice or incompetence, every Halferan bird had died. If there'd been any birds from other baronies, Minelas must have wrung their necks.

When those Licanin birds arrived, could she keep one in her withdrawing room, caged like a songbird? Zurenne never wanted to be without some means of summoning help ever again.

She looked at Master Rauffe, her new steward. The briskly jovial man had stepped up to Lord Licanin's stirrup, to exchange a few final words. He would doubtless be scandalised at the notion of a courier dove in the baronial chambers. Was it worth a quarrel, especially when any such wilful behaviour would be immediately reported to her brother-by-marriage? Zurenne had been allowed to choose her new personal servants but Master Rauffe was a Licanin man.

The grey-haired baron gathered up his reins. 'I will write before the turn of the season with my proposals for the Summer Parliament, to secure the grant of guardianship placing you under my care. Your other sisters' husbands have already sworn to endorse me. Saedrin save you, my dear, and your daughters.'

He waved up at the withdrawing room window. Ilysh and Esnina waved back. Zurenne had judged it safest for the girls to stay upstairs, after Neeny's tantrums at breakfast had tried Lord Licanin's patience to breaking point. Zurenne's only consolation was he had been sleeping in the gatehouse's freshly refurbished guest quarters, so the little girl's nightmares hadn't woken him from his sleep.

His personal guards drew up behind him, their horses restive after days in the stable. Impeccably liveried and every man alert, the well-drilled troop rode out through the gatehouse, following the fluttering pennant showing Licanin's bronze chevrons on a yellow ground.

The contrast with the Halferan guard was sadly marked. While they had turned up in twos and threes as soon as they heard Starrid and his brutes had been ousted, only greybeards and callow youths now wore Halferan's modest uniform of buff leather and undyed wool.

Licanin had not hesitated to chastise them, demanding that they account for deserting their lady in her time of such need. Zurenne's heart had twisted within her, as they stammered their excuses. They were no match for Minelas's hireling swordsmen. Some showed the scars they had suffered for defying his henchmen. Others wept openly for Halferan's chosen men, murdered with their lord in the swamp.

Whatever they had lost, at least they were free of Minelas. Even if he returned, his crimes had been uncovered. Zurenne looked up at the gatehouse, where Halferan's standard of three pewter bars slanted across a damson ground fluttered in the wind. No one would usurp this barony again. Even if the price of that was Master Rauffe's overbearing solicitude and his wife's irritating tendency to reorganise the linen closets without ever consulting Zurenne.

'Shall we take some air? Jilseth suggested brightly. 'Would you like to walk around the walls?'

Zurenne considered her options. That was a more inviting prospect than returning to her withdrawing room to deal with Neeny's sulks and Lysha's endless questions about what exactly Lord Licanin's guardianship would allow her, or forbid her, to do.

The noblewoman wasn't deceived though. Jilseth must have more questions about Master Minelas. Well, Zurenne didn't have to answer. She inclined her head to the lady wizard. 'Let's see how the pastures are faring.'

Rather than head for the main gatehouse, she turned towards the narrow entrance cut through the manor's encircling wall, tucked behind the great hall. That was how Starrid escaped. Licanin's men had discovered the gate swinging open as they routed the last of his hirelings.

Their path cut through the herb garden that separated the baronial tower from the kitchen and any risk of a spreading fire. Beside the kitchen, the laundry, brewery and bake house chimneys smoked steadily. Zurenne could hear the water that served them rushing through the stone-lined conduit that ran from the brook outside the walls.

A cloud of steam billowing from the laundry's latticed window told her that the maids had opened the sluice to let their suds wash along the channels to the stream a suitably discreet distance away. Snowy linen flapped in the breeze in the drying ground behind the household buildings, in front of the storehouses whose garrets accommodated those servants who didn't live in the village beyond the brook.

'Mistress Rauffe has the household well in hand,' Jilseth observed.

'Indeed.' Zurenne reminded herself to be grateful. She had her keys back, their reassuring weight swinging from the chain fastened around her waist. As long as she held those, she was content to leave hiring scullery maids and lackeys to Mistress Rauffe, a shrewd judge of character for all her appearance of rotund amiability.

Under Starrid's rule, most of the manor's maidservants had fled his henchmen's lustful attentions. Those few that remained were so self-evidently traitorous sluts that Zurenne had them thrashed from the gates with birch twigs, letting them take nothing but the clothes on their backs. That had left the manor inconveniently ill-attended until Master Rauffe had arrived.

'My lady.' The portly guard at the rear gate tugged his forelock and opened it for her.

Zurenne nodded to the guardsman at the sally gate. Jilseth followed her through to the top of the sloping bank supporting the wall on this side of the compound.

The grazing land that lay beyond was neatly divided with sturdy hedges. Spring grass was dotted with ewes and frolicking lambs. Dairy cows stood aloof, chewing their cud. Birdsong floated on the balmy breeze.

'Your demesne reeve tells me the herds are flourishing,' Jilseth remarked.

'Indeed.' Zurenne nodded.

The demesne reeve had also told her that the lady wizard knew nothing of animal husbandry, however learned she might be. That's how Zurenne had learned that Jilseth had been asking what the man knew of Master Minelas's intentions when he left Halferan. Anxiously twisting his homespun hood in his hands, the reeve swore he meant Zurenne's honoured guest no insult but he truly had nothing to tell her.

Zurenne studied Jilseth thorough her eyelashes as they rounded the curve of the roughly plastered brick wall. Why were a minor coastal barony's affairs of such interest to Hadrumal's Archmage?

Jilseth halted. 'You know I went to the marshes yesterday.'

'Indeed.' Zurenne shivered despite the warm sun. Ten leagues to the edge of the saltings and the lady wizard had gone and come back within the afternoon. A man on a fast horse would have been hard pressed to do that without ruining the beast for days.

'Would you like to know what I learned?' Jilseth offered.

'Of my husband's death? No,' Zurenne said tightly. 'You told Lord Licanin and that will suffice. He will lay the facts before parliament. I have no standing as a widow.'

That's what Licanin had said, when Jilseth had made the same offer the evening before. Zurenne had debated with herself long into the night, staring up at her bed's canopy, before deciding there was nothing to be gained by revisiting the grief that had so nearly destroyed her. Licanin was right. Now she must be strong for her daughters and look to their future. All her sisters said so.

Their letters bolstered Zurenne's resolve during the day, if she ever found herself unoccupied and that was seldom enough. It was at night in her lonely bed that she quaked with fear, lest Minelas reappear to challenge Licanin's guardianship. There were still sixty five days to go before the barons gathered at Solstice. Zurenne was crossing them out in her almanac. Even thinking of it now, she had to lace her fingers together to stop her hands from trembling.

'As you wish.'

As Jilseth replied Zurenne saw a shadow cross her brow. Had the lady wizard discovered something dire out there in the marsh? What could be more dreadful than Halferan's death?

'I should return to my daughters,' Zurenne said abruptly.

'May I join you?' Jilseth asked politely.

Zurenne narrowed her eyes at the lady wizard. 'To ask them more about Master Minelas?' Lysha had said that the woman wanted to know every word which had passed between her and the vile usurper.

Zurenne certainly didn't believe that Jilseth had any other interest in her children. She was as irritated as Licanin by Neeny's prattle. While she deigned to approve Lysha's copybook, she'd barely glanced at the embroidery which the girl had shyly shown her.

What of your needlework, my lady mage? Zurenne longed to ask. Who sews your seams so that you have the leisure to disparage such womanly virtues? Or is such honest toil done by magic amid Hadrumal's mists? What little Licanin had said of his visit to that unearthly isle sounded most unsettling.

Jilseth declined Zurenne's challenge. 'I hoped that Ilysh might play the clavichord,' she said.

That was as good as an outright lie as far as Zurenne was concerned. The lady wizard was as deaf to music as the stable cat. When Ilysh had shown Lord Licanin her proficiency on the expensive instrument, Jilseth's tapping foot had constantly stumbled over the beat.

Zurenne shook her head. 'We will be attending to the shrine.'

Since Starrid had gone, Ilysh insisted on helping her mother. A baron always served as the demesne priest, she argued and if she was the heiress to Halferan, this was her duty to her father's memory. Zurenne could no more deny her than she could stop Esnina trailing after them, to rumple the shrine table linen and dabble in the bowls of flowers.

'As you wish.' Jilseth inclined her head, apparently submissive.

Zurenne wasn't at all convinced, so made no reply. Walking onwards around the wall, she contemplated the reassuring vista of the horses grazing in the pasture on this side of the brook and the peaceful bustle of the village beyond, by the high road. They followed the curve of the sturdy wall and turned to see the manor's gatehouse.

As soon as they came into view, someone shouted high up in the gatehouse's turret. The gusting wind snatched away his words.

Zurenne looked through the open gate to see who the man sought to alert. The ragged guard troop in the courtyard looked uncertainly at each other. She realised with a cold shock that these men she must now rely on had no captain to guide them.

'My lady, the sentry is calling you.' Jilseth snapped her fingers and the man's panic sounded in Zurenne's ear as clearly as if he stood beside her.

'Riders, my lady, an armoured troop, coming through the woods on the north road.'

Zurenne's knees almost gave way. Minelas and his henchmen were returning.

'They must have been keeping watch from the cover of the woodland,' Jilseth observed with mild interest, 'until Lord Licanin was well clear. Very well, my lady Halferan, will you meet them on the steps of your hall or welcome them inside?'

Zurenne couldn't answer. Her mouth was dry as dust.

'That depends who they are, of course.' Firm yet unobtrusive, Jilseth's hand on her elbow propelled Zurenne through the shadowed entrance.

'My lady!' The sentry hurried to lean over the turret's inner parapet. 'They've unfurled gold lattice on a crimson ground!'

'Baron Karpis's standard.' Zurenne cleared her throat. 'We'll wait on the hall steps.'

She could not face Lord Karpis alone. Halferan had always said that he was a bully. He'd told Zurenne of debates among the barons when he'd been forced to shout their arrogant neighbour down, to make him acknowledge objections to whatever plan he had in mind.

'Shall we ask him how much Minelas paid, to purchase his testimony before the parliament?' Jilseth clapped her hands at a dithering boy in overlarge livery. 'Summon all the household to support your lady!'

Hurrying across the cobbles on nerveless feet, for the first time Zurenne was glad of the lady wizard's presence. Nevertheless she doubted she'd have the nerve to challenge Baron Karpis over his treachery. How were they to be rid of him without Lord Licanin's authority?

The fringe of the woods wasn't very far along the high road. The women had barely reached the top of the great hall's steps when their unwelcome visitors arrived.

Lord Karpis glared at the Halferan guards. 'Who will take charge of my horse?' The beast was lathered from the gallop, a blush of blood amid the sweat betraying cruel whip strokes.

No one moved. Every man looked to Zurenne for her order. She managed a curt shake of her head as their loyalty warmed her.

Red-faced with indignation, Lord Karpis kicked his horse towards the great hall's steps. 'This is no welcome, my lady!' Still in his prime though now tending to fat, he was as fussily dressed as Zurenne remembered, both gold fringe and embroidery decorating his costly riding cloak. The pomade in his hair was so thick that not even riding headlong had stirred his mouse-brown locks.

'I sent you no invitation.' Sudden anger lent a welcome edge to Zurenne's words.

'I need no invitation to do my duty.' Karpis dismissed her with a haughty gesture and turned in his saddle to beckon to his assembled men.

To Zurenne's utter astonishment, Starrid emerged from the knot of horsemen. With a repellent smirk, the man rode towards the steward's dwelling beside the stable.

'Where does he think he is going?' Zurenne demanded, outraged.

'You have no authority to dismiss Halferan's steward,' Karpis declared, as much to the assembled household as to Zurenne herself. 'He will resume his former duties.'

'He will not!' Zurenne almost started down the steps to bar Starrid's way herself.

Jilseth's unseen hand held her back. Her voice breathed in Zurenne's ear. 'Stay up here and he can't look down on you.'

As Zurenne froze, the lady wizard addressed Baron Karpis.

'You have only recently returned from the parliament in Duryea, I believe. How did you find the roads, my lord?'

'What?' The conventional courtesy distracted him. 'The journey was easy enough.' His belligerence returned. 'Who are you to ask?'

'She is my guest,' Zurenne snapped, 'which you are not. Kindly explain your presence and your impertinence!'

As she glared back at him, she was pleased to see a pensioned-off sergeant-at-arms plant himself between Starrid and the steward's house. Mistress Rauffe stood on the threshold with a birch broom. Her husband approached from the path by the brew house, tall and wiry and with a copper stick in his hand.

'What poisonous nonsense has this scoundrel poured into your ear?' Zurenne didn't hide her contempt for Starrid.

Baron Karpis ignored her, addressing the assembled household once again. 'Lord Licanin has no authority to dismiss Halferan's steward. There has been no new grant of guardianship approved by the barons' parliament.'

Jilseth stepped forward. 'On whose authority do you presume to reinstate him? On Master Minelas's behalf?'

The anger warming Zurenne deserted her. Did Karpis herald her tormentor's return? How soon could she get word to Lord Licanin? What might Minelas to do her and her daughters in the meantime?

Then she realised that Baron Karpis was glaring at Jilseth. He hadn't liked that question. However the pompous bully swiftly rallied. 'Master Minelas has been absent from the last three parliaments. When I learned he was no longer resident here, I realised my duty to settle Halferan's affairs.'

Zurenne found her voice. 'The barony's affairs are settled. Lord Licanin stands as my guardian.'

'In good conscience, I cannot approve that.' Karpis shook his head, his confidence returning. 'I will make my own case to the Summer Parliament. Until then, I will manage Halferan's affairs as the closest neighbouring baron and don't presume to gainsay me, woman,' he said with sudden venom. 'You will do as you're bidden. Begin by yielding to your husband's steward. Don't imagine Lord Licanin's guardianship will be approved,' he promised ominously. 'He lives far too far away to defend unprotected women in such uncertain times.'

Zurenne retaliated as best she could. 'Since you talk of neighbours, my lord, what does Baron Tallatt think of your proposals?'

Karpis smiled, malicious. 'Lord Tallatt and I discussed our concerns in Duryea. He and I will propose our mutual management of Halferan's lands.'

It was as she'd feared. They sought to divide her daughters' inheritance between them. Zurenne raised her chin, defiant. 'You will not.'

'As you make your case to parliament,' Jilseth enquired, 'will you explain why you supported Master Minelas? I fear the noble barons won't think much of your judgement,' she continued thoughtfully, 'when our witnesses give their testimony. How Minelas and his creature there—' she nodded towards Starrid '—dismissed the demesne's honest servants in favour of wharf rats and footpads with license to insult any maiden who came within reach.'

Zurenne saw that Karpis hadn't known that verse of this ballad. He narrowed his eyes at Starrid who was now hesitating between the baron's retinue and a line of Halferan men barring his way.

'If you give that thief houseroom, count your silver nightly,' Zurenne advised the baron. 'All he'll get here is a bed in the midden by the road.'

'Shall we chuck him in the muck heap?' The old sergeant stepped forward, several men eagerly following.

A handful of the Karpis men slid from their saddles, ready for a fight. It would be an unequal one. The newcomers wore chainmail hauberks and coifs. Barely half the Halferans even had a sword.

Starrid smirked while Karpis shook his head with insincere dismay. 'A master's hand is sorely needed, if Halferan offers violence to its neighbours.'

'Excuse me,' Jilseth said apologetically. 'My lord, do you have a penny?'

'What?' Karpis looked at her, perplexed.

'A copper penny.' Jilseth held out her hand. 'If I may.'

Bemused as he was, Karpis couldn't resist some petty spite. Not armoured himself, he rummaged in a doublet pocket under his cloak. With a flick of his thumb, he sent a single coin tumbling to the ground in front of his curious horse. 'You can—'

Before he could invite Jilseth to grovel for it, the coin darted to her waiting palm.

'My thanks.' She nodded at the startled baron and passed her other hand over the coin.

As astonished as everyone else, Zurenne watched the meagre copper disc rise into the air. As it began to spin, it began to grow. Golden magelight burned away the tarnish to leave the metal gleaming.

Jilseth gestured and a candle flew through the open door of the guards' hall, swift as an arrow. The wick kindled with scarlet sorcery as she plucked it from the air. The copper disc was now as broad as her hand, as brightly polished as a mirror.

'What—' Karpis's apprehension strangled the rest of his question.

'I must bespeak the Archmage.' Jilseth's expression suggested this should be obvious. 'He should know of your proposals, my lord.'

Unnerved, Karpis blustered. 'Caladhrian affairs are no business of Hadrumal's!'

'Forgive me, my lord.' Jilseth wasn't remotely contrite. 'Since you've been in Duryea for the parliament, you can't know that Baron Taine and Baron Saldiray have sought Hadrumal's aid in uncovering the depths of Master Minelas's deceptions. I know the Archmage wants to know how you and Lord Tallatt were duped.'

'What?' Karpis involuntarily reined his horse back a couple of paces. 'No. You cannot use magic against us.'

'Not even the Archmage can stop me using my magic however I might choose,' Jilseth assured Karpis, her hazel eyes opaque. 'He can punish me if he doesn't accept my reasons. But if I choose to risk his wrath, I can do whatever I wish.'

Like everyone else in the courtyard, Zurenne was agog. Was Jilseth going to turn Karpis into a toad like some hedge mage from a tavern tale?

Then Karpis's retinue began exclaiming. Their horses stamped and whinnied, sorely affronted.

'Talagrin's hairy balls!' One man swore, wrenching at his sword hilt. It came free with only a handspan of corroded metal below the cross guard.

More sword scabbards warped and split asunder. Brooches shattered and the Karpis men's cloaks slid off their shoulders. Their chainmail was crumbling away, leaving them clad in rust-smeared padded tunics. Halferan's guards began to jeer.

'I don't imagine the Archmage Planir will chastise me.' Jilseth smiled at Karpis. 'No one's been hurt, merely stopped from making mischief. Now, if you wish to ride home, I suggest you get on your way. Otherwise I can test my wizardry against your horse's harness and you can walk.'

'This is not an end to this!' Torn between fear and anger, Karpis jabbed with a shaking finger, unable to decide if his target was Jilseth or Zurenne.

Then he wrenched at his horse's reins and spurred for the gateway as if Poldrion's own demons pursued him. His men followed, all discipline abandoned. Starrid fled after them, scrambling back into his saddle, frantically shouting that he knew nothing of this terrifying stranger.

'That should give him pause for thought,' Jilseth said with satisfaction. 'You need not fear his kind while you're under Hadrumal's protection.'

As the reverberations of Baron Karpis's rout faded from the courtyard, Zurenne's delight at his humiliation faded as swiftly. She looked at her barony's guards; shavelings or grandsires.

'What do I do when Hadrumal's protection is withdrawn? When you've found out whatever it is you've come here to discover about Master Minelas?'

Without waiting for Jilseth's answer, she went into the great hall and walked its length to the stairs up to her private apartments. She had better have a letter detailing this encounter ready for Lord Licanin's messenger.

Would he send her some of his own troopers? Because Halferan was sorely bereft of worthy defenders.

— CHAPTER TEN —

Teio's Strand, in the domain of Khusro Rina
31st of Aft-Spring

CORRAIN GNAWED A ragged nail. Could he kill a wizard? He reckoned so, as long as he could get close enough, unsuspected. Then Minelas's death would be justice for Halferan and Corrain would argue his right to such vengeance with any man. Of course, he had to get home first.

'What is this place?' Kusint looked warily around.

'Don't draw the overseer's eye,' Hosh warned in low tones. 'Take this.'

Corrain shook off his distractions and accepted the basket of straw-packed bottles. Kusint took the next and they headed for the *Reef Eagle's* stern rail. This time their feet had been freed, just leaving their forearms burdened with manacles linked by clinking chains.

The rower who normally sat so silent beside him said something mocking.

Corrain smiled back at him. 'Pick up a basket, you slack-arsed goat lover.'

'Don't.' Hosh's nervous eyes darted towards the Aldabreshin overseer standing by the other ladder on the far side of the stern post.

'They don't understand.' Speaking in coastal Caladhrian, Corrain smiled amiably at the silent man.

'This would be a bad time to learn that they do.' Kusint handed his basket to another rower perched on one of the stern ladders. An Archipelagan crewman was supervising two others loading the net sling. Coffers and sacks from the hold were being lowered carefully to flat bottomed boats poling to and fro across this shallow bay.

A great many galleys were anchored within the curving reef. Ashore the sands were thronged with Archipelagan traders, from the humblest sitting on a blanket beside a spread of wood and shell trinkets to those relaxing beneath a shady canopy as their minions haggled with customers over silks, ceramics and metalwork.

'What is this place?' Kusint's eyes asked Corrain a different question. *Is this* the *place?*

'It's a trading beach, like a market.' Corrain held the red-head's gaze. *Yes.*

'This warlord, Khusro Rina, keeps a close watch on his waters,' Hosh quickly explained in clear Tormalin for the benefit of anyone listening. 'Galleys and triremes may only use the waterways which he has approved for their passage. Galleys may only land their cargo at these designated trading beaches.'

Corrain breathed a silent prayer to the gods he didn't believe in. *Don't let anyone suspect they planned to escape.*

Before they had embarked, chained to inconveniently separated oars, Corrain had told Kusint everything that they knew about these trading beaches and what they guessed about their customs and practise. Uncertainties still outweighed their knowledge. Corrain's hands shook as he passed the basket to Kusint.

The Forest youth held it between them. 'I heard they don't use coin. How can they have a market?'

'They bargain,' Hosh volunteered. 'Cloth for food or a ride to some other island in return for a cooking pot.'

The overseer was eyeing them. Corrain shrugged. 'What's that to us?'

But of course, it was vital. Because slave or free, a man must have something of value to trade to get ashore. He looked at Hosh.

The scrawny lad cleared his throat and went over to the other stern ladder. He waited meekly for the overseer to conclude his dealings with the Archipelagan in the flat-bottomed boat beside the galley.

If the overseer noticed the lad's pallor beneath his sweat, they just had to hope he'd take Hosh's cowering as his due from the wretched mainland barbarian. Corrain looked away, lest his anxiety betray them. He could only trust that the lad was saying what they'd agreed, meeting beneath the ugly tree on the anchorage beach in the dead of night.

The heavens offered propitious omens for trade. The Diamond, the Amethyst and the Opal were all in the arc of the sky that promised the Aldabreshi wealth and possessions. The shining stars of the Vizail Blossom would rise this very night on the eastern horizon, token of plenty alongside the heavenly Ruby, emblem of courage.

Hosh had a trade of his own to offer the overseer. He understood the mainland tongue so he'd understand the northern merchants as they strolled among the tented pavilions and modest awnings on the sands. He could tell the overseer what he overheard, to offer the Aldabreshin rogue an advantage when he had liberty to go ashore. All the galley master's henchmen had stolen mainland goods to trade on their own account.

Corrain could guess the overseer was asking Hosh what the boy wanted in return.

Hosh squared his narrow shoulders, only emphasising his painfully prominent ribs. He spoke up boldly nevertheless. He wished to be the slave collecting the leavings from those trading food; discarded scraps of flatbread, fruit with the first bloom of mould, the dregs of broth from cauldrons already emptied of stewed meat and vegetables.

Rowers were fed such garbage in return for the titbits of news which galleys carried between these trading strands. Humble islanders wanted word of neighbouring domains, however jealously their warlords guarded the tidings brought by their courier doves.

'Halcarion smiles today,' Kusint breathed as the overseer nodded.

Corrain grunted. The Forest goddess of love and luck had a great deal more to do if he were ever to revere her again. Even if fortune had favoured them so far. The blind corsair had come to trade in the Khusro domain which lay between the mainland and the corsairs' home isle. Had the skies decreed otherwise, he would have ordered the ships southwards to the welcoming beaches and merchants of the Miris domain. Desperate as their plan was, it would have been suicidal in more southerly waters.

Better yet, the trireme was anchored on the far side of the reef, along with a handful other such predatory craft. Khusro Rina wouldn't allow any warship close enough to launch an attack on the trading beach. That should win them a little more time once the overseer realised something was wrong. Once he decided the risks of not sending word to the blind corsair outweighed the dangers of being the herald of bad news.

There'd be few people on the galley whom he could ask for advice. The galley master and whip master had already gone ashore, shallow boats ferrying their personal loot. Barely a third of the corsairs remained to keep the slaves in check.

Now their hopes lay in Hosh's bony hands. Corrain hated that. If he wanted a job doing properly, he was used to doing it himself.

There it was! The signal they'd agreed. Hosh clasped his hands behind his back as he ducked an obedient head to the overseer. Now he gestured to Corrain and Kusint, ushering them to the stern ladder.

The silent man who shared their oar strode forward from the stern hatch down to the hold. He called out to the overseer. Corrain saw Hosh's dismay at the Archipelagan's reply.

'We have to take him with us,' he explained as he rejoined the two of them by the ladder.

'He's only a greedy son of whore.' Corrain pretended unconcern. They couldn't have Hosh panicking.

'I said I wanted to say who gets the first pick of the food.' Hosh waved to catch the eye of a shallow skiff's master. 'I said I'd be safer at the anchorage if the big men know I can see them fed or starving at sea.'

Although Hosh was gabbling, Corrain was impressed. The daft lad had learned to think on his feet.

'Let's get going.' Kusint climbed down the ladder. The silent man followed. Corrain studied their unwelcome companion with open suspicion. The man's light-skinned face gave nothing away.

In the skiff, they sat silent amid the hubbub of the waters. Ferrymen called out to each other, to men and women up on the galleys or on the smaller boats at anchor, triangular sails furled around angled spars.

More voices rose as they approached the beach, shouting everything from greetings to curses and mockery. Merchants were doubtless boasting of their wares, their quality and their value; however the Aldabreshi measured such things.

'Seen anything you like?' Corrain asked Kusint lightly.

The Forest youth nodded. 'Here and there.'

A metalworker with the tools they needed to break their chains? A boat that the three of them could crew out on the open seas? Corrain burned to ask but the silent man was watching him closely. Carrying out their plan would be thrice as hard with this bastard dogging their footsteps. It wouldn't be long before the overseer wondered where they were.

He considered grabbing the silent man's ankles and throwing him bodily into the water. But that would attract attention and they mustn't risk that any sooner than they had to.

The silent man said something to the ferryman as the shallow boat grated on the gravelly shore. The ferryman replied with alacrity. Hosh chipped in with a forced smile.

Corrain's stomach hollowed. 'What's wrong?'

Hosh spoke quickly in Caladhrian dialect. 'He asked this man to wait to take us and the food back to the galley. He says we won't be long.'

So now someone else would be watching and waiting for them. 'Let's get ashore.' Corrain mentally measured the chain linking his manacles, barely restraining himself from drawing it taut. Yes, it was long enough to wrap around the silent man's throat.

Kusint was already splashing towards the drier sand. The silent man followed close behind him.

Hosh plucked at Corrain's elbow. 'If the ferryman raises the alarm—'

'Only if he sees something to alarm him.' Corrain offered the waiting man a cheery wave. 'So let's lose ourselves in the crowd.'

That proved easier said than done. Traders were spread right along the broad sweep of the beach but their stalls were rarely more than two or three deep and all allowed their neighbours generous elbow room.

No one paid them any attention. There were a fair number of shaggy haired and bearded men ashore, marked as slaves by their chains and comprehensively ignored until they were needed to carry something for the Archipelagans they were trailing after.

Corrain slipped between three women examining a leather worker's wares. A bead-seller waved her colourful strings to entice the keen-eyed matrons in her direction.

Corrain didn't think anyone would recall them when the overseer came looking for straying slaves. Archipelagans couldn't tell one northern barbarian from another.

Hosh exclaimed with annoyance. Corrain saw the silent man grab the lad's shoulder. The Aldabreshin pointed at a ring of cook fires supervised by a brisk woman in tight-fitting tunic and trews. Underlings, surely her sons and daughters given their resemblance, fried sliced fruits and grilled meat and fish over glowing charcoal.

Their mother accepted a dark-wood box bright with mother of pearl inlay. She added it to a stash of wax-sealed bottles and lidded bowls before shaping a lump of cloud bread dough. She slapped it on a griddle to puff up as it cooked.

'Let him go begging there.' Kusint spoke up before Corrain could smack the silent man's hand from Hosh's shoulder. 'We'll go on down the beach.'

The silent man shook his head. 'No need to go on.'

Corrain stiffened. The bastard did speak some Tormalin.

'Corrain?' Kusint was looking inland towards the open ground beyond the ragged-fringed trees edging the beach. Armoured men were lounging on benches beneath twisted trees spreading shadier branches. 'They're Khusro Rina's guards?'

'Doing their duty to their lord.' Corrain wasn't fool enough to think they were as idle as they looked.

They wouldn't let anyone off this beach to wander the island's interior. Not traders, not visitors from other domains, definitely not curious slaves or even some overseer searching for strays. So if the three of them could possibly slip past the swordsmen unnoticed, they could benefit from the warlord's unwitting protection.

'Look there.'

Corrain saw Kusint's gaze fasten on a whitesmith's forge. The man was doing a thriving trade mending tin pots and pewter utensils. His tools could free them from their chains.

'You try to escape?' the silent man sneered. 'Now I know it, you are mine.'

Corrain had done enough soldiering to know that most plans fell victim to the unexpected. The mark of a good captain was keeping hold of the reins whatever misfortunes struck.

They'd hoped to quietly watch and wait and see if the guards' vigilance ever wavered. If so, all was well and good. If not, they'd wait for the galley's next landfall.

Sooner or later, Corrain swore, a sentry's attention would wander. He'd stood enough watches himself to know and Kusint had agreed. A slim chance but better than none.

So how well would a diversion serve them? Corrain only hoped that Kusint had his wits about him and Hosh's new-found talent for thinking on his feet held up.

Corrain shoved the silent man, both hands on his chest. As the man staggered, Corrain pursued him before he regained his balance. Another push sent the man further back. Startled Aldabreshi recoiled to leave their way open. So far, so good. Unlike his victim, Corrain could see where they were heading.

But the not-so-silent man fell over. As soon as he hit the ground, he thrust his leg between Corrain's ankles. Slamming his other foot against Corrain's shin, he twisted like a stamped-on snake.

Corrain fell hard, face down, sweat and dust searing his eyes. He rolled quickly onto his side and hauled up his knees. If he kept their legs entangled then the silent man couldn't escape him. He flung out his hands trying to catch the bastard in the face with the loop of his chain.

The silent man flinched away, arching his back. That saved him from the chain but he missed his chance to seize Corrain's hands.

Corrain got one knee beneath him and threw himself on top of the man. Both muscled from labouring at the oars, he was still the heavier. They lay motionless for a heartbeat, close as lovers.

So another man's death was the price of their freedom, of seeing justice for Lord Halferan. Corrain could live with that bargain. He wrapped the chain around his fists.

The man smashed his forehead into Corrain's nose, momentarily blinding him. The silent man wriggled free. Corrain snatched at his ankle but the chain on his own manacles pulled his hand up short. Their would-be betrayer opened his mouth to yell. Kusint silenced him with a double-fisted blow to the face.

Corrain seized his chance to assess their situation. This was nowhere near enough distraction. He sprang up with a roar and ran straight at the traitorous rower. The man tried to step aside but Kusint stopped him with another punch. Corrain drove his shoulder into the man's gut, ducking under his raised fists. He ignored the stinging slap of links on his back, the vicious gouge of the rower's manacles. This time the man would fall over when it suited them.

His bare feet skidded on the dry earth. A few more paces. There it was. Corrain threw his weight forward, lifting their betrayer bodily off the ground. The man screamed as he landed in the closest cook fire. Corrain rolled away, his own skin seared, hands and forearms worst of all. The woman in charge of the cook circle was screaming curses while someone yelled for help.

A dark swathe of cloth swept above Corrain's head. As he staggered to his feet, he saw Kusint had flung it at their betrayer, the man writhing as his clothes burned. But the Forest lad seemingly missed his mark, sending the heavy cloth into the next hearth where a pan of oil ignited with a flare prompting further panic. Kusint ran to drag the cloth away. Now the burning fabric landed close enough to a tent to stir fresh outcry.

Corrain saw the cloth merchant advance on Kusint, his snarl promising retribution. He scooped up a double handful of sandy soil and flung it in the man's face. The blinded merchant lashed out wildly, catching another trader a violent blow.

Confusion was spreading fast. Some sought to help the cook fire's victim. Opportunists snatched spilled food from the dust. The food sellers smacked thieving hands and heads with spoons and ladles. Outraged retaliation saw more pots upset, one fire quenched in a cloud of savoury steam. Another hearth erupted, the pot rolling away to scatter gouts of burning oil. Now those trying to get away from the flames were hampered by those drawing closer, curious to see the uproar.

Kusint grabbed his hand. 'The warlord's men are coming.'

'But Hosh—' Corrain couldn't see him amid the chaos.

'Move!' Kusint's merciless grip on Corrain's scorched arm was excruciating. He could barely think, his nose throbbing and his eyes raw. 'This way.' Kusint abruptly changed direction, pulling Corrain after him.

He could have screamed with the agony of it. 'We have to go back for the lad!' Between a securely pegged tent back and a spiny tree, Corrain wrenched his arm free.

'We'll only have this chance.' Kusint let his arm go, only to grab the chain between his manacles. 'To escape those swordsmen and lie low in the woods until we can find a boat.'

Corrain looked desperately around. 'But Hosh—'

'Go back and you will be flogged, most likely killed. Your bones will rot in these islands. Will that see your master avenged?'

In that instant, Corrain hated Kusint more than he'd ever loathed anyone. Even Minelas. But the Forest lad was right; curse him to Poldrion's demons.

— CHAPTER ELEVEN —

In the domain of Khusro Rina
31st of Aft-Spring

CORRAIN TOOK IN the uproar along the trading beach. He couldn't see how to retrace their steps to the cooking circle. Even if he went back for Hosh, he couldn't hope to find him in this commotion.

The Khusro warlord's guards ran past, ignoring them completely. The grassy expanse between the beach and the shady trees was left empty. Beyond, another rough sward ran to the foot of a brush-covered slope. From these shallow hills the island rose steadily to a distant peak.

'Come or not. It's all one to me.' Kusint ran.

Corrain followed. How could he not? If he'd had the breath he would have begged Hosh's forgiveness all the same.

Was that a warning yell behind them? Some cursed Aldabreshin alerting Khusro Rina's guards to fleeing slaves? What of it? Looking back risked fatal delay. They broke through the trees, skirting the guards' empty benches. Corrain ran faster, hating himself with every stride. How could he abandon Hosh? But how could he go back for him now?

'Get down!' Kusint flung himself into a gully carved by a stream. 'Are we pursued?' he demanded as Corrain crouched beside him. 'What can you see over there?' Peering over the gully's lip, he looked to north and west.

Corrain wiped anguished tears from his stinging eyes and scanned the trees to south and west. While there was plenty of commotion spilling out off the trading beach, none was heading in their direction.

As his pounding heart slowed, the deafening rush of his blood lessened. 'There's no hue and cry.' His chest ached with guilt as well as exertion. He wondered desperately what had happened to Hosh.

'We must head away from the shore.' Kusint shifted, ready to move. 'Will they set hounds on our trail?'

Corrain was dumbfounded to realise he hadn't seen the meanest mongrel among the corsairs.

'Do they use hounds to hunt?' demanded Kusint. 'By sight or scent?'

'I've no idea,' Corrain admitted.

Kusint grimaced and retreated to wallow in the shallow stream. 'We should break our trail regardless. Hurry!'

Kusint was already scouting ahead up the far slope. Corrain followed, barely pausing to douse himself with cool water.

This red-headed youth knew a suspicious amount about foiling pursuit. Well, Halferan's guards had always agreed Forest Folk were thieves and mountebanks, as they supped their ale. Forest women could warm the coldest bed and rouse the limpest manhood and only a fool would turn an invitation down, but their men were good for nothing.

Saedrin's stones! Where had he gone? As Corrain halted, stricken, Kusint appeared beside a stand of red canes, beckoning swiftly.

Good for nothing? Hardly. Kusint had the measure of this tangled undergrowth inside ten paces. Corrain followed quickly, intent on not losing him again. Thankfully the Forest lad soon found a deer path threading through the grey-trunked trees.

They crossed that first ridge on hands and knees to avoid being sky-lined. The far slope dropped steeply down, bare earth corded with roots. Kusint jumped from the last crumbling ledge to land beside a green-furred puddle. Yellow-veined leaves sprouted in clumps beside another stagnant slick.

Corrain saw movement through a cluster of red canes further along the gully. He was surprised to feel dull relief. They were caught. Hosh would know he hadn't been abandoned.

If Khusro Rina's men didn't kill them on the spot. They'd seen that straying slaves suffered no worse than a beating for breaking the bounds of a trading beach. No wonder. Kill a visiting ship's rowers and a warlord would have to recompense the vessel's master. They'd been relying on that, as they planned to test the Khusro guards' vigilance. But there could be no mistaking them for anything but runaway slaves if they were caught so far from the shore.

Corrain heard an odd barking sound. Dogs, after all?

'What are those?' Kusint moved for a better look, mystified.

Corrain could only shake his head. 'I have no idea.' The island harbouring the corsairs was a small one and he'd only ever seen goats among the trees. Starving slaves had long since trapped and eaten everything else.

Black-furred creatures were lapping from a bigger pond beyond the canes. About the size of a lurcher, they had dog-like muzzles but as one sat up on its haunches, it showed rat-like forepaws, long-fingered and sharply clawed. The largest stood upright, bow-legged and lashing a tail as long and lithe as a cat's. It barked again, inky lips drawn back to show formidable teeth. Corrain didn't take his eyes off the creature, lest it suddenly spring.

'No one's hunting us here,' Kusint said with satisfaction, 'or they wouldn't be drinking.' But as he spoke, the lithe creatures darted away, scurrying up trees to vanish among the leaves.

Corrain didn't wait to see if their arrival had startled the beasts or the creatures' large furry ears had heard Khusro Rina's men. Kusint was already running. They didn't pause until they put another tree clad ridge between themselves and the shore.

'Wait.' Corrain slowed. 'I need those.' He pointed at tight clusters of fleshy leaves in a patch of dappled sunlight. 'Leatherspear, the corsairs call them.' So Hosh had said, Corrain recalled with a bitter pang. 'Good for burns.'

Careful of the spiny tip, Corrain twisted a leaf free and tore it lengthways. He offered one half to Kusint, belatedly noticing that his antics with the flaming cloth had scorched his hands as well. 'Lay it pulp side down.'

He breathed slowly as the cool juice soothed his burns. These injuries should scab cleanly, as long as he could find more of these plants over the next few days. That was a relief because after all this travail, Corrain was not prepared to die from such trifling wounds. Not after losing Hosh. He breathed a savage prayer to Poldrion, hoping that the silent man died screaming after days of festering agony.

Twisting another leaf free, he used his teeth to split its tough base, spitting out the bitterness. This would be so much easier with a knife.

Kusint waited until he'd treated the burns on both his forearms. 'Let's go.'

By the time that the yellowing sunlight heralded the Archipelago's swift dusk, Corrain had wished for a knife a hundred times over, to strike back at the vicious leaves or to cut through knots of creepers. Hunger gnawed at his belly. With something to cut the thinnest, wiry vines, they could have rigged a snare, maybe caught one of the lapdog sized deer they saw or even a forest hog rooting with its odd spiral tusks. He was hungry enough to risk eating one raw.

Kusint interrupted his fruitless musing, his lean face taut with exhaustion. 'Let's get to higher ground before dark. Talagrin only knows what will come down to drink.'

They were following yet another narrow defile carved by a stream through the rumpled landscape. The Forest lad was right. Corrain looked for a route up the steep valley side and then at the streambed strewn with sharp-edged rocks, plenty of them large enough to snap a falling man's spine.

'We have to free our hands.' He looked around for a boulder to serve as an anvil. 'Spread your fists. Keep the chain taut.'

The first hammer stone he tried split clean in half. Cursing, he tried another. It held but so did the chain. Worse, every crashing strike echoed back from the ravine's sides.

Corrain's throat tightened with apprehension lest the noise drew some hunter's attention, man or beast. The stubborn metal finally yielded.

'My thanks for that.' Kusint stretched his long arms wide with a fervent groan of appreciation.

'My turn.' Corrain had no time to waste.

The shadows were thickening ominously before the second chain finally fractured. Night had truly fallen by the time they reached the top of the slope, grazed and dirty from heart-stopping slips as the plants that seemingly offered handholds proved perilously shallow rooted.

'Which way?' Corrain looked up. Precious little light was finding its way through the trees. There'd be little enough out in the open. The Greater Moon was dark with the Lesser only at her half. That's how they'd known this was a trading voyage, without the highest tides ahead to carry the corsairs onto the mainland and a raid.

'We had better sit tight till dawn,' Kusint said reluctantly. 'I don't fancy stumbling into some abyss.'

'True enough.' Corrain yielded to his exhaustion. 'They can't hunt us in the dark.'

'I wish we had a fire,' Kusint muttered some while later.

They were sitting back to back in the shelter of a bushy tree. Not too close to the trunk, for fear of snakes in the branches, on bare earth they had cautiously swept clear, for fear of scorpions amid the leaf litter.

The black night was alive with insects churring and chittering, hovering close before darting in to bite their sweaty flesh. Unable to see their tormenters, unable to see their own hands in front of their faces, neither man could swat the bloodsuckers.

Corrain grunted. 'I didn't see those rocks strike a single spark from our chains.'

They sat in silence through the interminable night. Small creatures squeaked and rustled through the undergrowth. Some larger beast passed slowly by, ponderous and ominous. They heard its heavy breathing, flanks brushing the leaves along one of the deer trails. Predator or prey? Corrain didn't want to find out.

Finally the first hint of day filtered through the leaves. His hunger reawoke, clawing at his belly.

'Let's find something to eat.' Kusint looked gaunt in the half-light.

But picking a cautious path through the grey jungle, they found precious little that Corrain knew to be wholesome.

'I'd settle for some water.' Kusint wiped sweat from his brow. 'We should find a stream heading for the sea anyway. Let's get our bearings.'

Before Corrain could ask what he meant, the Forest lad was climbing a tree, lithe as any squirrel. As he vanished, Corrain scowled at the thick green leaves. Fall and break a bone and Kusint might as well break his neck. Corrain had no hope of stealing a boat with an injured man—

Kusint dropped back down and grinned through his weariness. 'I can see the sea and a stream heading that way.'

'Any smoke?' Corrain demanded. Fires meant people and even if word of fleeing slaves hadn't reached these remote thickets, they were clearly fugitives, shaggy-haired and unwashed.

Was anybody hunting them? Had they beaten the plan out of Hosh? Not that the lad could betray which way they had gone. Corrain had no idea where they'd wandered by now. But would the whip master believe that before he'd flogged Hosh to death? Would they kill the fool boy just to warn the other slaves off planning such boldness?

Kusint shook his head. 'No smoke. No roofs. No noise.'

'Lead on.' As Corrain gestured, the last of the withered leatherspear fell from his arm. He kept his eyes open for more of the plants as Kusint forced a path toward the stream he'd seen. They were both bleeding from plenty of fresh scratches by the time they reached it.

The going was easier after that. Following the deepening rivulet, they emerged into the mid-morning sun above a narrow creek. Before Corrain could stop him, with a whoop that shook a flock of emerald birds from the trees, Kusint jumped feet first in the water.

Corrain hastily searched the banks for any sign of people. None to be seen. That was both good and bad news. They needed to find people to find a boat, unless they planned on paddling out to sea on a floating log.

He contemplated the darkly swirling water. Much as he longed to scrub off some grime and cool his itching insect bites, he decided not to risk some corruption from the mud on his burns.

'This way to the sea.'

As Kusint swam, Corrain followed on the bank. Reaching the mouth of the creek, they found waves breaking noisily on black shingle. Kusint clambered out of the water and Corrain found a path of sorts tracing along the coast. As noon approached, he was beginning to despair. The rocky cliffs were rising ever steeper, plunging sheer into waters deep enough to drown a man inside a heartbeat. They toiled through the vicious tangle of another tree-choked headland.

'Trimon be thanked.' Hoarse with thirst, Kusint pointed to a cove lying below them. Boats hung with nets were hauled up on the beach. Huts straggled beneath a line of nut palms well beyond the high water mark.

Corrain gripped his arm. 'Can you sail those?'

Kusint nodded. 'If we can steal one.'

Corrain gauged the sun overhead. This was the hottest stretch of the day. If the customs of the corsair anchorage were any guide, whoever lived in this fishing hamlet would be enjoying whatever shade they could find. With luck, the fishermen were sleeping off their night's labours. Women wouldn't emerge to cook or send their children foraging among the trees until it grew a little cooler.

He resisted the temptation to scramble down and rush across the sand to the boats. 'We need water.'

They found a meagre streamlet in a crevice shaded by an opportune tree. They each drank their fill and, once again, Corrain wished for a knife. With a blade he could have fashioned something to carry water for their voyage.

This was madness. They couldn't hope to make the crossing so hopelessly ill-supplied. Three weeks without food, three days without water. That's what his old sergeant-at-arms had told him a man could survive. Three days, that had always been the rowing time from the Khusro domain to their first glimpse of Cape Attar, southernmost tip of the mainland.

He looked down at the sandy beach. How could they steal a boat and be safely away in it before those fishermen saw them and chased them down?

What choice did they have? There was no going back.

Give up and they might as well jump to their deaths on the black rocks as die slowly lost in the forest. Give up and whatever Hosh was suffering for his sake would be for nothing. Whatever the lad was suffering for the sake of their oath to Halferan and the vengeance they sought on Minelas.

Corrain couldn't stomach that. He wiped stray drops from his chin. 'Come on.'

As they ran across the sand towards the boats, Corrain's mouth was as dry as leather. How was that possible with all the cold water sloshing in his belly?

'That one.' Kusint headed for the closest mooring post.

Lazy ripples of foam cooled his aching feet as Corrain fumbled at the rope with numb fingers.

'Let me.' Forest thief or not, Kusint was good with knots. He loosened the hawser inside a few breaths.

'Is it sound?' Corrain tried to see if the hull showed any damage, if the ropes were rotting, or the sail. This boat could kill them both out on the ocean. But if they didn't take it, death would surely find them on this island.

'It'll do,' Kusint assured him. 'Quickly, before we're seen!'

Together they dragged the boat hissing down the sand. As the eager sea nudged it, Corrain clambered aboard. Kusint had already found an oar to shove them off into these unknown waters. Corrain looked back towards the hamlet, but no one appeared among the huts and nut palms before the cove disappeared behind the headland.

'We did it!' He surprised himself by laughing out loud.

'Not yet.' Kusint wasn't amused. 'Help me raise the sail. Hold that. Now pull!'

Thanks be to all the gods that Corrain no longer believed in, Kusint hadn't been idly boasting when he'd said he could manage a boat.

The Forest youth guided the tiller and hauled on the ropes, shouting whenever he needed Corrain's hands or his dead weight hanging perilously over the boat's side. Corrain did as he was told. It saved him from having to think. It saved him from fearing that every sail they saw, every hull on the distant horizon, was going to bear down to recapture them.

As soon as they left the sheltering bulk of Khusro Rina's island, they were at the mercy of the winds. The fishing boat skipped across the waves like a nutshell tossed by a child. After a year as a galley slave, Corrain would have wagered a barony's gold that he was inured to seasickness. He would have lost his bet before sunset.

Endlessly trying to vomit on an empty stomach was so vile that he even forgot to fear being washed overboard or being knocked senseless by the triangular sail's erratically swinging spar.

Surviving that first night without the boat turning turtle and drowning them was victory enough. The next day was another ordeal of fear, hunger and thirst as they fought yet more violent winds and waves. After a second night of battering, another day that felt like half an eternity and a third night of exhausted terror, the rising sun finally showed them the mainland coast.

Salvation still lay far out of reach. The currents rounding Cape Attar were fierce and rightly feared. The most that Kusint could do was to keep their frail boat on an even keel as they were swept helplessly along below the towering cliffs.

— CHAPTER TWELVE —

Trydek's Hall, Hadrumal
34th of Aft-Spring

'HEARTH MASTER? YOU called for this meeting. Shall we get to business?' Planir sounded positively intrigued.

Jilseth might have expected Kalion to look annoyed by Planir's veiled amusement. Instead Master Kalion was smiling, taking his ease on an upholstered settle.

They were in the spacious sitting room where Planir was accustomed to confer with the island's senior mages. He also used the room to teach his own pupils and to offer guidance or discipline to lowlier apprentice mages, according to their needs and the wishes of whichever Hall Master or Mistress was guiding their studies. Jilseth and her fellow mages handpicked by Planir had perfected their nexus here, working quintessential magic together watched by the silent statues in their niches in the panelled walls.

The door was always open but Kalion had arrived escorted by three other wizards. That struck Jilseth as unwelcome boldness by the Hearth Master. That wasn't her only concern. Kalion had specifically requested her presence.

Planir nodded affably at Kalion's companions. 'How are your studies of quintessential magic progressing?'

Of course, Jilseth should have realised.

She would have expected to see Ely, who was in an emerald ribbon trimmed gown, sitting close to Galen on the settle beside the seat which Kalion had claimed. Broad-shouldered in dun wool, the earth mage's blunt-featured face was as impassive as always. It was no surprise to find him in Kalion's shadow either.

But Jilseth had been curious to know what Canfor's presence signified. Tall, thin and prematurely white-haired, the wizard bringing an air affinity to Kalion's scheming leaned against the window sill, a glass of the Archmage's wine in his hand.

He didn't follow the fashion of wearing his wizardly affinity's colour; his doublet a muted tan over black breeches. His shirt was Aldabreshin silk though, Jilseth noted.

She also saw his chagrin. Had he really thought another nexus working in Hadrumal would escape Planir's attention? She also wondered how Canfor's oft-voiced disdain for earth-bound magecraft sat with Galen.

Would that affect the working of their nexus? Planir said he'd taken some considerable care to find four mages who could work together in friendship, when he'd introduced her to Tornauld and then to Merenel and Nolyen, whose fire and water affinities now combined so effectively with her own.

Jilseth spared a moment to wish they were in this room now. Then she and Planir wouldn't be so outnumbered. Why weren't they here? It wasn't like the Archmage to be outmanoeuvred.

'Our explorations have resulted in some interesting discoveries.' Kalion smoothed his scarlet tunic. 'I gather that Mistress Jilseth has been to Caladhria to visit the

Widow Halferan. After you recently honoured those lordlings from their parliament with a personal audience in this very hall. Are you finally persuaded that we must curb this menace of the corsairs?' he demanded.

'No.' Planir looked unconcerned. 'Is that all?'

'Hardly,' Kalion said with some asperity. 'I take it you're aware of the way in which Jilseth humiliated Baron Karpis?'

Planir surveyed the other wizards with interest. 'I suppose I should be flattered that you've been paying such close attention to my dealings on the mainland. And in Hadrumal too?'

'There's no edict against it,' Kalion asserted.

'Indeed not,' Planir agreed. 'How else could an Element Master or Mistress, or indeed, an Archmage, fulfil all the responsibilities of office? One can hardly do one's duty without being fully informed.' This time his smile didn't reach his steely eyes.

Jilseth saw Galen redden. Ely lifted her pointed chin, her face bright with defiance. Over by the window, Canfor smiled and drank his wine, not catching anyone's eye.

'The Council is agreed,' Kalion said loftily. 'This business with Caladhria needs very careful handling if Hadrumal's reputation is to remain unsullied. Such foolishness as Jilseth indulged in discredits us all.'

Jilseth sat in the high-winged chair next to Planir's and looked calmly at the Hearth Master. That way she didn't have to see Ely's smirk or Canfor's scorn.

'You mean those members of the council whom you've spoken to individually have concurred,' Planir corrected Kalion. 'Or they haven't openly gainsaid you, which you naturally take for agreement. The full Council has yet to discuss any recent events in Caladhria.'

Kalion's face hardened. 'So when will you lay this matter before the Council?'

'Does it really warrant their time?' Planir plainly doubted it. 'There's little new to warrant taking our esteemed colleagues from their studies and obligations. Caladhrian barons are asking for wizardly aid once again. They've nothing to add to the ragbag of arguments which I reported to the Council after their last such appeal. And no, Kalion, I haven't changed my mind on that question. Hadrumal has no business fighting corsairs.'

The Archmage rose and went over to the side table to pour himself some wine.

'To return to the Caladhrian barons, I granted them an audience since dismissing their concerns by letter would hardly have been courteous. As you and I have long agreed, the mainland's nobles and princes deserve our respect.' Planir walked over to the empty fireside, wine glass in hand. 'On the other side of those scales, travelling to the mainland myself to tell them we cannot oblige, risks encouraging the Caladhrian parliament to believe the Archmage is at their beck and call. I thought it more fitting for the standing of Hadrumal to have their lordships come here as suppliants.'

Hoping that isolating and intimidating them amid Hadrumal's halls would convince them to accept the Archmage's refusal as final. If this wretched business with Minelas hadn't bobbed up like a dead dog in a well, Jilseth fully believed Planir's strategy would have succeeded.

'Then why did Jilseth go hurrying off to Halferan's manor?' Kalion persisted.

Planir smiled and looked across the room to Canfor. 'Your auditory spells proved inadequate at that distance?'

'Thus far, Archmage. I look forward to improvements as I draw on our nexus's power.' Canfor didn't look up. He appeared to be studying the white raven board on the gaming table by the window. Planir often invited apprentices and pupils to play and seemed to be half way through a game.

Jilseth was glad she had declined a glass of wine. She would have been tempted to throw it in Canfor's face.

'Well?' Kalion demanded. Jilseth was pleased to see frustration colouring his fat jowls.

'All in good time. I'm curious to know why you are so adamant that the Council must address this business of these corsairs. Do you believe that we're at risk here in Hadrumal? Is that why you've formed your own nexus, to defend wizardry's interests?' The Archmage's wave of his wine glass encompassed Ely, Galen and Canfor. 'You have my permission to sink any black galley stumbling through the wards that guard our waters.'

'Do not mock me, Archmage.' Kalion scowled. 'As long as these scavengers plague Caladhria, these appeals for our aid will continue. Obstinate rejection reflects ill on us all. Offering aid to the mainland can only enhance wizardry's reputation.'

'Feel free to propose some compromise to the Council, provided it avoids the grim consequences that prompted my predecessors' edict.' Now Planir's gesture took in the statues around the room. 'That challenge has defeated wiser mages than me.'

'The wisest Archmages knew to trust their Element Masters and Mistresses,' Kalion said, with rising ire. 'Perhaps if you had consulted myself and Troanna as well as Rafrid, this business could have been far better managed.'

Planir looked at Canfor again. 'Does your Element Master know that you're spying – forgive me, scrying on him?' He waved a careless hand before Canfor could even try to answer. 'I've no doubt he does.'

'As it stands,' Kalion continued forcefully through the interruption, 'Caladhria remains plagued by corsairs and the barons believe that we not only refuse to help them, but we're ready to make festival fools of them without provocation. You say we shouldn't interfere with mainland affairs yet Jilseth has done just that. You should see the letters I have had from the most influential barons,' he warned. 'They are outraged on Baron Karpis's behalf; that he should be so insulted when he only sought to protect a widow and her children once he learned they had been left unprotected.'

'Lady Zurenne is not unprotected,' Jilseth said hotly. 'She has an honest and competent guardian in Lord Licanin, or she will have once the parliament approves him. Whereas Baron Karpis sought to usurp the barons' authority through force of arms and threats.'

Planir sat forward in his chair. 'I will be very interested in those letters, Hearth Master. I'll be very interested to see how Baron Karpis explains his connivance in the forged grant of guardianship previously inflicted on the Widow Halferan. That's what Jilseth has been investigating.' Planir rubbed a hand over his chin. 'I'm puzzled, Kalion. You pride yourself on your acquaintance with the foremost barons in Caladhria's parliament. Yet you were wholly unaware of this deceit?

'What are you talking about?' Kalion was perplexed.

'A forger, a thief, imposed himself on the Widow Halferan as her guardian after her husband's death. By whatever means, Baron Karpis was induced to support the man's spurious claims. Once he had robbed this grieving widow and her children, he fled. Should I have refused Lord Licanin's request to help find the villain? It was mere good fortune that Jilseth was there when Baron Karpis arrived. I hate to think how he might have sought to cover up his collusion if he had ridden into Halferan and found himself with a free hand.'

'There must have been some misunderstanding.' Kalion looked troubled nevertheless.

'Let us be thankful that the Caladhrian barons don't know precisely who they're hunting.' Planir's voice hardened. 'Minelas, once of Grynth and more recently of Hadrumal.'

'The renegade?' Kalion stiffened with recollection. 'Who tried to sell his skills to Triolle?'

'The same,' Planir confirmed.

Jilseth saw that the notion of Minelas as a renegade came as a complete surprise to Fly, Galen and Canfor. She didn't have to feign her own startlement. When had Planir told the Hearth Master of Minelas's perfidy, and why?

'But Minelas is dead.' Kalion narrowed his eyes at Planir.

The Archmage nodded. 'Thanks to Jilseth.'

She managed to sit stony faced as the other wizards looked at her with sharp astonishment. Not Kalion however. Planir had evidently told him the whole story of her tracking Minelas down in Triolle, only to see him gutted by Sorgrad's unpredictable and thankfully non-mageborn brother, in the service of Lescar's rebels.

'However,' the Archmage continued, 'this theft predates his treachery in Lescar. If the truth were ever to come out, Hearth Master, your influence in Caladhria would go up in flames. A grievous loss for Hadrumal after your earnest endeavours.' He sounded wholly sincere.

'But Minelas is dead.' Kalion's relief gave way almost immediately to anger. 'When do you propose to lay this before the Council? We must determine just how thoroughly he has disgraced wizardry.'

'Perhaps Jilseth can be of assistance,' Canfor observed, beside the window, 'rendering the truth from his bones.'

Jilseth hoped her face didn't betray her nausea at that prospect. She also wondered what Canfor hoped to gain by needling her like that.

Kalion and Planir both ignored the lean wizard's remark. Kalion was frowning, deep in thought. 'As long as no one has reason to suspect Minelas was a mage, we should avoid a scandal. Halferan is a minor barony after all.'

'Quite so.' Planir nodded. 'Of scant concern to the principle barons whose estates and commerce look inland, north and east, to Ensaimin and to Tormalin. Jilseth has established that Minelas worked no magic while he was living in Halferan, before he went to sell his skills in Relshaz. With nothing to arouse suspicion, there's no reason why any of his misdeeds should have come to your notice through your noble Caladhrian acquaintance.'

Jilseth readily grasped the Archmage's unspoken warning. Accuse Planir of any failing before the Council and the Hearth Master must explain his own lapse, all the more embarrassing given his boasts of mainland influence. But Kalion seemed impervious.

'It's painfully clear that you underestimated Minelas.' The Hearth Master couldn't conceal his satisfaction. 'You and Rafrid both. I take it you did inform him of such duplicity by one of his own affinity?'

Kalion had never liked the Cloud Master, Jilseth recalled, even before he'd been elevated by the Council's endorsement of Planir's nomination. Naturally Kalion had favoured another candidate.

'Of course.' Planir seemed surprised that Kalion should ask.

'Not that I blame Rafrid, of course, since Minelas was apprenticed under his predecessor. A worthy element master would have curbed Minelas's arrogance from the outset,' Kalion insisted. 'Now we may all have cause to regret the way in which you allowed Otrick such licence to pursue his own flights of fancy at the expense of fulfilling his duties.'

'I believe the Council will agree that I showed fitting respect for a Cloud Master many decades my senior in office,' Planir mused. 'Besides, Otrick always warned me against reining in apprentices too tightly. Those with talent can become too cowed to realise their potential—' his gaze drifted towards Ely '—while those naturally inclined to rebel will be more likely to do so. If they leave Hadrumal half-trained as well as resentful, the consequences can be all the more perilous for mundane and mageborn alike.'

Planir wagged a chiding finger. 'You cannot run with the hare and hunt with the hounds, Kalion. If you want mainlanders to believe that wizards are not all

Hadrumal's minions, ready to do the Archmage's dread bidding, we must allow our prentice-mages the freedom to travel and to make their own choices about where they might live and hone their magecraft.'

'Suthyfer.' Kalion's snarl made a curse of the distant islands' name. 'Don't try to twist this debacle into some argument supporting your folly there. What new understanding of magecraft have your protégés there offered us? Those malcontents and ingrates whom you have allowed to scorn our teaching and set up their own haven of wizardry? How many more renegades like Minelas will such licence nourish?'

The Archmage's face hardened further. 'There are more mages than Minelas who find Hadrumal's stone walls more prison than sanctuary. I believe fewer will follow his path if they have some sanctioned route to a less oppressive place where we can still stay apprised of their conduct.'

Kalion grunted. 'So you say. But if we're reduced to swapping chimney-corner wisdom, let me offer this. He who hunts two hares catches neither.'

'By which you mean Hadrumal and Suthyfer?' Planir nodded. 'You don't see the folly of putting all wizardry's eggs in one basket?'

'The Council looks to you for single-minded guidance,' Kalion said with growing ire, 'on the future course of wizardry, on our relations with the dominions and realms of the mainland, on our dealings with this rival magic of Artifice. But we see you letting matters unfold however they may, in Hadrumal, in Suthyfer and clear across the mainland. Your responses are entirely haphazard, driven by events which you do not even attempt to influence!'

'If the Council truly believes that my counsel is lacking, they may challenge my tenure as Archmage.' Planir returned to his chair. 'If that's what you truly believe, perhaps it's time we reconsidered your tenure as Hearth Master—'

'You would not dare!' Kalion's booted feet slid back, as if he were about to spring to his feet. The dregs of wine in his glass ignited in a passionate scarlet flame. 'Do not mock me, Archmage!'

'Do not test me, Hearth Master,' Planir shot back. 'And don't let me keep you from debating how to present my choices to the Council in the worst possible light.' He gestured towards the door. 'You will, however, oblige me by taking your discussions elsewhere. Galen. Canfor. Ely. Good day to you. Hearth Master.'

Startled, Kalion had no choice but to rise and depart, Ely following, her face pinched with anxiety. Galen went after her, as impassive as ever. Canfor followed, with a smile that Jilseth detested as well as distrusted teasing his lips.

Planir drank the wine which he'd been holding untasted.

'Do you think Kalion will really try to discredit you before the Council?' Jilseth asked reluctantly.

The Archmage raised a warning hand. 'Canfor's skills with auditory spells are considerable, even if he couldn't reach all the way to Halferan.'

Azure haze filled the room, shimmering in the sunlight falling through the broad windows. Jilseth longed for such effortless control of the element so antagonistic to her own.

'The Council needs to know of Minelas's crimes.' Planir sighed. 'All his crimes, including Lord Halferan's murder, and that it was encompassed by the villain's magic. I cannot conceal such things from those who have entrusted me with Hadrumal's governance. I have no choice there.'

That said, Jilseth noted, the Archmage could usually choose when to inform the Council of some cause for concern. Had Kalion forced his hand before he was ready?

Planir grinned. 'Every rune bone lands to show one upright for each one reversed. If Kalion is fretting about what might happen if Minelas's crimes come to light, he can't be drumming up support for wizardly action against the corsairs.'

His smile faded. His hand tightened around the empty wine glass. It dissolved into fine white sand flowing to the floor.

'My compliments to Cloud Master Rafrid, if you please, and ask him to call me at once.'

'Archmage.' Jilseth hurried from the room. She had never seen Planir betray such anger before. She also wondered uneasily if the Archmage had intended to reduce that second glass to sand; the one which Canfor had left on the windowsill.

How much trouble could Kalion stir up, among the other members of the Council of Wizards? It was meagre comfort to think how much worse this could have been, if the Caladhrians had even suspected Minelas of magic.

— CHAPTER THIRTEEN —

THIS WASN'T HOW he'd imagined his homecoming; trudging barefoot along the high road wearing stolen clothes. Once he had been the envy of the guardhouse, drawing female eyes wherever he went with his fine linen, well-tailored clothes and polished boots.

Truth be told, Corrain had given up hope of getting home at all. Until, finally, around noon of that last terrifying day afloat, the Caladhrian coast relented. As the cliffs retreated inland, the sea met an expanse of windswept dunes. Once the tide turned in their favour, Kusint guided the boat into the surf. As soon as the hull bumped on the sand, Corrain yelled at him to jump over the side. He'd done just that before Kusint had a chance to ask why. As they spluttered their way ashore, fighting the buffeting waves, Corrain had explained.

'If we let the waves take the boat, it'll be cast ashore wherever the currents choose. No one gives a wreck a second look, not on this coast. But if we beach it properly, if some whelk picker stumbles across it, that could start a panic. I don't want to be beaten senseless for a corsair.'

'They could hardly think I'm Archipelagan,' Kusint had objected, 'and you're one of their own.'

'I doubt they'll let me get close enough to open my mouth with skin as dark as this.' Corrain had held up a hand tanned by the Aldabreshin sun.

Kusint had yielded; saving Corrain from having to tell him his Forest blood would be as suspect as any other foreigner's. Nor did he say, though he guessed it would be so, they wouldn't simply be beaten if they were caught. Not two unknown vagabonds, bare-chested in ragged trews, unshaven with knotted hair trailing down their backs and broken chains dangling from their fettered wrists. No. Corrain hadn't escaped the corsairs and an Aldabreshin warlord's swordsmen to be hanged by his own ignorant countrymen.

'The first things we need are shirts and breeches,' he had told Kusint. 'We'll arouse less suspicion if we're decently dressed.'

Then if they were challenged, if they couldn't escape being noticed entirely, he could explain away their presence with some bluff. With his familiarity with the region and its dialect, they should escape with only the usual insults and perhaps a beating, to keep vagabonds on their way.

Corrain wouldn't be telling the truth. He didn't want any whisper of his return to reach Minelas.

They circled right around the first village that they came to. Finally Corrain could steal them both some clothing from a goodwife's laundry spread on a buckthorn hedge. At the next hamlet, they raided a cottager's garden for the season's first turnips and carrots, tender and sweet.

Corrain didn't allow himself any qualm of conscience over the thefts. His first duty was to return to Halferan as swiftly as possible to avenge his dead lord. To return home unexpected, to cut that bastard mage's throat before the shitsucker even saw him coming.

So he insisted they walk through pastures instead of along the high road. They skirted any fields where herdsmen tended placid beasts. As each night drew on, they gave lit windows a wide berth, snatching what sleep they could in the indifferent shelter of hazel coppices.

Around the villages the fruit trees were thick with blossom while the coppices were cloaked with fresh green. Crops thrived in the fields and the verges were dense with flowers; the high white froth of Larasion's lace rising above clumps of blue quills, yellow hedge-bells and pink maiden's blush. Birdsong sweetened the air, only broken by the harsher shrill of some cock bird spoiling for a fight with a rival. There'd been no rain these past few days and the nights were warm enough to spare them any frost on their blankets.

Waking with the dawn they joined the rabbits raiding vegetable gardens, wary for the thump of an early riser's tools from some hamlet's workshops. As they walked, they plucked spring greenery from the hedgerows. Kusint had a sharp eye for the most tender leaves and Corrain recalled hearing that Lescari vagrants relied on such forage. The Forest lad had found wild birds' eggs and eaten them raw too. Corrain couldn't stomach the thought of it.

Now his guts twisted inside him. Ahead in the gloaming he could see lights in the windows of the baronial tower, and the breeze brought the tantalising scent of an evening's pottage from the village beyond the brook. But it wasn't only hunger knotting his guts.

'You're as tense as a bowstring,' Kusint observed.

'I need a sword if I'm to kill him.' Corrain looked

at the manor compound wall and the dark bulk of the gatehouse. 'I have to get in there unsuspected.'

Now he was here, either of those aims seemed an impossibility to rival their escape from the Aldabreshi. But of course, they had done that. Somehow the thought didn't hearten Corrain.

'You need to know if he's in there first,' Kusint drew him into the shadow of a chestnut tree a few discreet paces off the road. 'Is there anyone you could ask?'

'Not without them asking whatever befell me.' Corrain hesitated. The Spring Parliament would have come and gone, leaving Caladhria's barons free to return to their own firesides until they gathered at solstice, but who knew where a wizard's business might take him?

He contemplated the village where the manor's servants lived alongside a few craftsmen and those families who put bread on their tables with daily labour in the demesne fields. Hosh's old mother lived there.

Their questions would be endless. How could he return and tell them he was the only one? That their beloved sons and brothers and husbands were all dead? That he had witnessed Lord Halferan's murder?

'I need to see her ladyship,' he realised aloud. 'Before anyone knows I'm back.'

An owl drifted overhead, piercing the dusk with a querulous cry.

'Is there anyone you could trust to take your mistress a message?' Kusint prompted.

'I wonder.' The finest of Halferan's household guard had been murdered out in the marshes and the rest had vanished into the Archipelago. Who had that traitor Minelas hired to replace them? Home or not, Corrain must be as alert for danger as he ever had been among the Aldabreshi.

'We must arm ourselves.' He searched the hedgerow for some stick to make a cudgel. He tugged at a promising length only to find it wouldn't come loose.

'Whoever laid this hedge over winter made a handsome job of it.' With his longer reach Kusint managed to wrench a stake from amid the woven branches.

'Going in fear of the wizard,' Corrain said savagely.

Kusint hauled a second stave out of the hedge for him. 'So where are we going now?'

'An old friend.' Corrain swallowed. 'If he lives.'

If old Fitrel had kept his head below the parapet. He'd always told Corrain to remember that a miller can never change the wind but he can always turn his mill's sails to catch a favourable breeze. A long time ago, Fitrel's father had been a miller.

'This way.' Corrain gripped his stick, though he had no notion what he would say if he were challenged.

'That's the tavern?' Kusint wasn't suggesting they call in for some ale.

Corrain halted as laughter and music drifted through the evening. He looked down at the lane; dry and well tended with no ruts allowed to wreck an axle or an ankle. When they'd reached the outskirts of the Halferan demesne that afternoon, Kusint had remarked on the fine condition of the flocks.

Corrain ground his teeth. Of course Minelas would see the barony well tended, to fill his pockets with more gold.

But the revelry in the tavern unnerved him. He had been gone for more than a year. How much had changed in that time? Had everyone forgotten their dead lord so entirely? What lies had Minelas told about what had happened in the marshes? Surely Fitrel wouldn't have believed whatever that story had been?

They skirted the village, cutting across the rough grazing behind a row of placid brick cottages. A more disreputable wooden house lay some distance behind them. Rather than offering neat rows of vegetables, the garden was dotted with wooden cages. The inhabitants rustled, inquisitive.

'Rabbits,' Corrain explained as Kusint bent down to look. That reassured him. Fitrel was still raising meat and fur to supplement the grain and ale and copper pennies of his pension. Corrain rapped on the door with his purloined stake.

A glint through a crack in the planking showed a lamp approaching. 'Who's there?'

'Corrain, and a friend.' His voice cracked and he couldn't continue.

'Corrain?' The door flew open, nearly hitting him in the face. Incredulous, the old man thrust his lantern so close that Corrain could feel the candle's heat on his cheek.

'Saedrin save us,' the old man breathed. 'Everyone thinks you're dead, lad! Poldrion turn you back for lack of coin for the ferry to Saedrin's door?'

'I was taken by corsairs. We were betrayed—' Corrain bit down on his words. Lady Zurenne must be the first to hear this.

But the old man was nodding comfortably. 'By Master Minelas, that scum.' Fitrel spat casual contempt into the darkness. 'But we never expected to see any of you, not when the lady wizard said you'd been taken by the raiders' ships.'

He squinted at Kusint, hopeful for an instant then trying to hide his disappointment. 'You're welcome, friend, if you're a friend of this one.'

'That's good to know.' Kusint ducked his head, his eyes bright with equal amusement and curiosity.

'Where is Master Minelas?' Corrain could barely get the words out. Had someone already taken the vengeance he'd promised himself?

'Ah, now that's a very good question—' Fitrel broke off to step back from the threshold. 'But come inside, lad, you and your friend. You've had a hard time of it on the road, I'd say. Let me find you some bread and broth.'

The door opened into a kitchen warmed by an iron stove guarded by a brick built hearth and chimney. The room showed an old soldier's discipline, clean and mostly tidy but lacking niceties such as rugs on the flagstone floor or cushions on the wooden chairs. Fitrel lived alone as he always had. He'd been sharpening knives on the deal table.

Corrain's gaze lit on a wicked blade. 'What do you know of Minelas's treachery?'

'We did wonder what Lord Halferan could have meant by signing that grant of guardianship.' Fitrel's hand shook as he set the lamp on the table. 'But how could the likes of us gainsay it?'

He went to the stove and lifted the lid from a heavy pot. The aroma of stewed rabbit filled the room. 'Then he took himself off, last Aft-Autumn, leaving Starrid in charge, with a troop of scoundrels eager to break heads if anyone cared to argue. Then come Spring Festival, Raeponin finally sent us some justice. Lord Licanin came and drove Starrid out and hanged them of his men as didn't run. They're still rotting on the gallows.'

'And Minelas?' Corrain had to sit down. The flagstones underfoot felt as uncertain as a galley's deck.

'No one knows.' Fitrel took two bowls from a shelf. 'Even the lady wizard can't find him.'

'What lady wizard?' Taking a seat on the opposite side of the table, Kusint asked the question which Corrain couldn't begin to frame.

'Madam Jilseth.' Fitrel ladled chunks of meat into the bowls. 'From Hadrumal.' He startled Corrain with a sudden laugh. 'She made Starrid look a fool and a half. Shame you weren't here to see that, lad.'

'I thought you said Starrid was gone.' Corrain's hand moved towards a knife.

Fitrel chuckled again. 'Turns out he went scuttling to lick Lord Karpis's boots in hopes of getting his place here back again. As soon as Lord Licanin took to the road, they came riding in, ready to run roughshod over Lady Zurenne. But the wizard lady was here and they didn't expect that.'

The old man raised a warning hand. 'You don't want to go sniffing round Ralia again. Now she's rid of Starrid, she burned their marriage bed and she's keeping company with Brahen. They'll wed at midsummer.'

'I'll dance at the feast to wish them well.' Corrain had no interest in the steward's former wife. He'd only fallen into bed with her because he was drunk and she was weeping over the latest bruises which Starrid had given her. Hearing that gobbet of snot had turned his coat for Minelas came as no surprise. There was a far worse shock to contend with.

'What by all that's sacred and profane is a wizard woman doing here?' he demanded.

'She came to find out the truth with her magic, of what happened in the marshes.' Fitrel set the steaming bowls on the table and took a loaf of bread from an earthenware crock. 'Once Lord Licanin learned that Master Minelas had left us and there was every reason to doubt his appointment as guardian in the first place.'

Corrain could only stare as Fitrel told his tale, finally concluding with the widespread approval of Lord Licanin as the Halferan barony's guardian until Lady Ilysh was old enough to wed.

'So did you escape from some corsair ship raiding the coast? Where was that? South of here?' Fitrel sat at the end of the table, lacing his stained fingers tight. 'We've been fearing these high tides.'

It took Corrain a moment to realise what the old man meant. Of course, the galleys would be rowing north by now. The Lesser Moon had waxed to its full two days ago and the Greater would do so in four night's time. Even with the Lesser waning, the seas would be ripe for raids. He hadn't given that a second thought. Now he was back in Caladhria, the only thing he wanted to do was kill Minelas.

But here he was, like some lackwit who'd lost his almanac and turned up for a midsummer fair only to find the festival already over, solstice garlands wilted and tossed aside.

'Do you—' Fitrel hesitated. 'Do you have word of the others? The lady wizard said you were chained for slaves but her spells couldn't find you.'

Hunger beyond bearing prompted Corrain to take up his spoon and eat. The meat was tender, the broth rich with herbs and if the bread was a day stale, it soaked up the glistening liquid. None of it filled the hollow beneath his breastbone.

'Corrain, lad?' Fitrel tried again.

'I don't know anything,' he said dully.

Kusint cleared his throat. 'Hosh—'

'We've no word for Hosh's old mother.' As Corrain shoved the empty bowl away, the chain dangling from his manacle clinked against the pottery.

He glared at Kusint. There was no mercy in telling an old woman that her son was doubtless dead of a flogging. The fool boy must be shark shit by now. After Corrain had abandoned him, telling himself it was for Halferan's sake, for the oath they had both sworn.

Now it was all for nothing. Corrain's gorge rose and he feared he was about to spew that stew and bread back up again. He swallowed hard.

Whatever Fitrel saw in Corrain's face prompted him to turn to Kusint. 'Where are you headed, friend?'

'No idea.' Kusint shrugged.

'Will Lady Zurenne give us an audience?' Corrain rose to his feet. He couldn't face the prospect of an evening here by the stove fending off Fitrel's questions. Besides, he had some burning questions of his own.

'Now? It's late,' Fitrel said dubiously.

'Never mind.' Corrain was heading for the door undeterred.

'You put me in mind of the Dalasorian horsemen in Lescar.' Kusint stood up. 'Do you know what they always say?'

Corrain halted, half turned. 'No.'

Kusint grinned. 'When in doubt, gallop.'

Despite everything, Corrain's heart lightened a little. 'You're still with me?'

Kusint shrugged. 'Why not?'

'Why not?' Fitrel was caught between bafflement and outrage. 'Because you're filthy dirty, the pair of you, and barely dressed. You haven't even got boots to your feet and you expect admittance to my lady?'

Corrain was already out of the door.

Fitrel followed, hastily snatching his cloak from a peg on the wall. 'I'd better vouch for you at the manor. Arigo's got the duty and he's as blind as a mole these days.'

'Arigo?' Corrain was startled. 'He was pensioned off two years since.'

'Three years, him and me both,' Fitrel retorted. 'But we're the best my lady can call on to hold off the likes of Lord Karpis!'

As it turned out, Arigo was asleep by the guard hall fire. A youth who looked vaguely familiar opened the wooden slide to see who knocked on the gate.

'Open up, Reven,' Fitrel said briskly. 'Captain Corrain's back to whip you into shape.'

The boy stood gaping before scrambling to open up. 'Captain Corrain?' he called out as they hurried through the gate and across the cobbles. 'My Uncle Treche, do you know what befell him?'

Of course. The lad had the look of the man. Corrain almost turned but Kusint laid a warning hand on his arm.

'Answer him now and there'll be ten more tugging your sleeve. You must see your lady first.'

Corrain could already hear disbelieving voices repeating his name as the guard hall's opening door threw candle light across the compound. As the steward's door opened, a curtain rattled on its rings, hastily pulled back from the parlour window.

The door at the top of the great hall steps opened. 'What's amiss?' A woman called out. Not Lady Zurenne or anyone else whose voice Corrain recognised.

'Madam Mage.' Fitrel ducked his head in a nervous bow.

'You're this lady wizard they speak of?' Corrain couldn't see her clearly; a shadow against the lamplight inside the hall.

'I am.' The torch in the bracket beside the door flared scarlet.

Corrain wasn't impressed, either by the magic or what the firelight revealed. The magewoman looked like a dressmaker's maid. Then again, Minelas had seemed unremarkable. More than one trooper had thought him a milksop, before he'd called down lightning to kill Halferan's men between one blink of an eye and the next.

Corrain squared his shoulders. 'I wish to see Lady Zurenne.'

'I will see if she has finished dining.' The wizard woman stepped back. 'Come in and wait.'

Kusint glanced at him. What now? Corrain realised he'd never shared the details of Minelas's magic with the Forest youth. Come to that, he hadn't the slightest notion what Kusint knew of wizardry.

But what else could they do? He went up the steps. Kusint followed. The magewoman was walking back down the length of the hall. She had been reading, alone at the high table up on the dais. Reading and writing. Paper and ink lay beside the open books.

'Please, be seated. I will see if her ladyship is willing to see you.' She sounded like a maidservant. Though a maidservant couldn't have sent the outer door behind them slamming back into its frame untouched by human hand. Corrain shivered.

'So this is the pride of Halferan.' Kusint had paused to look around the hall. 'Truly handsome, my friend.'

'It looks better in the daylight.' Corrain's courage returned as he contemplated the lofty ceiling. The banners hung veiled in night's shadows but he knew them by heart; the standards of each Baron Halferan since time out of mind, blending the pewter and damson insignia with the emblems of those baronies whose daughters they had married.

'Captain Corrain?' Up on the dais, the door to the baronial tower opened. 'No, not captain. You were disgraced even before you were lost.'

Lady Zurenne walked forward. Hearing her disdain and distrust Corrain wished fervently for clean clothes, polished boots and a shave.

He dropped humbly to one knee. 'I was disgraced, my lady, through my own grievous fault. I am ever grateful to your husband, my lord, that he didn't dismiss me entirely.'

'Yet you are here and he is dead. How can that be?'

Corrain was shocked to see the difference in Halferan's lady. She had always been slightly built, short enough to tuck her head under her husband's chin, within the protective circle of his arm. Yet the curve of her hip and bosom had always promised every womanly virtue, her face as soft as a flower. Now her dark eyes were huge above cheekbones sharp against the dark luxuriance of her hair. A green gown made to her former measure hung in unaccustomed slackness at her hips.

He stifled his anguish. 'My life had the meagre value of a slave's, my lady, and that's the only reason I was saved. But your husband's death was of infinite worth to Master Minelas.'

'Indeed.' A crystal tear beaded Lady Zurenne's lashes. 'Very well, Guard Corrain, swear your loyalty to Halferan and you may return to your duties.' She regarded his dishevelment with distaste. 'Once you are bathed and clothed. You and your companion.' She contemplated Kusint with ill-concealed confusion.

'My lady.' Corrain clenched his fists behind his back. 'I must ask you. How does this lady wizard come to be here?'

'Madam Jilseth is searching for that thief Master Minelas.' Zurenne cocked her head, eyes bright as a bird. 'Why do you ask?'

Corrain wanted to ask what the noblewoman suspected. There was more here than met the eye, along with secrets on all sides. Corrain's anger was steadily burning through the unexpected torment of finding no target here for his revenge.

Listening to Fitrel's tale of what had gone on since Lord Halferan's death, Corrain had realised something. However ripe the obscenities the old man had heaped on Minelas's name, he'd never so much as hinted that the traitor was a wizard.

Corrain remembered that only Baron Halferan and his most trusted troopers had known the truth. Conspiring to suborn renegade sorcery, to outwit the Archmage himself; that was hardly something a Caladhrian noble wanted bandied around the taprooms. Baron Halferan wouldn't have burdened his wife with such knowledge.

'Is that to expiate Hadrumal's guilt?' Corrain had made his decision. If Minelas was no longer here to render up his life for his crimes, then someone else was going to pay.

As Zurenne stared at him, uncomprehending, the lady wizard stepped forward 'What—'

Corrain spoke quickly, before her sorcery could silence him. 'Master Minelas was a mage, my lady. My lord Halferan promised him gold in return for his spells against the corsairs, after the Archmage of Hadrumal refused us any such aid. Your husband, my lord, he begged the Archmage time and again for help.' He spared a scowl for the lady wizard.

'Then Minelas betrayed us to the corsairs. They'd offered him more gold than Halferan could and he was more than willing to sell his wizardry. His magic killed men and beasts alike in that fight in the marshes.' Now Corrain was shouting, his voice raw with hatred. 'He wouldn't face my lord in a fair fight. The coward had one of those corsair scum stab him in the back!'

He wished those words unsaid as Lady Zurenne buried her face in her hands. She swayed and for one heart-stopping moment, Corrain feared she would fall headlong from the dais to the hall floor below.

'Let me—' The lady wizard reached out to save her.

'I knew you lied about something!' Lady Zurenne sprang away, fending her off. Then she went on the attack, one hand raised to slap Jilseth. At the last, Zurenne's nerve failed. She hugged her clenched fists to her breast.

'Time and again, you have lied to me!' she screamed at the grey-gowned woman. 'He was a wizard? Invading my home, threatening my daughters? One of your own and you did nothing? Worse than nothing! How could you?'

'We did not — I have not lied.' The lady wizard stood her ground, just barely.

'Truly?' Zurenne demanded, suddenly icy with contempt. 'You say you don't know where he is? Why should I believe you?'

Now she was shaking. Corrain couldn't tell if that was from wrath or fear.

The lady wizard was gathering up her papers, closing the books lying on the table. 'Granted, my lady, I have not told the whole truth. I will ask your forgiveness for that. Though I could not. I do the Archmage's bidding first and foremost.'

'You won't get my pardon, now or ever,' Zurenne snarled. 'Nor will your Archmage. His name will be spat upon across Caladhria once this tale is known.'

'You must talk to the Archmage. Let him explain.' To Corrain's vengeful satisfaction, she couldn't look Zurenne in the eye.

'The Archmage can give us Minelas.' Corrain stepped forward.

'To hang for his crimes,' spat Zurenne.

'I—' Whatever the lady wizard might have said was lost as she disappeared in a blinding flash of white light.

Zurenne screamed and screamed again, incoherent with rage and grief. Fitrel charged into the hall, the rest of the ragged guards at his heels. They fanned out, searching the shadows, shouting angrily to each other. Kusint went to explain what had happened to Fitrel and to fat Captain Arigo puffing after the rest of his men.

Corrain stood looking up at the high table. He had seen a candle flicker before the lady wizard had vanished. Her hand had shaken as she'd picked up a parchment. See such a tell-tale in a swordfight and a warrior knew he had the upper hand.

Yes, these wizards would pay.

— CHAPTER FOURTEEN —

'MY LADY, OH my lady. Please sit down. Please drink some of this.'

It was her new maid, Zurenne realised, beseeching her through the uproar that filled the great hall. Raselle was plucking at her sleeve, offering a goblet of wine in her shaking hand.

Down on the floor of the hall, Master Rauffe and Captain Arigo were standing toe to toe, shouting at each other. Mistress Rauffe was trying to listen at the same time as darting back and forth to rebuke the household's maids.

The women were largely ignoring the steward's wife, skirting around the tables and benches to demand explanations of the troopers. Who were these newcomers? What crisis threatened? Were there tidings of corsair raids out on the coast?

Whatever explanations the red-headed youth could offer were only compounding the confusion. Corrain was standing motionless, his face empty of emotion. He might have been deaf and mute for all the heed he took of those clustered around him, demanding answers.

Up the stairs in the baronial quarters, Zurenne could hear Esnina wailing, drowning out her nursemaid's efforts to soothe her.

'Mama?'

Zurenne spun around to see Ilysh in the doorway to the stairs. 'Go back to your room!'

Something in her tone cut through all the commotion like a hot wire through wax. Shocked silence echoed from the dais to the doorway and up to the banner-hung rafters. All eyes turned to Zurenne.

Unable to bear their scrutiny, she took the goblet from Raselle and drank deep. A fit of coughing nearly brought her to her knees. The wine had been fortified with what tasted like half a bottle of white brandy.

As she allowed the maid to help her to a nearby chair, Zurenne dimly realised Master Rauffe and his wife were clearing everyone out of the great hall. So the pair of them had some uses.

'My lady?'

Blinking away tears prompted by the coughing, Zurenne looked down to see Corrain still standing before the dais. She waited for him to continue but he only gazed helplessly up at her. Then he started forward, his hand going to his hip for a non-existent sword hilt.

'My lady Halferan.' A courteous voice spoke behind her.

'Who are you?' Ilysh was in the doorway to the stairs.

Zurenne twisted awkwardly in the chair. 'Who—'

She saw Jilseth had returned with an older man. Older than Halferan would have been, had he lived. Not as old as Lord Licanin. Or was he? Zurenne looked again and saw fine creases at the corners of the man's grey eyes, his hairline receding though there was barely any silver in his close cropped black hair and beard. Lean-faced, his wiry build was emphasised by his plain black doublet and breeches. He could have been a merchant's clerk from Trebin or Ferl.

'Lady Halferan.' His smile softened the intensity of his expression, before his next words stripped away any such reassurance. 'I am Planir, Archmage of Hadrumal.' He bowed to her and then to Ilysh. The girl clapped her hands to her mouth, eyes wide with wonder.

Zurenne gripped the goblet so tightly she feared the glazed ceramic would crack. She fought to set it on the table without spilling the contents, before accusing Jilseth. 'You said a wizard can only go where he's been before!'

Why had she said that? Because it was the first thought that came into her head. Zurenne nearly reached for the goblet to hide her confusion in it. But her head was already spinning from the liquor, the shock or both.

The Archmage was answering as if her question were perfectly reasonable. 'It's possible in theory, for those with supreme proficiency in their scrying spells as well as confidence in their other abilities, to travel somewhere they have never been. However, over the generations, there have been far too many instances where an apprentice wizard's self-belief has led to disaster.'

Planir shook his head, rueful. 'Consequently, translocation through scrying is so thoroughly discouraged that it is effectively forbidden.'

'But not to the Archmage,' Corrain challenged.

'I am also the Stone Master. If my scrying erred—' Planir gestured as though the hall masonry wasn't there '—if I found myself in the midst of your outer wall for example, my command over stone and earth would allow me to walk through the brickwork into the open air. Most people would be so impressed, they wouldn't realise I'd made a mistake.'

Zurenne thought she saw a warning buried in Planir's smile, like the blade concealed within a swordstick.

He shrugged. 'I had no need to run such a risk. Jilseth's magic brought me here.'

Once again, the shock or the liquor prompted Zurenne to speak, where she should have kept silent. 'I wish I could say you are welcome, but that would be a lie to dishonour Ostrin.'

'I am pleased to be here nonetheless.' Planir inclined his head politely, to her and, once again, to Ilysh.

Zurenne caught her daughter's eye. 'Go to bed. Now.'

Ilysh hesitated then fled. Zurenne was relieved to hear the door to the upper hallway close on Esnina's shrieking.

'My lady, may I sit?' Planir made no move to take a chair without her permission.

Zurenne didn't know what to say. She settled for a curt nod. As the wizard sat, she turned to Corrain, still down on the floor of the hall before the dais. 'You, come up here.'

Like the Archmage, she sat in silence as he made his way up the steps at the far corner. Corrain made no move to sit when he approached the table. Nor did Jilseth, remaining in the spot where her magic had brought her back to Halferan.

Zurenne wondered if she should send word to Lord Licanin. But Lord Licanin couldn't get a reply to her any faster than a horseman could carry it. Halferan still had no birds to carry messages back to the barony. So Licanin would only learn of this unforeseen visit in the same message that told him of its outcome. And announced Corrain's return and the revelations he had brought with him.

Zurenne looked at the far end of the dais. Her husband's chair stood there, vast, ornate with its carved wooden canopy. It was shrouded with an embroidered mourning pall which had grown dull with dust thanks to Starrid's neglect. One of the first things Mistress Rauffe had done was to set maidservants to work with dusters and beeswax and have them beat the heavy velvet clean.

It was the baron's formal seat where her husband had sat to hold his courts and to deliver his judgements like his sire and grandsire before him. Tangible embodiment of his hereditary rights over this barony and the lives and deaths of those dwelling within its boundaries.

She turned to the Archmage. 'This man is one of my husband's chosen guard. He says that my husband asked for magic's aid against the corsairs.'

Zurenne had always known that Halferan took his duties seriously. She would never have guessed that he had been driven to such extremes.

The Archmage nodded. 'Your husband and others since, most recently the deputation to Hadrumal that included Lord Licanin, when he told us of Minelas's treachery.'

Zurenne guessed that explained the lady wizard's arrival, so curious about what Minelas had done and said. She wondered what else had gone on at that meeting. Which other barons had been present? Was there any point in asking Lord Licanin? He would only tell her what he judged she needed to know and that would be very little.

Zurenne clasped her hands in her lap. As she looked down, she saw her white knuckles betray her anxiety. 'Do you have any news of Master Minelas?'

Planir nodded. 'You may rest easy, my lady. He is dead.'

'Dead?'

Before Zurenne could exclaim, the guardsman Corrain took a long stride from his place by the end of the table.

'How did he die? When? Are you certain? Tell me!'

To Zurenne's surprise, Jilseth stepped forward, her voice ringing through the empty hall. 'He died hard and painfully, caught in the very act of misusing his magic.'

'Where's his body?' the guardsman raged.

Planir gave no sign that he'd heard, still addressing Zurenne. 'Minelas left here intent on yet more grievous treachery in his search for wealth and gratification. He was pursued in accordance with my oath as Archmage. He paid in blood and agony for his crimes in this life and you may trust that Poldrion's demons torment him now.'

'Where is his body?' Corrain was advancing, his face twisted with anger. He halted, his expression slackening with fear.

Zurenne saw Jilseth's raised hand stop him in his tracks. A chill of unease sent a shiver down the noblewoman's back. She raised her chin, squaring her shoulders.

'When did Master Minelas die?'

Planir's slate-grey gaze didn't waver. 'Last year, towards the end of Aft-Autumn. My lady—'

'Last year?' Zurenne was too astonished to continue. Overwhelming relief swept through her. After so many seasons of misery, oppressed by constant dread, she need never fear the villain's footfall on the stairs again. Then sheer fury overcame her, shattering every lifelong habit of caution and propelling her to her feet.

'Last year? Yet all this time I have been left friendless and helpless? I have been subject to abuse and humiliation from ruffians and traitors to my husband's memory! I have been beset by direst fears and doubts, for myself and for my innocent children! And all this while you knew that my tormentor was dead? Did you never think to tell me?'

'We had no notion what he had done here,' Planir offered sincere regret. 'If I had known—'

'If you knew?' Zurenne swept his apology aside with the goblet. It flew off the table, toppling through the air before smashing into shards on the floor. 'Yet you didn't.' She teetered between contempt and disbelief. 'So much for your oath as Archmage.'

Planir didn't respond, simply sitting and looking calmly at her.

'Where is his body?' Zurenne repeated the guardsman's question, gesturing at Corrain as she did so. 'I have learned not to believe that a man is dead unless I see his pyre. How can you be so certain that Master Minelas is dead? Your very presence here proves how easily wizards can slip from place to place.'

As she spoke, her voice trembled. How desperately she wanted the Archmage to convince her that the monster could never return. Yet how could she believe any mage, when she had been duped so thoroughly, twice over now? Incensed, Zurenne silently accused the lady wizard with a fulminating glare.

Once again Jilseth startled them all with the vehemence of her answer. 'I saw him gutted like the swine you know him to be. A dagger ripped him open from navel to neck.'

Planir nodded, his lack of emotion doing did little to blunt the shock of this story. 'We saw his body wrapped in a sailcloth shroud and weighted with stones. He was dumped in the deepest waters of a lake in the dead of night.'

'You were there?' Corrain demanded.

Jilseth nodded. 'I was there when he died.'

Which wasn't precisely answering the guardsman's question. Zurenne considered how skilfully Jilseth had already deceived her. She knew at once when Neeny was trying to conceal some mischief, if the little girl persisted in avoiding a direct answer. These wizards were just as deceitful. Zurenne felt that chill down her spine again.

Then the Archmage shook his head. 'I saw his body disposed of through a scrying spell. His death had undone the magic which he customarily used to hide himself and his crimes.' He looked at her intently. 'Which is why we had no notion what he was doing here.'

Zurenne judged that much was true. She was far less inclined to believe it was the whole truth. 'You say you could stand unharmed in the middle of a brick wall. Can a wizard not escape a drowning?'

'He was already dead,' Planir reminded her. 'But we continued to watch, believe me. He did not resurface.' Now the Archmage smiled, grim as a death's head. 'We could recover his corpse if you wish to see it. We know the lake in question. That's to say, we could recover what the fish haven't eaten.'

As Zurenne recoiled, Corrain took another furious step forward. 'You dare to mock my lady?'

Planir turned in his chair, ominously fast. 'I only seek to reassure her that Minelas is truly dead. That this business is finished. If she does not believe me, Hadrumal's necromancy will wring the truth from Minelas's bones.'

'No, this business is not finished.' Looking at her husband's empty chair, Zurenne was inspired to challenge the Archmage's assertion with unexpected resolve. 'Not until we have agreed on terms.'

'Terms?' Planir leaned forward, his elbows on the table. 'You intrigue me, my lady.'

Was that amusement in his tone? Was he trying to intimidate her? To embarrass her into silence? Did he think she should leave such matters to Lord Licanin?

Zurenne couldn't tell. All she knew, with unanticipated certainty, was she was utterly sick of deferring to men who presumed authority over her.

'My terms, Master Archmage. Your magic can find the Halferans lost along with Corrain into the Archipelago.' She folded her hands in her lap. 'Aye and rescue every last man, since it was one of your own who condemned honest men to slavery. That is only justice.'

'Or do you want Hadrumal's reputation shredded from Peorle to Relshaz,' Corrain snarled. 'I'll see this tale of your renegade mage's frauds and murders repeated in every tavern and market place along the highroads and byways'

Zurenne silenced him with a frown before addressing Planir once again. 'You had also better make sure that no corsair sets foot in Caladhria. That no black ship appears on our horizon this summer or any other. This is my price for my silence over Hadrumal's part in my husband's death, for the terrors and humiliations heaped on my innocent daughters.'

That was what her husband had sought. What better way to honour his memory? If it wouldn't make his loss any less grievous, perhaps his death wouldn't have been entirely in vain.

'Or Hadrumal will be disgraced,' Corrain hissed, 'from the Great Forest to the Tormalin Emperor's court!'

Zurenne wished he would shut up. Would he obey her if she rebuked him? No. Better not to risk showing either weakness or dissent to these mages of Hadrumal. She folded her hands tight in her lap and gazed steadily at Planir.

The Archmage smiled. 'No.'

'No?'

Corrain's fury matched Zurenne's disbelief like two sides of the same coin.

'My lady,' Planir said coolly. 'I explained to your lamented husband. I explained to Lord Licanin and his fellow barons. The defence of Caladhria is a Caladhrian affair and none of Hadrumal's concern. Wizards do not involve themselves in warfare.'

'One wizard did.' Zurenne rallied. 'And betrayed my husband to his death!'

Planir shook his head, more in pity than denial. 'Lord Halferan's own actions betrayed him—'

'Not so!' Corrain stepped forward again, one fist clenching.

He was far too close for Zurenne's peace of mind. He also reeked of sweat and salt and worse.

'Take care, trooper.' Planir stopped him with a look more menacing than any gesture. 'By all means, spread the tale of Minelas's treachery. Once it's understood that those corsairs needed magical aid to win their victory over this barony's finest men, I have every hope that the coastal barons will rally as I have urged them to do for so long. Caladhrian strength of arms should be a match for these raiders if you stand together.'

He paused, his gaze holding Corrain.

'But do you really want to betray your dead lord's memory? You talk of Hadrumal's disgrace, but what of Halferan's? You cannot tell this tale without letting all and sundry know that your lord tried to suborn sorcery with silver and gold. How many people will reckon he merely reaped the trouble that he had sown?'

He turned his attention back to Zurenne, grey eyes flinty.

'What will your daughters think of that tale? What will it do for their marriage prospects? You don't think that barons and their ladies alike will look askance at daughters of a man so headstrong, so convinced that he alone was right, that he defied Caladhria's parliament and the Archmage alike? How many husbands and mothers by marriage would welcome such wilfulness at their fireside? Blood will out, isn't that what they will say?'

Now he smiled without a trace of warmth.

'You say Hadrumal will be disgraced from the Great Forest to the Tormalin court. Believe me. I have the personal goodwill of Emperor Tadriol and the respect of the great and the good in every city and fiefdom. I am the Archmage of Hadrumal and these people will believe what I choose to tell them of this whole affair. Do you imagine anyone will discount my words in favour of some swordsman with a grievance from a minor barony on Caladhria's coast?'

'We'll see, won't we?' Corrain countered, defiant, even though he'd taken a wary step back.

All at once, Zurenne felt exhausted. She looked at her dead husband's vast chair. What manner of fool had she been, to think that she could presume to take his place? What a brave and noble fool he had been, to imagine wizards would share any of Caladhria's concerns or sympathise with their pains.

Zurenne had seen for herself how utterly heartless these mages were. If they weren't outright villains like Minelas, they were sly deceivers like Jilseth. The Archmage felt no guilt for everything that she had suffered. All he was prepared to promise was her daughters' ruination, if not as brutally as Minelas had done. Whatever else she might contemplate, Zurenne could not risk that.

'Get out,' she said quietly.

'Forgive me—'

Before Planir could say anything further, Zurenne rose to her feet and walked towards the door to the stairs. 'Go away. Just go away.'

'As you wish.' The Archmage's words were cut short as white light flared.

Zurenne couldn't help looking over her shoulder. She could only see Corrain. Left alone on the dais, he was looking from side to side.

He stared at her, oddly bereft. 'Where's Kusint?'

Zurenne couldn't find the words to tell him she neither knew nor cared. She just wanted to see her daughters. At least they were safe now. She could hold fast to that.

— CHAPTER FIFTEEN —

Halferan, Caladhria
41st of Aft-Spring

CORRAIN HADN'T SLEPT, not to speak of. He'd wandered dazed out of the great hall after Zurenne's challenge to the Archmage had been so comprehensively rebuffed.

His first thought had been to find Kusint. That had been easy enough. The red-headed lad was by the laundry door, joking with the gaggle of maidservants offering to help him soap his back. Or anything else that might relish a gentle touch after whatever he'd had to endure as a galley slave.

Corrain couldn't face that gathering. He'd headed for the guard hall, for the broad room that served the men as dining hall, gambling den, workshop for making and mending their gear, even their practise floor through the rainy halves of winter. Only to be unceremoniously rejected.

He stank like a dead squirrel, according to the chorus of protest. Corrain didn't argue. He went out again, not to the laundry, but round to the well behind the storehouses. Stripping beneath the indifferent shelter of its pantiled roof supported on four brick pillars, he hauled up bucket after bucket of water and poured them over his head. He didn't care how cold they were. He couldn't care about anything now.

He only stopped when his arms were too tired to continue. Then he'd seen Fitrel waiting in the darkness, beyond the reach of the splashing water. Without a word, the old man set down a bundle of clean clothing. Corrain found soft, darned linen, buff breeches and a woollen tunic. A guard's uniform, along with socks and boots.

Where had Fitrel found boots to fit him? After pulling on the clothes, heedless of how damp he was, Corrain had picked one boot up. Turning it in his hands, he recognised the stitching around the buckle. This was his own boot. 'How—?'

He didn't know how long he wept, silently huddled by the well house. When the storm wracking him finally passed, he managed to put the boots on with shaking hands. Rather, he did once he'd discovered the knife tucked inside the other one, sheathed on a stretched leather belt. He knew that for Fitrel's own and was nearly unmanned again. He only headed back towards the guard hall when he was sure he had himself in hand.

The guard's barrack hall was empty. Everyone had gone up the open stairs to the dormitory above. Corrain wasn't ready to assert his own right to an empty bed space. What if there wasn't any such space to be had? That didn't bear thinking about.

Looking through the diamond paned window, he contemplated the single lamp burning by the gatehouse. No, he couldn't face finding out who had that solitary duty. That would mean questions.

So he had spent the night sitting beside the cooling woodstove in the barrack hall. No need to waste good fuel keeping it alight through the night, not at this season. He guessed he must have dozed, since the night sky didn't usually shift from black to the first blush of dawn inside the blink of an eye.

As the light strengthened, he found a pouch of rune bones discarded on a table and cast idle trios for a while, sword hand against his off hand.

Roll the heaven bone first, to see if it landed with the Sun showing, to give the strongest runes the upper hand. Of all the runes, only the three heavenly symbols were the same whichever way up they landed, without any upright or reversed aspect. No, with Sun on the bottom face unseen, the Greater and Lesser Moons joined forces to remind any players that strength alone never promised success. So the Pine Tree outweighed the Plain and the Calm outlasted the Storm. The Forest need not yield to Water.

Corrain played on simply to occupy his mind. He didn't want to think about anything else, only of the familiar symbols wrought from neatly incised lines. The Sea, last of the four domains, alongside Mountain, Forest and Plain. Drum, Horn and Chime to make music alongside the Harp. Reed and Broom, token of more womanly concerns, complementing the masculine virtues epitomised by the Oak and Pine. Then a bone landed to show him the rune for the Air.

Four lines so easily struck by a chisel or carved with a knife, to make up a lightning strike. Symbol for the element. Token of the wizard who had ruined his life.

Corrain sat staring at the rune bone, unable to look away, until a maidservant came bustling in to rake out the stove's cold ashes. The rattling roused him with a shock like another bucket of water. Realising he was thirsty, he went out into the compound and headed for the well.

'It's Corrain, isn't it?' A thickset man was already busy lighting the smithy's hearth. 'I'm Sirstin. Do you want rid of that?' He gestured towards the broken manacle on Corrain's wrist. 'Let me get some long-handled pincers and I'll have you free in no time.'

Corrain didn't recognise the smith. He wondered what had happened to Pask. Twisting the manacle around his wrist, he contemplated the man's kindly-meant offer. He looked up with a forced smile. It was as much as he could muster. 'Thanks but no. I think I have another purpose for this.'

'As you like.' Sirstin shrugged and returned to the business of firing up his forge.

Corrain hauled up the well bucket and dipped water with the cup chained to the handle. Yes, he decided. He had another purpose for that manacle.

The household was beginning to stir. He nodded as lackeys and maids called out their greetings but didn't slow as he loped across the cobbles towards the manor's shrine. He didn't want anyone engaging him in conversation. He had a task in hand.

The manor shrine door was closed but unlocked as was customary. Men had nailed their pennies to the outside in token of their oaths. Whole pennies, Corrain noted, some even silver. None of the usual cut-pieces that everyone ended up with in their purse, when hard bargaining drove merchants to cut pennies into halves and quarters, which prudent goodwives hoarded against the day when they had nothing else left to buy bread.

The inner face was soft with countless scraps of ribbon and lace, even humble calico, the women's oaths no less sincere. Corrain closed the door behind him. He had something far less reverent in mind.

The shrine was dimly lit by a single lamp. It stood before a funeral urn of costly green crackle glaze. It could only be Lord Halferan's. Corrain nodded an acknowledgement before turning to Talagrin's statue.

'I won't thank you for seeing me home safe. Not till I see Hosh at his mother's fireside and that's not likely to happen. But what about seeing this land and its folk safe from those cursed corsairs? No, I don't ask you for that boon. But you can witness my oath to make sure of it without any god's assistance and without any poxed Archmage!'

He brandished his fist at the god, the shackle's chain rattling. 'When I'm done, you can have this iron and I'll tell everyone who cares to hear that you've done nothing to earn it. No more than you did anything to save my lord from being murdered. We'll see who reveres you then!'

As he stormed from the shrine, the sun was rising over the manor wall. Blinded, Corrain very nearly walked straight into Captain Arigo.

'Well now.' The old man shook himself like a fat hen in a dust bath. 'Good day to you.'

Corrain contemplated Arigo's broad shoulders and the flesh rolling generously over the top of the wide belt buckled tight around his hips. As long as he could remember, Arigo had been counting off the days till he could lay down his sword to sit in the sun and fish in the brook above the village.

Arigo looked Corrain pointedly up and down, his gaze lingering significantly on his mane of unkempt hair. 'Do you want to rejoin the Halferan guard? Will you toe the line this time?'

If that was supposed to be a challenge, it sounded more like an appeal. Corrain could see some of the younger men, Reven in particular, watching from the gatehouse archway.

Corrain was sorely tempted to make the old man look a fool by shrugging off any such notion. But he couldn't contemplate doing that even for a joke. Where else could he possibly go?

'Yes Captain, I do and I will.' He nodded dutifully.

Arigo's relief was tempered by some consternation, before the old man got his expression in hand. 'Then you must come up to scratch, groomed as befits the barony's dignity,' he said sternly 'Get your hair cut and get rid of that slave chain.'

Corrain looked down at the manacle. 'No, captain.'

'What did you say?' Arigo wasn't feigning the question. He was taken aback. A moment more and he coloured, enraged. 'If you expect to claim the privileges of food, fuel and shelter—'

'I've sworn an oath to Talagrin.' Corrain looked up at him. 'I'll lay this chain and my hair on his altar when the corsairs are defeated.'

He knew the old bladder of lard couldn't argue with that. A vow was sacred, though Corrain did not propose to detail his angry impiety. A gust of wind drew a knotted lock of hair across his eyes and he regretted that impulse to claim his hair as well as the manacle, as he threw the fat old man's orders back in his face.

No, he was glad he'd done it. Who did Arigo think he was to scold Corrain like some soil-stained ploughboy?

The old man narrowed his eyes, before glancing over towards the guard hall. A worm of doubt gnawed at Corrain's certainty. He had been away for so long; did he have any allies left in the barracks? What about those men who'd been quietly satisfied to see him brought low after the utter folly of slipping between Starrid's bed sheets?

Because fat old man or not, Captain Arigo didn't seem ready to back down. Well, Corrain wasn't going to. If he did, he might as well leave here and keep walking.

'Captain!'

Both men turned their heads at the shout from the gatehouse. Fitrel was hurrying in, dragging a pimpled youth with tousled brown hair and on the verge of weeping.

'Corsairs!' Fitrel called out. 'No,' he added scornfully as two maidservants fluttered their white aprons like ducks catching a fox's rank scent. 'They won't come this far inland. But the lad brings news from the shore.' His glance swung from Arigo to Corrain and back again.

'Inside, boy.' Arigo flung his hand towards the guard hall door, convincingly commanding.

Corrain let the old man go ahead and followed after with a handful of other guards hurrying from all over the compound. He wondered privately if Arigo was as relieved as he was. They could have ended up stood there, like duelling swordsmen with their hilts in a bind, until the sun went down again. Corrain wouldn't have thought old Arigo had that in him. He decided he could show the fat old man some respect, at least.

'Fetch me the map!' Arigo was calling out to one of the guardsman over by the shelves where such things were stowed, along with whetstones, oil for weapons and leather, waxed thread and anything else a trooper might need.

Corrain went to search the shelves. The lad Reven came to what he sought. 'What do you want?'

'An almanac.' As Corrain searched the next shelf, he caught sight of Kusint. Freshly shaved and with his hair cropped back to coppery fuzz, the Forest youth was eating a hearty breakfast of fresh bread, cheese and bacon. One of the kitchen maids was idling beside him.

Meantime, the messenger was telling Arigo of a raid on a village to the south and west of the manor where the farmland met the saltings. Seven or eight leagues away. Corrain could see the map where the old man scratched a careful mark with his charcoal. Raided the day before. Corrain tallied up the charcoal marks. Already far too many and increasingly too close for comfort.

Over the next few days, more frightened boys like this one, from villages further afield, would straggle in. By the time the final reports of remotest theft, rape and murder arrived, ten and fifteen days later, the next high-springing tides would almost be upon them, promising fresh waves of raiders.

This was the endless litany of misery which had driven Lord Halferan to the desperate act that had been the death of him. With every man he trusted to tell of it encouraging him, Corrain included.

He needed an almanac, curse it. Corrain shoved rags and other detritus along a shelf. He'd lost track of the days and, besides, the parliament decreed the turn of the seasons from year to year, in between the fixed points of Solstice and Equinox. Every so often the barons added a day or so here and there when the calendar had to be rebalanced.

'Here.' The lad Reven offered him a little book printed on familiar coarse paper and bound with imperfectly shaped boards.

'What day is it today?' Corrain leafed swiftly through it, looking for the pages charting the phases of the moons. With the Greater circling the sky eight days faster than the Lesser, keeping track of both waxing and waning in relation to the other was a complex business. Easiest by far to look it up. 'When's the turn of the season?'

'Forty first and For-Summer's four mornings from now.' Reven peered at the crudely printed pages. 'What's to do, captain?' He sounded as frightened as the lad now weeping into Arigo's ample embrace. 'It's been a bad year so far. Is it going to get worse?'

Corrain studied the course of the moons laid out on the smudged page, from full round to curved paring and back again. Never mind Archipelagan superstitions about coloured jewels in the sky. If the blind corsair had his fingers on the beat of this heavenly dance, no wonder he was promising a summer of plunder for his galleys.

From the start of For-Summer and right through the Solstice into the aft-season, the highest tides would surge time and time again. This summer the moons would favour the corsairs like no other year until their five year pattern had run its full course again, the end and new beginning marked by that rarest of nights, one with no trace of either moon.

So much for that. What use was him knowing that such tribulation lay ahead? Caladhrians had no way to know where the corsairs would land.

'Captain? I mean, Corrain?'

He looked up at Reven. The lad's resemblance to his dead uncle was more striking than ever and, worse, he was of an age with Hosh. It was too much to bear.

'I need some air.' He shoved his way out of the crowded barrack hall into the courtyard. But there was no escape for him there.

'Corrain, is it?' A woman had entered through the wicket cut into the double gate beneath the archway. 'I'm Abiath—'

'I know.' Corrain wished he could walk away but his cursed boots felt nailed to the ground.

'What of my boy?' The woman looked at him. Not with any hope or even a hint of appeal. Her resignation was ten times worse.

'I—' What could Corrain tell her?

Then Kusint was at his side. 'He was alive, the last time we saw him,' he told Abiath. 'More than that?' He shook his head with honest regret. 'We cannot say.'

'The thirty first of Aft-Spring,' Corrain managed to tell her. 'He was alive then.'

'Ten days?' Abiath pressed the back of one shaking hand to her mouth. 'Ten days since and my boy was alive? Saedrin save him—'

She hurried away, first walking then running for the manor shrine, skirts and shawl flapping frantically.

Corrain couldn't watch. Turning away, he saw Kusint's gaze following her, his green eyes hooded with sympathy.

'How did you know she was Hosh's mother?'

Kusint shrugged. 'She has the look of him. Or rather, he has the look of her.'

Corrain realised the Forest youth was right, at least around Abiath's eyes. Personally he'd always thought that Hosh favoured his father more; a demesne labourer who'd died, struck by a falling tree when the lad was barely out of leading strings.

'Bread?' Kusint offered him the heel of a loaf fresh from the oven, lavishly smeared with butter. 'And you should get your burns cleaned and salved.' He showed Corrain his own hands swathed in gauze sticky with ointment.

Corrain looked at his forearms, realising for the first time how sore the cracked and oozing scabs were. Salt water, wind and sun had saved his raw flesh from festering but that was all that could be said for it.

'You're making yourself at home here.' Despite his grudging words, Corrain took the bread. It was marvellous beyond words. He'd never thought to taste butter again and this was its finest season, with the cows grazing on the richest grass.

'They're making me welcome.' Kusint was watching Abiath, now the centre of a cluster of women by the manor shrine door. 'Since there's nothing they can do for their loved ones lost to slavers or worse. Doing what they can for me is better than doing nothing.'

Corrain realised the red-headed youth was right. That lass from the kitchen, she was Orlon's sister's girl. Theirs was a large and loving family.

'Don't you have kin to welcome you home?' Kusint picked a shred of bacon from his teeth.

'No.' Corrain shrugged. 'My mother died in childbirth, along with a sister, in the year of my ninth summer. Yellow ague killed my father a few years after that.' He looked around the compound. 'That's when Fitrel took me in. I signed on the Halferan muster as soon as I was tall enough.'

His gaze strayed to the measuring post secured to the wall of the shrine. The crowd around Abiath was growing.

'What use is such news to her?' he demanded angrily. 'She'll never see her son again. You heard what the Archmage said.'

'I did,' Kusint said thoughtfully, 'and there's something we should discuss.'

Corrain looked at him, nonplussed.

'I want to help you and these good people,' Kusint said with growing passion. 'You freed me from those slave chains when I thought that I would die in those accursed islands. Everyone here has welcomed me, a stranger, a wanderer, as though I were one of their own. I cannot bear the thought of more lives or livelihoods being lost to those foul raiders.'

'Then what do you suggest?' Corrain felt the first stirrings of hope and fresh purpose in his heart.

— CHAPTER SIXTEEN —

Halferan, Caladhria
41st of Aft-Spring

ZURENNE STARED UP at the pale linen canopy above her lonely bed. This was a puzzle to set before Arrimelin. Minelas was dead. The Archmage himself had sworn it. Her fears should be relieved. So why would the goddess of dreams deny her sleep?

She had spent the whole night slipping into a fitful drowse only to stiffen, wakeful, as recollection of the previous day pummelled her. Whenever her eyelids grew leaden with the hope of rest a fresh thought would startle her anew.

She shouldn't have wished to be rid of the Archmage. How heartless of him to take her at her word, she thought resentfully. He owed her more than that inadequate apology.

Someone should pay; for the empty expanse of linen beside her, for the loving father her children had lost. Though what recompense could possibly match such grievous losses? Her husband's life couldn't be reckoned in coin.

She sat up and reached for her bedroom gown. The curtains were closed, the room dim despite the morning bustle outside. Zurenne picked her way carefully to the window and drew back one edge of the blue brocade. Sunlight warmed her as she looked down into the courtyard and saw the servants about their duties.

The two men stood in the shadow of the guard hall caught her eye; the newcomer unmistakable with his coppery head and Corrain, ragged-haired and unshaven. Their lives had been measured out in coin.

Zurenne caught her breath with sudden curiosity. How much coin had Master Minelas been paid for the enslaved Halferan guards? Where was that gold and silver now? What of the barony's revenues which he'd misappropriated?

She looked around her bedchamber. Halferan had always made good on his wedding vow to see her kept in comfort. Their private furnishings were renewed at the first sign of shabbiness while each festival brought her fresh linen and new gowns, her cast-offs a welcome windfall for her maids. It was only Starrid who'd begrudged her rightful due.

What of the future? Would Lord Licanin be as generous? Or would he decree that her widowhood only warranted new gowns half-yearly? Once a year? When would he decide that Ilysh was of marriageable age and so entitled to adornment? Would Zurenne have to beg for every copper penny she wished to spend on treats for her daughters?

What of the demesne folk and the tenants in the barony beyond? Halferan had always been generous with solstice and equinox gifts, especially to those celebrating their birth festival, embarking on married life or bidding their farewells at a loved one's pyre.

That was to say, Zurenne corrected herself, Halferan had rightly been generous to those whose character and deeds had earned his favour. How could Lord Licanin know who was worthy of his goodwill? Wouldn't he be more likely to keep the coin in Halferan's coffers, to be spent by Ilysh's as-yet-unknown husband?

Zurenne shivered despite the warmth of the sun through the window. There was no point in thinking so far ahead when much more immediate dangers threatened. Whatever else Minelas had done, however the renegade mage had done it, he'd kept those cursed corsair ships at bay. No longer.

Was it her duty to send Lysha and Neeny away to safety? As long as she stayed here herself, that would safeguard Ilysh's inheritance. Her other sisters lived far beyond the reach of corsair raids. Of course, the thieves had never ventured this far from water.

'My lady!' Her new maid, Raselle, halted in the doorway, startled to see her mistress by the window.

'You may enter.' Zurenne went back to bed, pretending to doze. That allowed Raselle to draw the curtains fully open, to pour hot water into the ewer on her washstand and lay out a clean shift and stockings. Finally the girl went to fetch a pan of glowing charcoal from the kitchen, for the little water-stove set in the withdrawing room hearth now that daily fires were no longer needed.

Zurenne tossed aside the shift she had slept in, washed and donned fresh linen before wrapping herself in her bedroom gown once more. She was sitting in the withdrawing room, unplaiting her hair from its night braid when Raselle returned with a tray; fruit bread and a dish of new butter together with Zurenne's crystal glass in its silver holder and the makings of a morning tisane.

If the girl had been raised to quench her thirst with small beer in her family's farmhouse, she had soon learned to appreciate the niceties of tisanes. Zurenne nodded approval as Raselle spooned judicious measures of dried hawthorn leaves, sweet briar and cowslip blossoms into the pierced silver ball and snapped it shut. Now the water in the reservoir surrounding the stove's central chimney was boiling. Raselle filled the polished kettle from the spigot and brought it over.

'Thank you.' Zurenne poured hot water into the glass and swirled the ball around with the spoon. Smoky tendrils seeped from the steeping herbs. 'I will wear my almond green gown with the short ruffled sleeves.'

Lord Licanin had allowed her to summon her dressmaker when he'd seen how shamefully worn her clothes had become. Though Zurenne still faced the problem of finding something suitable to give to Doratine the cook by way of reward for finding Raselle among her numerous nieces. She could not give away a new gown but her old ones were too worn or stained to be fitting thanks.

'My lady.' The girl bobbed a curtsey. Once she had laid the dress ready she hesitated by the clavichord.

'Yes?' Zurenne's smile invited her to continue. While she'd made it clear to Raselle that she didn't wish to be bothered with idle gossip, the girl had readily understood that she should keep her eyes and ears open, to alert her mistress to things of significance and to be able to answer whatever questions Zurenne might have about the demesne's affairs.

'Your pardon, my lady, but Corrain of the guard says he wishes to see you.' Raselle smoothed her spotless apron.

'He can wait.' Zurenne had no wish to be reminded of the previous evening. She stirred her tisane one last time and fished the silver ball out of the glass.

She contemplated her writing box on the far side of the polished table. It had been a gift from her sister Celle on her wedding day. Cunningly hinged, it opened into a slope with paper, pens, ink and blotting sand safely stowed in its two halves.

She had to tell Lord Licanin about the Archmage's visit and of the revelation of Minelas's death. Zurenne had no doubt that Master Rauffe had loosed a Licanin courier dove at first light. But a dove could carry precious few words on the onionskin paper in the silver cylinder screwed safely to its leg band.

Even without the parliament's seal of approval, everyone would consider a widow without father or brother answerable to an older sister's husband. So Zurenne could not lie or dissemble in her dealings with Licanin if she wished him to trust her with her daughters' education, let alone any of the barony's business in his absence.

'Mama?' Ilysh peered around the half-open door from the hallway.

'Sweetheart.' Zurenne summoned her with a smile and Neeny followed her sister. 'More plum bread, Raselle, if you please.' Zurenne deftly moved the steaming tisane glass as Esnina's hand reached across the breakfast tray.

'What shall we do today?' Ilysh asked hopefully.

Zurenne couldn't recall when she last saw her daughter so carefree. As far as Lysha was concerned, she realised, word of Master Minelas's death was good news to outweigh any word of corsair raids.

Esnina was spreading butter on a slice of fruit bread, oblivious to their exchange. Zurenne doubted she even remembered Minelas after half a year's absence. Did her little daughter remember her father, she wondered with a pang. Well, that was a rune showing two faces, one upright and one reversed. If Neeny didn't remember her father's love, she wouldn't suffer the enduring agony of his loss.

'Mama?' Ilysh prompted.

'Music, I think.' Zurenne nodded decisively. 'You and Neeny should practise a duet to entertain Lord Licanin.'

'A duet?' Lysha couldn't hide her scepticism.

'Then you and I will play together,' Zurenne allowed. A knock sounded on the doorpost.

'Raselle?' Zurenne looked round. 'You need not—'

But it was not Raselle. The guard Corrain stood in the hallway, his red-headed companion at his shoulder. Zurenne was momentarily too astounded to speak.

'My lady—' he began.

'How dare you?' Zurenne's astonishment had turned to anger. 'Be about your duties, churl, until I send for you.'

He dropped to one knee, his shaggy head bowed. 'My lady, I beg you.'

Zurenne wasn't beguiled. She'd seen the determination in his eye. 'Be off before I order you thrashed from the gates!'

'Were you truly kept as slaves?' Lysha was looking at both men, avid with curiosity. 'Among the southern barbarians?'

'Jora says so.' Neeny nodded, mouth full and butter glistening on her cheek.

'Jora says more than is good for her.' Distracted, Zurenne wiped Esnina's face and pushed her towards Ilysh. 'You may let her know that I said so. Now take your sister and dress. Ring for Jora.'

Mistress Rauffe definitely need not be rewarded for finding that freckled, gap-toothed nursemaid for the children.

'My lady.' Corrain edged aside to let the girls leave, awkward on one knee. 'This is Kusint. We escaped the corsairs together. I would never have succeeded without him.'

Zurenne nodded, reserved. 'So I understand.' She wasn't about to trust any strangers, not after Minelas. More immediately to the point, this red-headed lad could well share the vices commonly attributed to his people.

To her surprise, the young man dropped to one knee beside Corrain. 'I am Forest born, my lady, from the Soluran side of the woodlands.'

'The corsairs raid that far?' Zurenne was horrified.

Kusint looked up, perplexed. 'No, my lady.'

She blushed as his tone implied that was a foolish question. 'How did you fall foul of Aldabreshin slavers then?' she snapped. 'Through bad luck or bad judgement?'

He smiled at her, unabashed. 'Something of both, my lady.'

'You're fortunate to live to learn that lesson.' She dismissed them both with a backhanded gesture. 'Now leave. I have urgent affairs to attend to.'

Corrain rose to his feet but made no move to depart. He stood twisting that manacle around his wrist. 'Do you wish to be revenged upon those wizards, my lady? All of them, not just Minelas.'

Zurenne couldn't believe her ears. 'What? How?' Common sense rescued her. 'Are you drunk or dreaming? Be gone, the pair of you!'

Corrain stood his ground. 'We can show Archmage Planir that he cannot dictate to us. Aye, and see Halferan and this whole coast defended against the corsairs. I swear it, my lady.'

Zurenne could only wonder at his certainty. 'How by all that's holy could we hope for such marvels?'

Corrain's smile boded ill for the Archmage. 'Hear what Kusint has told me.'

The red-headed lad stood up. 'My lady, there are more wizards in this world than those of Hadrumal. Mages who owe your Archmage Planir neither allegiance nor obedience.'

Zurenne was lost for words.

'In Solura,' Kusint explained, 'wizards govern themselves quite differently. Any mage whose skills command respect may found an Order. The mageborn come to study whatever he or she may teach them. They may stay or they may move on. A revered Order can endure for generations, producing many mighty wizards.' He smiled. 'While the reverse of that rune soon sees a mage with more ambition than skill begging for bread by the roadside.'

Zurenne struggled to recall what she had learned of Solura, so remote and irrelevant to Caladhria. 'Do you people not have a king? Does he truly permit wizards such licence?'

'Royal law does require the mageborn to have their potential assessed by an established Order,' Kusint admitted. 'Anyone with effective magic must be apprenticed to an older wizard. All the wizards of an Order are guarantors for their fellow mages' good conduct and each Order must secure a noble patron.'

'They do that readily enough,' Corrain cut in, 'since Solura's lords see the value of wizardry in their warfare.'

'The northern mountains separate the Kingdom of Solura from the realm of Mandarkin.' Kusint's green eyes hardened. 'That's a hard land, rocky and cold through their long winters and baked to scorching dust in the summer. Mandarkin's tyrants rule through fear and pain and keep serfs bonded for life in their villages.'

'They're slaves,' Corrain interrupted again.

Kusint shot him an exasperated glance. 'Mandarkin's tyrants covet Solura's lowlands. They launch attacks through the passes time and again. In generations gone, they even succeeded in holding territory south of the mountains for years at a time. Mageborn in Mandarkin are compelled to serve their tyrants on pain of death, so the wizards of Solura have long stood shoulder to shoulder with our kings and armies.'

Corrain clenched his fists with a rattle of his manacle's chain. 'We can invite a Soluran mage to defend Caladhria against these corsair slavers. Planir of Hadrumal has no right to gainsay us.'

Zurenne was enthralled by the thought of defying the Archmage. Of securing her daughters' future. Of safeguarding the humble folk of Halferan from future ordeals.

'But Solura is so far away.' She had only the vaguest idea how distant. 'Winter would be upon us before you could return with such a wizard, even if you could find one to help us. I must suppose that any such mage would want some reward for his endeavours,' she continued bitterly. 'Even if I held the Halferan purse strings, Master Minelas has beggared the barony.'

'The corsairs have loot enough to satisfy ten Soluran mages,' Corrain assured her. 'We don't only seek to defend the coast. As long as this mage agrees to rescue those enslaved, we can guide him to an emperor's ransom in the raiders' lair.'

Truly? And coin was the key to all locks. Halferan had always said so.

'Burn out their nest and the coastal baronies may rest easy for years to come,' Kusint pointed out.

'With a fast ship, we can reach Solura by the middle of For-Summer,' Corrain promised.

Kusint nodded. 'With magic swelling the sails, we'll return in half the time.'

'Where will you find such a ship,' Zurenne challenged. 'Never mind pay for its hire?'

Corrain's grin unnerved her. 'Corsair ships are the fastest. We'll take one of those.'

Stranger or not, Zurenne looked to Kusint for explanation.

'We know where the raiders land to take on water—'

'Once we've cut down the bastard Archipelagans, we'll offer their rowers their freedom,' Corrain said with satisfaction, 'in return for a summer's service. They'll see us to Solura and back before Solstice.'

Zurenne was already shaking her head. 'Halferan cannot raise a force to fight corsairs for a galley.'

'No,' Corrain agreed, 'but Saldiray, Myrist and Taine have troopers to be reckoned with, aye, and Karpis and Tallat.'

Zurenne scowled at him. 'Their lordships of Karpis and Tallat seek to carve up Halferan between them. Haven't you heard?'

But Corrain was still grinning. 'No baron can act without men to back him and I know those barony's guard captains of old. They'll help us for the sake of their own kin living along the shoreline.'

Despite herself, a tantalising vision filled Zurenne's thoughts. She recalled Jilseth's magic stripping Baron Karpis's men of their chainmail. Her pleasure at his humiliation turned to resentment. The lady wizard had done that so easily. How little magic it would have cost the Archmage to save her beloved husband.

She recalled one of Halferan's favourite sayings. A man can stand by the river and wish for a fish or go home to weave a net. But the net he had woven had been the death of him.

'Will you tell these barons or their captains that you intend to suborn Soluran magecraft?'

Corrain hesitated. 'No,' he admitted.

'Telling them we know how to strike at the raiders should secure their aid,' Kusint said quickly.

'Once we bring back a wizard, do you imagine they will argue the point?' That wicked grin spread across Corrain's face again.

Could this mad plan possibly succeed? Zurenne shook her head. 'Lord Licanin will never permit this.'

'He's not Halferan's guardian yet,' Corrain pointed out.

'Don't be a fool.' Zurenne narrowed her eyes at him. 'He will be as soon as midsummer when the parliament approves his grant. Whatever I do between now and then will determine my role in my children's future. Such folly as this could see them taken away from me. We're wholly in his hands until Lady Ilysh is wed.'

'Then let me be wed.'

The two men sprang forward as if a dog had snapped at their ankles.

Appalled, Zurenne saw Ilysh standing in the hallway.

'What are you doing? Where is your sister?' As she spoke, she was belatedly relieved to see all the other doors to the hallway closed; to both the girls' bedchambers, to the rooms opposite given over to clothing stores and to their servants since no sons of the barony needed them.

'Go to your room, Ilysh.' Zurenne was on her feet. 'This is no concern of yours.'

'Yes it is. I am the heiress to Halferan.' The girl's voice shook, colour rising on her cheekbones. 'I don't want to hear the maids weeping because their villages have been raided. I don't want anyone else's father killed by these corsairs.'

'Lysha—' Zurenne's heart was breaking.

'I don't want anyone else telling us what we can do and where we can go, even inside our manor, or what dresses to wear or what music to play.' Ilysh's grief gave way to anger. 'Not even Lord Licanin. He knows nothing about us.'

Now Zurenne was growing cross. 'You must have a guardian.'

'Why?' Ilysh shot back.

Zurenne wasn't having this defiance. 'Because it is the law!'

'The law gave us to Master Minelas.' Ilysh's contempt was palpable.

Whatever the furious girl said, her eyes accused her mother. Zurenne took an irate step forward. 'Who would you give yourself to, you silly little fool? And me, and Neeny? As soon as you are wed, we must submit to whoever it is!'

'To someone chosen by Lord Licanin?' retorted Ilysh. 'Will I even be allowed to meet him before he cuts my wedding plait? Will Halferan be traded away to suit Licanin and his allies in the barons' parliament?'

'Ilysh!' Once again, her accusations stabbed Zurenne to the heart.

'I have no father to choose my husband as my heart might wish it,' Ilysh said bitterly. 'So let me be wed and before midsummer, to someone we can trust here in Halferan. Then no one can tell us what to do anymore. We can fetch a Soluran wizard to kill the corsairs and no one can do anything to stop us!'

'I could—' Corrain licked his lips. 'I could wed Lady Ilysh—'

Zurenne sprang forward and slapped Corrain's face with all her strength. As her hand bounced back, her rings caught in his hair. As she tore herself free, he grabbed her wrist with a stable yard oath.

'You swine!' She spat full in his face. 'You're no better than him. Claiming to serve Halferan when you only serve your own lusts! I know your reputation of old, bedding every woman fool enough to fall for your lies. Unspeakable!'

As she raised her free hand to claw at Corrain's face, Kusint stepped in to seize her wrist.

'My lady, I believe you do him disservice.' Though Kusint was looking askance at the Caladhrian.

'A proxy marriage!' Corrain threw Zurenne's hand back at her and Kusint immediately let her go. 'To be dissolved when she's of an age to marry a man worthy of her and the barony.

'If you think I would lay a finger—' His face twisted, repelled. 'I only offer the protection in law afforded by marriage, no more. Then neither Lord Licanin nor any other baron need be appointed as

Halferan's guardian. No one could ever take your children from you!'

For a moment he couldn't continue. 'Granted I have bedded plenty of women and none too wisely at times. I paid for Starrid's wife with bruises and humiliation. But I never—' His voice roughened as he struggled to find words fit for Zurenne and Ilysh's ears. 'I never took a slice from an uncut loaf!' he said furiously.

So he didn't share Minelas's proclivities. What was that to her?

'I will not countenance such a thing.' Zurenne plucked torn hairs from the settings of her rings with savage precision.

'Think on it, my lady.' Corrain ground his teeth, flushed with resentment at being so grossly misunderstood. 'I would be responsible in law for bringing this wizard here. The parliament would have no cause to remove you from your daughters' lives. I will face whatever penalties might follow, for my dead lord's sake. I already owe Lord Halferan my death in his service. I owe you no less, nor Lady Ilysh and Lady Esnina.'

His fervour unnerved Zurenne. She shook her head.

'Mama!' Ilysh cried out in reproach.

'If you can gather a force from the coastal baronies, to seize a corsair ship, then you may go in search of this wizard.' She would not lightly cast aside that possibility, if there was the remotest chance it would succeed. 'That is as much of this madness as I will countenance. Now, be gone, all of you. Not you, Lysha!'

As the two men quickly retreated to the stairs and down to the great hall, Zurenne grabbed her daughter's arm and pulled her into the withdrawing room. The girl's face was alight with defiance.

Zurenne said nothing. She wasn't going to give Lysha another opportunity to attack her. She waited until she heard the door at the bottom of the stairwell close.

'Go to your room and dress,' she said quietly. 'Ring for Jora and Raselle. Then we will choose some music and practise.'

Ilysh looked uncertainly at her. This wasn't the reaction she had expected. Zurenne raised her eyebrows in silent query. Ilysh fled.

Zurenne walked over to the window and looked down into the manor courtyard. She watched Corrain and Kusint striding towards the guard hall. They weren't wasting time.

Even if they succeeded, Lord Licanin would call this madness. What would the Archmage say, come to that? Zurenne quailed at the thought of confronting either man.

A treacherous thought soothed her fears. Distasteful as the prospect was, she could divert Lord Licanin's wrath by claiming those two vagabonds had duped or menaced her. She was nothing but a helpless widow.

— CHAPTER SEVENTEEN —

Trydek's Hall, Hadrumal
43rd of Aft-Spring

JILSETH STEELED HERSELF to knock on the tower door. This was Planir's private study, not his audience room. Everyone knew that his bedchamber lay beyond the connecting door.

Ely would assume that was her destination. Jilseth couldn't decide which part of that notion was more insulting; that she couldn't look after Hadrumal's interests without the Archmage's assistance or that she would secure such help with sexual favours.

She discarded that irritation as a thought creased her brow. Ely could only focus a scrying spell on one of them at a time. Would she have followed Jilseth here or already be scrying on the Archmage?

Jilseth decided to mention that to Planir. If one of them wanted some privacy, the other could draw Ely's suspicions, or Kalion's, so that he would direct her magic to follow it.

As she raised her hand to knock, Jilseth hesitated, hearing voices within. But the Archmage had summoned her.

'Enter!' Planir answered the rap of her knuckles.

Jilseth lifted the latch and went in. It was a serenely comfortable room. Bookcases framed tall windows with upholstered chairs set either side of the hearth and a polished table and ladder-backed chairs on the other side of the room. A matching sideboard offered crystal glasses and jewel-like decanters as well as a silver tisane service mellowed with age and use. Simple watercolours of flowers and birds decorated the walnut panelled walls.

'Cloud Master Rafrid, good day to you. Master Herion.' She greeted the two men sat at the table with Planir.

'Jilseth, always a pleasure.' Rafrid smiled genially. Not overly tall, he sat long backed and broad shouldered in a midnight blue woollen tunic. When Jilseth had first begun her studies, his tousled hair had been as dark as midnight. Now it was the pale grey of a clouded dawn, his face weathered.

'Good day to you.' Herion smiled amiably, a mild-faced man with faded brown hair, perhaps a handful of years younger than Planir or Rafrid. He was a mage who felt no need to blazon his water affinity, wearing a rust-coloured doublet and grey breeches.

'Madam Sannin.'

Strictly speaking, Jilseth need not offer the courtesy of that title to the woman sitting across from Planir. Sannin held no office whereas Herion was the Master of Hiwan's Hall, guiding apprentice and pupil mages of all four affinities and with a broad range of ability.

However anyone studying wizardry soon knew of Sannin and not merely for her glorious chestnut tresses, her shapely figure flattered by her elegant gowns in every vibrant shade of red.

For the last decade and more she'd travelled between Hadrumal and the mainland, wherever and whenever some curiosity hinted at an elemental mystery as yet unfathomed by wizardry. Pupil mages would swap stories of their studies being sent down unexpected paths after Sannin had accosted their mentor. Apprentices longed for such a privilege.

Jilseth had also heard more than one middle-ranked fire mage, indiscreet after a glass of white brandy, looking forward to the day when she might serve as their Hearth Mistress.

'You've been working quintessential magic.' Jilseth was surprised into uttering her sudden realisation aloud.

Planir's smile deepened the creases around his eyes. 'You think we should let Kalion run around stirring up trouble without keeping an eye on him?'

Sannin laughed with rich amusement. 'Forgive me.' She waved an apologetic hand. 'But the notion of our esteemed Hearth Master running...'

Jilseth couldn't help a smile. The thought of Kalion hitching up his flowing mantle to scurry across a courtyard was funny. Which was all very well but Planir had summoned her. 'You sent for me, Archmage?'

He nodded. 'Indeed—'

A sonorous bell interrupted him. It tolled a second time, and a third, the sound rolling across the rooftops to echo back from Hadrumal's towers.

'The Council bell?' Herion looked puzzled.

Rafrid leaned his weight on broad, workman-like hands as he stood up from the table. 'Kalion's been threatening to summon us for days.'

Sannin rose to her feet. 'Shall we be prompt to unsettle our esteemed Hearth Master or tardy so he can irritate as many people as possible with his pomposity?' The glint in her eye spoke of no great respect for the Master of her affinity.

'Does it matter?' Planir turned to Jilseth. 'We'll talk later. Let's see what our honoured Hearth Master wishes to lay before the Council today.'

'Archmage.' Jilseth moved aside to let the other mages through the doorway.

'After you.' Planir gestured.

As she went ahead, Jilseth noticed him locking his door with a brush of his fingers. She couldn't recall seeing him do that before.

He didn't lock the door at the base of the tower. As they walked out into the sunshine, Jilseth could taste the dusty heat rising from the flagstones. For-Summer still lay ahead and then the Solstice festival, when the full heat of the year would bear down on them. Thankfully Hadrumal's encircling seas would soften its ferocity.

The four wizards and Jilseth walked out of Trydek's Hall's outer quadrangle in silence. The Council Chamber wasn't far, a modest building compared to the later edifices hemming it in. The sweeping curve of its walls defied their rigid angles, undaunted by their lofty towers.

The bell tolled one last time, no rope to stir it. Only the magic of those granted a Council seat by their peers could give it voice.

The age-darkened oak door stood ajar, mages of all ages and affinities filing through it and up the stairs beyond. As she followed Planir and the others, Jilseth noted spots of rust on the iron banding. She brushed them away with a scour of magic.

A second door at the top of the short flight of steps was further slowing the assembled wizards' progress into the council chamber. Questions rose to the barrel vault.

'Were you told of this meeting? This morning?'

'Comair mentioned getting a note. Did you?'

'I thought we were gathering tomorrow? That's the turn of the season.'

'Perhaps Kalion misread his almanac.'

'Oh, I knew there was something in the wind.'

Jilseth shifted to see who said what. Sannin caught her eye and leaned close to confide in her ear.

'Walever's pretending he's more important than his friends might realise. But Kalion has definitely been gathering allies.'

Jilseth nodded. She could see for herself how many faces showed no hint of surprise but rather expectation and even some spiteful anticipation. Were they expecting to see Planir finally worsted?

Sannin strode ahead, skirts flowing seductively as she headed for her own seat on the far side of the round Council Chamber.

Forty-eight seats, the number fixed by Trydek himself. When a vacancy arose through death or retirement, each new council member inherited a wooden chair set in a niche carved into the stonework. The pilasters between each one soared upwards, branching into an austerely beautiful vaulted ceiling.

Jilseth ran a finger over the moulding of the doorframe. Like those niches and the roof vault, the golden stone had been carved by magic, not tools. She never came here without wondering which early mage sharing her birthright had wrought such beauty.

Despite the lack of any record, some insisted it must have been Loynar, first Stone Master and staunch ally of Trydek. Jilseth would have thought a Stone Master had more urgent calls on his time. She liked to think that some lesser earth mage had taken on the tedious task of fitting the masonry close together against whatever storms might buffet the island, in return for the opportunity to work such glorious artistry with his, or her, magic.

Not all the encircling wall was carved. On either side of the door three chairs stood against plain stonework, for the ease of any guests or witnesses invited by the council members.

Jilseth wasn't going to get a seat. Canfor and Ely already occupied two of them. Galen was standing beside them, glowering at the oblivious back of a thin-faced magewoman in blue. Perched on the edge of the third chair she was intent on her conversation with a balding wizard absently combing his beard with stained fingers. A double handful of other men and women were trying not to block the doorway. The Council rarely saw so many attending their deliberations.

Forty eight council members and one Archmage. Jilseth watched Planir cross the flagstones, pausing to greet someone, to lay an apologetic hand on a silken sleeve, to acknowledge a knot of self-conscious wizards breaking apart as they saw him approach.

He skirted the dais in the middle of the room. A ball of magelight hung above the stone platform, offering illumination as bright as the sun outside this windowless room.

'Are we all present?' Planir didn't need to raise his voice to command silence. Those wizards who'd been deep in conversation broke off and quickly headed for their chairs. While every seat was filled, Jilseth noted more than a few proxies. Every council member had the right to send such a representative, though in theory any wizard deemed worthy of this coveted rank should be able to return to Hadrumal the instant they heard the Council bell. Quintessential magic would carry its ringing to their ears, however many thousand leagues distant they might be.

Jilseth looked across the room to Sannin and saw her own questions reflected in the fire mage's face. Why weren't those mages here? To stay aloof from whatever quarrel Kalion might try to force on the Archmage, or to avoid lending Planir their support?

She looked as discreetly as she could at Flood Mistress Troanna but saw nothing in the thickset woman's face to give any hint as to what she might be thinking. Not that that was in any sense unusual. Troanna kept her own counsel more effectively than any other mage of Hadrumal.

Planir nodded. 'Let us secure against interruption.'

Every seated mage looked at the entrance. The door's metal bonds shone with subtle magelight. Running together like quicksilver and glowing like molten bronze, the iron remade itself into a solid sheet.

Jilseth looked at Canfor, Ely and Galen. Even quintessential scrying wouldn't penetrate the ancient enchantments warding this place, so they must be present to see whatever transpired. With luck one of their faces would betray something useful for Planir's purposes. That said, Jilseth realised, she didn't know what Planir's intentions might be.

'Hearth Master.' Planir wasted no time, gesturing towards the central platform. 'You summoned us here.'

Kalion was more than ready for this challenge. He strode to the centre of the chamber and stepped onto the dais so promptly that Jilseth would swear he used a jolt of ensorcelled air beneath his kidskin half-boots.

He spoke without preamble. 'All of us in this chamber know how thoroughly Minelas has disgraced wizardry by offering his sorcery for hire to Triolle, even if that knowledge is not yet common gossip in the wine shops.'

He shot a warning glance at those standing by the door.

'When we last gathered to discuss this shameful episode, we could hope that mageborn and mundane alike might long remain ignorant of the details. Our Archmage assured us that all who knew the truth could be trusted or otherwise convinced to remain silent.'

He shook his head. 'Alas, he was wrong. There's a man in Caladhria, one of Lord Halferan's household, who's escaped from the corsair galleys and returned home.'

Kalion paused to allow astonishment at that to run its course, his fleshy lips pressed tight together.

'This man knows that Minelas was a wizard. He saw magic openly used to kill and to betray Lord Halferan to these corsair raiders. Minelas had taken their gold as well as Lord Halferan's coin, long before he sold himself in Lescar.'

Kalion paused once again to allow indignation free rein. Then Rafrid rose to his feet a scant breath before the Hearth Master would have continued.

'Minelas is indeed proven a traitor thrice over,' he said dourly. 'I offer no excuses as to why those of us sharing his affinity had no inkling of his true depravity.' He looked around the chamber. 'It may be offering hay to a dead donkey but I've let it be known I'm eager to learn of any straws in the wind that we might have noted in the past. I will share my conclusions in due course.'

As he moved to sit down, Kalion drew breath. This time Herion beat him to it.

'Thank you, Cloud Master. All those of us involved in the governance of Hadrumal's halls—' his sweeping gesture encompassed almost everyone present '—will do well to learn whatever lessons we may from this sorry business.'

Kalion flushed with annoyance. 'A far more immediate concern is this disgrace spreading across the mainland!'

'You fear this captain will tell tales?' Sannin evinced more doubt than concern. 'How far can one man's voice reach before its echoes fade away?'

Satisfaction narrowed Kalion's eyes. 'We are no longer dealing with one man's voice. This captain of guards is rallying troops from every neighbouring—'

'Excellent.' Planir clapped soft hands.

'Archmage?' Kalion rounded angrily on Planir.

Planir stood up, entirely at ease. 'We've long hoped that the Caladhrians would form an alliance to safeguard themselves.'

'Quite so, Archmage,' Rafrid agreed. 'The news of their sufferings has distressed me sorely; for all that I acknowledge Hadrumal's edicts make it impossible for us to offer aid.'

Jilseth was pleased by murmurs of agreement on all sides. Then she caught sight of Galen's obdurate expression and looked a second time, for those who didn't share the Archmage's satisfaction.

'Whatever success this alliance may or may not achieve,' Kalion said bitingly, 'this captain will be spreading word of Hadrumal's disgrace to tens of men, to hundreds before he's done. What of wizardry's standing on the mainland then?'

Sannin raised a hand, silver bracelets sliding down her forearm. 'This remains a tale of only one man's misdeeds. We've all encountered a bad egg from time to time. The folk of the mainland know as well as we do that one cannot tell the addled from the wholesome still in the shell. I don't make light of Minelas's crimes, far from it.' She offered Kalion an elegant bow. 'I will keep an open ear on my travels to see how much discredit is laid to Hadrumal's account. But we must address the most serious questions first. If you'll forgive more kitchen wisdom, one bad apple can spread rot through a whole barrel. We must make certain that no future pupil mage's lusts evade our suspicions as Minelas so clearly did.'

Jilseth saw the magewoman's words prompt widespread agreement.

'Quite so.' Kalion said, with ill-concealed irritation. 'But to return to our disgrace on the mainland—'

'How thoroughly are we insulted?' Rafrid was on his feet again. 'What do your mainland allies say, Hearth Master?'

Jilseth was intrigued to see Kalion's already high colour deepen.

'I have no specifics,' he replied stiffly.

Rafrid folded his arms. 'Then what prompts your concern?'

Kalion squared up to him. 'I am reporting what I have seen on the mainland.'

'Through scrying?' Rafrid looked pointedly at Ely over by the door.

'Obviously,' Kalion said testily.

'Your nexus has had no success with auditory enchantments?' Rafrid's gesture taking in Canfor and Galen provoked a wider murmur of interest and some indignation.

Jilseth tried to assess who had already known of the Hearth Master's quintessential magic. Some Council members hadn't looked seriously affronted.

'Not thus far,' Kalion admitted with ill grace.

'Forgive me, Cloud Master, Hearth Master.' Herion rose though Rafrid showed no sign of sitting down. 'What prompted you to scry after this man in the first place?'

Kalion lifted his chins. 'I have been scrying along the Caladhrian coast since the turn of For-Spring, to gauge these corsairs' depredations. I think a case can be made for intervention which doesn't challenge Hadrumal's historic edicts.'

More than one groan rose to the vaulted roof.

'That debate is done and dusted.' A white-haired fire mage withered by his years reached for his silver-topped cane. 'If you wish to waste your time again, you won't waste mine.'

'Master Massial, by your leave,' Sannin interjected, 'I see a far more pertinent question. What will these mainland barons think, Hearth Master, when they discover you've been spying on them? You know how jealously the Caladhrian parliament guards its dignities.'

Rafrid was on his feet again. 'They'll be wondering where you've blabbed their secrets. You speak often enough of your friends among the noble and wealthy from Selerima to the Tormalin Imperial Court.'

'I do not blab,' Kalion said indignantly. 'Nor am I beholden to any mainland prince or power.'

'But will you convince mistrustful Caladhrians of that?' Sannin looked anxious. 'They may even ask where you've sold their secrets, if they think all wizards are as venal as Minelas.'

Rafrid's laugh was a harsh bark. 'I'll wager any coin that tales of wizardly snooping will spread further and faster than any Caladhrian trooper's claims of Minelas's malfeasance.'

Kalion's chest swelled with outrage. 'How dare you—'

'You dared to scry on me.' Rafrid's jaw jutted, belligerent. 'On Madam Sannin, on Master Herion and even on the Archmage. How many more Council members float across your minion's scrying bowl?'

Jilseth saw Ely pale at the disdainful flick of the Cloud Master's hand. Galen scowled.

'It's a shame you weren't scrying after Minelas,' Sannin observed unhappily.

'That's hardly fair,' Herion objected. 'No one had reason to suspect him, as we've already established. Unless you're proposing that every mage be subject to constant scrutiny?'

There was an instant of silence as the assembled mages tried to decide whether to laugh at that ludicrous notion or to voice their disapproval in case anyone might seriously consider it.

Planir stood up. 'We are not here to question the Hearth Master's motives. He acts, as he always has, in Hadrumal's best interests.' The Archmage looked pensive. 'If we cannot get the measure of mainland sentiments through our own magic, perhaps we should consider alternatives. Aetheric adepts—'

'Artifice?' Appalled, Kalion jabbed a fat finger at Sannin. 'She fears mundane outrage if they discover that we keep watch on their coastal waters with our magecraft? How much more offended would the mainlanders be, to have their innermost thoughts rifled through from afar?'

Jilseth saw more than half the wizards shared the Hearth Master's astonishment that Planir should suggest such a thing.

'You misunderstand me.' The Archmage raised placating hands. 'I would never advocate such a gross intrusion. But our friends in Suthyfer tell me that Artifice can read a gathering's mood without any need to invade an individual's thoughts.'

'That would require a gathering of Caladhrians who've heard this trooper's tale.' Herion looked thoughtful. 'As well as an Aetheric adept brought from Suthyfer.'

'I think we can learn all we need to by more usual methods,' Sannin objected.

With most of the wizards nodding, one of the youngest councillors raised a hand. At Planir's nod, he stood, his aptitude for elemental air discreetly declared by his unbuttoned grey jerkin's sapphire lining.

Jilseth remembered his name. Urlan, a mage who divided his time between Hadrumal and the distant ports of Tormalin's east coast, using his skills to guide ships across the far ocean to the unexplored lands beyond.

'Our friends and colleagues in Suthyfer have discovered many ways for Artifice and elemental magic to complement each other. We should not be so quick to dismiss aetheric magic merely because its mysteries are closed to us. I would not be standing here if Artifice's healing hadn't salvaged my broken legs.'

Jilseth recalled hearing he'd suffered appalling injuries when his ship had fallen foul of a catastrophic storm.

'That's another debate which I have no wish to revisit.' An ancient magewoman rose laboriously to her feet. Despite the heat outside she was wrapped in a mossy cloak. A mage by the door stood up, ready to hurry forward and assist her.

'I have no interest in mainlander affairs.' She looked around the great chamber, her sunken eyes glittering. 'Let us not forget why Archmage Trydek brought his first apprentices here, those men and women in whose chairs you sit. Look at the defences enveloping this hall which they wrought with the first quintessential magic, blending their spells in desperation born of fear for their very lives.'

She shook her head, white hair as fine as thistledown barely concealing her bony skull. 'Mainlanders have always feared us, even when they've sought to make use of our skills. At least we knew where we stood when the mageborn were beaten and exiled, if they weren't hanged outright.'

'Forgive me, Madam Shannet.' Herion bowed respectfully. 'But those days were long gone even before your birth.'

'You don't think such persecution could return?' She teetered alarmingly as she thrust her stick at him. 'For us and for these adepts of Artifice—' her disdain was palpable '—if they're fool enough to share their secrets. I've lived long enough to see how vile the mundane multitude can behave to one another, especially when they fear for their land or livelihood. We have nothing to gain by interfering and far too much to lose. The proper business of wizards is

wizardry and that is the business of Hadrumal!'
Her voice echoed back from the encircling wall,
unexpectedly forceful.

'Archmage? By your leave?' She gestured towards the
door, still an impenetrable barrier.

Some of the mages looked towards Planir. As he sat
back down with a casual wave of one hand, Jilseth
saw the metal cloaking the door flowing back into the
everyday bands of iron. The heavy portal creaked and
swung open now that the will of the majority inside
commanded it. She hastily stepped aside as council
members began to leave.

One of the first, Jilseth noted, was Flood Mistress
Troanna, as silent as she had been throughout the
meeting, her expression as unrevealing as ever.

'How much of that charade did Planir rehearse
beforehand?'

Jilseth found Canfor at her shoulder, looking down
at her.

'I don't know what you mean.'

'No?' He smiled maliciously. 'Then he does just keep
you to run his errands. Well, Sannin, Rafrid and Herion
all played their parts admirably. My compliments,' he
offered, sarcastic.

'Then Ely is teaching you to suspect slights and
connivance where none exist.' Jilseth would have
walked away but too many wizards were leaving the
council chamber.

'When did so few wizards last speak at a Council
meeting?' Canfor stooped, his twilight blue eyes
unblinking. 'Where was the usual discussion, weighing
the argument on either side of the scales, a consensus
agreed among all those present?'

'Why is that remarkable?' Jilseth retorted. 'So many mages have lost patience with Kalion forever disputing the Archmage's decisions.'

'How many are losing patience with Planir's perpetual refusal to act?' Canfor pressed a hand against the wall to stop Jilseth squeezing through a gap. 'What will your Archmage do when the mainland loses all patience with wizardry? When his lack of leadership has destroyed all unity among the mageborn? What good does it serve to have such senior mages undermine the Hearth Master's concerns and distract everyone from the real issues at hand?'

'Kalion's notion of unity is everyone doing his bidding.' Jilseth ducked under his arm. 'I prefer to think for myself.'

'A single strong voice commands respect.' Canfor took a step to stay in front of her. 'A bickering multitude invites contempt.'

Before Jilseth could counter that, Canfor vanished into the throng. She pressed her back against the wall, allowing the gathering to disperse. As the chamber emptied, she saw Planir in the centre, conferring with Sannin, Rafrid and Herion.

Planir saw her and beckoned. As Jilseth joined the quartet, she saw that Herion was looking glum.

'So we have curbed Kalion's interference at the cost of giving rein to Shannet's prejudices against everyone and anyone not mageborn.'

Rafrid agreed with a heavy sigh. 'While seemingly endorsing Master Massial's oft-stated dismissal of anything beyond these shores.'

'Giving those sharing such bias or blindness the perfect excuse of following their elders' example,'

Sannin concluded sardonically, 'thus deepening the dissent already rife in our halls. A good day's work, Archmage?'

'Deplorable as Hadrumal's divisions might be, that's a lesser evil than magical tyranny, no matter how honourable its motives.' Planir caught Jilseth's eye. Whatever he saw in her face prompted a wry twist of his mouth.

'We don't disagree with Kalion. Wizards must engage with the mainland if we're to escape the non-mageborn's fear and suspicion. If a fraction of the hatred that drove Trydek to this sanctuary ever takes hold again, no wizard's life will be worth a copper cut-piece on the mainland.'

'But Kalion's approach would reap resentment by the bushel basket,' Rafrid said with sincere regret, 'which would rapidly ferment into hatred.'

'Let us be thankful that our Hearth Master is such an honest man.' Sannin's remorse was just as genuine. 'Much as it pains me to use that against him.'

'He could have lied about his nexus scrying on the mainland,' Herion explained to Jilseth, 'or claimed that exaggerated calumny is being heaped on wizardry in Minelas's name.'

'No, he couldn't,' Planir said heavily. 'Another mage perhaps, but not Kalion. He's far too principled.'

'What now?' Sannin looked around the empty council chamber.

'We must get the measure of our esteemed colleagues' true opinions.' Planir looked even more weary. 'Most of them will keep their coin safe in their purse until they see which way these runes will roll. We must also keep a close eye on Captain Corrain,' he added with asperity.

Jilseth wondered at that. 'Archmage—'

'I don't trust him any more than Kalion does.' Planir shook his head. 'He wears that broken manacle as a remembrance; I've no doubt of it. He is not a man looking to forgive or to forget anyone who's done him wrong. I suspect we're all in that number thanks to Minelas.'

'I saw that for myself.' Jilseth wanted to say something different. 'Archmage, since Kalion's nexus will be watching you more closely than ever, could we be of assistance; myself, Merenel, Nolyen and Tornauld? We could watch Corrain for you, in case he does something untoward?'

With luck they'd hear some clue to the ruffian's intent. Jilseth would wager gold against brass on Tornauld's magic being able to listen a thousand leagues further than Canfor's.

Planir considered this before nodding. 'Very well.'

— CHAPTER EIGHTEEN —

Siprel Inlet, Caladhria
1st of For-Summer

CORRAIN YAWNED. THEY'D been keeping watch since early light, when the stream oozing from the marshes was a braided silver thread cutting across brown mud fringed with green, like the rot edging putrid meat. The stink lurked in the back of his throat even now that the returning tide had drowned the flyblown cordweed.

'You're certain of this?' Captain Mersed sat beside him on a mat of lousewort.

'As sure as I can be.' Corrain looked seawards through the tangled branches of a salt-thorn bush.

Mersed stirred uneasily. 'No word from the watchmen?'

'They'll come at high water.' Kusint sat hugging his shins, chin resting on his knees. His talent for making himself comfortable, whether he'd learned that living in the Forest or campaigning with the Solurans, was something Corrain could only envy.

'An hour or so after noon.' Kusint checked the shadow of the stick he had set up for a makeshift sundial. 'A Caladhrian hour.'

Corrain had been surprised to learn that the Solurans divided every day from dawn to dawn into twenty equal hours, as the Archipelagans did from sunset to sunset. Perhaps that made more sense in the southernmost

Archipelago where the islands saw days and nights of equal length year round. But Solura was to the north of Caladhria, even more subject to the vagaries of the seasons.

However you measured it, nothing could hurry the sun's passage across the sky above these trackless, midge-filled marshes. He shifted to ease the ache in his buttocks, careful not to shake the salt-thorn. A corsair galley might already be approaching. Any sentry in the prow would be able to see significantly further than those on the shoreline, even if they weren't hiding in the bushes. The Caladhrian swordsmen must lie concealed until the raiders sailed right into their trap.

Mersed sucked his teeth unattractively. 'You're sure this is the right place.'

Corrain carefully folded his arms. Throttle the Tallat captain and some vengeful god would surely send them the galley at that very moment, to be alerted by the sound of choking.

'You saw the tracks and barrel marks by the stream. This is the place.'

He had no doubt of that. He'd tallied up the summer's raids marked on Arigo's map against the almanac, double-checking his own recollection of the phases of the moon against Kusint's memories of that stop to replenish the *Reef Eagle's* water casks. Together they had scoured every map of these remote shores and sought out every greybeard guard's reminiscences of hunting trips.

From the dates of those first raids and the distances from the despoiled villages, Corrain and Kusint concluded this was the corsairs' favoured inlet, deep in the saltings between Halferan and Tallat, so remote that there was no point in wondering where the border between the baronies might lie.

So Corrain had bullied Captain Arigo into saddling up the Halferan guard and they'd gone southward in search of allies among the charcoal marks on his map. They'd soon found Mersed and his troopers riding beneath Tallat's black and white chequer-cloth. Those men had been readily convinced to plan this assault on the raiders. They'd spent the previous six days riding the coast only to arrive each day amid the devastation the corsairs had left, sometimes so recently a burned house was still smouldering.

Faint doubt tormented Corrain all the same. It had looked different at night from the deck of a galley, insofar as anywhere in these endless vistas of reed and scrub could look different from anywhere else. And they were wagering that a galley would arrive before Captain Mersed gathered up his men and rode away. He certainly wouldn't stay beyond the first despatch bringing word of another ravaged Tallat village.

Corrain saw the tension in Kusint's angular jaw, as well as a darkness behind his eyes. Corrain recognised that unspoken fear. It had visited him in the cool grey light of dawn.

'They won't take us again,' he murmured to the Forest lad. 'We outnumber them three to one. We know when they'll be weakest—'

'A brindle owl!' Mersed uncoiled his long limbs to crouch, alert.

Corrain's hand was already on his sword hilt. 'We don't move till they're split between ship and shore.'

That first call meant a corsair vessel had been spotted off shore. The next signal would indicate it was making for the inlet.

Absurd uncertainties quickened Corrain's heartbeat. Someone aboard that ship might know that supposed owl for a counterfeit. Brindle owls only hunted among the forests inland. He thrust away such foolish misgivings. The Aldabreshi would be as ignorant of Caladhrian birds as he had been of the twittering in Archipelagan trees.

Kusint offered Corrain a swig from the water skin slung over his shoulder. He sucked gratefully on the horn mouthpiece.

He refused to indulge in more foolish speculation. There was no chance they'd find Hosh chained to an oar. The fool boy was doubtless dead, murdered when Corrain had escaped with Kusint. He would have to answer for that whenever he finally stood before Saedrin.

The brindle owl called a second time. Corrain watched the corsair galley advancing cautiously up the inlet. The platforms at prow and stern were both crowded with armed and armoured Aldabreshi, vigilant in every direction. The slow oars barely raised a whisper in the sluggish water, obedient to the flute's steady rhythm.

Corrain glanced at the clumps of sea reed marking the uncertain margin between mud and more solid ground. Chest high to a tall man, the tufted green and brown stems offered sufficient cover to hide the Tallat troopers. Mersed had promised they could contain their hatred. He'd threatened to personally castrate any fool ruining all their hopes by attacking too soon.

Corrain knew the Halferans wouldn't give in to their outrage, not and risk his and Captain Arigo's boot so far up their arse that they'd be sucking on hobnails. The galley was drawing ever closer to the broad wedge of firm ground, where the stream offered untainted water. With deftness impossible for any ship under sail, it spun around inside its own length, the oarsmen on one side backing while those on the other flank rowed forwards. Now the galley lay sternward to the shore.

'It's not the *Reef Eagle*,' Kusint breathed.

Corrain saw the disappointment deep in his eyes. He had hoped to rescue Hosh too.

Every oar rose clear of the water, drops pattering down from their blades. The whip master blew his whistle. With a crash, each oar descended and backed the galley so close to firm ground that Corrain could hear the keel grate on the mud.

The corsairs were shouting briskly, no alarm to stir the salty air. The oars were drawn inboard with a rumble like distant thunder, leaving the blades bristling along the oar ports. The crude anchors hit the shallow water, splashing loudly.

'We've got them,' Mersed whispered, exultant.

'Lay an egg before you cackle.' Corrain crouched, tense as a bow string.

Attack now and the corsairs would cut those anchor ropes, whip the rowers to their oars and be away to warn their allies never to venture here again.

The galley's master was visible in the stern, gesturing as he ordered the hatch opened to the hold. Some Aldabreshi were already climbing down the ladders fixed at the galley's stern. Corrain watched as a gaggle of slaves began filling leather flagons from the stream while others manhandled the little barrels to be filled with water.

He took a carved horn whistle from the pouch of oddments on his belt and blew a raucous blast.

The corsairs looked around, more curious than concerned.

Every Caladhrian recognised the sun-faced duck's call. They erupted from the thickets and reeds. Mersed ran to join his men, all concealment abandoned.

Those raiders already ashore readied their own weapons. Curved Archipelagan steel clashed with straight mainland swords. Cries of pain mingled with abuse hurled by both sides, mutually incomprehensible.

Every muscle in Corrain's body urged him to join the fray. No, that first assault was Tallat's task. If the Caladhrians were to win the day, they must stick to their plan.

More Aldabreshin raiders poured down the galley's stern ladders, shining blades in hand. Tallat's troop began retreating. The first of the fallen, Caladhrian and Aldabreshin, were trampled underfoot.

Corrain gritted his teeth. Men died. It was the way of battle. At least those heroes of Tallat had struck a blow to avenge Caladhria's sufferings.

Now they were relying on Captain Mersed's mastery over his men. The Tallats must hold off from striking back long enough to draw the corsairs far enough from the ship.

Good enough. The second wave of Caladhrians, led by Mersed himself, surged forward from concealment to cut the raiders off from their ship. Seeing they were now caught between the two troops, the corsairs quickly drew close together.

That left them wrong footed when Mersed's men rushed up the stern ladders instead. Now the Tallats' initial retreat stopped dead. Those swordsmen sprang forward to prevent the corsairs on shore from falling back to defend their ship. However, there were still enough raiders on the galley to make a fight of it and these southern barbarians had other resources.

'Corrain,' Kusint said warningly.

'I see it.' Corrain was watching the prow platform, jutting out from the shore. Pale smoke rose, teased by the summer breeze.

He took the crossbow that Reven offered him. Tucking the stock tight into his shoulder, he sighted along the length of the weapon, through the fine ironwork lattice set in the centre of the curved arms. Several men were stooping over the source of the smoke.

Corrain saw one straighten up. The Aldabreshin drew back his arm, intent on making his throw. Corrain pressed the crossbow's trigger and felt the bolt's discharge rush through his body like a physical release.

As the corsair fell, he saw the others in the prow looking wildly around their feet. 'Reven!'

The boy took the spent crossbow, handing Corrain a second with its sturdy hemp string already drawn, deadly bolt loaded. Reven bent to thrust his foot through the stirrup at the front of the empty crossbow. Snagging the string on the hook on his belt and standing upright, his action drew the weapon ready for use once again. He reached into the quiver slung from his shoulder for another bolt, only to realise Corrain was still watching and waiting.

'Captain?' Reven had started calling him that, along with a fair few of the other lads. Thus far, Arigo had chosen to ignore it.

Corrain saw a raider in the galley's prow pounce like a cat on a mouse. The man sprang up, his arm swinging wildly. Something small soared through the air; no bigger than a man's fist. It burst in a flash of flame, sending fragments spattering into the water.

That was a relief. He didn't want the fools to burn their own ship to the waterline. The relief was short-lived. The next fire pot flew straight over the galley's stern to smash on the shore. While it fell too short to shower them with flames, the Tallat men recoiled with cries of alarm.

Corrain raised the crossbow and as quickly as he could, aimed bolt after bolt at the galley's prow. Other Halferan bows joined him. Hunters like Fitrel and Arigo were deadly accurate, their skills born of years of hunting.

The Archipelagans' short wooden bows had no hope of reaching the archers equipped with either crossbows or mainland bows in the Dalasorian style, masterfully crafted with bone, horn and sinew. After seeing how readily Aldabreshin wooden bows warped through their rain-filled seasons, Corrain had realised such intricately wrought mainland weapons could never survive the damp. So the raiders would have no answer for Halferan arrows.

Now younger men were emerging from cover to hurl grapnels clear across the inlet, not at the ship but to each other. Each one trailed a rope. As the barbed iron teeth bit into the mud, swift-footed lads ran forward to haul on the ropes. Nets followed, edging across the mud and through the water to be lashed securely to the deepest rooted thorns on either side. Soon a double layer of heavy mesh would frustrate any attempt to row the galley away to the safety of open water.

Corrain saw one of the Halferan lads fall backwards into the ooze. The boy clutched at the garish Aldabreshin arrow piercing his chest. The corsairs were loosing sheaves of arrows to drive the net riggers off and some had carelessly strayed within range.

One of the men in the prow threw a smoking pot towards a thorn bush tangled with ropes. A Halferan man recoiled, arms flailing madly as golden fire blossomed on his chest. The flames spread with impossible speed. Another trooper grabbed the man, trying to force him into the muddy water to quench the flames. The greedy fire surged up the rescuer's arms, devouring his face. Sticky fire; as vile as travellers' tales promised. Corrain had warned them.

Up on the galley, the Tallat men had seized control. Now they were charging down the walkway. The men in the prow abandoned the pots of sticky fire, seizing swords to fight for their lives. Corrain saw Caladhrians among the rowers' benches. Blades rose, casting off scarlet showers of blood. Did they know who they were killing? Or was every dark-skinned man fair game?

'Come on!'

Corrain ran, Kusint at his side. Yelling for the Tallat troopers ashore to clear the way, he slashed at any Aldabreshin too slow to evade him. Kusint was hacking his own path. They reached the stern ladders together.

'Go on.' Kusint sprang half way up, looping one arm through the upright, sword ready to foil any attacker pursuing them.

Corrain scrambled up the ladder. The noise up on the deck was making his blood run cold. The Tallat men must have forgotten what their captain had agreed, overcome by bloodlust.

'Don't kill the rowers! Don't kill the slaves!'

He nearly skewered a hapless trooper as he half-jumped, half-fell onto the stern platform. The man recoiled with an obscene oath.

'Do you think we're muttonheads?' Captain Mersed jumped up onto the walkway, just as insulted. 'You can lay any dead on this ship to the corsairs' account!'

Corrain saw that most of the rowers were alive, cowering between their benches. Those few who lay dead were obscured by Aldabreshi corpses. The whip master and overseers had been killing the oarsmen themselves before the Tallat men cut them down.

'What now?' Kusint appeared at the top of his ladder.

Ashore, the Tallat men were prevailing. Even Aldabreshin ferocity was no match for Caladhrian weight of numbers. The ground was sodden with blood, fresh puddles shining as grey-headed Halferans cut any fallen enemy's throat.

'Captain Mersed!' Corrain hurried up the walkway. 'Forgive me. I meant no offence but I need this ship and these men to row it.'

'Do you now?' Suspicion coloured Mersed's sardonic tone. 'Why?'

Corrain didn't blink. 'To be about the Archmage's business in return for him telling us where to lay our trap today. Beyond that, I'm sworn to secrecy.'

He and Kusint had racked their brains over how to convince some Caladhrian captain to hand the galley over. Finally they had concocted this bare-faced lie.

'Let's talk without too many ears flapping around us.' Corrain ushered Mersed to the galley prow. 'You've heard that Lord Licanin travelled to Hadrumal after the Equinox?'

'With the barons of Saldiray and Taine?' Kusint added, 'to ask for the Archmage's help.'

'Aye and those noble lords were sent home with their tails tucked between their legs.' Mersed's face betrayed the same resentment that Corrain had felt when he'd heard the story.

Corrain forced himself to smile. 'The Archmage cannot break his own edict.'

Mersed folded his arms. 'Then why do you look like the pig with the deepest spot in the wallow?'

'Perhaps we should say,' Kusint reflected, 'the Archmage cannot be seen to break his own edict.'

Mersed looked at him with sudden suspicion.

'As long as no one speaks out of turn,' Corrain said with spurious innocence, 'Baron Tallat has allied with Halferan purely out of shared concern over these corsair raids.'

'Like Lord Taine,' Kusint nodded, 'and Baron Saldiray too, before the turn of the season.'

'Stop talking in riddles.' Mersed was getting annoyed. 'You say the Archmage is willing to help us? As long as it's a secret?'

Corrain grinned. 'How do you suppose my friend and I escaped the Aldabreshi?'

'Impossible to believe. As incredible as—' Kusint pretended to search for an elusive word '—as magecraft?'

'Magecraft?' Corrain pretended surprise. 'But using magic to help Caladhria would threaten the wizards' edict.'

Kusint nodded. 'No mage would ever do such a thing,'

'Any more than a lady wizard could send men away in rags and rust,' Corrain remarked, 'when they'd been fully armoured.'

Much as he distrusted the Hadrumal woman Jilseth, he could kiss her feet for that flourish. What better to persuade Mersed of this supposedly undeclared alliance?

'Truly?' The Tallat captain looked at them, awe-struck. Then he looked around the inlet, his expression one of savage delight. 'So we can catch them all like this?'

'The Archmage cannot risk his involvement being discovered,' Corrain said quickly. 'Not yet.'

Kusint was alert to his cue. 'But he has shown us how the corsairs rely on this inlet, and we know they must have other such lairs where they take on water before they row south.'

'If you ride to confer with the other baronies' captains up and down the coast,' Corrain looked straight at Mersed, 'Caladhrian swords can ambush them coming ashore in the days after every high-springing tide.'

'Best not to mention the Archmage though,' Kusint advised.

Corrain nodded. 'You wouldn't want to risk his wrath. Not when you can enjoy your lord's favour for solving the riddle of catching the corsairs.'

'Along with the gratitude of those other captains who'll be so praised by their lords of Karpis and Saldiray, Myrist and Taine,' Kusint agreed.

Mersed looked at Corrain for a long moment. His troopers were gleefully heaving the dead Aldabreshi over the galley's side to bob clumsily in the inlet.

Corrain winced as one corpse struck the oar blades with a potentially damaging thud. 'Make sure you net those bodies when you clear the inlet, if you want to spring this trap again. If corpses float out to sea, raider ships in these waters will know that something's amiss.'

'That's what the Archmage says, is it?' Mersed chewed his lip. 'We should lay this snare again while you're about his business?'

Corrain gestured at the dead Aldabreshi ashore now being kicked and abused by the exultant Tallats. 'Won't your lord want more of the same, once you tell him how you've avenged his losses? But you won't lure any more raiders in here if they see a galley already moored. How else will you be rid of it if we don't take it away?'

Mersed looked at the cowering rowers, whip scars cutting across their protruding ribs, crusted sores beneath their fetters and manacles. 'You don't let those vermin loose, not anywhere in Caladhria. I want your oath on that.'

'You're rid of them, I swear it,' Corrain assured him.

'You've some way to be sure they won't cut your throat as soon as you're out of sight of land?' Mersed looked unconvinced. 'What's to stop them raiding on their own account when they've fed you to the fish?'

'The Archmage doesn't leave us unprotected.' Corrain smiled with a confidence he didn't feel in the slightest.

He could already see some of the apparently craven oar slaves watching this conversation, ominously intent. He and Kusint knew they would have to sleep turn and turn about on the voyage to Solura, for fear of a knife in the night. Always assuming they could get these slaves to co-operate in the first place.

'Captain Corrain?' It was Reven, running up the walkway. Gaping at the chained men on either side, he nearly tripped and fell headlong. 'For you,' he gasped, offering a folded and sealed letter.

'What's this?' Corrain turned it over, to see only his name written in elegant strokes.

'Captain Arigo gave it to me.' Reven shrugged.

Corrain looked ashore but could see no sign of the fat old man. As he snapped the seals he noticed Lady Zurenne's rune sigil stamped in the wax. The nobility liked to use their birth runes thus, to distinguish private business from their barony's affairs.

If you have received this, you have succeeded. So I will hold you to your offer of protection for me and mine before you depart. Come at once and make good on your oath.

Corrain read and reread the curt words with growing disbelief. How could he go? He had no time to waste on this. The galley had to catch the ebbing tide, to avoid any other corsairs heading this way to refill their water casks. How long would it take to ride to Halferan and back? What would happen to these rowers left here undefended against the menace of Tallat's troopers? This was ridiculous.

He read the note again. How could he not go?

— CHAPTER NINETEEN —

Halferan Manor, Caladhria
1st of For-Summer

ZURENNE LOOKED UP at the faint silvery *ting* of the timepiece on the mantel shelf. Was it still so early? But of course, it had been turned to show the summer faceplate; the graduated scale spaced more widely as the sliding arrow counted off the day's ten chimes, before the ten shorter divisions of the night.

Since the days of the Old Tormalin Empire, everyone had seen the sense of dividing darkness and daylight as evenly as possible, adjusting for the season. Zurenne wasn't about to deny the wisdom of it but the turn of the seasons did always catch her unawares for a few days.

Time to ring for Raselle, for a night tisane before she made ready for bed. Even with a full branch of candles lit, Zurenne's eyes were too tired for more embroidery. She couldn't concentrate on reading any book. What was happening out on the coast?

Hooves sounded loud on the cobbles beneath her window. Zurenne sprang to her feet so fast that she knocked the table, the candles shedding hot wax to mar the polished surface. She didn't care, running to the window to pull back curtains drawn against the dusk.

It was him. It had to be. Alone? Through the window she could see two horses in the light of the gatehouse lamp, but neither of the crop-headed lads tending them could be Corrain, and she had thought his Forest-born ally was taller.

Voices below told her he was at the great hall's door. Taking a single candle, Zurenne hurried out into the hallway. She blessed Drianon in passing that she hadn't already shed her own gown to go to bed.

'Lysha, my love.' Zurenne opened the bedchamber door as quietly as she could. The last thing they needed was Esnina waking.

Ilysh was deeply asleep behind light summer curtains hung to foil insects rather than drafts. Zurenne stuck the candle which she carried in the empty stick by the bed.

She drew the curtain aside and knelt, her mouth so close to her daughter's ear that the girl's curls tickled her cheek. 'Lysha, wake up.'

'Mam—'

Zurenne stifled Ilysh's exclamation with a gentle hand, her other forefinger raised to her lips. 'Hush, my love.'

Ilysh stared at her, uncomprehending. 'Corsairs?' Terror strangled her whisper. 'Neeny—'

'No, no.' Zurenne reached for her daughter's hand. She could have slapped herself for a fool, not thinking of Ilysh's fear, startled out of a sound sleep. She drew a determined breath.

'I have decided you were right. Seeing you wed will safeguard Halferan.'

'What?' Ilysh sat up, astounded. 'Now?'

'Hush!' Zurenne gave her hand a warning squeeze. 'We mustn't wake Neeny!'

Thankfully that dire prospect silenced Ilysh, giving Zurenne a chance to summon up her resolve. 'Corrain is here. That means he must have captured a galley. If he is to sail to Solura, we must do this tonight. Now, we must dress you quickly, and don't make a noise.'

As Ilysh threw back her satin coverlet and the linen sheet beneath, Zurenne allowed herself a measure of relief. Having to wake Ilysh like this was no bad thing if the undoubted need for silence meant she couldn't ask awkward questions.

Zurenne hadn't yet decided how she might explain what she was about to do. But she had this first half of summer before Lord Licanin proposed his guardianship to the Solstice Parliament. She need not dismay him with this sham of marriage before any grant was approved. When she should have some idea if Corrain could make good on his promises to rescue them from the corsairs with unsanctioned magic.

If so, Zurenne would defy the outrage that her actions tonight would undoubtedly cause, for the sake of seeing Halferan and its people safe. And as long as Corrain was Ilysh's husband in a correctly witnessed ceremony, the parchments signed and sealed, no one could punish Zurenne by taking her children away, for letting him bring a Soluran wizard here.

Ilysh's husband only in name. As Ilysh went to her washstand, Zurenne saw her daughter's budding breasts through the gossamer-fine fabric of her summer chemise, and the first swell of her hips.

Corrain wouldn't see a hint of such nubile allure. Zurenne took one of Ilysh's festival gowns from its chest and shook fragrant snakestraw from its velvet folds.

Ilysh hurriedly donned a clean shift and stockings. 'Mama, my hair?' She tugged agonised at her tousled night plait.

'Sit.' Zurenne took up brush and comb and quickly unbraided the girl's long locks. 'Now, dress.'

'Mama?' Ilysh looked puzzled at the high-necked violet gown, ill-suited to these humid nights on the cusp between spring and summer.

'Hurry up.' As Ilysh stepped into the violet gown, Zurenne's hands were shaking so badly it took all her concentration to lace the back securely.

What if Corrain simply vanished from their lives after tonight? They would never know if he were to end up dead in some Soluran ditch or at the bottom of the sea, his throat cut by a corsair's blade.

Zurenne's hands grew steadier. She would hardly be any worse off. As long as Corrain's fate remained unknown, provided she was armed with legally binding documents to shield her daughters in his name, she could resist any attempts by Licanin or anyone else to impose their will upon her.

That might even be preferable until Ilysh was old enough to wed in name as well as on paper. By then Zurenne could have found some noble protector whom they could trust.

'My lady?' Raselle peered around the bedchamber door, at a loss to understand what she saw.

Zurenne very nearly dismissed her, but changed her mind. 'Fetch my writing box from my bedchamber.'

When she had decided to do this, she had drawn up the marriage contracts, referring time and again to the parchments binding her to Halferan. If the legalities weren't correctly detailed, signed and sealed then this wedding wouldn't be valid. Zurenne would have no defence against Lord Licanin's wrath.

Then her nerve had failed her and she had called Raselle to light the fire, burning the heavy paper and smashing the ashes into oblivion with the poker. Before thinking it through again and drawing up a second set of contracts.

'Ilysh.' She took hold of her daughter's shoulders, looking deep into her eyes. 'This night's work is to remain a secret, as far as anyone else is concerned. Corrain will only stand as your guardian until you're of an age to wed by your own choice.'

When Ilysh would wed as a virgin, Zurenne was absolutely determined. She had a knife purloined from the carving platter when they had last dined on roast lamb, to make sure that Corrain kept to that part of this scandalous bargain.

'He will not lay a finger upon you. He leaves tonight, to fight the corsairs, as soon as you are wed. Lord Licanin may never need to know what's transpired,' Zurenne added hastily. 'We'll only have to tell him if he insists we agree to something untoward.'

'Until Corrain returns.' As Ilysh looked back with equal determination, Zurenne was startled to realise her daughter had grown almost as tall as she was.

'My lady?' Raselle hesitated in the doorway, the ornamented writing box in her hands. 'The captain, that's to say, Corrain, he's waiting below.'

'I know.'

Zurenne ushered Ilysh into the hallway. The door to the stair was open, where Raselle had answered the summons of the bell below. The door to the maids' room was closed and she could hear Jora snoring. So much for the nursemaid waking at any hint of mischief by her noble charges. That would be yet another pennyweight in the balance of Zurenne's dislike for the girl, if it wasn't such a relief not to have to order her back to bed, to stay dumb and blind about whatever she might see tonight.

'Downstairs.' Zurenne waited for Ilysh to follow Raselle and then locked the door after herself. Whatever else, Neeny couldn't follow them now. No secret could survive that.

At the bottom of the stairs, she saw Corrain waiting by the high table, beside the only lamp burning in the entire great hall. For a man who'd ridden all day and into the night, he didn't look too badly dishevelled. He had not shed that broken manacle nor cut his disreputable mane but his hair was brushed back and neatly bound at the nape of his neck. Zurenne winced at the thought of wrenching a comb through those knots and tangles.

'You came.' She hadn't entirely believed that he would.

As he stepped forward and the lamplight struck him, she saw his face was tight with emotion. 'And near killed two good horses riding them without a break.'

Zurenne refused to contemplate that. 'Have you gathered a force from the coastal baronies? Have you captured the ship you sought?

'I have.' He nodded. 'That's to say, I have the ship and Tallat's men are ready to snare as many corsairs as they can after this victory, and to set the rest of the coast hunting them as well.' He took a step forward. 'If I am to make use of that ship, my lady, we cannot afford any more delay.'

Zurenne heard desperation as well as exasperation in his warning. She spoke quickly before her nerve could fail her again.

'I will agree to you marrying Ilysh, in name only, before you depart for Solura. You will leave a sealed grant of regency authorising me to manage Halferan in your absence.' She fought not to look round as Raselle gasped in shock.

'No one else is to know of it and only I will decide when and if to make any of these dealings public.' Now Zurenne did look round, to fix the maidservant with a piercing gaze. Raselle nodded with fervent, mute assurance.

'Of course,' Corrain agreed.

'Then we must go to the shrine.' Zurenne thrust away the thought of Licanin's wrath if he discovered her audacity.

Why didn't she submit to his kindly dominion and trust the assembled wisdom of the barons to save Caladhria from the raiders? Because their noble lordships had shown no sign of defending the coast despite five years of corsair raids, more widespread and destructive each successive summer. Because their parliament's debates on the subject had proved as worthless as echoes in an empty room. That's what her husband had said and Halferan had been the wisest man whom Zurenne had ever known.

Her heart was pounding as she twisted the ring to open the door into the shrine from the dais. The glow of candlelight embraced them.

Zurenne looked at Halferan's urn. He had put his trust in magecraft, even if vile treachery had led him to his death. Now Zurenne had seen what even a lady wizard's magic could accomplish and knew that her husband had been right. Let Corrain prove his worth and redeem his oath to his dead lord by finding a mage who could be trusted.

She walked over to the shrine table and picked up the flowers she'd laid before Drianon that very morning; the delicate froth of Larasion's lace and the milky bells of honeysilk. If she was doing the right thing, she had prayed to the goddess, then let Corrain come. If not, let Poldrion's demons take him so he never showed his face in Halferan again.

Well, here he was but the goddess's blank marble gaze offered Zurenne no reassurance that she wasn't committing a heinous crime in this holy place. She turned to see Ilysh looking uncertainly at Corrain.

'Where is your companion?' Lysha's voice trembled.

'Kusint?' He smiled down at her. 'He's keeping the boat safe, so we can go to Solura.'

'My lady?' Raselle was standing with her back to the great hall door, as if to bar it against attackers. She hugged the writing box in her arms. 'If there's to be a wedding—' she sounded as though she didn't entirely believe it '—where is the priest?'

Zurenne had asked herself the same question, when she'd been unable to shake off this outlandish notion. Her husband had been the hereditary priest of this manor, as was custom and practise across Caladhria. Every shrine within the barony had been within his gift, their priests owing him their allegiance. That was all very well but she wasn't about to trust anyone else to keep this secret. Wasn't that an end to it?

Not when she realised she would be performing the rites to welcome For-Summer. Any baron's wife could do so in her husband's absence. It was essential when the lords were travelling to gather for the quarterly parliament.

Any widowed mother could give her child in marriage in her husband's stead. That was one of a mother's very few privileges enshrined in law.

Did those separate decrees mean that Zurenne could perform this marriage? Well, she would do it and if their lordships didn't agree, they could argue custom and precedent until their tongues turned black and, all the while they did so, Halferan and Ilysh would be safe from their interference.

'We don't need a priest,' Zurenne said firmly.

Corrain nodded. 'Then let's get this done.'

But as he stepped forward, Ilysh didn't move. She pressed her chin to her chest, her unbound hair falling forward to curtain her face.

'My lady.' Corrain had to sink to one knee in order to look up into her eyes. 'I owed your father my duty even at the cost of my life. I swore that in this very shrine. Now my lord is dead, you are his heir and my duty is to you. To keep you and this barony safe.'

He offered her his open hand. 'Marry me, in no more than name, and no one can forbid me from saving this barony as your father intended. I will see his name redeemed even if I die to do it.'

As Ilysh laid her slender white hand in Corrain's calloused palm Zurenne was torn between relief and a frantic urge to rip her daughter away from this man.

It was so unlike her own wedding, when the shrine had been decked with flowers. The whole compound was bright with late-flowering blooms and the first sheaves of corn to herald the harvest, in honour of Drianon, goddess of hearth, home and storehouse.

Music and merrymaking filled five full days. The manor was full to bursting with Zurenne's relatives and the Halferan barony's friends and allies joining in the feasting, along with those neither friend nor ally but who might take dangerous offence at the insult of not being invited.

Those nights had been filled with the private bliss of discovering for herself what her mother had merely hinted at as a wife's duty, and which her sisters had explained in more useful and intriguing, if unnerving, detail.

No, this wasn't the wedding Zurenne had planned for her daughter: given to a man she could love and respect, with Halferan performing the rites and reminding that unknown bridegroom whom he would answer to in this life if he failed to cherish and adore Ilysh, regardless of any goddess's chastisement.

'My lady?' Corrain prompted.

Zurenne cleared her throat. 'Ilysh, come here.'

As well as the flowers, she had laid a comb and silk ribbons at the foot of Drianon's statue. She deftly plaited Ilysh's dark tresses, the ribbons golden in the candlelight. With her hair drawn back, Ilysh looked both more adult and more vulnerable.

Zurenne refused to falter. The shrine's table was already laid with a linen cloth and unlit candles, while a new pair of scissors lay beside flint, steel, a loaf of bread and a shallow bowl of honey.

As Ilysh went back to stand beside Corrain, Zurenne lifted her chin. 'Corrain, do you declare before all here present and in the eternal sight of the gods that you wish to take Ilysh beneath your roof as your beloved wife?'

'I do,' he replied.

'Do you swear that you are free to do so, with no wife living under your protection?'

'I do.'

Customarily, these questions were merely a genial invitation. Zurenne found herself looking Corrain in the eye, challenging him with the ritual's demands.

'Do you swear to provide her with shelter, fire and food even if you must go naked, cold and hungry?

'Do you swear to comfort her in times of sorrow or sickness and to cherish her in times of joy?

'Do you swear that your arm will always defend her and the children she may bear you?'

She nearly choked on those words but the ritual must be followed to the last detail if she and Raselle were ever to need to give their own oath on it.

Corrain didn't blink. 'I do so swear and may Drianon scourge me if I prove false.'

Zurenne couldn't look Ilysh in the eye. She fixed her gaze on a nail head in the shrine's door, left behind when some cloth token had fallen or been torn away, now snagging a glint of candlelight.

'Ilysh, do you declare before all here present and in the eternal sight of all the gods that you wish to tend Corrain's hearth as his obedient wife?'

'I do,' Ilysh whispered.

'Do you swear that you are free to do so, not subject to any man save for the guardian who brings you here today?'

Zurenne didn't wait for her daughter to answer, running swiftly through the rest of the rite, so meaningless in these circumstances yet so necessary for Halferan's protection.

'Do you swear to take diligent care of his hearth and household and to see him and the children you may bear him always clothed and fed before yourself?

'Do you swear to comfort him in times of sorrow or sickness and to cherish him in times of joy? Do you swear never to shame him with inconstancy or profligacy?

'Do you swear that you will be guided by his wisdom just as you are guarded by his strength?'

Zurenne couldn't help it. She looked at Corrain. Did he see the question in her burning gaze?

Was this plan of his wisdom or arrant folly? Could he possibly return with a wizard to safeguard them all?

'I do so swear and may Drianon scourge me if I prove false,' Ilysh murmured with something perilously close to a shrug.

Zurenne was startled to see Corrain's grim expression crack with a grin. She recovered herself.

'Come before Drianon, that she may know you for man and wife. Always remember that the goddess is as sure-sighted as the eagles sacred to her.'

Had the goddess ever seen such an ill-assorted couple? What did she think of a mother bringing her daughter to such a wedding? Zurenne felt a new qualm. Never mind Lord Licanin. How might the goddess chastise her?

But it was too late. The oaths had been sworn and now Corrain was striking a spark from the flint, to light the candle set before him. He smiled as he handed it to Ilysh and she set the second one alight.

As her hand shook and the candle flame wavered, Zurenne caught her breath. If it were snuffed in this crucial moment, such misfortune would cast a pall over any true marriage. No matter. The flame had strengthened and the second candle was safely lit.

'Ilysh—'

The girl had already handed Corrain the scissors, a plain workaday pair nothing like the gold ornamented ones that Zurenne treasured in her sewing box.

'Not too short!' Zurenne said hastily as Ilysh turned to offer him the ribbon-decked plait of her hair. 'We can hardly keep this a secret if everyone sees her with a cropped head.'

'Not too short.' Corrain's grin came and went again. He carefully cut barely a thumb-length and laid the dark hair at Drianon's feet.

As Ilysh turned, he gave her back the scissors. According to the usual ribald wedding jokes, Drianon insisted that every wife kept hold of the means to geld a straying husband.

Candlelight dissolved into haze as Zurenne's eyes filled with tears. She had revelled in the unaccustomed brush of the breeze on her neck, in the heady sensation of being relieved of the unexpected weight of her hair. Like every other bride, Zurenne had delighted in everyone seeing that she was newly married, welcoming well-meant advice from friends and strangers alike. That was what marriage should be, not this deceitful counterfeit.

Ilysh giggled and Zurenne blinked furiously to rid herself of the sparkling tears. What was going on?

Ilysh sought to feed Corrain the scrap of bread which she had torn from the loaf and dipped in the bowl of honey. He caught the sop between tongue and lip as she dropped it, snatching back her fingers as if she were feeding a hound of uncertain temper.

'Thank you,' he said drily. 'Your turn.'

Ilysh watched as he pulled a morsel from the loaf and dipped it in the bowl. She giggled as he made a feint to stick it on her nose. Then she opened her mouth, as trusting as a nestling. As he fed it to her, his stained fingers brushed her cheek.

'Good girl,' he said absently.

As Zurenne looked at her daughter, a most unwelcome recollection struck her. Ilysh had often looked at her father like that. The girl missed him so desperately. Might this so-called marriage prompt some foolish daydream of Corrain somehow replacing Halferan?

Drianon was the goddess of hearth and home, of practical, sensible marriages. Larasion was the maiden goddess of love and luck, her symbol the moon so full of change and possibilities. Countless ballads wove her praises through tales of improbable romance, of brave deeds undertaken for the sake of beauteous maidens. Zurenne would cull those songs from their stock of sheet music, as soon as she got back to the clavichord.

Corrain bowed low, to Ilysh and then to Zurenne. 'My lady. My lady. Forgive me but I must leave and ride through the night. If we sign and seal the contracts, this business can be done with.'

'Of course.' Zurenne breathed a little easier. 'Raselle?'

The obedient maidservant brought the writing box to the table, setting out documents, ink and pens. Corrain carefully inscribed his name, once, twice and thrice, in a neater hand than she had expected.

Zurenne watched Ilysh sign her name, no trembling in her script. That was all to the good, should this marriage ever be challenged.

All the same, Zurenne silently swore to Drianon, to Larasion and any other gods taking heed. She would make certain that Ilysh knew this wedding was no more than a paper fiction, before the dust of Corrain's departure had settled out on the road.

Zurenne wrote her own name. Taking up a stick of sealing wax, she melted the end in a candle's flame. Fat drops fell sluggishly below her signature. She pressed Halferan's baronial ring into their pliant sheen.

Not that these contracts were going into the barony's archive, where Lord Licanin might stumble over the secret, searching for something in the muniment room. Zurenne had already decided to hide them among the shrine's ledgers in the chest under the table. No one would find them there among the faded records of sanctified urns.

And she would see Corrain's blood spilled, as darkly red as this wax, if he ever tried to seduce her daughter on the strength of this night's work. He would wish he had never escaped those cursed Archipelagans.

— CHAPTER TWENTY —

Black Turtle Isle, in the domain of Nahik Jarir
6th of For-Summer

HOSH FELT HORRIBLY exposed, walking between the
lapping wavelets and the smudged line of dead seaweed
that marked high water's reach. His eyes darted
constantly from the sand to the fringe trees lining the
shore.

He stooped to pluck a white shell from the grimy
beach, chipped and broken from tumbling in the surf.
That didn't matter. He dropped it into the bag he'd
fashioned from a rotting rag.

Standing upright, he looked out across the anchorage.
No more galleys had returned since the morning. So
two ships were still missing. That wasn't good, not
under these skies. The *Reef Eagle* had returned four
days ago, the galley master cutting their voyage short
to make sure of getting away from the mainland before
the Ruby moved into the arc of Death, where the stars
of the Sea Serpent currently writhed.

Both the Amethyst and the Diamond were in the arc
where the Hoe would be lurking below the horizon, and
where for some reason which Hosh couldn't fathom,
Brotherhood was somehow tied to short-term ventures.
All of this warned of wasted effort, apparently.

For the present the jewels were scattered around the
heavenly compass, their positions off-set and irregular,

and two ships were missing. The entire corsairs' encampment was full of men on edge. Every Aldabreshin could read the heavens, as easily as a Caladhrian could read the temper of a dog or a horse.

'What are you doing there?' One of a trio of slaves hailed Hosh from the tree line.

Hosh sighed and stood there, waiting for the men now approaching him. There was no point in running. That would only provoke them and he had nowhere to go. Besides, once a rival slave had established that Hosh had no food to steal, or had stolen it if he had, even the worst bullies tended to lose interest. Where was the prestige in defeating such a wretched specimen? So Hosh took care to look as wretched as he possibly could.

'What have you got?' The first tore the makeshift bag from Hosh's hand, spilling the shells on the sand.

The second man dropped to his knees to grab them before looking up, his face ugly with dashed hopes. 'Dry and empty.'

'What are you doing, fool?' The third didn't wait for an answer. He just punched Hosh hard in the belly.

He dropped to his hands and knees, waiting for a knee in the ribs, a brutal fist to the back of his head. Instead he heard a tumult of silver whistles sounding along the shore. His would-be tormenters ran inland, slipping on the loose sand in their urgency.

Hosh quickly scrabbled for his scattered shells. He didn't get them all but they weren't worth the risk. Not when Grewa had sent his envoy. Getting to his feet, ignoring the pain in his gut, he ran up the beach and across the dusty expanse edged by the fringe trees.

No one paid him any heed as he ran through the noisome encampment between the pavilions and through the ironwood trees now sadly tattered by axes. Everyone was hurrying. It wouldn't be wise to be late to the bloodstained hollow, not under the current skies.

The slopes were already crowded, corsairs and slaves alike intent on the man bringing word from the trireme's blind master. He surveyed them, impassive, the sunlight striking iridescent green shot through his blue silk tunic.

'Grewa has assessed the portents,' he declared without preamble. 'The most favourable day to strike north will be the first new shining of the Opal.'

A cheer greeted his words, albeit somewhat muted. Hosh raised his own hurrah while doing his best to tally the days without anyone seeing him count on his fingers. The Opal shining meant the reappearance of the Greater Moon ten days from now.

The envoy fixed his pale-eyed gaze on those around the hollow who weren't applauding this news.

'The stars of the Bowl with their promise of plenty will rise on the eastern horizon as the Opal shines in the arc of Wealth between south and west. Directly opposite, the Pearl will join the Ruby in the arc of the sky which promises Death to our foes.' He smiled with cruel satisfaction. 'While Amethyst and Diamond offer solid reassurance once they have moved together into the arc of Home.'

Where, if Hosh didn't miss his guess, the stars of the Hoe would also have shifted, by Aldabreshin reckoning anyway. With the Hoe below the horizon and warning of wasted effort, Hosh reckoned he could see more than one raider in the crowd who would have disputed this reading of the heavens. No one voiced open disagreement though. Not with Grewa.

The envoy smiled serenely, apparently oblivious to those scowls. 'Grewa will lead us north on the first tide after the Pearl slips from view.'

Four days until dark of the Lesser Moon. Until Hosh was chained to his oar in the *Reef Eagle* again. He sighed.

'Hosh.' A hand clapped him on the shoulder as the crowd began to disperse. It was Nifai, the overseer.

Hosh knew he owed the man a considerable debt. Nifai left him in no doubt that he fully intended to claim his due.

After the chaos of Corrain's escape, the *Reef Eagle's* whip master was ready to flog every slave senseless, whether or not they'd been ashore. When he'd recognised Hosh as Corrain's broken-faced shadow, he'd drawn a blade to cut his throat there and then.

Hosh had thrown himself at Nifai's feet, snivelling piteously as he spewed desperate lies. He'd only followed Corrain for fear of being murdered by the brute. But Hosh had outsmarted the dull-witted mainlander. He'd learned the Aldabreshin tongue.

Hadn't he promised to help Nifai in his trading? Would he have made that offer if he'd been planning to flee? Truly, he was glad that Corrain was gone.

Trimon be thanked, Hosh had already heard a few choice titbits of news before uproar flared around the cooking fires. Those must have tilted the balance in his favour. So now he was Nifai's pet.

The overseer was nodding with careful approval. 'Grewa is a wise leader and reads the heavens with great wisdom. Don't you agree?'

'Without doubt,' Hosh concurred. He also knew Nifai would want to know anything Hosh heard to the contrary.

Well, Hosh's mam had always said that Misaen made folk with two ears and two eyes and just the one mouth. So listen and look for four breaths before you think of drawing one to speak. That was proving good advice.

Did Nifai truly believe in Grewa's interpretation of the sky? Had the man believed him, back on Khusro Rina's trading beach? Hosh wasn't sure. But the overseer had defied the whip master. The tail only follows the *loal*, so Nifai had said. It has no wits of its own. Hosh had followed Corrain without sharing in his scheming.

A loal was one of those dog-faced beasts with man-like hands and long furry tails. Hosh had seen one caged on the trading strand. He'd fallen behind to get a better look, so a gap had opened up between him and Kusint, filled with thronging Aldabreshi. That was why Hosh had been taken wholly unawares when Corrain attacked their unwanted oar mate.

Amid the Archipelagans recoiling from the chaos engulfing the cooking circle, Hosh had been seized by panic. He'd lost sight of Corrain entirely. Which way to go? Which way was inland? Which way lay the shore?

Before he could decide where to run, men with staves had waded into the mêlée. Hosh guessed they had the warlord's sanction for subduing a riot at the cost of broken bones or cracked skulls. Whether the stars were shining kindly upon him, or Ostrin or Trimon or some other god from home, he had made it back to the beach.

Nifai's grip tightened on Hosh's shoulder. 'When the rains close the sea lanes to the north, we will double our wealth in trade with the western domains. Grewa will see our losses made good.'

It hadn't been losing a couple of slaves that had so enraged the whip master. Hosh had learned later how heavy the penalties were for disturbing the Rina domain's peace.

The blind corsair had paid a crippling price in metal looted from the mainland. All his galleys were ordered to quit the trading beach at once. The only reason the whip master hadn't reached for his scourge was because the slaves were needed to row. Fail to reach the sanctioned sea lanes fast enough and the *Reef Eagle* and all aboard it would be forfeit to Khusro Rina. They would be the warlord's slaves, from the galley master down.

Hosh stood patiently as the overseer's eyes grew distant, contemplating his likely gains.

'There will be new mainlander slaves from these next raids.' Nifai gave Hosh one last pat on the shoulder. 'You will tell me what you learn.'

Heartsick at the prospect, Hosh nodded nevertheless. He had no other choice.

Nifai's gaze sharpened as he saw Grewa's envoy head for the ironwood trees. 'You may go.' Dismissing Hosh, he sauntered over to contrive a casual encounter with Ducah, who'd also come to hear the envoy's pronouncements. The bare-chested corsair was frowning ominously.

Hosh definitely wanted to keep well out of that vicious brute's way. He weighed his shells in his cupped hands. He had enough to be going on with. He joined the slaves dragging their feet back to the corsairs' encampment. Unnoticed amid the crowd, he made it to spurious safety in the shadow of the *Reef Eagle's* master's pavilion.

'Hosh.' A woman was sitting on the back steps.

'Imais.' He offered her a tentative smile.

She was one of the more approachable of the women. Mixed blood by the shade of her skin but Aldabreshin by her speech and from some distant domain. Her dialect was very different to that of these northern reaches so she spoke slowly and sparingly to him, to be sure he understood.

Corrain had insisted that the pavilion women whored themselves but Hosh had never seen Imais seek some corsair's attention. It was easy enough to see which girls were ready to spread their legs. They relaxed on the shaded steps running across the front of the pavilion, draped in silk and drinking wine.

Latterly Hosh had concluded that Corrain didn't always know what he was talking about. Since he'd learned the Archipelagan tongue, since he'd been here alone, he'd learned more about the other slaves than he ever had under Corrain's thumb.

Most of the Aldabreshin slaves had been born to slave parents, granted, but a good number had been left without home or family after storm or disease ravaged their island home. Surrendering their freedom in return for shelter and food seemed entirely customary in such circumstances, as incomprehensible as Hosh found it.

Even the younger ones had travelled or been traded across any number of domains. Some, to Hosh's horror, reckoned this blighted isle offered a far better life than whatever brutality they had endured thus far. Those were the keenest to shed an oar's chains for a raider's curved blade, to swear their allegiance to the blind corsair.

He saw Imais was studying a tall glass jar with a spray of vizail blossoms hanging upside down inside it. 'What have you got there?'

As she turned it, Hosh saw something move. 'Is that a mouse?' He moved closer and saw there was indeed a small rodent clinging unhappily to the stems.

'Mouse and scorpion.' Imais held the jar out so he could see.

Even though the top was secured with tightly tied cloth, Hosh shuddered. He'd never imagined there could be such vile things as scorpions before he'd come to this island. Back home he'd thought spiders were bad enough.

'Vizail wilts.' Imais gestured at the jar and then up at the sky.

Hosh nodded his understanding. The Vizail Blossom constellation currently held the most portentous position on the eastern horizon, gradually drifting away until the Bowl appeared.

Imais nodded at the jar. 'Last day, we see which is alive. Mouse or scorpion.'

Hosh wondered what meaning would be read into that omen. Would it be something he should pass on to Nifai?

Every corsair conversation that wasn't about the practicalities of managing ships and slaves eventually turned to portents. The Archipelagans scrutinised everything from the spread of jetsam cast up on the shore to the way that goat bones cracked, cast into the fire at the end of a feast.

Men scratched circles on the ground as soon as the setting sun kissed the horizon. They hurried to turn their backs before casting peeled twigs over one shoulder. They barely let them settle before reading their alignments. Any lit candle was watched for the hue and vagaries of its flame. Hosh had seen candles set in triangles and circles, sometimes with shards of coloured glass cast between them, every reflection studied.

Imais put the jar carefully down and reached for a shallow bowl. It held a thick waxy leaf with a small ember in its hollow. She sprinkled a little powder onto the charcoal and inhaled the sweet-smelling smoke. 'We share?' she offered.

'No, thank you.' Hosh smiled apologetically.

He had tried the dream smoke once, when he'd been returned to this accursed island. When he'd been driven to utter despair by his fear and loneliness. Corrain had always forbidden it, offered in their early days here. He told Hosh he knew of strong men dying from their first sniff of the disgusting barbarian vice. Yes, and he'd insisted that Archipelagans shunned any form of liquor or narcotic. So much for that.

Hosh had decided he didn't care. Since he was going to die, he might as well do so insensible. Alas, he'd discovered that while the dream smoke had soothed his cares, it hadn't killed him. Worse, the after-effects of inhaling it left his face throbbing with as much pain as when his nose and cheek had first been broken. The passing relief of the sweet-scented daze wasn't worth that, not again. Not when the daze would pass and he'd wake to this same relentless misery.

'No ships back?' Imais blew on her ember to stir a little more smoke.

'No ships back,' Hosh confirmed.

The woman shrugged and sprinkled more resinous powder on her coal. 'You bring shells?'

'I do.' Hosh sat down in the shade and spread his rag on the ground. He used a handy stone to smash the white shards into smaller pieces. A little more work and he'd have a useful heap of coarse, clean sand.

Offer to scour a kitchen's pots with it, once the *Reef Eagle's* master and his men had been served the choicest dishes, and Hosh could hope for some food from the women. That task and any others he could find to earn their goodwill would take him till midnight. By then slaves and raiders alike should have sought some rest in the cool of the night. Hosh could find a quiet corner and risk some sleep himself.

The door behind Imais opened and two more of the pavilion women emerged to share her smoke. Hosh concentrated on pounding his shells.

You can't roll a rune without one showing reversed. That's what his mam always said. Hosh did miss her so. Skulking behind the pavilion might be safer than mingling with the other slaves but seeing these women with their work-roughened hands and age-thickened bodies as they snatched their brief respite did remind him—

Hosh sniffed crossly. An aggravating trickle of mucus was sliding from his nose. He threw his head back to try and stem it. As he did so, he caught sight of the jar with the wretched mouse clinging to the vizail stems.

Did the poor creature realise that venomous peril lurked beneath the blossoms? Would it starve first or be stung to death? Was there any way it could survive being trapped in there? Poor little mouse.

Hosh ground the crushed shells with his stone. He sniffed harder but couldn't stem his miserable tears.

He was trapped as surely as that mouse. Even if he escaped the myriad things that could kill him, he would eventually die here alone. His beloved mam would never know what had become of him. None of these godless barbarians would give his body a decent burning. He'd suffer the torments of Poldrion's demons until the last of his bones crumbled to dust.

— CHAPTER TWENTY-ONE —

The Tresia Estuary, Caladhria
9th of For-Summer

CORRAIN AWOKE WITH a start. He had dreamed he was back in chains, the stink of the galley seeping into his sleep. No, he was enjoying the dubious privilege of the galley master's bunk in the cramped stern cabin.

He swung his feet to the planking and stretched his arms to ease the stiffness in his shoulders. Feeling the tug of the healing burns on his arms, he found the jar of ointment which Hosh's old mum had given him and Kusint to share. They didn't want those scars to heal stiff, she had warned. Corrain worked the pungent salve into the tender skin.

How long had he slept? He'd come below deck just after midnight, as far as he could reckon it. Rousing Kusint to take his place up by the steersman's oar, he'd rolled into the musty bunk and been asleep within moments.

Was it morning? With the door securely wedged shut, the fetid gloom gave Corrain no clue. He didn't feel particularly rested. That meant nothing. This voyage was proving as exhausting as any he'd ever made chained to a rower's bench.

The galley wasn't moving. Anger burned through Corrain's weariness. If they were to reach Solura this side of Solstice they must row from dawn to dusk and on into the night if the moons permitted it. Belting on his sword, he stooped to pull the wooden wedge out from under the door and went into the hold.

The stern hatch was open, bright sunlight showing him two rowers sharing a cup of water in the shadows of the main hold. Ignoring them, Corrain climbed the ladder. Where was Kusint?

The Forest lad was sitting in the galley master's chair up on the stern platform. He was fiddling with one of the Aldabreshin compasses which they'd found in the galley master's cabin. It was a dauntingly complex instrument compared to a straightforward Caladhrian roundel with a needle indicating north. A circular brass plate as big as Corrain's splayed hand was engraved with a web of lines and numerals. A second pierced disc overlaid that with more interlaced circles while two brass pointers swivelled around the whole thing, all joined together by a central pivot.

'Why aren't we under way?' Corrain demanded.

Kusint took a breath before answering. 'See here? I know where all the heavenly jewels and constellations are at this very moment.' He held up the gleaming device, apparently expecting its display to mean something to Corrain.

'Why aren't we under way?' He repeated with some heat. It wasn't quite as bad as he'd feared; the sun was low in the sky and the morning cool had yet to lift, which was far better for rowing than the oppressive heat which would soon be building. 'We're wasting the best part of the day!'

'You need to persuade the men that taking the westward course is wise.' Kusint's gaze warned him that something was awry on the rowing deck. Not for the first time.

Corrain turned to look at the benches. A few of the laggards glared back at him. Others were looking studiously away, over the bulwarks towards the open seas on one side, at the green coast of Caladhria on the other.

A handful huddled together in a manner which Corrain had come to know all too well. He walked towards them, staying up on the raised planking, one hand on his sword hilt.

A rower lay on the deck below a bench, curled around a corsair dagger driven straight into his heart. There wasn't much blood. From his unmarked hands, Corrain judged the man had been taken so completely by surprise that he hadn't had a chance to fight back.

'What happened here?' he asked dispassionately.

The knot of slaves looked up at him, Archipelagan born, dark of hair and skin. How many could understand him? It was hard to say. Not for the first time, Corrain wished fruitlessly for Hosh who could have translated his threats and promises.

Imposing his will on the rowers had proved an unforeseen challenge. All Corrain could do was cajole and browbeat and hope to the gods he didn't believe in that none of the freed slaves would actually force him to draw his sword.

It had been a shock. Restored to his rank of captain in Halferan, if only unofficially by the likes of Reven and Fitrel, Corrain had readily slipped back into the habit of command. But the Halferans were willing to obey him, albeit with grumbles.

After casting off their chains, the galley's former slaves chafed at even the slightest order. Tempers were as raw and tender as their shackle welts at wrist and ankle.

Bloody arguments flared, with few of those involved paying any heed if Corrain or Kusint tried to mediate. None of the rowers would surrender the blades which they had seized from the dead corsairs.

'What happened here?' Corrain repeated himself slowly and clearly in formal Tormalin. He knew full well that some of these slaves had picked up a little of that tongue in the course of their misadventures. But this handful merely shrugged, their faces calculatedly uninformative.

'Are you dumb beasts or free men?' Corrain demanded with barely restrained anger. 'Have you been chained for so long that you can only behave like the animals the Aldabreshi called you?'

'Enough!' Kusint's voice carried the length of the galley. 'Have you no respect for your equals, Corrain? Have you forgotten your own sufferings as a slave? Do you propose to use an overseer's whip to loosen their tongues, while you bear such scars on your own flesh?'

'Never!' Corrain was shocked into furious denial. 'How can you think that?'

But as he brandished his broken manacle, he saw the other rowers looking up from their benches. For some, that very fear lurked in their hollow eyes. Others looked at him with veiled menace, warning of dire consequences if they even suspected he would try it.

Corrain looked back at the corpse. 'Get rid of that before it starts to stink.'

The men standing around grabbed arms and legs and hauled the body over to the bulwark. Heaving it over to throw it clear of the oars was something of a struggle.

Corrain had been appalled to realise he and Hosh and Kusint had fared significantly better than these unfortunates when they'd been chained aboard the *Reef Eagle*. Whoever this galley master had been, he'd expected his slaves to row on an Aldabreshin stodge of steamed grain mixed with rancid shreds of meat and a few crudely chopped potherbs. The stuff had either been prepared or stored so imperfectly that it was full of weevils. Dead rats had been floating in the water in the casks in the hold.

No wonder he and Kusint had discovered the galley's master, the whip master and both the overseers dead in the hold. Their necks had been broken, the flesh purpling with the imprint of links from the chains that had strangled them.

The killers managed to hurl the dead man away to vanish in a fleeting splash. Corrain saw the other Archipelagans looking anxiously for whatever might rise from the shallows to claim the body. To his relief, nothing ruffled the water. There were no sharks in these waters accustomed to follow galleys for an easy meal. Nothing to encourage Aldabreshin superstitions which were proving yet another thorn in his foot as this cursed voyage progressed.

He began counting heads. How many had they lost on Kusint's watch this time? Four, including the one just tossed overboard. Corrain knew better than to rebuke Kusint. Men died or disappeared between most sunsets and the following dawn. He'd seen some killed openly, a fatal misjudgement prompting violent retaliation ending in shattered skulls or knife-torn bellies. If he or Kusint tried to intervene, they risked the rowers turning on them. Better to leave well alone, they had agreed behind the galley master's cabin's securely wedged door.

What had happened to the others? Corrain looked over towards the green Caladhrian shore. Whenever the tides and currents brought them within sight of land, a few more starved and brutalised men decided to try swimming ashore. He had no idea how many had succeeded. Or how many might escape being hanged out of hand by the Caladhrians who caught them.

Corrain couldn't help wondering what might become of those who survived. Particularly those too long adrift to ever return to the lives they'd led before they were enslaved. Those too ashamed to go home with the scars they now bore.

On the other side of the scales, he was relieved whenever he saw the missing men included one or more of the troublemakers they'd been lumbered with. Losing them was worth even the cost of the oars being stripped of their strength. But now the galley was becoming dangerously weakened. Its progress these past few days had been infuriatingly slow.

He walked back to the stern platform as the killers returned to their rowing bench. 'When can we get on our way?' He was asking the sullen oarsmen as much as Kusint.

The Forest lad held up the Aldabreshin compass again. 'We'd be better served by a rest day.'

Corrain saw that warning in Kusint's eyes again. He looked at the rowers. 'Is that what you want?'

The Archipelagans nodded emphatically, even the ones who'd pretended not to understand him earlier. So this was something to do with their stars. Corrain swallowed his exasperation. There was no use arguing. He'd learned that much in the Archipelago.

What about the rest? Despite their grime and the

sun's bronzing, plenty of the others were mainlanders. It turned out that Aldabreshin slavers prized the crews of mainland merchant ships almost as highly as the corsairs valued their cargos.

'Why can't we head northwards?' Someone called out amidships; a Lescari voice.

'We're headed for Solura,' Corrain shouted back. 'That's what we agreed. When we reach their Great River, you can leave this ship with an equal share of the plunder to make what you can of your freedom. Any who'd rather return to the Archipelago can take this galley and their chances, and may the gods and the omens favour you.'

Kusint had found plenty of loot in the holds; lightweight linens, dyestuffs, brassware, even woollen carpets from Dalasor and leather and fur from the mountains, traded right down to the coast. All much sought after by the Aldabreshin warlords and a grievous loss for whatever merchants had entrusted their goods to the ship which this galley had caught following the sea lanes towards the southerly waters.

It had been easy enough for Kusint to persuade these paupers to conceal the bulk of it from Captain Mersed and his men on that first day. After handing over some sacks of grain, three casks of wine and leather pouches of jewellery and prized possessions from ravaged villages, they had begun hauling out the barrels of the sour-smelling pottage garnished with dead rats. That had been enough to dissuade the Tallat men from searching the holds. It had also been the start of the Forest lad gaining the rowers' trust, far more than Corrain had managed.

And of course, while the galley had wallowed in that inlet, the newly-unchained slaves could see the

Caladhrians were ready and willing to cut their throats if they so much as set foot ashore without permission to refill the water barrels or some such innocuous task.

Would they prefer gold or cold steel? When Corrain had got back to the inlet, after riding all night and ruining two more good horses for the rest of the summer, he'd found Kusint had already made that proposal to the rowers, as well as seeing that their worst hurts were tended and their bellies were filled with swamp deer hunted down by Captain Mersed's men and freshly roasted on buckthorn fires.

'Solura. That was agreed,' one of the Archipelagans called out, prompting vigorous nods from the rest.

'Piss on that.' The Lescar was on his feet, fists bunched. 'We want to go home. Row north from here and we'll be in the Gulf of Peorle. We can head for Peorle itself or cut across to Col. Their merchants will give us good coin for our share of the goods and we'll be set fair for a new life.'

'You think they'll deal with you fairly?' Corrain challenged him. 'Filthy and starving, marked for life by whip and chain? If they don't confiscate your goods outright and hang you for corsair thieves.'

Kusint came to stand beside him. 'In Solura, all of you, even those of Archipelagan blood, will be judged only by your willingness to work and the skills which you can offer. No one will pay any heed to where you might come from.'

'Put us ashore with our share here and we'll take our chances.' An Ensaimin man spoke up. His bulk spoke of a hard-working life even before he'd been chained to his oar.

'No shares!' A tall Archipelagan stood to look across the walkway's divide. 'You go ashore, you go empty-handed!'

Voices were rising on both sides of the deck now. Corrain quickly estimated who was in favour of rowing on to Solura and who was finding the lure of the coast too enticing. The balance was in favour of heading west but it was uncomfortably close to tipping.

'I have sat in your place and rowed for my life and felt the sting of the slaver's lash.' He rattled his broken chain at them. 'Don't you want to reclaim your manhood? Don't you want to be avenged on those who've stolen your lives and made your every waking moment a misery? That's what I seek in Solura. We have a plan to bring such grief down on the corsairs' heads that they will be utterly destroyed!'

He broke off. Desperation had made him careless. But there could be no going back to Halferan. Not after the promises he had made and the lies he had told. Not without making good on everything he had sworn to do.

Then Corrain saw, with rising hope, that plenty of the rowers looked interested in this unexpected prospect of revenge.

'What is this plan of yours?' Another mainlander stood up, Ensaimin by his accent.

'Prove that we can trust you and we'll tell you,' Kusint said quickly. 'First we need to know if you'll row west.'

'Into open waters across the neck of the gulf?' A seated rower of mingled blood was caught between defiance and apprehension. 'What if we will not?'

Corrain looked the man straight in the eye. 'Then my friend and I go ashore today with our share of the spoils. No one there will give us a second glance.'

Everyone could see that was true. His clothing and Kusint's, even grubby and creased, looked like a warlord's silks compared to the rowers' rags.

He looked around the galley. 'If you don't want to be hanged for corsairs, I recommend you beach this tub as soon as you can and use what's left of the sticky fire to burn it down to the keel.'

That suggestion prompted more uneasy looks among the rowers. To Corrain's intense relief, he saw the first nods of agreement, some grudging, more relieved. Even that Ensaimin man ducked his head, albeit with a scowl.

'Then let's have no more argument!' Corrain warned them with a forceful finger. He'd nearly reached for his sword, only realising at the last heartbeat that could hardly help matters.

'And no more killing! If any of you have a grievance against another man, whatever his blood or birth, we'll hear testimony from all who wish to speak on the matter. We'll come to a reasoned judgement like honest men, not savages. Otherwise we're no better than those cursed raiders!'

Whatever Kusint might think, Corrain felt responsible for these men, however much they might resent or reject his authority. When the galley's cargo was finally divided up, he would be truly glad to see them depart with the means of starting some new life. Until then he had to keep the whip hand over them, if only as a figure of speech.

They looked at him, sullen, but no one voiced dissent.

'How long do we row west?' one of the Archipelagan rowers with fluent Tormalin broke the silence.

'If we start at first light, we should see land again by dusk,' Kusint assured him. 'Then we can follow the Ensaimin coast past Dusgate to the Bay of Teshal. If the weather stays set fair, we can cut across that in four days, maybe.' He shrugged. 'If we have to stay close to the shore, it'll be eleven days to reach the same point. Then we can follow the coast all the way to Solura.'

Corrain wanted to protest. They couldn't afford the time to round every cove and headland around the Bay of Teshal. They had to get to Solura as quickly as they could. He kept silent nonetheless. The rowers, especially the Archipelagans, disliked being out of sight of land for any longer than was absolutely necessary.

'Then all's well.' Kusint's smile won a few grudging nods from the closest oarsmen.

Corrain heard his unspoken words. *So far.*

'Then we rest today and row at first light. Check your oars and wash down the decks before we take to the open seas. Once that's done we can try for some fresh fish.' The muck the slaves had been fed had proved unexpectedly good for luring better food. Fashioning hooks and line was no great challenge.

Corrain stood for a moment until he saw the rowers begin to move, to follow his orders. He turned to Kusint.

'We'll run short of food if we can't cut across the Bay of Teshal,' he warned quietly. There was leathery flatbread, dried meat and pickled fruit in the hold, provisions for the dead galley master, his crew and his swordsmen, but far less than Corrain would have liked.

Kusint shrugged. 'If we must, we can trade along the western Ensaimin coast. That far away, no one will be bothered about buying goods from a corsair galley.'

'We'll lose half these oarsmen,' Corrain objected. 'They'll run away ashore.'

Kusint shrugged again. 'Then we hire on more rowers once we reach the margin between the Great Forest and the sea. There are always bored boys looking for adventure.' He looked rueful. 'I should know. I was one.'

And look where that landed you, Corrain was tempted to say. He didn't, looking westward instead.

Because that was the way to Solura, his route to finding a wizard to sink every accursed corsair galley and, aye, that old blind bastard's trireme. Corrain would see him drown for Hosh's sake. If that arrogant Archmage didn't like it, that was too bad.

— CHAPTER TWENTY-TWO —

JILSETH SEARCHED THE tables crowded with pupil and apprentice mages. This idle time between afternoon and evening customarily saw Hadrumal's wizards washing away the dust of a day's study in the libraries or easing throats dry from debating with their elders and betters.

Before she found Tornauld and Nolyen, she saw Ely waiting by the counter. The slender mage was drumming her painted nails impatiently on the polished wood.

'Jilseth!' In the far corner, Nolyen stood up to make sure she'd seen him.

Avoiding gesticulating hands, Jilseth eased her way between chairs and tables.

'Tresia blush.' Nolyen handed her a glass frosted with condensation. Mageborn or mundane, no one in Hadrumal drank tepid wine even in the height of summer. 'You'll like it.'

'Thank you.' Jilseth didn't doubt it.

Nolyen's choices were always excellent, which wasn't so surprising. No expense had been spared on his education, as befitted a Caladhrian baron's son, until the inconvenience of his water affinity could no longer be ignored.

He waited for Jilseth to sit before resuming his own chair. While a decade in Hadrumal had taught him the folly of assuming that women were mere ornament or entertainment, such courtesies remained instinctive. Jilseth had no quarrel with that.

'I think they'll raid tonight.' Tornauld looked over to include her in the conversation they were already having.

Ensaimin born, of merchant stock, he was always straight to the point, as if delay would cost him coin. Jilseth knew some found him abrasive but he was always willing to yield to anyone matching his directness, so she and he had always been friends.

'You're talking of the corsairs?' She knew Nolyen was scrying towards the Caladhrian coast morning, noon and night, to keep their nexus and Planir informed. 'But both moons are nigh on dark tonight.'

'And tomorrow and the night after, but a dark of both moons brings a high-springing tide.' Nolyen absently twisted peridot studs linking the cuffs of his linen shirt. While he scorned outward display of his affinity, he had an impressive collection of ornaments set with green gemstones, from the costliest to the merely gaudy. 'They can make landfall during the day.'

Tornauld leaned forward, elbows on the table, broad shoulders hunched. 'The heavenly compass takes a decisive turn tomorrow. They'll want to land with the omens on their side, before the balance shifts in the mainlanders' favour.'

'What are you talking about?' Jilseth looked from Tornauld to Nolyen in hopes of an explanation.

'I've been talking to Velindre Ychane.' Tornauld took a swallow of the aromatic pink wine. 'She's made a particular study of Aldabreshin predictions.'

'Is she back in Hadrumal?' Jilseth asked cautiously.

She had heard no end of rumour about the magewoman Velindre. Supposedly she'd been the lover of Cloud Mage Otrick, holder of that office before Rafrid, and no one was entirely sure how that feared and fabled wizard had met his end. Velindre was said to have left Hadrumal in a fury at being passed over by the Council, convinced she should have been Cloud Mistress. According to some, she'd helped drive dragons out of the Archipelago.

Jilseth had never given that tale much credence, reckoning it was speculation spun out of ignorance of Velindre's true dealings with the southern barbarians. All the same, the magewoman must have enough courage to face down a dragon if she was prepared to travel in the Archipelago, where the penalty for magebirth was death.

'No, she's in Relshaz. But this is what she was telling me.' Tornauld was drawing a circle on the table, his fingertip wetted with the drops beading their carafe. 'This is the last day when the Vizail Blossom sits on the eastern horizon. The constellation they call the Bowl rises tomorrow evening. That shifts the other crucial stars into the next arc around the heavenly compass as the Archipelagans draw it. Tonight, the Ruby sits in the arc of Death along with the Sea Serpent's stars. That's a formidable omen promising them victory in battle.'

Jilseth watched him dot fresh marks around the circle.

'Tomorrow, the Sea Serpent drifts away from the Ruby. The night after that, the auguries become even worse. The Diamond, for strength, joins the Amethyst which lends resolve, in the heavenly arc governing omens for home and family, with the constellation they call the Hoe, token of labour rewarded.'

Nolyen stroked the small pointed beard he was cultivating, in hopes, Jilseth suspected, of compensating for his prominent nose. 'The wandering stars can be seen clearly enough but that Hoe constellation is below the horizon.'

'Exactly.' Tornauld nodded. 'Which sets signs in that arc of the sky in opposition to whoever might be reading these portents. In this instance that means luck will favour the corsairs' opponents. They won't risk that, not while they're wondering what's happened to those two galleys which the Halferans and their allies have ambushed.'

'They've caught another one?' Jilseth hadn't heard.

'Just yesterday.' Tornauld grinned. 'They've found another of the corsairs' watering stops, and troops from Myrist, Taine and Saldiray are riding up and down the coastline looking for more places to set their snares.'

'And Karpis?' Jilseth reminded herself that however obnoxious a baron might be, his innocent populace deserved protection from the corsairs.

'And Karpis,' Tornauld confirmed.

'But none of this has any bearing on reality.' Nolyen was unconvinced. 'The moons influence the tides but wandering stars in the remotest heavens cannot possibly have any material effect on an event's outcome.'

'I don't suppose that has any bearing on what the Aldabreshi believe,' Jilseth observed. 'Do the Caladhrians know of this Archipelagan practise of reading the skies? Surely we could share such knowledge without infringing on our edicts?'

'Alas, poor Caladhria has few scholars worth the name.' Nolyen smoothed his beard. 'Anyone with an unhealthy obsession with books is usually shipped off to Vanam or Col. Isn't that right, Tornauld?'

The burly wizard wasn't listening. A sharp line deepened between his dark brows. 'Madam mage? No longer content to eavesdrop from a distance?'

Jilseth turned in her chair to see that Ely had slipped through the crowded room to listen to their conversation.

'Take a seat,' Tornauld offered, sarcastic. 'Oh, forgive me. You're running Canfor's errands now.' He nodded at the bottle of wine which Ely held. 'What does Galen think of that?'

Though Ely's colour rose, she didn't retreat. 'You're scrying the Caladhrian coast, I hear. Even if you won't warn those unfortunates who'll see their homes and storehouses ravaged tonight. Not even to repair the damage that Hadrumal's aloofness has done to wizardry.' Her contempt was a match for Nolyen's rising indignation.

Suspicion soured the sweet wine on Jilseth's tongue. 'I hope the Hearth Master doesn't intend raising an alarm.'

What would Planir do if he was so openly defied? How successfully might Kalion argue that merely offering a warning didn't outrage Hadrumal's edicts? Was that so very different to passing on the interpretation of the skies which Velindre had given Tornauld?

Jilseth grew more concerned as she realised Ely was hesitating too long before replying.

'The Hearth Master will act as he sees fit,' the lissom magewoman said stiffly.

Tornauld wasn't going to let that evasion pass. 'Always acting in accordance with the Archmage's wishes?'

Ely ignored him in favour of challenging Nolyen. 'Are you still scrying after that trooper who escaped the slavers? To see how far he's spreading his tales to discredit wizardry?'

Jilseth noticed drinkers at several nearby tables were glancing in their direction, their curiosity caught by this ill-tempered exchange. Before she could warn Ely off openly discussing matters better reserved for the Council chamber, Nolyen had already spoken.

'What do you make of his present course? Do you think he's making for Col or Peorle now that the galley's turned into the Gulf?'

'You can't make out his conversations any longer?' Ely commiserated.

'If I can't, nor can Canfor.' Tornauld's belligerence dared her to say different.

Ely ignored him again. 'He's making for Col. Where else? So many Ensaimin merchant traders have been losing ships at sea to these marauders. The Halferan trooper will be rallying vessels and men to patrol the sea lanes, to lend weight to the Caladhrians' defiance on land.'

'Exactly as the Archmage predicted,' Jilseth said firmly. 'The mainlanders can take care of themselves once they put their shoulders to the wheel.'

'Don't let us keep you.' Nolyen nodded to the bottle of wine in Ely's hand. 'You're letting the Hearth Master's wine get warm!'

'I am not!' Affronted, Ely looked down at the bottle in her hand.

Unfortunately for her, Nolyen was entirely correct. The green glass was dry, the wine within already matching the day's heat.

'A first season apprentice could do better.' Tornauld mocked.

The bottle turned milky with frost. Nolyen winced. 'You had better ask for another. That vintage is ruined.'

'Mind your—' The bottle shattered in Ely's hand. The wine, a solid lump of ice, slipped from her lacerated fingers to smash on the floorboards amid the shattered glass.

Smears of blood coloured the frozen wine. Alarmed, Jilseth sprang up, reaching for Ely's hand. 'Let me—'

But Ely fled amid cheers and laughter, heedlessly raised according to custom whenever a pot man or serving maid dropped a loaded tray. The affronted sweep of the magewoman's gown left a trail of melting ice and broken glass.

'I suppose that wasn't very kind of us.' Tornauld was callously amused nonetheless.

'I'm curious to know why her magic betrayed her.' Nolyen remarked as conversations resumed around them.

'It's not as easy as you might think.' Jilseth could see more than one mage was gesturing at the shattered glass or towards the door, after Ely. Sympathy for her humiliation seemed balanced with derision.

Jilseth recalled her own shock at learning first hand not to cool a sealed bottle too rapidly. She'd had no notion that even a gentle knock could turn the contents to ice demanding far more space than the water that made it. But Ely was a water mage. her instincts should surely have warned her.

'Why were you asking her about Col?' Tornauld emptied the carafe of blush wine between their glasses.

Nolyen leaned closer. 'That trooper captain Corrain hasn't sailed into the Gulf of Peorle. He's heading along the Ensaimin coast.'

'Where's he going?' Tornauld was baffled.

'Wherever it is, Ely won't know.' That was Nolyen's point. 'He's beyond the reach of her scrying. She had no idea that I was lying to her.'

Whereas, Jilseth realised, Ely's lies to them had distracted her sufficiently to let the wine warm in her hand.

'So she's not the fabled scryer that she'd like us to believe,' Tornauld commented with curt satisfaction.

'She's never had any personal dealings with Corrain.' Jilseth felt obliged to judge Ely fairly. 'Without holding something once in his possession, focusing her magic over such distances must be a challenge, even with a water affinity.'

'When will the galley sail beyond your reach?' Tornauld asked the Caladhrian wizard.

Nolyen was unbothered. 'If we scry as a nexus, since you've met the man—' he glanced at Jilseth '—our spell should reach at least as far as the Great Forest.'

'What could they possibly go seeking there?' Tornauld shook his head, perplexed.

Jilseth frowned. 'Corrain's companion looks Forest born, but the Folk have no quarrel with the Aldabreshi. Archipelagan traders don't sail so far north, never mind corsairs.'

'Of course!' Tornauld snapped his fingers.

'What?' Jilseth saw his outburst drawing curious eyes.

'I was watching Kalion and his nexus yesterday.' Tornauld was too exultant to lower his voice.

'Scrying on the Hearth Master?' Jilseth wondered uneasily who at nearby tables had heard that admission.

'Only when he summons his lackeys.' Tornauld was unrepentant. 'To see if Canfor and Ely are spying on the Archmage.'

Nolyen nodded his agreement. 'What were they doing, Kalion and the rest?'

'Using a diamond pendulum over a map.' Tornauld leaned back, folding his arms in satisfaction. 'They're trying to find the galley that way.'

'Quintessential magic, and not an easy working at that. All to keep track of an errant slave? I wonder what Kalion suspects.' Something that meant losing sight of the galley seriously threatened Ely's composure, Jilseth concluded. But what?

'How were they faring?' Nolyen asked with interest. 'With the pendulum.'

But Tornauld was looking towards the door. 'Here's Merenel at long last.'

'Good day to you.' More handsome than pretty, she was taller than average, with olive skin and curling black hair to proclaim her Tormalin blood. After a recent journey to Suthyfer, she'd taken to wearing breeches, shirt and jerkin rather than gowns. Many women did so on the islands in the eastern ocean, or so it was said.

Jilseth wasn't convinced that it was the maroon linen tunic fitting so closely to her generous curves which was drawing so much attention their way. Not when the simmering dispute between the Archmage and the Hearth Master was such favoured gossip.

'Let me get more wine.' Tornauld raised a hand to attract Master Noak's attention.

'Not on my account.' Merenel made no move to sit. 'The Archmage wants to see us.'

Jilseth swallowed the last of her wine. 'Of course.'

Nolyen ran a nervous hand through his wavy brown hair. 'Is there something amiss?'

Merenel raised her brows. 'Should there be?'

'Come on.' Jilseth was already heading for the door. 'Where is he?'

'In the Physic Garden.'

Outside, Merenel headed down the gentle slope of the high road. As Jilseth fell into step beside her, she could hear Nolyen and Tornauld a few paces behind.

'Could you see if Kalion's nexus was able to focus the pendulum?'

'It didn't look like it.' Tornauld was more thoughtful than triumphant. 'I'm not sure that particular nexus has the right balance for quintessential magic.'

'In balancing the respective strengths of the four affinities?' Nolyen queried. 'Or on account of differences in proficiency?'

'I think it's a question of temperament.' Tornauld considered this as they walked on. 'Ely has the talent but she's always lacked confidence in her own skills. She's followed Kalion's lead for years and Galen commands what loyalty she has left over. Can she hold her own in a nexus when Canfor's so overbearing?'

Their common affinity with elemental air did nothing to lessen Tornauld's dislike of the white-haired mage.

Nolyen was silent for a few more paces. 'A good many texts on quintessential magic also advise balancing a nexus equally with two men and two women, as we four do.'

Merenel looked over her shoulder. 'Sannin holds her own in the circle with Planir, Rafrid and Herion.'

Tornauld chuckled. 'Sannin could hold her own against the entire Council.'

'Is there much study of quintessential magic in Suthyfer?' Jilseth asked Merenel.

'Not much,' she admitted. 'Master Usara is more interested in trying to fathom why elemental magic and aetheric enchantments are so irreconcilable.'

'I thought the wizards and the adepts were finding ways to work together,' Tornauld objected.

'Wizards and adepts are exploring how their different spells might complement each other,' Merenel corrected him. 'The magics remain fundamentally opposed.'

'Trying to square that circle doesn't seem a worthwhile use of Master Usara's intellect.' Jilseth knew that many of the Council hoped to see him as Stone Master, if Planir ever yielded that office. She had even contemplated making a visit to Suthyfer, to see if Master Usara's insights offered any new perspective on her own affinity.

Making the arduous journey would be a waste of time and effort if his attentions had strayed to that pointlessly intractable puzzle. Jilseth couldn't decide if she was more relieved or disappointed.

'How far can aetheric enchantments reach,' Nolyen wondered aloud, 'compared to a scrying?'

Jilseth guessed he was wondering if Artifice could secure some insight into Corrain's inexplicable voyage.

'Between adept and adept?' Merenel considered the matter. 'Easily as far as a scrying. As far as a bespeaking wrought between mages and beyond. But without aetheric learning on both sides, as I understand it, an adept can only send their thoughts to someone they already know very well indeed.'

'Not so different to scrying then, for all the differences between our magics.' Nolyen sounded reassured.

They walked on in silence, absorbed in individual contemplation. As they entered the alley leading to the physic garden, Jilseth gestured to unlock the gate.

Within the enclosing walls, the air was heavy with the scent of myriad flowers, alive with the hum of bees. Planir was cutting back a tangle of honeysuckle threatening to overwhelm an espaliered apple tree.

'Did anyone take note of you coming here?'

Nolyen was taken aback. 'I don't know, Archmage.'

'No one paid us heed.' Jilseth hastily qualified her answer. 'I don't believe so, anyway.'

'Unless Ely's scrying after us.' Tornauld glowered. 'With Canfor drawing our words along the breezes.'

'I've nothing to say that Master Kalion's friends cannot hear.' Planir looked around as though acknowledging unseen watchers before turning to the four of them.

'I have decided that you will work with Master Kalion's nexus. Exchange your insights into quintessential magic for whatever Galen, Ely and Canfor can offer. You'll benefit by furthering your understanding of your own elemental affinity and that of your fellow wizards who were born to other disciplines.'

Tornauld gaped. 'Archmage?'

Jilseth shared his astonishment. 'May we ask what prompts this request?'

Not that there seemed to be any room for refusal, and that was unlike Planir.

'I'm seeing too much rancour and acrimony in Hadrumal,' the Archmage said crisply. 'I'm hearing of quarrels in the quadrangles when a handful of pupil mages declares for Kalion and the cause of intervention on the mainland while another gaggle of apprentices proclaims their support for me and the justice of Hadrumal's detachment.'

Nolyen nodded, troubled. 'Wizardry cannot thrive amid division.'

Planir startled them with a chuckle. 'On the contrary, division is an excellent thing. Why do you suppose I spend so much of my time encouraging every mage, from highest to lowest, to pursue their individual passions, to travel wherever their fascinations might take them? Why do you suppose I urge anyone chafed by Hadrumal's harness to see what free rein Suthyfer offers?'

His expression grew more serious. 'It's factions of mages banding together that would threaten wizardry most, if I ever allowed them to become established. Master Kalion and I are agreed on that, even if his preferred solution is everyone abiding by the Archmage's dictates.'

Tornauld was startled into a laugh. 'For a wizard with firelight at his fingertips, he's as blind as a man in the dark!'

'Show some respect for my element master,' Merenel said swiftly. 'Take him for a jackass and you only prove you're a donkey yourself.'

'Our Hearth Master is no fool, Tornauld,' Planir agreed. 'He is however an idealist, which is why he's so confident that any dissent would be set aside in Hadrumal's best interests. That's what he would do himself.'

Planir shook his head. 'As I've told you more than once, Kalion seeks only good for Hadrumal, and after that, for the mainlanders. As far as he's concerned, that's easily achieved. Once the princes and powers of the mainland yield to Hadrumal's guidance, everyone's best interests will be secured.'

Jilseth recalled Ely's unguarded words in the wine shop. 'He thinks they'll yield if we save them from the corsairs?'

Planir inclined his head. 'Unfortunately, I don't share his confidence that the next crisis would be so readily answered. So I'll do without the mainland's gratitude this summer for the sake of avoiding its disillusion and anger in some unforeseen season to come.'

'While we go to work with the likes of Canfor, to persuade everyone that you and Master Kalion are the firmest of friends?' Tornauld evidently loathed that prospect.

The Archmage grinned at him. 'I'll settle for the hotheads realising that Kalion and I will settle our differences of opinion without anyone's interference.' His eyes hardened. 'I want it understood that anyone bold enough to play advocates in the alleys and taverns will feel the scorch of Kalion's wrath from one side and the full weight of my anger from the other.'

Jilseth was glad she wasn't the object of his censure. She only hoped their word carried enough weight to tilt the scales of opinion around Hadrumal's halls.

Nolyen's thoughts were elsewhere. 'Are we to work with Master Kalion's nexus to follow that slave galley you've had us searching for?'

Planir nodded. 'Until we're convinced that malcontent trooper isn't going to spring some unforeseen surprise.'

'While we continue to scry along the Caladhrian coast?' Merenel asked.

'For all the evidence you can gather,' Planir confirmed, 'to convince the Council that the barons can manage their affairs without our interference.'

'And as long as we're working with them, Canfor, Galen and Ely won't be able to deny such evidence.' A slow smile spread across Tornauld's face.

Planir's grin answered him. 'Quite so.'

Jilseth found her own spirits rising. Hadrumal had escaped being entangled in Lescar's wars. Now she could reasonably hope wizardry wouldn't be dragged into Caladhrian affairs. The last echoes of Minelas's treachery were finally fading away.

— CHAPTER TWENTY-THREE —

HOSH WAS TREADING very carefully, and not only because the noon sun made the ground hot enough to scorch the soles of his feet. Not just because he was carrying a heavy bucket brim full of water.

The anchorage was crowded with unfamiliar vessels; twelve galleys at last count and three triremes. Wasn't Grewa, the blind corsair, worried that one of their masters might threaten his dominion over these raiders? Or had he brought more triremes here to make sure that none of the galley masters could try to usurp his authority?

Hosh had more immediate concerns. Most of the arriving ships' slaves were kept afloat but some had to be allowed ashore to fetch water. Though the Aldabreshi swordsmen and crewmen were supposedly restricted to the beach, every day saw some of them wandering across to the encampment between the resident captains' pavilions. That rough and ready settlement had doubled in size since the start of the spring as more ships had chosen to sail in the blind corsair's wake.

How many of them were regretting that choice now or second-guessing the portents that had urged it? Since that first raid when two galleys had failed to return, there had been two more expeditions northwards. Under high tides and dark skies, two more ships had been lost and when both moons had been at their full, three had disappeared.

Corsairs prowled the shore at dusk and dawn, disputing the patterns of clouds and studying the moons and constellations and the jewelled stars wandering the heavens most intensely of all.

There were daily clashes between corsair and corsair, between raider and rower, between slave and slave. Not that anyone ever hurried to break them up, not even Ducah, whose whip and blade enforced such rigid discipline between the *Reef Eagle's* rowers ashore. When he found such a fight, the brute would hold off anyone trying to intervene. Then he'd take wagers from anyone gathering to see the sport, until one of the wretches lay dead at the other's hand.

Without Corrain, Hosh had no one to watch his back. So he was spending as much time as he could lurking around the *Reef Eagle* pavilion's back steps.

Now he was paying the price, summoned to fill this bucket from the jealously guarded well in the pavilion's courtyard. Now he had to carry the cumbersome burden across the searing dust between the encampment and the shore. Every blade of grass had long since been worn away by uncounted feet.

Spill this water and what might happen to him? Hosh was trying to look in all directions, for fear of some passerby intent on slyly tripping him or an openly malicious shove. He'd learned the hard way that too many slaves resented the favour that Nifai showed him. Not that Nifai cared. Hosh had learned to keep such bruises to himself.

The corsairs were even more dangerous. Plenty of them were looking at mainland rowers with hate-filled eyes. The wealth that Grewa had promised on these recent raids had largely failed to materialise. Pickings ashore were lean, with deserted villages stripped of anything worth stealing. The only raiders to return with full holds were those who'd been prowling the sea lanes to catch fat merchants sailing from Col or Peorle to Relshaz.

Struggling on with the heavy bucket, Hosh could only be thankful that those not seeking some shade from the noon sun were watching the horizon for any sign of the missing vessels.

So much for the blind corsair's envoy declaring that the current skies promised death to the mainlanders, with the Ruby for strength of arms and the Opal talisman for truth in that very arc of the sky. In some other significant alignment which Hosh couldn't quite fathom, the Pearl apparently led the Winged Snake against their foes.

Half a season ago, as far as Hosh could reckon with no hope of an almanac, no one would have questioned Grewa's interpretations. Since then though, even with so many newcomers to the anchorage, these losses couldn't be denied.

Whispers mingled with the breezes among the fringe trees. Was some new nest of mainland pirates preying on their galleys? But Grewa himself had led the attacks leaving those barbarians dead in the surf a handful of years ago. Perhaps one of his own galley captains had ignored the blind corsair's strictures against attacking Aldabreshin merchants. Some outraged warlord could have sent his own triremes to safeguard Archipelagan trade.

Hosh paused and set the bucket down to ease his aching shoulders. A splash over the rim slopped welcome coolness on his feet. Even the breeze from the sea was a furnace blast these days.

Presumably some tide would wash up the answers. For now Hosh could breathe a sigh of relief as he reached his destination without incident. He showed the bucket to a bored-looking swordsman sitting under a tree. 'Water for the captives.'

He couldn't take much comfort from the corsairs' losses. Those galleys that had returned had done so with both booty and slaves. The men had already been subjected to their ordeal in the ring of stones, the survivors hauled off in chains to the waiting galleys. Now the women and children were loosely penned some way along the shore, a prudent distance from the pavilions and the encampment.

The galley masters weren't concerned with preventing escape. They merely wanted to keep their goods from further soiling before the slave traders of the southern and eastern reaches arrived to take their pick. Then the corsairs would get their leavings, to be plucked for a night's passing pleasure and discarded. Women and children who survived that degradation and any diseases that followed would be kept in servitude until, sooner or later, they were traded away.

The swordsman nodded absently. Then he looked up at Hosh with more interest. 'What say you to the news, mainland man?'

'What news?' Hosh asked warily.

'You know the *Red Heron* rode the tide into shore in the north?' The swordsman studied his face. 'They found one of our missing galleys as a black and broken skeleton. They're saying those craven mainlanders burned it.'

'More likely some fool dropped a pot of sticky fire.' Hosh managed a half-hearted shrug even though his heart twisted with hope almost too painful to bear. If the Caladhrians were finally fighting back, that could that be the answer to the puzzle of the corsairs' lost ships.

Corrain had sworn he'd rally the barons to avenge Lord Halferan. His return with Kusint would prove that the Aldabreshi weren't so great a foe, if they could be outwitted by mere slaves. More fool them, to underestimate a free man of Caladhria and a Soluran mercenary. So Corrain had said. Could he have possibly have found a way home to make good on his words?

No, Hosh couldn't allow himself to hope that Corrain had escaped Khusro Rina's isle, still less that he'd managed to make good on his oath. Not until he had some better reason.

He looked along the paltry fence of laths and woven vines. Women sat desolate within, not even trying to escape. They knew full well how much worse they would fare beyond that illusory defence.

'Shall I share out the water?' Hosh offered as casually as he could. 'I hear these cats claw at each other if they're not kept in check. Grewa won't want too many dying of thirst.'

'True enough.' Unsurprisingly the swordsman was content to let Hosh take on that task in this punishing heat.

Hosh carried the heavy bucket as far along the fence as he dared, in hopes of getting beyond earshot of the swordsman. The women within watched him with dull and lifeless eyes. What little shade they could contrive with sacrificed clothes and boughs torn from the trees had been given over to the children.

Hosh dipped a nut husk cup into the water. He offered it over the fence. One woman forced herself to her feet.

'Where are you from?' His heart sank as she looked at him, uncomprehending. Not Caladhrian then. He repeated himself in Tormalin.

'Relshaz,' she mumbled, her tongue thick with thirst. 'Sailing for Ensaimin.'

Hosh's hopes fell further. 'You're Lescari?' He thought he recognised her accent, like some beggars whom his mother had once fed at her scullery door. She scorned Steward Starrid's order that vagabonds must not be encouraged to linger in Halferan. Let him answer to Ostrin for scorning such unfortunates, she had said. Let him discover too late that he'd spurned the god of hospitality travelling in human disguise.

Corrain had said that any mainlanders enslaved in the Archipelago would be thieves or debtors fallen foul of the Relshazri magistrates. Hosh had been troubled by that. His mother had always warned that debts could as easily mount up from misfortune as they could from folly. She always kept a pot of coin buried beneath a pantry flagstone against the day when Raeponin was looking elsewhere.

The woman had gulped down the water. She looked longingly at the bucket, clutching the nut shell with dirt-encrusted hands. 'Parnilesse,' she said more clearly.

Hosh recalled Corrain saying that any Lescari's first loyalty was to their dukedom. Well, to their purse and to their own self-interest and then to their dukedom. That was why the realm's festering divisions so often burst into bloody strife. That and tolerating rulers too arrogant and selfish to yield to a parliament's collective wisdom. As Hosh's mother always said, thank Saedrin we were born Caladhrian.

'Lost my home and my husband to the war,' the woman said, desolate.

'I'm sorry,' Hosh said helplessly.

The woman merely shrugged, handed back the husk cup and stepped aside so that another could drink. So much for Lescari selfishness.

Hosh refilled the cup and handed it over. His hand trembled as he saw one girl urging another to get up and join the silently patient line. The girl on the ground shook her head, scraping up dust and cramming handfuls into her mouth.

'What is she doing?' Hosh protested.

The next woman in line shrugged. 'Eating dirt so she'll die the sooner.'

Before Hosh could respond, a harsh voice hailed him.

'Hosh!' It was Nifai.

'Can you reach the bucket if I leave it here?' He looked along the fence line. The swordsman on guard wasn't about to leave his shade to come and dole out the water.

He thrust the cup into the Parnilesse woman's hands and hurried over to Nifai.

'Carry this.' Impatient, the overseer thrust a bundle at him; a rug wrapped around a sunshade and a crackling frond of fringed leaves dried to the colour of salt fish. 'I am summoned.'

Nifai was speaking in the Tormalin tongue which he'd asked Hosh to teach him of late. There wasn't any sound of whip masters' silver whistles, so whatever was stirring, Hosh realised, the overseer didn't want this gathering noised among the swirling whispers.

He ducked his head, obsequious, and followed Nifai
back towards the dusty expanse by the shore, through
the driftwood huts and then past the ragged stumps of
the ironwood trees that had previously separated the
pavilions from the killing ground. They had all been
felled and hauled away for firewood. Now the far
slopes beyond the grisly hollow were being laid bare to
feed the rapacious hearths.

This definitely wasn't an open meeting. Swordsmen
sat on the tree stumps, warning off those who hadn't
been summoned. Head humbly ducked, Hosh looked
through his eyelashes to see who had come. They were
all galley masters and slave overseers.

Grewa's personal slaves were setting up a silken
canopy on hardwood poles on the far side of the
constellation stones. The blind corsair had yet to arrive.

Hosh could see the dark stain by the fringe trees
where a slave had been disembowelled for daring to
raise a hacking blade to those sacrosanct branches. Had
the man been merely ignorant or calculatedly suicidal?
Hosh couldn't decide.

'Here is honour enough for me.' Nifai gestured to
the ground.

Hosh wasn't deceived by this show of self-effacement.
The canny Aldabreshin wanted to be close enough to
hear while sitting sufficiently far away not to have his
reactions scrutinised by the blind corsair's slaves. They
were always their master's eyes and ears.

The overseer settled on the rug and accepted the
sunshade that Hosh offered. Hosh stood behind him
and began fanning the fringed frond to cool Nifai's
sweating brow. He kept up a steady rhythm even when
a stir heralded Grewa's arrival.

Then Hosh saw who accompanied the blind corsair. Despite his efforts, he shuddered like a man struck with palsy. Nifai looked up as the dried frond rattled, curious as well as annoyed.

Hosh feigned a stifled fit of coughing. Surely there was enough dust in the air to make that convincing? If the gods and stars were merciful, he must be far enough away to escape being noticed by those beside the canopy. If not, he was a dead man.

Thankfully, Grewa began speaking, drawing every eye. Shunning the silken shade, he stood before the assembled corsair masters. Turning his head this way and that, it almost seemed he could see the gathering before him.

'Six sunsets from now we will see the highest and swiftest tides to carry us to the northern barbarians' shores. As the Mirror Bird spreads its starry wings on the eastern horizon, so the stars of the Bowl will cup the Ruby for valour and victory where the sky promises death to our foes. Opposite, the Spear lends us strength, promising wealth under the unifying light of the heavenly Opal.'

The blind corsair nodded with satisfaction. 'Caught half way between these two portents of our victory, we see the Amethyst for meekness with the Pearl for compliance with the stars of the Hoe below the horizon, a tool for farmers, no weapon for warriors, in that arc of the sky where we look for omens of childhood. These northern barbarians will prove as weak as infants as they face our attack.'

Hosh had to fight to contain his misery. If he'd kept his count of the days right, Grewa was talking about an attack during the summer solstice festival. A truly wretched celebration lay in store for some poor villagers.

'Honoured commander?'

Hearing Grewa interrupted was as startling as hearing a horse burst into song. Hosh turned with everyone else to see who had spoken. He didn't recognise him; an Aldabreshin with a shaven scalp, wearing plain blue tunic and trews.

Those sitting near were already drawing away, to shun such effrontery or to avoid being splattered with blood when this fool lost his head.

'What of the Diamond, honoured commander?' Though the man's voice shook, he pressed on. 'That token of strength sits alongside the Amethyst and the Pearl with the stars of the Hoe?'

One of Grewa's attendant warriors was already advancing, naked blade in hand. The old raider lifted a hand and the swordsman halted.

Could that old bastard really see? Hosh had wondered more than once what lay beneath that cloth hiding Grewa's eyes. Regardless, the fabric alone looked thick enough to blind a man.

'The Diamond does betoken strength,' the old corsair said calmly. 'It will strengthen the influence of other heavenly jewels. So the northern barbarians will be left all the more enfeebled.'

Most of the galley masters nodded hasty agreement. Then another voice called out.

'These northern barbarians are not be so bereft of fighting skills.' This light-skinned man was bold enough to stand up. 'What of our lost ships? Did any omens warn against sailing inshore? Is there no word of their fate?'

'By your leave, Grewa.' A man stepped forward from the group of corsairs, slyly claiming the shade which their blind master scorned.

Hosh had to summon all his strength and will to keep steadily fanning Nifai. He dared not risk a single faltering stroke that might draw anyone's eyes towards him, least of all this vile brute's.

This newcomer was head and shoulders taller than any man here and massively muscled beneath a faded brown tunic in the Aldabreshin style. He might have been of mixed blood or a mainlander deeply tanned by the sun. His flowing black hair was swept back and his long beard was plaited with gold chains. One broad hand on his sword hilt asserted that no enemy would ever get close enough to seize hold of those braids.

'Some of these northern barbarians have finally found their manhood.' He shrugged, unconcerned. 'I know where to find them. Cut the head off a snake and it dies. I will avenge our lost allies while the heavens look so favourably upon us.' He smiled with cruel anticipation. 'Let us plan our attack.'

As the galley and trireme masters seized on this, eager to show their loyalty to Grewa, Hosh bit his lip so hard that he tasted blood. He could have sobbed aloud with the horror of it, if he hadn't known the outburst would be the death of him.

This was the bearded raider who'd captured him and Corrain. He'd commanded the Aldabreshin warriors who'd ambushed them in the marshes, when that traitor Minelas had led so many good men to their deaths. This very corsair had killed Lord Halferan, stabbing him in the back as he lay face down in the mud, unable to defend himself. Hosh remembered Minelas gloating as the baron sprawled helpless at his feet.

Then he remembered something else which nearly made him drop the frond. This bearded brute hadn't turned a hair when a mage-spawned lightning bolt had killed Captain Gefren, desperately fighting to save his lord. As Hosh and Corrain had lain unheeded in chains, they'd heard Minelas and this very corsair remind each other of the bargain they'd struck.

The raider had killed Lord Halferan so that Minelas could steal his fiefdom. That debt would be repaid by the wizard granting the corsairs a safe haven on the Caladhrian coast. As long as the raiders shared their loot, his magecraft would keep them hidden from view.

But the Aldabreshi detested wizardry. Corrain had always said so and everything Hosh had learned since only went to confirm that. Imais had once told him that even the humblest mageborn must be skinned alive, his hide nailed up on a doorpost. She couldn't explain why but Hosh had seen enough cruelty to believe anything of the Aldabreshi.

Hosh forced himself to count slow, measured strokes as he fanned Nifai. What would the overseer make of this knowledge, if Hosh chose to share it with him? What might Nifai win by way of reward if he told Grewa the truth? Would Hosh see the bearded raider killed, Lord Halferan finally avenged?

Or did the blind corsair know that this galley master consorted with wizards? How swiftly would Nifai be killed, so the old man's deceit wouldn't be revealed? Would Nifai die quickly enough, before anyone thought to ask who had told him?

If not, Hosh would be the next to die. Despair beat down on his head, as relentless as the hot sun.

— CHAPTER TWENTY-FOUR —

Port Issbesk, Kisbeksar Province, in the Kingdom of Solura
30th of Lytelar (Soluran calendar)

SO MUCH FOR getting home by Solstice. 'It is midsummer day tomorrow, isn't it?' Corrain had tried to keep track, marking off each dawn with a notch on the galley's prow post.

Once again, Kusint was intent on one of the Aldabreshin compasses. He looked up, triumphant. 'It is indeed.' He held up the instrument. 'See?'

'You said those are valuable enough to sell?' Corrain had no objection to Kusint indulging his fascination on their voyage but now they had reached Solura, they needed to turn the galley and its contents into sound coin.

'Indeed.' Kusint sounded regretful all the same, still absorbed in reading the device.

'How far will we have to travel to find—' Corrain checked himself, looking around the people idling outside this dockside tavern. 'An ally?'

These streets were thronged with more people than he had ever seen, even in Trebin or Ferl when Caladhria's nobility gathered for the seasonal parliaments. It was a surprise, given everything he'd ever heard about Solura's remote and scattered villages.

This was a port to rival Relshaz, as Kusint had promised. Wagons and coaches rattled along, unloading at warehouses and inns. Many of those arriving would soon be embarking on the substantial ships moored at the broad stone quays where the river met the sea. Tall, many-masted vessels would carry goods and passengers further west along the Soluran coast to other ports where the realm's great rivers carried water from the northern mountains down to the boundless sea.

Meantime, everyone was revelling for the two days their king granted for Solstice celebrations. Songs, laughter and incomprehensible conversation bounced back and forth between the wooden-walled buildings as folk enjoyed the cool of the lingering twilight now that the day's sultry heaviness had passed.

Corrain couldn't even read the letters that formed the angular writing above the shop fronts, never mind the words of the handbills pasted on the buildings' walls.

'I need to talk to some people.' Kusint made a careful adjustment, sighting along the compass's pointer.

'Who? When?' Corrain sipped his ale; dark and flavoured with summer berries. Not much to his taste but all there was to be had unless he was fool enough to risk well water and three days squatting on a bucket.

Looking inland, sail barges crowded around the wharves and jetties extending upstream as far as Corrain could see. He couldn't even see the far bank. In between, vast rafts of great logs floated, brought down from the Great Forest. Some of the rafts even carried wooden huts with smoking stove-chimneys sticking through shingled roofs. Truly, the mighty Rel, the greatest river that Corrain had seen, was indeed a stream by comparison.

'Kusint?' he demanded, exasperated.

'All in good time,' Kusint said absently.

'We have no time to waste,' Corrain insisted. 'Any more delay—'

Kusint looked up. 'You think we could have got here sooner?'

'No,' Corrain said curtly.

They had finally arrived, with barely enough men to manage the galley's oars. Deaths and desertions had continued through the voyage. The other face of that rune meant those who endured to the end had been rewarded with an even greater share of the loot in the galley's holds.

The scum-sucking bastards could have been more grateful. Corrain took another swallow of the darkly fruited beer. 'Have you any idea how much coin the services we seek will cost us?'

He had absolutely no notion how much gold a Soluran mage would ask for and no idea what other expense might lie ahead as they searched for such a wizard. They had already had to pay out for fresh clothes and travelling gear to avoid being scorned as beggars or worse.

Granted, they had a heavy coffer of gold and silver between them, from selling their share of the galley's cargo and better yet, it was locally minted coin. All the same, so much uncertainty made Corrain tense.

'Kusint!' He plucked the accursed compass from the Forest youth's hands, barely restraining himself from hurling it out into the roadway.

Kusint almost snatched it back, before thinking better of it. 'We need to go north, and the river will be quickest, but there will be no boats to take us until the Solstice is done. I'm sorry, but there it is.'

'We can buy horses.' Corrain wondered what that would cost.

Kusint shook his head. 'There'll be no one selling, not tonight, tomorrow or the day after.'

Corrain looked at the crowds enjoying the balmy evening. 'You're sure we have to travel? Surely, among all these people—?'

'Can you tell a mage from the rest?' Kusint queried. 'I can't, and besides, if we find one to help us we still need consent from the Order's elders. After we wait out the Solstice, we can go straight to an Order's tower.'

'Where's the closest?' Corrain demanded. 'We can start walking.'

Kusint took a drink of his own beer. 'The closest wizards' Order will be beholden to Lady Kisselle, whose province this is. She won't countenance any mage heading for Caladhria. None of the coastal lords will.'

'What have wizards' affairs to do with her?' Frustration burned Corrain's gullet.

Now Kusint looked exasperated. 'I told you. Soluran wizards have no Archmage. Each wizardly Order is bound by fealty to their province's ruler.'

'Can't we seek an audience with this lady?' There had to be something they could do instead of sitting here drinking peculiar beer. 'Explain Caladhria's plight to her?'

Corrain was beset by more and more irritations, flocking around him like the gulls following the fishing boats into the dockside. If Caladhrian-born wizards answered to the parliament instead of the Archmage, then Corrain would never have had to make this desperate journey. Lord Halferan need never have died in the first place.

'We could wait thirty days or more even to see her port reeve.' Kusint gestured at the busy street. 'We'd be lucky if he gave us a chit to take to her castle door before the end of the year. Lady Kisselle has far more important things to fill her days than granting audiences to travelling strangers. She has more important things for everyone to do, wizards included. Kisbeksar may be one of Solura's smallest provinces but trade makes it one of the richest. And she's a ferocious old woman by all accounts. We won't find anyone willing to sacrifice her goodwill just to help us out, however much coin we offer them.'

Corrain grunted. Kusint had explained how women could both inherit and rule without any man as their guardian, but he found it an outlandish notion.

Kusint delved into a pocket and found a map he'd drawn for Corrain while they were on the galley. It turned out that the cargo included a quantity of the finest quality paper, heavy with rag. The Aldabreshi prized it highly for recording their astronomical observations and the intricate calculations that followed.

'Here's the Great River of the East and the Great Forest, your Land of Many Races beyond it.'

'You mean Ensaimin?' Corrain interrupted.

'Here's Kisbeksar's northern boundary.' Kusint sketched in a larger province above it embraced by a broad sweep of the river. 'This is Brawathar, where Lord Brawen is very weary of seeing the trade from the forest and the mountains heading downstream and seldom even bothering to pay him for an overnight berth. But if he could secure friendly ties with Caladhria and Caladhria's merchants, then Lady Kisselle would at least have to pretend to treat him with some respect.'

Everything always comes down to self-interest, Corrain reflected sourly. No need to waste time appealing for succour for Caladhria's suffering innocents. 'So he'll tell a wizard to help us?'

To his growing annoyance, Kusint shook his head again.

'We wouldn't be able to get an audience with Lord Brawen any sooner than we could with Lady Kisselle. If we find a willing wizard on the other hand, there's every chance he'll know exactly how to secure his Order's permission and those Elders will have no trouble tugging on Lord Brawen's sleeve that same day.'

'If?' Corrain fastened on that word. 'What if we can't find a willing mage?'

Kusint ran a hand through his hair, barely. It was short enough after its cropping in Caladhria to turn heads in Solura, where Forest Folk in particular favoured much longer styles.

'Then we'll have to head further north, most likely to Pastamar. Mandarkin holds these mountains, north of Resdonar.' He stabbed at the map with his finger. 'This region here, north of the Great Forest and west of your Land of Many Races, is always being disputed. The Mountain Men usually drive back Mandarkin incursions but they've had their own troubles of late. Last summer, Mandarkin forces—'

'Why Mandarkin?' Corrain snapped. 'Why not 'Men of the North' or some such? You don't grant any other land the courtesy of a name!'

Kusint was more taken aback than affronted. 'Why should the Solurans bother with names for anyone else? They have no real interest in whatever might lie beyond their great rivers of east and west. A simple description suffices for strange places far away of which they know little and wonder less.'

Corrain felt himself reddening, obscurely ashamed of his outburst. But words once spoken were as far beyond reach as a loosed crossbow bolt. He seized on a different question. 'Who are these Mandarkin?'

'A brutal people ruled by tyrants.' Kusint scowled. 'If Solura's wizards didn't take a stand against their enslaved mages, Mandarkin soldiery would pour through the mountain passes and lay waste to everything between the pine woods and the sea.'

His vehemence took Corrain by surprise. The youth's hatred for these unknown northerners sounded equal to his own loathing of the Aldabreshi.

'The Mandarkin often test Solura's resolve in the summer,' Kusint continued, glowering, 'especially when the Solstice sees so many border nobles travelling to Solith to renew their fealty to King Solquen.'

He took another swig of beer. 'I know this delay galls you but I'll be able to hear the latest news rumoured round the taverns. If we know where there's been trouble, we'll know where to look for a mage.'

Corrain contemplated the map. 'How many days' travel to Pastamar?'

'To the southern end of the province? Ten days by road, far less on a sail barge and there'll be plenty of those heading north after the Solstice,' Kusint assured him.

'Very well, if that's how it must be.' Corrain sought to wash away his irritation with more beer. 'What do we do in the meantime? If no one's trading over the Solstice, I take it we can't sell those cursed things?' He nodded at the discarded compass.

Kusint looked around. 'We can eat some dinner, for a start.'

Corrain was about to say he wasn't hungry, but Kusint's words might as well have been someone cutting the pastry lid of a pie right under his nose. Now the evening air was luscious with tantalising spices and the scents of roast suckling pig. Corrain's stomach growled.

Kusint laughed. 'Lightning liquor will lift your spirits, if you don't like our local ale.'

Corrain managed something close to a smile. 'That should take care of tonight. What about tomorrow? Don't you have Solstice rituals to attend?' he asked belatedly.

As he spoke, he found he desperately wanted to be back in Halferan, where fire and water would be rededicating each threshold to Saedrin. Everyone would gather for the festival feasts where men and boys raced burning hoops against each other, rolling them into the brook between the manor and the village amid cheers and steam.

Corrain had always been among the victors. A little scorching was a small price to pay for the admiration of some young wife giddy enough to be reckless while her husband drank himself insensible.

Would Halferan see such celebrations this year? What of the other coastal baronies? Had corsair raids put paid to their jollifications, despite whatever successes Captain Mersed and the Tallat men might have achieved?

Recalling the corsairs prompted more unwelcome thoughts.

Was Hosh looking up at the skies and marking the solstice, even more bereft than Corrain? Or was the fool boy answering to Saedrin at the door to the

Otherworld, explaining Corrain's failure to save him, to see him safe home again? Corrain grabbed for his tankard and hid his distress in the sickly beer.

Kusint was shaking his head. 'Solurans will be gathering at their own firesides after settling their debts. Some may offer thanks at their local sanctuary for goodwill and good fortune among family and friends or seek counsel from the priests if they've had illness in their household.'

'You don't worship the gods as we understand them?' Corrain hesitated somewhere between a question and confusion.

'The Solurans don't,' Kusint corrected. 'My father was Soluran but I follow my mother's religion. The Forest Folk revered Trimon and Talagrin, Larasion and Arrimelin long before their reputation spread east to your people. We were the first to teach the lore of the runes to those once ruled by the Tormalins.'

'Runes?' Corrain drained his tankard and slammed the battered pewter down on the table. 'Let's find a game.' That would be one way to pass the time, if there was nothing more constructive to do.

Kusint looked sideways at him. 'What do you plan on spending to buy your way into a game?'

'Those things.' Corrain nodded at the Aldabreshin compass. 'You think I'd touch our coin coffer?' He challenged Kusint with a look. 'That gold's to buy us a wizard, and as soon as we can.'

His fingers tightened around the tankard's handle. Lady Zurenne would be expecting him any day now. Lord Licanin would be laying his claim before the barons' Summer Parliament, to be acknowledged as Halferan's guardian.

He and Kusint had to get back with a wizard in tow before Lord Licanin arrived to impose his will on Lady Zurenne. If they didn't, what would she do?

— CHAPTER TWENTY-FIVE —

ZURENNE HAD YET to decide if she welcomed Lysha's growing independence over this past half season. She felt they both hesitated on a threshold far more perilous than this entrance to the manor's shrine.

She closed the door from the great hall's dais behind her. 'What are you doing?'

'Who told you I was here?' Ilysh laid a garland of leafy green stems and bright blue flowers on the pedestal before Saedrin's statue.

'Never mind.' In fact, Jora had told Raselle, all fond amusement and the dutiful maid had hurried to rouse Zurenne. 'What are you doing here?'

'If I am now truly wedded, then my claim to Halferan is secured.' Ilysh's composure and determination reminded Zurenne painfully of her dead husband. 'Whatever the parliament might say.' Her eyes flashed with a hint of the indomitable will she had inherited from her father. 'So I must undertake the duties expected of a baron's lady while my husband is away. Just as you have always done, Mama.'

'But no one must know of your marriage.' Zurenne forced herself to speak calmly. 'We agreed on that and you promised me, in this very shrine.'

As soon as Corrain had departed, she'd been tormented with doubts, demanding oaths of utmost secrecy from Ilysh and Raselle, before Saedrin's statue and Drianon's.

Ilysh laid fennel stalks and an elder spray on the shrine table. 'No one need know of my marriage. The demesne folk will only see a daughter honouring her father and his legacy.'

The girl went towards the shrine's outer door. She paused with her hand on the iron ring, looking at her mother, unblinking.

'At this season above all others, we must see the rites observed. Saedrin's door must stand open for those who've been released from the flesh and bone that binds us to this world, especially for those who've died unnoticed and unburned. Half the village still mourns their men folk taken by the corsairs.'

Zurenne longed to protest. Lysha was a child and such matters should not concern her.

'You saw to the rites last year, Mama,' Ilysh reminded her. 'Even after Master Minelas forbade it, and you did the same at Winter Solstice.'

'Who told you that?' Zurenne had gone walking alone in the night time pastures, chilled with fear as well as the frost. She had cut the rowan spray and blackthorn twigs with a shaking hand and a purloined knife, hiding everything beneath her cloak before scurrying back to the manor.

Starrid had caught her sneaking back in through the rear gate, pouncing like a triumphant cat on a mouse. What if she had fallen and hurt herself, or been lost to some other misfortune? Whatever would become of her daughters? Master Minelas was sure to punish her when he returned.

Zurenne had gone in dread of the monster's retribution for the rest of the season, long after she had crept to the shrine at midnight on the winter solstice and honoured Poldrion with whispered rites.

Her nostrils flared. She need never have endured such fear. Minelas had already been dead. That was one more weight in the scales against the wizards of Hadrumal. Surely the demands of justice would see Raeponin deliver Corrain safely back to repay the Archmage for that deception.

Ilysh opened the shrine door and a muted cheer startled Zurenne. She took a few steps forward and saw the household servants and troopers gathered outside. Though the sun was barely risen, their approval of their lost lord's daughter and heiress taking up his ritual duties was as warm as the midsummer morning. There was Jora, whose busy tongue was doubtless responsible for bringing them here.

Zurenne retreated back into the fragrant shade of the shrine. Whatever her own misgivings, she realised the demesne folk's testimony would strengthen Halferan's case if she and Ilysh ever found themselves arguing for this clandestine marriage before the parliament.

Lord Licanin had sent her a whole series of letters, detailing the arguments that he would be making before the barons. He was confident that his guardianship would be approved. Shutting the letters inside her writing box didn't alter their words.

Zurenne could only be grateful that the parliament was meeting in Kevil, so far to the north and not on good roads. He couldn't pester her while he was there, not even with brief notes sent to Master Rauffe. It took a full half year to raise courier doves from egg to reliable messenger.

But as soon as the parliament was over, he would be heading southward, waving the parchments supposed to seal their fates. Had she been an utter fool to trust in Corràin, a man of such flawed reputation, even if he had escaped the Aldabreshi?

Zurenne watched as Ilysh carefully removed the rowan spray and blackthorn twigs that had protected the shrine since midwinter from the hooks beside the shrine's door. She stooped to lay them on the threshold.

Now the shrine door would stand open from dawn to dawn, the chicory wreath before Saedrin a sign to any uneasy shade that their way to the Otherworld lay open.

Ilysh knelt and struck sparks with flint and steel. The dried leaves of the rowan flared into flame and an appreciative murmur stirred the household.

Zurenne blinked away tears. Ilysh looked so like her father. It was agony to remember Halferan doing this, just as calm and assured. So long and his loss was as sharp a knife to her heart as ever.

She wondered how a could child show such strength of purpose. But Lysha's words had shown that she understood the ritual. Her daughter was less a child with each passing season, soon to become a young woman.

Neeny was still her baby. Zurenne caught sight of her younger daughter, fidgeting by Jora's side. All the festival meant to her was honeyed sweetmeats and scampering in the pastures by the brook with the children from the village.

Jora tightened her grip and Esnina's squirming subsided. Now Ilysh was taking the elder and fennel from the shrine table and hanging them on the doorpost hooks. The door to the Otherworld might be open but no one wanted the troubled dead lingering here, or worse, any of the Eldritch Kin, until some rainbow offered them a door back to the Otherworld.

Ilysh paused to smile shyly at the watching household before going over to Larasion's statue. The serene goddess gazed at them all, her armful of enchanted boughs bearing bud, blossom and fruit at the same time.

After curtseying to the goddess, Ilysh carefully lifted up the jug of wine which Zurenne herself had set before Ostrin's statue on the final eve of For-Summer, giving thanks for the grape, his bounty, and for that season spent in his care. Now Ilysh set the wine before Saedrin, adding garlic and rosemary, rue and wormwood, just as her father had always done.

Zurenne had laid those herbs ready herself, just as she had always done. No, not quite. She pressed her lips tight together. They had none of the cracked blackspice which Halferan had always used, brought all the way from the remotest islands of the Archipelago. Even if they had Zurenne would not have used it. Nothing from the Aldabreshi was welcome here. So she had gathered sage, expecting that she would be the one to add it to the souring wine.

Ilysh dipped a sprig of hyssop into the jug and drew it carefully across the width of the threshold, brushing aside the ashes of rowan and elder. The line wavered, damply dark on the stone, running from door jamb to door jamb.

'Saedrin see us safe through the year to come.'

The household echoed her words in a ragged chorus. Some of the demesne men murmured prayers to Larasion as well. The goddess of weather might not take up her watch over Aft-Summer until the festival was done but there could be no harm in beseeching her favour for the harvest a few days early.

Zurenne saw the uncertainty which prompted those fervent prayers. This was far from the carefree festivals which they'd enjoyed when Lysha was Neeny's age, Halferan generous with the barony's largesse.

Cracked blackspice wasn't the only thing she could no longer afford to order from the markets or travelling merchants. She had almost no coin left for anything beyond necessities. None for more than a token towards the gifts customary at this season for loyal servants and tenants. The manor's feasting, open to all-comers on the solstice eve, had been far from lavish.

She searched the demesne folk's faces for any sign of resentment. Did they realise how empty her coffers were? Or did they condemn her miserliness? Did they grumble among themselves and wonder why she didn't appeal to Baron Licanin now that he held the purse strings?

Because she dared not draw his attention back to Halferan any sooner than she must. Where was Corrain? He'd promised to be home by midsummer.

'My lady.' Captain Arigo had stepped forward, his age-spotted hands reaching for the jug and the hyssop.

'No, thank you.' Ilysh held the herb-steeped wine close.

Zurenne caught her breath, for fear of a spill on Lysha's dress. She realised with a shock that the girl was wearing the violet gown which she had been married in.

'I will anoint every doorway myself.' Ilysh managed to convey her apologies to Arigo at the same time as making it clear this was not open to further discussion. 'By your leave, mother?'

She turned to Zurenne who hastily cleared her throat. 'With my blessing, my love.'

She forced a wide smile but could not follow as the crowd moved away, heading first for the manor's gatehouse.

Zurenne had seen Jilseth, standing motionless as the kitchen maids flowed around her.

'My lady Zurenne.' The lady wizard advanced inexorably to greet her. 'Fair festival.'

'Fair festival to you.' The courtesy was out before Zurenne could curb it. 'As you see, we are busy with our festival rites. What brings you here? More threats? More deceits to acknowledge?'

Jilseth stepped over the drying wine stain into the shrine. Zurenne could hear the people outside, accompanying Ilysh on her progress to anoint every doorstep in the manor. They might as well have been a hundred leagues away, leaving her in this quiet gloom with the lady wizard.

'I came to see how you and your daughters are faring.' Jilseth straightened a posy of cornflowers laid before Drianon's statue. 'And to thank you for Captain Corrain's continued silence. We're glad that you saw there was nothing to be gained by Hadrumal's humiliation.'

'Don't thank me,' Zurenne said waspishly. 'Thank your Archmage's threats.'

The lady wizard had the grace to colour at that reminder. Jilseth looked out through the door into the manor courtyard. 'I don't see Captain Corrain. Is he pursuing the corsairs? We've been most impressed by your men's recent successes, and the others along the coast.'

So the wizards were spying on the coast. Zurenne supposed that shouldn't come as a surprise. She folded her arms, suddenly bold.

'Naturally Captain Corrain and his men are keeping watch in the saltings. This solstice brings the highest tides and we know full well those often bring the corsairs. Are you telling me that you don't know that, after all your magical spying?'

Zurenne saw that the lady wizard knew that she was lying. She felt a surge of triumph nevertheless. She could also see Jilseth's disappointment. By all that was sacred and profane, Corrain had somehow escaped the Archmage's scrutiny.

He had escaped the Aldabreshin slave galleys, which everyone said was impossible, and now the mighty wizards of Hadrumal had no idea where he was. Perhaps Zurenne could dare to hope Corrain would return to make good on his promises. To stand between her and her daughters and those men who would rule their lives. No one else would ever know that he was no more Ilysh's true husband than a straw man from the fields.

In the next instant, dread chilled her. If the wizards couldn't find him, did that mean Corrain had been killed? Was that why he hadn't returned? Could mages scry for the dead? Zurenne dared not ask.

She saw Jilseth was studying her face with unnerving intensity. 'I'm curious to learn what you know of Captain Corrain's strategy, my lady.'

Zurenne smiled sweetly. 'Such matters are hardly a womanly concern.'

'Perhaps not in Caladhria, though I know a great many women elsewhere who'd say different.' Jilseth pursed her lips. 'No matter. I can wait until Lord Licanin comes here to take charge of the barony. I imagine he'll want to know where Corrain has got to.'

'I'm sure he will,' Zurenne said placidly.

Jilseth considered that before persisting. 'Is there nothing I can do for you, to persuade you to trust me? I know you have good reason to mistrust wizardry but I stood by your side when Lord Karpis would have foisted that villain Starrid on you again.'

Zurenne hesitated. Jilseth looked more hopefully at her. 'There is something I can do for you, isn't there?'

As Zurenne spoke, she spared a fleeting prayer to Saedrin that she wouldn't regret this. But for all her mistrust of magic, this festival's display of her poverty had shamed her beyond endurance. 'If you really wish to make amends, you can find Starrid for me.'

'He's no longer in Lord Karpis's service, I take it?' Jilseth was all business now.

'He was whipped from his lordship's gate,' Zurenne said curtly, 'and last heard of bleeding on the road to Saldiray.' She saw her opportunity to get an answer to her earlier question. 'He may not have survived such a thrashing. Can you scry for a dead man?'

'If you can provide me with some of his possessions, I can. Why do you want to find him?'

'Because he might know where that thief Minelas has stowed Halferan's wealth.' She gestured furiously towards the door to the great hall. 'I have spent almost the last of my silver just to offer the demesne folk a plain wafer cake and cup of ale.'

'That's certainly a service which Hadrumal should render you, as some recompense for your sufferings at

Minelas's hands.' Jilseth was nodding. 'Little enough and too late, I know.'

She meant it too, though Zurenne was getting her measure now. She could see what lay behind the lady wizard's eyes. Jilseth was thinking she could worm her way into her confidence, once Zurenne was in her debt.

Zurenne would happily encourage Jilseth in that delusion, as long as the wizards of Hadrumal hunted Starrid down.

Once the treacherous steward was in her hands, the prospect of wizardly retribution should shake whatever he knew of Minelas's thievery out of the villain. After Jilseth's humiliation of Baron Karpis, Zurenne was certain that Starrid wouldn't risk his own skin by testing that threat for a bluff.

Moreover, if the Archmage and his subordinates were busy looking for the coward, they couldn't be hunting Corrain, wherever he had got to. Perhaps there was a slim chance that the vagabond trooper and his Forest ally could make good on their promises.

Now Zurenne could hear the affectionate crowd escorting Ilysh back towards the great hall's steps.

Once again, anguished doubts assailed her. Was there any chance that Corrain would return before Baron Licanin arrived to assert his guardianship? If not, did she dare to admit to the clandestine marriage without his presence to strengthen her hand?

How would Licanin react to the news? What would this loyal household think of their barony's heiress married so young to a guardsman of such tarnished character? What if Corrain never actually returned, after Zurenne had publicly linked Ilysh's name to his, swearing they were truly wed?

Who would ever ask for Ilysh's hand in marriage after that? That night's hasty work could have ruined her daughter's hopes of future happiness. Was it worth making that sacrifice for the sake of escaping Lord Licanin's undoubtedly benign control of their affairs?

'You may join us for ale and wafer cakes before you depart,' she told Jilseth politely, hiding the feverish turmoil of her thoughts. 'Forgive me, but I cannot offer any guests fitting hospitality until our household's fortunes improve.'

— CHAPTER TWENTY-SIX —

WHATEVER HAD POSSESSED the Caladhrian barons to hold their Summer Parliament here? Jilseth slapped at a tickle on her neck. She was relieved to feel a trickle of sweat beneath her fingers, not one of the pestilential flies which emerged as the day cooled. If there was some quadrate cantrip to soothe the reddened itching which their bites provoked, she had yet to find it.

The whole town reeked of decay as the breeze blew in from the fens. While this whole coast was fringed with salt marshes, a great swathe of land lay waterlogged hereabouts. The vast swamp stretched a full thirty leagues inland at its widest point, extending to the north of Kevil from the river that gave its name to the town right the way to the River Tresia flowing down from Trebin far inland. The shortest route between the two rivers would be fifty leagues, if such a path could ever be found amid the shifting channels and treacherous bogs.

Only the locals seemed immune to the smell. Perhaps that was why they had such a reputation for stupidity. If those in the other countries that had once made up the Old Tormalin Empire told jokes about slow-witted Caladhrians, the Caladhrians told the same jokes about Kevilmen.

Jilseth was more inclined to think their nostrils simply gave up the unequal fight with the fetid odours in childhood. Could they even taste the subtleties in the celebrated wines of Trebin's hills? Or were the finest vintages as tasteless as spring water? Jilseth took a sip and wished the blush wine tasted as fragrant as it had in Hadrumal. No chance of that with the stench clogging her palate.

She contemplated the Merchants' Exchange on the far side of the market square. The spacious entrance had been built to accommodate the widest wagons bringing goods to be sold and traded. A full season's produce from leagues around could be stowed safely in the undercroft's storerooms while deals were done in the great hall up above.

Now those double doors were spilling Caladhria's barons out onto the cobbles. The nobles' deliberations had finally been completed for the day. It had taken long enough but the Caladhrians did take their parliaments very seriously.

An equal voice for all the barons hallowed by custom and enshrined in law saved their realm from the ruinous rivalries that had beset Lescar as those six dukes constantly sought supreme power. It protected smaller, poorer baronies from being overridden by wealthier ones, in the way that the lesser fiefdoms of Ensaimin were so often bullied by the great city states of that fragmented country.

It was far superior to the Tormalin Convocation of Princes, in the Caladhrian barons' opinion. However much influence the men rising to lead the empire's noble houses might have over their vast dominions, the lesser branches of their extensive families and their countless tenants, they were all still subject to the Tormalin Emperor's ultimate authority over the laws enforced within their boundaries and his final say on any decision to send the Imperial legions beyond them. No Caladhrian need yield to such tyranny.

In theory, each new emperor's authority rested on his acclamation by the Convocation. If they wished to, the other leading princes could designate a different noble house to provide a guardian of their rights and freedoms. In practise, the same dynasty would sit on the imperial throne for generations until some calamitous decision or egregious stupidity forced the Convocation's hand. They'd learned nothing since the days of Nemith the Reckless, whose folly had brought the Old Empire crashing down into the dark generations of The Chaos.

That's what Ilysh had solemnly told Jilseth, when the magewoman had idly probed the girl's understanding of the world beyond Halferan. Jilseth forbore to tell her how the inhabitants of those other countries routinely mocked the Caladhrians' interminable, inconclusive discussions that kept the baronies and all their inhabitants retracing their fathers' and forefather's steps as dumbly as a donkey in a harness endlessly circling to drive a mill wheel.

All around the market square, innkeepers shooed their prettiest serving maids forward to smile demurely and curtsey, promising the finest dining in Caladhria within the welcoming shade of their particular hostelry. Kevil hadn't seen such a gathering inside two generations and the locals were determined to make the most of it.

Jilseth wished them luck. The stink from the marshes had killed her appetite. Then she realised fine dining was the last thing the barons were considering. A dark haired lord walked past without as much as a glance in Jilseth's direction. He was arguing hotly with his hook-nosed companion.

'You think we should have sat on our hands behind our manor walls and let the corsairs plunder our domains as they pleased?'

'I know that every merchant whom I have dealings with tells me of outrage in Col, Peorle and Relshaz,' the hook-nosed baron said with equal passion. 'If these corsair raids on their vessels continue, they will send their goods by road and river next season.'

'They will not,' the dark-haired lord scoffed. 'A ship can carry fifty times the weight of a wagon and make the journey in a quarter of the time.'

'Then these merchants will buy fifty wagons and endure the delay, for the sake of seeing their goods actually arrive,' the hook-nosed baron assured him. 'Better that than lose both stake money and profit to some Archipelagan raider. What happens to your lordships' revenues then, from harbour dues paid in Attar and Claithe and Pinerin, with no coastal trade between Relshaz and Ensaimin?'

'Those revenues are no recompense for our losses,' the dark-haired lord assured him.

'Then perhaps we should consider my lord of Prysen's proposal,' the hook-nosed baron snapped. 'Perhaps if Lord Halferan had brought that whole business to the parliament as he should have in the first place, we would not be tangled in this coil!'

'If their lordships sitting comfortably a hundred leagues from the coast had agreed to pay the necessary levy to raise an army, we would have seen an end to our losses long since.' The dark-haired lord was growing angry.

'Who would this army of yours have fought? Where? When?' the hook-nosed baron demanded, his wrath rising equally swiftly. 'This isn't Lescar's war with dukes and their militias neatly drawn up to face the rebels on either side of a battlefield. When we get wind of a corsair raid, we only ever arrive after they've fled and we never have any notion where the villains will strike next!'

For a moment, Jilseth actually thought the dark-haired lord was about to punch the hook-nosed baron in the face. He certainly clenched his fist. Then he drew back with ill-concealed satisfaction. 'This business will be resolved without paying these corsairs a copper cut-piece. You have my word on that.'

He strode away with a superior smile on his face, leaving his associate glowering after him. The baron waved away an obsequious pot man trying to entice him towards a seat. He headed across the market square for a different tavern where more gesticulating barons had gathered.

Jilseth considered going after him. What was this business which Lord Halferan should have laid before the parliament? It couldn't be approaching the Archmage for wizardry's aid. That was all done and dealt with and the whole parliament knew of Hadrumal's refusal.

What was Lord Prysen's proposal? Who was he? Jilseth didn't know the man by sight or reputation, any more than she knew that hook-nosed baron's name.

But she had no standing to prompt any unknown noble into conversation. Not unless she revealed herself as a magewoman of Hadrumal, and that wasn't something she wanted to do. She had come here to find out as discreetly as possible what Lord Licanin might know of Corrain's whereabouts.

Jilseth found herself much less inclined to dismiss the Archmage's instinct to keep an eye on that potential troublemaker after her recent visit to Halferan. Lady Zurenne was definitely hiding something.

She rose to her feet, leaving a silver penny to pay for her half-drunk glass of wine. She had seen the barons of Saldiray and Taine emerging from the market hall's shadowed entrance.

As she crossed the cobbles to meet them, they were as deeply engaged in heated conversation as those first lords. They didn't even notice her approaching.

'If the inland baronies won't countenance paying a levy so we can raise a coastal army, what makes you think they will open up their coffers for the sake of buying off these accursed corsairs?' Lord Saldiray demanded.

'Warfare is one thing. This is commerce.' Baron Taine sounded disgusted.

Whatever his quarrel was, Jilseth saw it wasn't with Lord Saldiray.

'Fair festival, my lords.' She smiled at them both.

'What are you doing here?' Lord Saldiray was brusque to the point of rudeness.

Baron Taine overstepped that mark by a long stride. 'Don't imagine that you are welcome.'

What prompted this hostility? Jilseth wondered for an instant if the parliament had learned the full extent of Minelas's treachery. But surely that scandal would have been on every baron's lips, not this Lord Prysen's proposal, whatever that might be.

'Then forgive me, my lords.' She took a step backwards, ready to walk away.

'Not so fast, madam mage!' To her utter astonishment, Lord Saldiray seized her wrist.

Jilseth was so taken aback that she couldn't even translocate herself. All her instincts reached for earth and stone rather than the elemental air. Then the spell came rushing back to her. Let him find his hand as empty as a winter nutshell—

'What has the Archmage promised Halferan?'

The desperation in Saldiray's voice gave Jilseth pause. She let the swirl of enchanted air dissipate.

'What do you mean?' she asked warily.

'Besides guiding them to these victories over the corsairs,' Baron Taine said impatiently. 'Have you any notion how foolish we looked in there?' he asked with mounting wrath.

'My lord, I have no notion what you're talking about,' Jilseth assured him with increasing unease.

Lord Saldiray stared at her, uncomprehending. 'The corsair galleys which the men of Halferan, Tallat and Myrist have captured and burned over this past half season. The Archmage told Halferan's captain where they would make landfall.'

'He most definitely did not,' Jilseth assured him. 'Nor any other mage.'

It was inconceivable in the current circumstances that any renegade mage, however well-meaning, could possibly escape the Archmage's vigilance, or Hearth Master Kalion's.

Baron Taine spun around with a comical flounce of his lightweight cloak. Jilseth could have smiled if she hadn't felt such dire misgivings.

'Lord Licanin!' Baron Taine's hail turned heads clear across the market place. 'If you please?' he added belatedly.

Lord Licanin had turned aside as soon as he left the Merchants' Exchange, heading for a side street rather than any revelry. Jilseth thought he might keep on walking until Baron Saldiray added his own plea.

'A word, by your leave?'

Visibly heaving a sigh, Lord Licanin crossed the market place. He nodded to Taine and to Saldiray. 'My lords. Madam mage.'

His antagonism was cold enough to drive off the evening's midges.

Jilseth offered her warmest smile. 'Fair festival, Lord Licanin.'

'So what have you to say for yourself?' Lord Licanin wasted no time on courtesy. 'Come to that, why are you here?'

'I came in case you might need my testimony that Master Minelas is dead,' she said carefully. 'In support of your proposed guardianship of Halferan.'

That was as good a reason as any for her presence, with the added virtue of being true. Even if it was not the whole truth.

As well as looking to find out what Lord Licanin knew of Corrain's westward voyage, Jilseth had come to listen to the idle conversation around the inns and taverns. She'd been profoundly relieved to hear no whisper of scandal hanging around Halferan, no rumour of any unknown wizard's malfeasance.

Not that she'd doubted Lady Zurenne's word, but Jilseth reckoned Corrain was about as trustworthy as a Lescari silver mark and no one had to be a mage to know those were almost entirely made out of lead.

'Halferan.' Lord Licanin looked wearily at her. 'Please, madam mage, what purpose has been served by keeping us in ignorance? Did you think we would object to burning corsair galleys? Is the Archmage entertained to see us congratulated by our peers and made to look utter fools when we know nothing of such things? When we have already told them time and again that Hadrumal offers no aid to the mainland?'

'Believe me, my lords, I don't understand what you're accusing the Archmage of doing.' Jilseth hoped she could convince them. 'We know that Halferan men and others have been burning corsair galleys but they've had no help from any wizard of Hadrumal.'

'You expect us to believe that?' Baron Taine looked at her with outright accusation. 'When Baron Tallat is openly hinting of more help to come?'

'If you are not involved, how do you even know that these galleys have been burned?' Lord Saldiray asked suspiciously.

Jilseth was wishing she'd never spoken. What was it they said in Caladhria about unwise words? When one pig gets through the hedge, there'll be no stopping the rest.

'We have been scrying along the Caladhrian coasts.' She tried for the dignity befitting an envoy of Hadrumal. 'It behoves us to know what's afoot on the mainland.'

'Does it?' Baron Taine's chin jutted aggressively. 'So you can feel safer on your magic-swathed island, knowing that the corsairs have sated their appetites by ravishing innocents and looting their humble homes?'

Jilseth wasn't about to answer that. She addressed Lord Saldiray. 'We have seen Halferan's men riding regular patrols through the salt marshes, along with troops from Tallat and Myrist. Whatever they've learned of corsair habits, which has enabled them to lay in waitsnares—' she spread helpless hands, '—they've done so without magical aid. Lord Licanin, I expected to be congratulating you on your Halferan captain's initiative.'

'Which captain?' He asked at once. 'Who is hunting corsairs so effectively? What is his secret?'

'I don't know that.' She could only apologise. 'But it was Captain Corrain who first rallied Halferan and Tallat to capture a galley.'

He looked at her blankly. 'The reprobate who escaped the corsairs?'

'Could he know some secret that makes them vulnerable?' Lord Saldiray wondered, uncertain.

'Why have we had no word of this?' Baron Taine sought a target for his ill-temper. He turned on Licanin. 'Has Halferan's widow said nothing in her letters?'

'Not beyond detailing the affairs of her children and household,' Lord Licanin retorted. 'As is entirely right and proper. Does your lady wife converse with your guard captains?'

Baron Taine bridled, outraged. 'My captains know full well I'd see them birched for such insolence!'

'My lords.' Lord Saldiray stepped forward to intervene. 'There's no quarrel to be had here. A noblewoman has no business dealing with guardsmen; we're agreed on that. This man Corrain must be acting on his own initiative. However irregular that might be, any successes must be welcomed.'

'Even when they have caused so much commotion?' Lord Licanin plainly wasn't convinced. 'Well, the man can answer for himself when I reach Halferan. That's where I will be going as soon as this parliament is concluded.'

Before Jilseth could find out what "commotion" Licanin was referring to, Baron Taine turned to her.

'Baron Tallat's hints of magical aid to come? There is no substance to that?'

'None,' Jilseth said crisply. 'And I would welcome an introduction, my lords, so I might ask him to explain such hints himself, to me or to the Archmage.'

The silence between them was filled with the chinking of glassware and laughter amid the rattle of rune bones and the chink of carelessly wagered coin.

Lord Saldiray grunted. 'He's over there.'

Jilseth followed his pointing hand and saw the dark-haired lord who'd been talking to the hook-nosed baron. 'Thank you, my lord.'

She hid her own annoyance, with Baron Tallat and with these other noble lords, who evidently had no idea what Corrain might be doing. They didn't even know that he had taken a galley and left Caladhria, if Licanin was expecting to find him in Halferan.

Baron Taine was hardly placated. 'It's high time you asserted your authority,' he told Lord Licanin.

'I will do so as soon as I have the parliament's grant of guardianship.' Lord Licanin glared at him. 'If we can be done with this nonsense of Lord Prysen's and proceed to some other business!'

'Excuse me, my lords,' Jilseth broke in, 'what is Lord Prysen's proposal?'

Baron Taine was too irate for discretion. 'It seems these accursed corsairs offered Lord Halferan a bargain fit for Poldrion's demons. If he would pay them half of his revenues, they would leave his lands untouched. When he refused, as you know full well, madam mage, they murdered him.'

'That scoundrel steward, Starrid, knew of this offer.' Licanin's face twisted with contempt. 'He told Baron

Karpis when he was under his protection, in case Karpis might like to defend his barony in such a craven fashion.'

'Why Karpis was fool enough to tell Lord Prysen—' Lord Saldiray shook his head, appalled. 'Now Lord Prysen proposes a levy from all the baronies, to pay these corsairs to sail away to plague the southern reaches of the Archipelago and leave our sea lanes safe so that merchants may ship their goods from Col to Relshaz unmolested.'

'The inland lords are not inclined to congratulate us for burning corsair galleys,' Baron Taine said acidly. 'Rather we coastal lords are being rebuked for inciting corsair violence against the merchants.'

'There's no chance anyone will vote for this proposal.' Lord Licanin was adamant. 'We know the corsair demands would grow with each passing year until we were all beggared.'

'I'm very sorry for your troubles,' Jilseth said sincerely. So much for any hope of Caladhria returning to its usual peaceful torpor this side of winter solstice.

'Your sympathies are worth as much as anything else we've had from Hadrumal,' Baron Taine snapped. 'Precisely nothing.'

Jilseth hoped her face didn't betray her dismay. Hearth Master Kalion's apprehensions seemed increasingly justified. It didn't even need Corrain spreading the poisonous truth of Lord Halferan's fate for Caladhrian resentment towards Hadrumal to fester.

'Excuse me, my lords.' She smiled tightly. 'I will leave you to your evening's entertainments.'

But before she went back to Hadrumal, there were two things she could do. She could find out why this

Baron Tallat was spreading rumours of the Archmage's promised aid and she could make him rue the day he'd first opened his mouth.

She walked briskly across the market place to the tavern where the dark-haired lord was dining with a handful of others around a table beneath an awning.

'My lord Tallat?' She stood in front of him to demand his attention.

'Whatever it is you're selling, beyond the obvious—' he looked her up and down with some perplexity, his smeared knife poised in the air '—I'm not in the market. Nor for the obvious, either.'

One of his companions chuckled. 'Oh, she looks clean enough and doubtless cheap.'

It took Jilseth a moment to realise what he meant. They thought she was a whore.

The chair which Lord Tallat was sitting on vanished in a flash of amber magelight. As he sprawled on the ground, the table followed suit, along with his companions.

Jilseth heard the startled lords exclaiming on the far side of the market place where they had just arrived, drenched in spilled wine and covered in food. Let them go bleating to Hearth Master Kalion and see if he thought she should have swallowed this insult.

'I am not selling anything,' she said, with quiet menace. 'But I would like to know why you have been peddling lies about the Archmage of Hadrumal.'

'What?' Lord Tallat looked up at her, aghast. 'No, I never would.'

'You have told your friends that Hadrumal will save your barony from the corsairs.' Jilseth took a step forward. With him flat on his back, she could loom over him most satisfactorily.

'I never said Hadrumal,' he insisted in a strangled whisper. 'I never said the Archmage.' His eyes darted frantically from side to side. 'I know it's a secret.'

He was telling the truth, Jilseth realised. He was also more afraid of this conversation betraying whatever it was that he thought he knew than he was of her.

She summoned up a veil of silence. Azure magelight flickered as the elemental air escaped her control. Sending those sniggering lords all the way across the market place had taken more effort than she realised. These mainlanders might gaze, wide-eyed and amazed, at the very thought of magic, never mind their astonishment at seeing actual wizardry, but none of them ever appreciated how draining the most dramatic spells could be.

She wrapped the magic tighter. 'Listen to that silence? No one can hear us now. Tell me what you know,' she ordered.

Lord Tallat sat up, looking at her like a rabbit in front of a stoat. 'Captain Corrain of Halferan,' he said nervously. 'He told my own Captain Mersed, that's to say, he didn't tell Mersed in so many words, and he told Mersed not to tell me, only the man is loyal as he should be, and he told me alone. But we know there is help coming. No one will ever know where it comes from,' he insisted, agonised.

So in fact, he knew nothing, Jilseth concluded. Except that he had helped spread whatever rumour had started with Corrain, spawning even more outlandish stories as it passed from hand to hand.

She would have been tempted to dismiss it as nonsense. Only Corrain was definitely up to something, taking charge of that galley and somehow persuading those erstwhile slaves to row away towards Solura.

'Whatever you have heard, you have been misinformed,' she said tartly. 'Hadrumal's position remains the same. Caladhria can expect no aid against the corsairs from the Archmage or any other wizard. We will look to you to correct this misunderstanding among your fellow barons before this parliament is concluded.'

She stooped, reaching forward. He scooted back over the cobbles on heels, hands and backside. That didn't stop her snagging a brass button from his doublet with a flare of scarlet magic. She closed her fist around it. 'We will know if you don't, thanks to this token.'

If he didn't, she wasn't at all sure what would she do. But Lord Tallat was nodding frantically, struck dumb without any need for magic.

Jilseth let the silence fall away, to realise that she could probably have heard a rat scampering across the far side of the market square, if not on the other side of the town. Everyone was looking at her, awestruck, from lofty lords to beggar children.

There would be courier doves on the wing from Kevil well before the late-falling summer dusk turned to night. No baron would have come to this gathering without home-reared birds to be let fly to their nests with any vital news. How soon before Hearth Master Kalion learned of Jilseth's latest folly?

Not before she could go and confess her day's work to Planir. She had the advantage over these lords and their doves. A mage could travel from place to place faster than even the swiftest hawk.

Never mind Hearth Master Kalion's rebukes. She must also tell Planir what she'd learned of the pestilential Corrain's antics. The sooner they caught up with him, the better.

'Good day to you, my lord of Tallat.' Jilseth inclined her head and vanished between one breath and the next.

— CHAPTER TWENTY-SEVEN —

Nadrua Town, Pastamar Province, in the Kingdom of Solura
9th of Slekinar (Soluran calendar)

CORRAIN HAD NO idea what Kusint was saying to the sailing barge's captain. More and more, the Forest youth had to be reminded to speak in Tormalin. It wasn't as if he only spoke in Soluran. He slipped as readily into the Forest tongue whenever they encountered one of his own folk, and the further they travelled upstream, the more of the Folk they met. Which was doubtless very nice for Kusint but Corrain was getting sick and tired of not knowing what was being said around him.

Kusint's conversation continued and Corrain itched with frustration. Thankfully that was the only thing causing him irritation. Solurans might live in thatched wooden buildings that looked more like barns than houses but they kept their homes and themselves scrupulously clean. Every cabin's floor on this sailing barge was freshly strewn with rushes, each footfall stirring fleabane and other unknown herbs mingled with the long leaves.

Corrain longed for the familiar smell of meadowsweet. How much longer before he could go back home? What would he find there? The stench of burning after a season of corsair raids?

It should be Aldabreshin galleys burning, for as long as their masters were fool enough to go looking for water along the Caladhrian coast. If fat old Arigo's resolve held firm without Corrain to give him some backbone. If Captain Mersed of Tallat had the wits and the troopers to set more such traps and successfully spring them. If he managed to persuade other captains in neighbouring baronies to adopt such tactics.

Or would Corrain return to find more Halferan villages looted and smouldering? To meet with accusing stares, before everyone from Lady Zurenne down looked past him, searching for the help he had promised to bring.

He broke into a pause in the exchanges between Kusint and the sail barge captain. 'So where are we, and what happens now?'

'This is Nadrua,' Kusint said, unnecessarily, to Corrain's mind. He'd already told him that morning that they'd be stopping at this town to offload the barge's cargo of grain before loading up with marten pelts, deer horn, pine resin and other such Forest goods destined for the Soluran coast.

'The Mare's Tail joins the main flow of the Great River here,' the Forest youth continued.

'The Mare's Tail?' Corrain interrupted.

Kusint grinned. 'That's the name of the waterfall up in the mountains where Solura's kings yield their claim on the land. The river that bears the same name cuts almost due south and since Resdonar and Pastamar provinces were settled, it's been the easternmost border of Solura in these reaches. It's navigable up to—'

'Pastamar?' That had caught Corrain's attention. 'You said—?'

Kusint nodded. 'I'll ask around and we'll see what scents we can find. So let's pay Captain Waire and say our farewells.'

'The price as agreed?' Corrain asked quickly.

'Of course.' Kusint's brow wrinkled. 'Why—?'

'Never mind.' Corrain headed for the ladder down to the cabins, to fetch his gear and their coffer of coin.

It was securely wedged under his bunk. He hadn't been too worried about it being stolen on board. Where could a thief run? Besides, the lock was a Mountain crafted puzzle which no pick would easily defeat. An expensive rarity in Caladhria, such things were readily purchased in Solura and Corrain and Kusint had the only keys around their necks.

But it had crossed Corrain's mind that their captain might demand more than the price he'd first quoted before he would let them disembark unmolested. Every Caladhrian trooper had heard the stories of such sharp practise among the boatmen along the River Rel and around the Gulf of Peorle.

He laid the coffer on the bunk, unlocked it and counted out the silver they had settled on. No need to run any foolish risks by opening it up on deck. He was relieved to see the cost of their passage wouldn't deplete their funds too much. He and Kusint had worked every day of this voyage, even if they could only offer unskilled muscle.

Corrain had been glad of the toil. It stopped him brooding on the possible disasters that might be unfolding at home. But now the time had come to go and find a wizard to put paid to such threats to Halferan once and for all. The sooner the better. It was already midday.

He put the pouch of counted coin in his pocket, hefted his own travelling bag onto one shoulder, Kusint's on the other, and took the coffer in both hands.

Back up on deck, he handed the silver over to the captain, still in amiable conversation with Kusint.

'Thank you. We're truly grateful,' Corrain said, looking intently into the captain's eyes. The man spoke no Tormalin. 'Make sure he understands, will you?'

At first, when Kusint had told him this broad, flat-bottomed barge was the boat they'd be taking upstream, Corrain had very nearly refused to board. Surely they'd be quicker walking? Before the end of that first day, he'd realised his error.

The barge's dramatic expanse of rusty-red sails had swelled readily in the winds that rippled across the burgeoning crops of Solura's rich farmland. For the first handful of days anyway. Then Corrain had woken to find both banks of the river were thick with trees and not merely coppices supplying the Soluran hamlets and farms with firewood, tool handles and wattles. Mature timber came right down to the water, fit for building sea-going ships or supporting the roofs of halls far greater than Halferan's own.

The barge hadn't slowed. Corrain hadn't reckoned on the deftness of the crew. With five separate sails on the massive main mast and the stubby mizzen towards the stern they could capture every fickle breath dancing through the branches.

Corrain found being so enclosed horribly oppressive. Looking eastwards as they worked their way upstream he had studied the unbroken woodland. He saw no wisp of smoke, no scars from felling, no sign of the people whom Kusint assured him lived and loved and thrived behind that brown and green paling running along the bank.

As they quit the barge however, Corrain could see a goodly number of copper-haired men and women along the wharves or in small boats criss-crossing the turbulent water. They wore clothing no different to the Solurans and, like them, evidently considered the vast river as no more than a minor obstacle.

Kusint concluded his farewells and the captain chuckled, tossing the purse in his hand before walking away to supervise some lads who were working the hoist to haul a sack of grain from the fore-hold.

'Let's find an inn,' Kusint said briskly.

As the youth led the way into the town, Corrain spotted a few Forest Folk in well-worn leather garb with bone and feather adornments. He guessed they were denizens of remoter woodland than this. He wasn't about to ask, lest he make himself look foolish.

'This will do.' Kusint pushed a door open.

Corrain was taken unawares. This didn't look like any tavern to him, more an ordinary dwelling with a holly bush planted in an old half-barrel outside. But inside, he found a taproom with barrels racked behind a sturdy deal counter, tables, stools and benches and a lively crowd slaking their thirst after a morning's work.

Kusint headed for a corner table. 'You wait here with the gear while I go and ask around.' He dumped his bag by a stool and went over to the counter, leaving Corrain with no option but to set his own bag down. He put the coin coffer securely between his feet and scanned the gathering for any lingering glances in their direction.

Thankfully, no one was taking any undue interest insofar as he could tell. Corrain hoped it would stay that way. The last thing he needed was someone picking a quarrel for entertainment. Every man in Solura seemed to wear a sword, from spotty-faced striplings to dotards needing their other hand for their walking stick.

Kusint returned with two pewter tankards of ale. Corrain drank deep and very nearly spat the whole mouthful out again. He forced himself to swallow before glaring at Kusint. 'That's not fruit in there.'

'Fruit for flavour? No, not so far from the coast.' Kusint grinned. 'Hereabouts the local brewers toss evergreen twigs into their tuns.'

Corrain looked into his ale. Was the Forest lad teasing him? He wasn't entirely sure. Kusint's spirits had been rising with each successive dawn as they travelled north.

He looked up from the tankard. 'What now?'

'I go and see if I can get word of any wizard staying in the town.' Kusint finished his ale with every appearance of enjoyment. 'Stay here, and try not to look eager for female company,' he added as he got to his feet.

'What manner of fool do you think I am?' Corrain curbed his annoyance. Slapping the youth would definitely attract unwanted attention.

Kusint shrugged and walked away. Not for the first time, Corrain wondered exactly what stories the youth had heard during their brief stay in Halferan. Well, those gossiping stable hands and scullery maids could choke on their words, when he came back to make good for his follies and misdeeds.

Besides, even if he felt inclined to dalliance, which he didn't, how exactly was he supposed to go dallying when he didn't speak the language? As their walk from the wharves had proved, he couldn't reliably find a tavern in this place, never mind a brothel.

Corrain took another swallow of ale. He had yet to get the measure of Soluran women. Most went openly armed, if only with a long dagger belted over their skirts. A good number wore breeches and boots, not only those crewing the river's boats or those vast rafts of logs. No one seemed inclined to remark on what would have been scandalous attire in Caladhria.

He'd made the mistake of mentioning that to Kusint. The youth had begun reminiscing about the female mercenaries whom he'd met fighting in Lescar's civil war. Such women would hardly favour skirts for battle, he'd pointed out, or when fighting off the unwanted advances that were a common hazard of their lives. As though Corrain had never heard of such a thing. He scowled into the tankard. Of course he had heard plenty of stories from other captains when he'd accompanied Lord Halferan to the quarterly parliaments.

So what did it mean, seeing so many women dressed like that hereabouts? Was life in Solura so perilous? Didn't this mighty river supposedly defend the Kingdom from whatever threats lurked in the Great Forest? What threats might those be?

He had no way of knowing, nor even of asking. So he must sit here and stay out of trouble, nursing this tankard of peculiar ale until Kusint returned. He lifted the tankard again, before setting it down untasted. Finish it and he'd lose his excuse for keeping this table. He didn't even know how to ask for a refill.

As he had put the tankard down, the broken chain dangling from his manacle had scraped noisily across the scarred wood of the table. Corrain slid the manacle as far up his wrist as he could and tucked the chain back up his shirt sleeve. He really didn't want someone coming over, curious for an explanation. At least plenty of the Soluran men wore their hair long.

How long would it be before Kusint returned? If they couldn't find the ally they sought, was there any point in Corrain returning to Halferan? He picked at the splinters around a gouge in the table, determined to resist that dispiriting conclusion.

He was still searching for some alternative strategy when Kusint reappeared at his shoulder.

'Good news.' He dropped onto the stool beside Corrain's own and reached for the tankard. 'You're not drinking that?'

Corrain shook his head, so Kusint drained it.

'Well? Have you found a wizard?'

'Not in the town,' Kusint raised an apologetic hand, 'but three passed through here two days after the Solstice.'

'Where?' Enduring this enforced idleness, Corrain had also calculated the date. According to a civilised almanac, it was already the seventh day of Aft-Summer. Saedrin save them all. So much time was slipping through his fingers.

'I said there were far too few Mountain Men to be seen.' Kusint leaned forward, his grin conspiratorial.

'You said they're either fighting off the Mandarkin or fighting among themselves.' Corrain readily recalled their conversations as the sail barge slid through the dusk, golden reflections of its lanterns slipping away astern.

'There are Mandarkin in the hills across the river.' Kusint brandished the empty tankard to summon another drink from the tapster.

'You're certain?' Corrain demanded. As Kusint had predicted, they'd had no luck asking for news of a wizard at any of their halts upstream.

Kusint's freckled hand gripped his forearm. 'Lord Pastiss sent a detachment of his own mercenaries across the river escorting three wizards from the Order of Fornet.'

'Seven days ago?' Corrain stared at the knots in the tabletop and considered the vastness of the Forest. 'How will we ever find them?'

Kusint looked quizzically at him. 'With a handful of men-at-arms leaving here yesterday to take them fresh supplies I'd say we can follow their trail.'

He might as well have slapped Corrain in the face. Had he betrayed his self-doubt so plainly, for this lad half a generation his junior to humour him?

'Three wizards, you say?' Corrain looked up. 'Then we should be able to persuade one of them to come south.'

One face of a rune always landed right side up. He clung desperately to that hope.

'With your silver tongue and that box of coin? Let's hope so.' Kusint accepted a refill from a serving maid with a jug.

He said something that made her laugh and flipped a silver coin into the air. She caught it and sauntered off with a distinct swing of her hips.

Corrain ignored her. 'Where can we buy horses and gear? Can we get across the river without swimming for it? What can you tell me of these wizards?'

'Equipping ourselves for a hunting trip and buying a ferry crossing will be easy enough.' Kusint sampled the fresh ale and nodded approvingly. 'As to these wizards, they're of the Order's most junior rank—'

'Will they be at liberty to come with us then, if we can persuade them?' Fresh misgiving assailed Corrain.

Kusint nodded, confident. 'Such mages are always looking to prove themselves. I spoke to the ferryman who took them to the far bank. From what he overheard, they're hoping for a chance to show their worth to Lord Pastiss. Then they'll be invited to profess their loyalty to him in person, not merely through their Order. Until then, they can hire out their skills to whoever is willing to pay, as long as what's asked of them doesn't challenge their duty to the Order,' he qualified.

'Will they be as skilled as a mage of Hadrumal?' Corrain recalled Minelas's lethal magic.

He realised he had no idea if the traitor had been a prentice mage, a journeyman or a master. Though he thrust that uncertainty away, he was nevertheless relieved to hear Kusint's next words.

'They wouldn't have been sent across the river if they weren't well able to defend themselves and any men they're riding with,' the Forest youth assured him.

A mere lady wizard like Jilseth had put Baron Karpis and his troopers to flight, Corrain reminded himself.

'We need food.' He reached for his travelling bag and pulled the coin box forward with his heels. 'To eat now and to take with us, and we'll want some means of hunting once we're into the woods as well.'

Now he had the whip hand again, and he'd be astride a decent horse before nightfall, if such a beast was to be had anywhere in this tree-choked country.

It was those endless days sitting on the barge that had unmanned him, Corrain realised. On the galley watching for the ever-present perils of mutiny or murder had kept him alert.

Kusint drank his ale with maddening slowness before counting out copper coins to pay their reckoning. He set the tankard on top of them before standing up. 'Let's go.'

— CHAPTER TWENTY-EIGHT —

Trydek's Hall, Hadrumal
7th of Aft-Summer

'Good day to you, Jilseth.' Hearth Master Kalion entered the Archmage's spacious sitting room, rubbing his hands together. 'Since we have the benefit of your presence, let's see if we can finally find this scoundrel Corrain.' His smile was distant, his thoughts already focused on the magic they would be working. 'If our errant adventurer is already dead, that greatly simplifies matters.'

'Let's hope so, Hearth Master.' Jilseth had been wondering why Kalion had specifically requested her attendance this morning. That was now clear. Galen could no more scry for the dead than any other wizard. Only an earth mage who was also a necromancer had that particular talent.

Canfor didn't say anything as he left the window seat for the chair opposite Kalion's own.

'Nolyen.' Kalion acknowledged the water mage. 'Please, take the lead.'

'Hearth Master.' Nolyen's smile was taut enough to betray his nervousness. This was the first time he had shared a nexus with the Hearth Master himself, never mind directed the magic.

Canfor smirked. Jilseth would have liked to have kicked him under the table but she knew the white-haired mage would only exclaim to call attention to her childish behaviour. She wouldn't give him that satisfaction. More to the point, she wouldn't subject Nolyen to such foolishness.

She offered the erstwhile Caladhrian noble an encouraging smile as she and Kalion took their seats around the table. A shallow silver bowl in the centre was half filled with water.

Nolyen cleared his throat. 'I've been consulting with Mellitha Esterlin of Relshaz. I would like to try her practise of using perfumery oils in scrying. In particular, she suggests that I use some scent tied to the man we're seeking. Since Jilseth recalls tansy on his linen, I've added that to the mix. '

'I commend your initiative.' Kalion leaned forward, keenly interested. 'Let's see what we may learn, of the man himself and of this particular magic.'

These past few days, Jilseth was finding herself more at ease in Kalion's company than she had expected. When the Hearth Master's attention was fixed on his magic, or on anyone else's come to that, he proved mercifully free of his usual pomposity.

'Indeed, Hearth Master.' Some of the tension left Nolyen's neck and shoulders.

Jilseth was amused to see Canfor swallow whatever critical remark he'd had on the tip of his tongue. Doubtless he thoroughly disapproved of Mellitha Esterlin, the independently-minded and independently wealthy magewoman who'd made her life in the trading city for decades now.

Canfor should consider how valuable Mellitha was to Hadrumal, keeping the Archmage informed of every rumour and scrap of news that washed up on the tides or drifted downstream from all the countries of the Old Empire and beyond.

'Jilseth?' Kalion was looking at her.

'I'm ready, Hearth Master.' She hastily gathered her wits as Nolyen uncorked a small vial. He let a few drops fall, not even enough to tint the water if they had been ink. Since this was magic, the clear water turned emerald green. The radiant magelight was bright enough to outdo even the summer sun pouring through the windows.

Canfor rested one long-fingered hand on the rim of the bowl. The magelight shimmered turquoise, the water rippling as if a breeze toyed with it though the air in the room was quite still.

Jilseth reached forward and laid her own hand against the side of the bowl, the silver cool against her palm. The magelight warmed with a golden hue, scenting the air with perfume. She smiled appreciatively at Nolyen. This smell was so much more pleasant than the acrid fumes from the rock oils she was accustomed to using in her necromancy.

She could feel the ensorcelled water through the silver bowl. To an earth wizard, the metal was no barrier. The water itself was so much more than she was used to sensing whenever she worked a scrying alone. Working with others, water magics that usually tested her powers would prove a mere trifle. Arcane spells normally a tantalising finger's width beyond her reach would fall easily into the palm of her hand. This was quintessential magic.

She felt the resonance of elemental air with every breath she drew. It was usually so antagonistic to her own affinity. Working its complex spells required all her concentration. Not now. That magic linked her to the dancing breezes outside these closed windows, to the winds shepherding the clouds above the city and beyond to the sweeping currents of air beyond Hadrumal's shores, all the way to the great vortex of a circling storm far away across the open ocean.

Was this what Canfor felt every day, from first waking moment to last dozing thought? What was he feeling in turn? Was he aware of the stones of the building, of the foundations reaching down through rich soil to the bedrock? Could he feel the rise and fall of the seabed surrounding Hadrumal's island? The crests and troughs where the living rock buckled or split as the cold sea met the banked fires beneath?

She could sense the furnace heat many leagues deeper down. The Hearth Master was holding his hands over the bowl now. The water was swirling round and round, the motion hollowing the middle. The gold of her own magic warmed further to a fiery orange.

It would be the work of mere moments for this nexus to draw the molten ores upwards from deep beneath Hadrumal, sundering the very land the city was built on. As long as they all agreed on it, which of course, they never would.

'Nolyen,' the Hearth Master prompted.

The younger mage slid his outstretched fingers into the water and the swirling magic stilled. Magelight rose like vapour, rainbow hues sliding over and under each other. Nolyen gestured and the magelight formed a ring floating above the silver bowl's rim.

Kalion leaned forward to study the image reflected in this magic mirror. 'Do any of us know this place?'

It was a town of wooden buildings with wide, well-made streets. Jilseth could see that, just as she could see that no one else in this nexus had any more notion where it might be than she did.

'Let's see look for some clues,' Nolyen murmured.

He sent the spell scudding along the road. Jilseth only wished doing this didn't make her feel quite so nauseous. She should be more sympathetic to sea-sick Caladhrian barons.

'It must be Solura.' Canfor's voice sharpened with anticipation. 'That's their script.'

Jilseth saw an inn had some bold proclamation painted on its whitewashed wall. 'This is the furthest anyone's scryed after him so far.' She caught Nolyen's eye and grinned.

'Fine food and clean beds. Horses and carriages for hire.' Kalion looked at the three of them, challenging their surprise. 'Solurans visit Hadrumal from time to time. I have long considered it folly that more of us don't learn their tongue and their script.

'No knowledge is ever wasted,' he went on with something of his usual superiority. 'Nolyen, kindly find me the main market. There will be proclamations posted there with the local lord's seal and insignia.'

Jilseth sat as quietly as Canfor, both focused on maintaining their part in the magic while Nolyen did as the Hearth Master instructed. The water mage soon found a stone pillar nearly invisible beneath layers of broadsheets, the last to be pasted up detailing entertainments for the Solstice feast.

'Pastamar,' Kalion said. 'Nolyen, please show me the course of the river.'

As the town shrank away, the magic soaring like a bird, Jilseth had to close her eyes.

'Nadrua.' Kalion's satisfaction was tempered by perplexity. 'Why is this vagabond swordsman travelling so far from home?'

Jilseth opened her eyes to see the magical reflection searching along the wharves of a riverbank crowded with sail barges and humbler scows.

'Is he there?' Kalion peered into the spell. 'Or has he already moved on?'

That was a refinement of quintessential scrying which Jilseth had come to value. Where the customary spell merely showed where someone or something was to be found, this enhanced magic could trace out their path.

'Is he still alive?' Canfor wondered. 'Jilseth?'

Outside the nexus, she knew, his question would fall somewhere between a taunt and a challenge. Within the magic, he was honestly curious.

She concentrated on Corrain and as she did so, Jilseth found she could pick out the individual note of the tansy oil amid the heady mix of perfumes. She teased it out of the circling magelight. Focusing her own magic through it overlaid the vivid image with a pale golden veil. It was both like and unlike working necromancy. Instead of drawing on some scrap of flesh or bone, now she was seeking such carrion.

Not any carrion. Only Corrain's dead body. Could she do this at such an incalculable distance? No, this was no time for self-doubts.

As Nolyen surrendered control of the spell, she sent it searching this way and that. Jilseth was conscious of Kalion watching her intently. She could feel his elemental affinity reaching through the fire woven into the quintessential scrying. The Hearth Master sought some understanding of the magic she was working.

Canfor's pale eyes were avid. She could sense tension in the elemental air threaded through the spell. His instinct was to take control of the spell, even as wizardly reason must tell him that the magic would be torn asunder if he did. Jilseth recalled her own struggles with this unnatural intimacy of affinity.

She had to find Corrain, if he was there to be found, before Canfor's innate self-importance triumphed over his conscious intellect. But she was only sensing emptiness.

'I'm sorry, Hearth Master. I don't believe he's here, dead or alive.' She swept the golden haze away from the magical reflection of the distant town and felt the tansy oil merge with the perfumed scrying once more.

Canfor opened his mouth, doubtless ready with some cutting criticism.

Kalion spoke first. 'I regret to say I must agree. My compliments, madam mage. The clarity of your magic is such that there can't be any doubt of it.' He looked up, not to Jilseth but to Nolyen. 'Can we follow his trail from here?'

'Let's see.' But after a few tense moments the emerald magelight in the scrying bowl glowed with Nolyen's chagrin. 'I regret not, Hearth Master.'

Canfor opened his mouth. Jilseth was ready to kick him if he sneered at Nolyen. Instead he surprised her.

'Let's try the pendulum, Master Kalion, now that we can start with a specific point on the map.' He gestured at the ensorcelled reflection.

Kalion pursed his fleshly lips. 'We've had no luck with that magic at such a distance.'

'We haven't tried with this particular nexus,' Canfor countered, 'and Archmage Planir is insistent that we find this man.'

The Archmage had agreed, when Jilseth had returned from Kevil and told him what she had learned, and what she suspected after her visit to Halferan. She looked at Canfor and wondered what Planir had told him. Or what Kalion had told him, though of course that depended on what the Archmage had told the Hearth Master.

Kalion considered this and then nodded. 'Very well. Nolyen?'

'Hearth Master.' The water mage deftly disentangled the scrying magic.

Canfor was on his feet, carrying the bowl to a side table before the water stilled. He snapped his fingers, summoning a rolled parchment with a crackle of azure magelight. His other hand already held a faceted diamond pendant on a silken thread.

He'd come prepared, Jilseth noted, intent on winning the prestige of finding the fugitive. She didn't say anything, instead joining Nolyen in fetching small statues from their niches to weight the corners of the stubbornly curling map.

Kalion contemplated Solura's coast, so far away to the west beyond the Gulf of Peorle, the long thrust of Ensaimin into the Southern Sea matched by the Great Forest on the far side of the Bay of Teshal.

'Here.' He pressed a plump finger on the junction of a lesser stream from the mountains and the mighty river separating the kingdom from the forest.

'Let's see where he went after that.' Canfor stretched out his hand, the silk thread held between finger and thumb. The diamond's pointed tip hung over the town's inked symbol. The gem glowed with blue light.

Kalion laid his palm over the back of Canfor's hand and the radiance shifted to lavender before Nolyen's magic darkened the magelight to an ochre hue. Jilseth rested her own hand on top of the water wizard's and saw the enchantment lighten as golden radiance poured down into the stone.

She drew a startled breath. Now her wizardly senses extended for leagues above this tower. She could feel different layers and densities within the air, just as she was accustomed to sense the myriad seams and veins in the rocks beneath her feet. This was disturbingly different to the weighty reassurance of soil and stone. The sky was an ever-changing turmoil of wind and weather assailed by the sun's heat and suffused with water vapour rising from land and sea alike.

The gem began to swing back and forth. Jilseth swallowed baleful resentment at the thought of Canfor succeeding. What mattered was finding Corrain.

The pendant glowed more brightly until the white light was too painful to look at. Jilseth squinted at the map and seriously considered using her free hand to shade her eyes. Before she was forced to reveal such weakness to Canfor, the pendant faded. Now it was merely a diamond in the sunlight, its facets edged with shifting rainbows owing nothing to quintessential magic.

Kalion sighed. 'It was worth a try.'

'Hearth Master?' Nolyen's question saved Jilseth from asking.

'All this tells us is the man was here, as your spell did.' Canfor spoke through clenched teeth. 'We'd see an uneven oscillation if the pendulum was going to lead us towards him.'

Jilseth realised the lingering perfumes in the room had been burned away by the light emanating from the gem stone. She had felt the diamond magic's intensity evaporating before it could pick up their quarry's scent. Something about that felt significant but she couldn't identify what.

'Forgive me, Hearth Master.' Nolyen withdrew his hand, forcing Jilseth to do the same. The water mage wiped sweat from his brow.

'Kindly warn me before you do that again,' Canfor snarled and Jilseth saw an unhealthy blue pallor around his lips.

She was glad to take her own seat unnoticed. Tremors ran through her, from fingertip to fingertip and from head to toe. She was as fatigued as if she'd just run from the bottommost step of this tower to the top without pause for breath.

Kalion was apparently unperturbed by their spell's sudden rupture. He was leaning over the map, peering ever more closely through a lens of ensorcelled air. That was how these wizard maps could be drawn with the finest detail, with a pen nib as fine as a single hair.

'I will bespeak the Soluran mages I know,' the Hearth Master announced. 'They may have travelled in that area recently or some of their own acquaintance might have done so. I'm owed a few favours which should buy us some Soluran scrying.'

'Then this hasn't been all in vain.' Nolyen's drained eyes brightened a little.

Canfor grunted, rising from his chair. 'With your permission, Hearth Master?'

'Of course.' Kalion favoured him an absent smile before returning to the map.

'Please excuse me as well.' At the Hearth Master's nod, Nolyen followed Canfor to the door. 'Some wine?'

Jilseth thought the taller wizard would rebuff him. Then he nodded curtly. 'Why not?'

Jilseth considered following but her legs felt as heavy as lead. She would sit here a little longer.

Kalion was still absorbed in the map. He brushed aside the diamond which Canfor had discarded, the thread mimicking Solura's rivers. The gem was worthless for further magic now, whatever price a jeweller might put on it.

As Jilseth looked at the stone, she felt for her own pocket, hidden within the light twill of her skirt. That lump inside the linen pouch was the ensorcelled lodestone she had used to find Minelas, forgotten among her folding knife, her keys and a mesh purse holding a few coins for a wine shop or the bakery. Why was she carrying the stone? Minelas was long dead.

Why was she thinking of it? Because she was recalling the shining grey stone pulling on the pewter chain. The sensation was reminiscent of the diamond pendulum's swing. But quintessential magic or not, that particular working had to be initiated by an air mage.

Jilseth frowned. There was some insight to be had here, if she could only puzzle it out. 'Excuse me, Hearth Master.' She rose to her feet.

'By all means.' Kalion was removing the statues from the map and rolling the parchment with a noisy rattle.

Jilseth nearly stumbled as she went down the stairs; her knees were unhelpfully inclined to buckle. She concentrated on getting safely out into the quadrangle before returning to her inner deliberations.

Kalion was welcome to try persuading some Soluran mage to scry for Corrain. Even if the Hearth Master's reputation was sufficient to secure such co-operation, none of those distant wizards had even laid eyes on Corrain. The best they could do was scry at random in hopes of seeing a man of his description. If he had the sense to cut his hair and lose that broken manacle, they had no chance of success.

The manacle. How might that feature in the magic she was groping for?

Jilseth hurried back to her own room. She wanted peace and privacy and the tools of her affinity around her. If she could refine this inkling of a spell, she might succeed where Canfor and his pendulum had failed.

If so, that scoundrel Corrain would learn that no amount of distance travelled could take him beyond the reach of Hadrumal's wizardry.

— CHAPTER TWENTY-NINE —

The Great Forest
8th of Aft-Summer (Caladhrian Parliamentary Almanac)
10th of Lekinar (Soluran calendar)

CORRAIN COULD HAVE followed the Soluran contingent's trail himself. Not as quickly as Kusint, he silently acknowledged. Not when the track through the woods branched and the summer soil was too hard and dry to be dinted even by an iron-shod hoof. Corrain knew he wouldn't have been nearly so swift to spot the bent grasses and ruffled leaves which were the only traces to show which route their quarry had taken.

This was nothing like the roads he was used to riding through woodland. Caladhrian undergrowth was cleared for a plough-length on either side, allowing the sun and wind to dry out the ground as soon as any rain ceased. In Ensaimin, so he'd been told, the vegetation was cut back as far as an arrow-shot from the highways for fear of bandits. This track could be mistaken for a game trail, if not for the occasional rut from a wheel's metal rim where shade left the soil softer.

'How far are we from the Great West Road?' Corrain had only the vaguest idea of where that mighty highway arrived in Solura after cutting through the trees from Selerima, most westerly of Ensaimin's great trading cities.

'Fifty leagues north of here,' Kusint said absently. 'Sixty perhaps.'

He had dismounted beside a tree stump hollow with age and rot, marking another divide in their route. The Solurans could have gone either way.

The Forest lad looked around, brows knitting. Corrain felt uneasy. That was more than a squint prompted by the sunshine.

'Did you hear that?' Kusint stiffened. 'I think,' he said warily, 'that we should stop here.'

Without waiting for Corrain's agreement, he perched on the frayed stump. His horse, a sturdy dun cob, nosed at the long grass flourishing around its base.

'Why?' Corrain searched the shadows beneath the trees. What had Kusint seen?

'Because he knows that's it's courteous to wait for an invitation into somebody's home, Caladhrian man.'

Corrain's rough-coated mount stamped, startled. A Forest man had stepped onto the track a stone's throw beyond the stump. Where had he come from, silent as a deer at dawn?

'You understand our tongue?' asked Corrain. The stranger was speaking Tormalin with an accent strongly reminiscent of Ensaimin.

The Forest man smiled. 'I know all manner of speech, from east to west and from north to south.'

Maybe so, but his clothing was wholly unfamiliar. Tight leather leggings were criss-crossed with leather thongs while a sleeveless leather tunic, close-fitting as a second skin, was cropped short at his waist. His pale arms were as mottled with freckles as the track was dappled with leafy shadows.

He wasn't as tall as Kusint and to Corrain's eye, the newcomer's leanness owed as much to hunger as it did to a wiry frame. With autumn's bounty of nuts and fruit half a season away, the woods offered meagre forage in high summer. Kusint had bought plenty of dried fruit and meat and travel bread for their saddle bags back in Solura.

Corrain noted the short bow slung on the man's back and a pigeon's feather caught on the woven quiver strap across his chest. The quiver was made from spotted deer hide. How many folk was the man hunting for, if he went hungry despite such proof of success? How many of those might be lurking in the trees?

'I'm Corrain and he is Kusint. May we know your name, friend?' he asked cautiously.

The Forest man angled his head. Corrain was put in mind of a fox; sharp-eyed and quick-witted. Crafty too.

'You assume that I offer friendship?'

Something in his tone reminded Corrain of the way Kusint had been teasing him of late. 'I can only speak for myself,' he replied. 'I am assuredly no enemy to you and yours.'

The Forest man's gaze darted to Kusint. He was old enough to be the youth's father, Corrain reckoned, his hair faded from burnished copper to something closer to gold, and drawn back in a tightly plaited braid. 'What have you to say for yourself?'

He added something in the Forest tongue which prompted a blush furious enough to obscure Kusint's freckles. He replied hotly in the same language before checking himself and explaining to Corrain.

'He says that I sound like a boar piglet from last year's litters moving through the underbrush, while you make more noise than a sow rising from her wallow.'

Corrain refused to be provoked. Not now that he had this seemingly endless journey's end in sight. Or the halfway point where he could turn for home, once he'd secured a wizardly ally. As long as this Forest man knew where the Solurans were.

'How noisy are the men we're tracking? The men-at-arms from Pastamar?'

Kusint spoke up before the man could answer. 'Have you seen any Mandarkin in these woods?'

Idle birdsong drifted through the treetops. The Forest man visibly made a decision.

'The Solurans whom you seek are half a league or so ahead. Shall I show you where they're making camp? That might be safest, since there are indeed sneaking Mandarkin hereabouts. Your Solurans are hunting them. My name is Deor,' he added, an apparent afterthought.

Something was amusing the man which he wasn't about to share with them. Again, that didn't matter, not for the present. As long as he could take them to the Solurans.

'Please, lead the way.'

Corrain dismounted to lead his horse beside Kusint's, since the Forest youth showed no sign of resuming his saddle.

'What do the Mandarkin want in these woods?' Kusint queried.

Deor led the way along the narrower of the track's forks. 'They've been coming down since the spring, never too many and never staying long.'

'The Mountain Men have done nothing to stop them?'

Deor laughed derisively. 'They're too busy travelling from valley to valley, jingling their coin and wrestling their rivals for the right to court the fairest maidens. Can you explain that to me?'

Kusint smiled wryly. 'You have the Lescari to thank.'

Corrain looked to him for an explanation. 'How so?'

'You know of their marriage customs?' When Corrain shook his head, Kusint explained. 'Mountain Men don't own land as you do in the lowlands. Blood counts for all, for the women that is. They live out their lives in the valleys where they're born and each daughter is granted a share in the wealth above and below the ground; in the forest's furs and timber, in the iron or tin from the mines.'

'The women?' Corrain was astonished.

'They don't work the land or the mines.' Kusint corrected Corrain's misapprehension. 'That's for their husbands and brothers and sons to do, and to travel and trade what they win with their labours while the women stay to tend hearth and home. So when a woman's looking for a husband, she wants a man with a strong back and shoulders to show he's fit to work her land grant, and a heavy purse at his waist to show that he has the wit to make a good profit once he's done so.'

Corrain was still puzzled. 'What have the Lescari to do with this?'

Kusint grinned. 'It wasn't only Solurans who came east with Captain General Evord, to put an end to the Lescari Civil Wars. He recruited score upon score from the Mountains, promising a far quicker route to enough coin to impress a bride.' His smile faded. 'Those who survived to go home won't be wasting any time now that they've seen how short life can be.'

Deor was walking half-turned to take a part in their conversation. 'The Ensaimin sheep men will likely be surprised next year, if they persist in driving their flocks into the hills without leave.'

'Indeed,' Kusint agreed.

That hardly mattered to Corrain. Quarrels in remote northern mountains had no bearing on Caladhrian suffering.

But that wasn't what was amusing their Forest guide. Deor was definitely keeping something from them.

'You don't mind these Mandarkin prowling your woods without asking leave of you?' he challenged the Forest man. 'I hear nothing good of them in Solura.'

'Solura's affairs are Solura's own and we have no quarrel with Mandarkin,' Deor said airily. 'They don't want our woods when Solura's grain lands lie over the river. They'll slink off home before the first snows close the passes. Wolves coming down from the heights in a hard winter are more to be feared.'

'They hardly show the Folk the same forbearance!' Kusint broke into the Forest tongue, vehement in his outrage.

Deor's answer lay somewhere between indifference and a taunt. Corrain laid a firm hand on Kusint's arm. He wasn't about to lose a guide to those Solurans, no matter what was upsetting the youth. 'Let's not—'

Kusint snatched his hand away, scarlet faced. 'The reason I'm merely of the Blood, as he would call it, rather than truly of the Folk, is because my mother's camp was burned when she was a child. Her family were all killed and only Halcarion knows how she survived wandering alone. When she reached the Forest fringe, a family of woodcutters took her in as a fosterling.'

'Halcarion's hand must truly have sheltered her.' Corrain really would rather the two didn't get enmeshed in some quarrel.

Deor was strolling onward. Corrain left Kusint to brood, glowering at their guide's oblivious back. He concentrated on the narrowing path, lest his horse lame itself stumbling over a tree root or stray branches snag his gear. Even these stocky beasts weren't suited to the depths of the forest.

After a long stretch of silent walking, Corrain grew prey to doubts. This Forest man could be leading them astray. Deor would be hard put to rob the two of them single-handed, their two swords against the skinning knife sheathed on his hip. If he were to lead them towards lurking allies—

'Wait.' Deor stopped dead, his attention to the fore.

Corrain looked to the rear, lest any attackers catch them unawares. Then a gust of wind blew shouts and the clash of steel down the track.

Deor reached for an oak tree's branch and swung himself up into the greenery. 'Your Solurans have found the Mandarkin.' Inside a few breaths, he'd disappeared with no more rustling than a squirrel.

Kusint drew his sword. 'Shall we lend a hand?'

'Let's see what's afoot first. Tie up your horse. I don't want to be walking all the way back to the river.'

As he knotted his own reins around a sapling, Corrain peered up into the foliage. Was Deor waiting to come down and steal their food and coin? A Forest man accustomed to travel and trade would know the value of the gold they carried.

The sounds of battle grew louder. Kusint shifted impatiently from foot to foot. 'Come on!'

The dun cob snorted nervously. Corrain scowled. They couldn't risk taking the horses closer. They would have to leave them here, long enough to see what was afoot. If Deor was a thief, they'd just hunt him down. He could hardly get the horses up into a tree.

Corrain drew his own blade and gave Kusint a quelling look. 'We haven't come all this way to lose life or limb in someone else's quarrel.'

'Any foe of the Folk is a foe of mine.' Kusint was already questing ahead, slipping deftly through the trees.

Corrain followed, trusting that the sounds of fighting would cover any noise of their approach. The clash of swords and bellowed insults grew louder though he couldn't yet see who was skirmishing amid these accursed trees.

'There,' Kusint breathed.

Corrain looked along the Forest youth's pointing blade to see an open stretch of deer-cropped turf ahead. A forest lawn, that's what Kusint called such an open space.

Kusint dropped into a crouch. Corrain did the same. Together they edged closer. While the trees grew thinner, the flourishing summer undergrowth offered effective concealment.

Corrain gripped Kusint's shoulder. Kusint turned, his mouth opening with a protest. Corrain shook his head, his forceful fingers silently forbidding the youth to go any further.

After a tense moment, he felt the youth's muscles yield. They both hunkered down behind a tangled bramble.

In the centre of the treeless glade, a handful of men stood back to back in a circle. They were surrounded by twice their number, fending off these foes' determined assaults. All were equally skilled with their swords.

Neither side showed any blazon. Those under attack wore heavy boots and coarse flax-cloth breeches beneath buff leather tunics overlaid with chainmail hauberks. Two wore coifs while helms obscured another two's faces. One fool went bare-headed, a russet cloak swirling around him despite the summer heat.

Their assailants favoured black leather tunics reinforced with metal plates overlapped like fish scale. Every man wore an open-faced helmet.

Kusint tugged at Corrain's sleeve and scratched a circle on a scrape of bare earth with his forefinger. He stabbed at it five times and mouthed a single word. *Soluran.*

Corrain nodded. He was already bracing himself to stand, his spirits rising as he gripped his sword hilt. Their unexpected arrival would tilt the balance of this fight. What better way to put the Solurans under an obligation?

A crack of brilliant light shot across the clearing. Its unnatural violence left Corrain reeling. Cold sweat beaded his forehead, his shirt clammy beneath his armpits. Blood pounded in his ears as he struggled to catch his breath.

Such light on the edge of sight could only be magic. His mind's eye saw Caladhria's marshes, the sedges exploding as Minelas's vile wizardry brought down lightning to kill them all—

'Talagrin's hairy arse!'

Kusint's gasp of astonishment startled Corrain out of that nightmare memory. 'What is it?'

'Watch their swords.' Kusint's mouth hung half-open.

The blinding crack seared the sunlight again. Corrain flinched but this time he saw what happened.

A Mandarkin sword lay in shards on the grass, as shattered as some dish dropped by a careless servant.

The rest still had their blades. They drew closer around the beleaguered Solurans. Corrain saw that they were intent on the man in the cloak.

He must be the wizard. Corrain planted one boot on the ground, ready to rise, to run and attack the closest Mandarkin's unwary back—

'No!' Kusint grabbed his wrist. 'See?'

The Mandarkin who'd lost his sword to the shattering spell stood over his broken weapon, looking down expectantly.

'There!' Kusint stabbed with the point of his sword.

Corrain saw several figures crouched on the far side of the glade. One, short and slightly built stood up and gestured. Blue light flashed across the turf. The Mandarkin swordsman scooped up his blade and ran to rejoin his fellows. Razor sharp steel gleamed in his hand, as whole and as lethal as when it first came from the forge.

The sweat on Corrain's brow froze. He recalled Kusint saying that the Mandarkin had wizards too.

'Halcar—' Kusint's exclamation died on his lips.

Darkness as absolute as a moonless night enveloped those Mandarkin lurking beneath the trees. Azure magelight crackled through the shadow, giving it an eerie solidity. The Mandarkin wizard's spell trying to counter the black shroud?

If that was what it was, the attempt was to no avail. The Mandarkin swordsmen could only run out of the blinding darkness, three of them with their blades levelled lest some foe awaited them.

Corrain watched for the wizard but he didn't emerge. Was he sheltering inside the darkness? There was no way to tell. If the Mandarkin mage couldn't see out, no one else could see in.

His swordsmen met no opposition. On the far side of the glade, the Solurans were hemmed in by their attackers. Those first Mandarkin had redoubled their efforts to cut the men-at-arms to pieces, to reach the Soluran wizard.

The only thing weighing in the Solurans' favour was while their first attackers pressed them so hard, there was no room for new swords to join the fight.

'We have to help.' Despite his grip on the hilt, Corrain's blade shivered.

Their presence wouldn't tip the scales so decisively now. The Solurans were even more badly outnumbered and although they had a mage to back them, so did their Mandarkin foes.

He forced himself to his feet nonetheless. Kusint rose slowly enough to betray his own fears.

The turf rippled clear across the glade. Corrain looked into the cloud of magical shadow. Where was this wizardry coming from? This grass was too short to be stirred by the wind and there was no breath of a breeze.

One of the Mandarkin who'd fled the magical darkness sprawled full length. He planted a hand on the ground to push himself up. As he did so, another fell, as if he'd stepped in a rabbit hole. He landed hard enough to be left winded. A few paces behind, a third tripped and went headlong. The first man yelled, outraged.

Corrain's eyes widened. The grass was growing around the Mandarkin. Already finger length, in the next blink, it was a handspan long. More to the point, the green blades were twining around his wrist like pea fronds.

The man scrabbled at his belt with his free hand. Corrain guessed he was reaching for a knife. Too late. His outspread hand was hidden by knotted stems. Now a swathe of green surged over his waist. There was a repellent cracking sound and the man screamed in agony.

The other two were as securely pinioned. Corrain swallowed abrupt queasiness. The man with the breath knocked out of him lay motionless with a woven veil of grass obscuring his face. Only the third was fighting the clinging greenery. He had managed to sit up, using his sword on the tendrils tangling around his boots.

'Saedrin!'

Kusint and Corrain both recoiled as sapphire radiance burst through the darkness beneath the trees. A ferocious wind carried off black rags of shadow and whole sprays of leaves ripped from the branches.

The Mandarkin mage stepped forth, flanked by two wary swordsmen topping him by a head and more. The Soluran wizard was still ringed by battling men-at-arms.

Corrain could see that the opposing contingents were evenly matched in skills and ferocity. As soon the first Soluran was wounded, the scales would tip decisively.

The Mandarkin mage thrust a bony hand upwards. A thunderclap tore the blue sky. Recollections of Lord Halferan's death assailed Corrain once again. He shivered, anticipating a murderous lance of lightning.

Instead, the ground shivered beneath his feet. Loose earth and little stones rattled against his boots. They surged into the air. As slack-jawed as Kusint, Corrain saw the skinny Mandarkin mage and his escort surrounded by swirling soil threaded with amber magelight.

Corrain recalled a travelling jester providing festival-tide entertainment. The man had flourished a lump of amber as big as a grown man's fist. He'd polished it diligently with a handful of wool and offered it to Lord Halferan. As the baron took it, breadcrumbs had sprung up from the high table's cloth to cling to the clouded gold lump.

Fiery light seared Corrain's eyes. He blinked and realised it hadn't come from the Mandarkin mage.

'No!' Kusint exclaimed with disbelief.

One of the Solurans now brandished a sword outlined with flames. The Soluran wizard slapped a second man-at-arms on the shoulder. The man's blade kindled instantly. As the blazing steel sliced through the metal scales on his opponent's shoulder, the Mandarkin reeled away screaming curses. His sword arm hung limp at his side.

Corrain imagined such a fiery sword biting into Aldabreshin flesh. He gripped his sword. Make haste and he could win Soluran gratitude by stabbing some Mandarkin in the back. Or he could cut the throat of that man slashing at the grass snaring his ankles.

Thunder shook the trees and a knife of lighting slashed open the cloud of earth. The Mandarkin mage sprang forward, leaving his two burly guards lying dead, soil filling their mouths, eyes and ears.

Four of those attacking the Solurans had already fallen victim to the burning blades. The Soluran wizard broke off from kindling his last defender's sword and hurled a handful of fire at his foe.

A single step took the Mandarkin mage three long strides in the blink of an eye. The grass that had sought to trap him was left curling around empty air.

The Mandarkin flung a dart of lightning, his arm swift as a whip. Deadly sorcery pierced a Soluran swordsman's eye. Blue magelight glowed through the links of his chainmail coif before he collapsed with his face blackened, the skin split to show the skull beneath.

The Soluran mage yelled. A voice answered from behind Corrain and Kusint.

Corrain spun around, his sword at the ready. 'What did they—'

His words were cut short, but not of his choosing. He could feel the breath in his throat and knew his mouth and lips were moving but he couldn't hear a thing.

He wasn't the only one silenced. He saw Kusint shouting, exertion swelling the youth's throat. No murmur escaped him. There was no birdsong to be heard, no rustle of the leaves overhead.

The Soluran men-at-arms continued valiantly defending their wizard. The remaining Mandarkin warriors hacked at them with renewed savagery. All in silence. Their antics might have been a masqueraders' dumb show, though bladders of fake blood couldn't hurl scarlet into the air as violently as the stump of a Mandarkin's severed hand.

Kusint seized his arm and pointed. Corrain saw a second cloaked Soluran advancing through the woods, escorted by a handful of implacable men-at-arms.

Corrain raised his hands wide with his sword pointing downwards. He wasn't about to relinquish the weapon so he could only hope that they would accept he was no threat.

A sideways glance showed him the Mandarkin mage flitting around the lawn flinging his lightning bolts at the embattled Solurans. Except their wizard had ringed the men-at-arms with sorcery of his own. The Mandarkin spells bounced off a shimmering shield as insubstantial as the haze rising from a sun-baked road.

The Solurans advancing through the woods ignored Corrain and Kusint completely. They only had eyes for the fight in the glade.

An errant shaft of lightning scored a burning gash in a tree trunk far too close for comfort. Branches all around the lawn were smouldering. His shirt sodden with cold sweat, Corrain's every instinct urged him to drop to the ground or just run. Any sane man would flee ordinary arrows, never mind these enchantments.

He forced himself to stand. There'd be no hope of enlisting Soluran aid if they thought he was a coward.

The newcomers' wizard strode forward, intent on the Mandarkin swordsmen and cradling ochre magelight in his cupped hands.

Corrain saw an attacker fall backwards. The man's arms flailed wildly as he hit the ground. As his head arched back, his screaming face was visible within his helmet. Thankfully the unnatural silence saved Corrain from hearing his sickening agony.

A Soluran stepped forward to drive the point of his sword into the fallen man's gaping mouth. The blade went so far that he must have driven it through the back of the man's neck and into the ground beneath.

Kusint turned away, revolted. Corrain watched more of the Mandarkin fall, writhing in that same inexplicable agony. He saw their legs were twisted grotesquely beneath them, limp and useless.

'Shit!' Kusint clapped his hands over his ears so hard he nearly stunned himself with his own sword hilt.

Corrain had already dropped his weapon, shoulders hunched and hands cupped to defend his own hearing. Crippled and wounded men were screaming. Solurans yelled furious questions. Those few Mandarkin still alive shouted what must be appeals for mercy.

The wizard who'd just arrived bellowed at the mage who'd survived in the heart of the fight. A third cloaked figure appeared on the track leading from the clearing escorted by more men at arms. Her voice added a shriller note to the cacophony.

'Where's the Mandarkin wizard?' Kusint looked wildly around.

'He must have escaped them.' If the Mandarkin mage had fled, that was of little concern to Corrain. Despite the noise making his head ring, despite his gorge rising at the stink of spilled blood and seared flesh, he smiled.

He only had to convince one of these Soluran wizards to bring such lethal magic to Caladhria.

— CHAPTER THIRTY —

Trydek's Hall, Hadrumal
8th of Aft-Summer

NOLYEN CLEARED HIS throat. 'Do you suppose this is why Hadrumal's Council prefers wizards not to wage warfare?'

Tornauld sat, his face cupped in his hands, and stared into the scrying bowl deep in thought.

'Earth magic crippled those men.' Merenel looked across at Jilseth. Like Nolyen, both magewomen had sprung to their feet, as startled as the other two to see such magecrafted violence.

Tornauld looked up, keen-eyed. 'How?'

Despite her revulsion, Jilseth was equally intrigued. 'I don't know,' she was forced to admit, 'but my guess is that second wizard broke the bones in their legs.'

'Those swords were shattered with elemental air, which required impressive concentration by the lad in the midst of that mêlée.' Tornauld's heavy brows knitted as he contemplated the vision floating on the ensorcelled water. 'But the earth mage couldn't see what he wished to break.'

'I don't know how he did it.' Jilseth disliked repeating herself. 'I will give it some thought.'

'I take it that woman works with water, if she roused the grasses to snare them?' Merenel sought Nolyen's confirmation as he resumed his seat. The Caladhrian water wizard nodded.

415

'You noticed that air mage could barely summon more than a handful of fire?' Merenel murmured. 'I'd like to see what a mage with true fire affinity might do in such a situation.'

'Who are these men who attacked them?' As Nolyen laid his hand on the scrying bowl's rim, the water shimmered and the emerald radiance strengthened.

'If you please, master mage.' Tornauld grinned, looking up. 'The spell held true. Let's not overlook that.'

'Indeed.' Jilseth allowed herself a moment of euphoria. This was a splendid new achievement for their nexus.

'We must show Planir.' Merenel said decisively.

'How we worked the spell or what we've scryed through it?' Nolyen frowned.

'Let's watch a little longer.' Tornauld contemplated the aftermath of the carnage in the glade. 'These are Soluran wizards, wouldn't you say? Fighting among themselves?'

Nolyen looked more troubled. 'What do you suppose this man Corrain wants with them?'

Merenel snapped her fingers and a perfect circle of scarlet flame appeared above her hand. Fire mages had no need of candles or mirrors for their bespeaking. 'Archmage? Please join us as soon as possible. We have made some important discoveries.'

Jilseth found her mouth unexpectedly dry. Planir would surely wonder why they hadn't consulted him as they explored her new theory. In his role of Stone Master if not as Archmage.

On the other side of those scales, now she had another wholly new spell to her name fit to be recorded in Hadrumal's libraries. She looked at the scrying bowl. Two more spells, one could argue.

'What is so important?' The Archmage appeared at her side, as silently and unobtrusively as someone stepping through an open door.

Nolyen and Tornauld immediately began talking, gesturing at the bowl, at the map of distant Solura.

'We've devised a means of finding the man Corrain and then tying that spell into a scrying—'

'These are Soluran mages. That greybeard works earth magic while the younger man has an air affinity—'

'The woman seems born to water—'

Planir looked at Jilseth. 'Please explain,' he invited.

She couldn't help clearing her throat. 'I was thinking about pendulum magic, Archmage, after working with the Hearth Master's nexus and trying to find Corrain by dowsing with a diamond. Though such efforts have been unsuccessful, that prompted me think about the lodestone magic which we devised to hunt Minelas. To follow him in particular,' she amplified, 'rather than just finding any magic being wrought, as the former spells could.'

She paused, expecting Planir to comment. The Archmage simply looked at her, silently expectant.

'Corrain wears that manacle around his wrist.' Jilseth pointed at the bowl. 'We found a way to search for him with a modified version of the diamond magic and using a lodestone pendulum focused on that specific piece of iron.'

They would never have been able to do that if she hadn't encountered the man back in Caladhria. As it was, it had taken her a sleepless night to recall the precise resonances of the manacle whose presence she'd barely registered with conscious thought. But her affinity with earth and stone had noted the metal's properties, born of the ore that made it.

Planir inclined his head. To Jilseth's apprehensive eye, that merely indicated his understanding. She had yet to win his approval.

'And this scrying?' The Archmage looked at the bowl.

'Nolyen said something interesting when we were discussing lodestones.' Jilseth smiled at the water mage and hoped he realised that she sought to share credit rather than blame. 'We were talking about the rare earths contained within rocks. Some respond to his innate affinity with water even when he's working with stone magic just as others speak to Merenel's sense for fire.'

She caught Tornauld's scowl. Did he think she would deny him his due? It was unfortunate that his innate magic had played no direct part in these new spells; Air and Earth were too fundamentally opposed. But they could not have worked the nexus without him. The Archmage would know that.

'What did Nolyen say?' Planir prompted.

'He remarked on the oils to be found in black shales. We'd already been experimenting with ground oils and scrying,' Jilseth explained, 'to see if that offered any new prospects of scrying over such a great distance. Not with any success, I'm sorry to say. But then I recalled that red shales can have fragments of lodestone within them.'

Which Planir knew full well. She hoped he didn't think she was trying to school him. Jilseth blushed, talking quickly.

'We found a shale with traces of both oil and lodestone. Once we had successfully used such a pendulum to find Corrain, we drew the oil out of the stone and into the water and managed to scry for him through that.'

It sounded so simple in summary. Planir would surely appreciate the endless deliberation and trial and error it had taken the four of them to achieve this. When they had been putting the first shale pendulum into the water with Merenel's magic warmly resonant within it, the thing had exploded, showering the room with searing splinters. Without Tornauld's quick thinking and quicker magic sweeping up the fragments in a quenching curl of fog, one of them could have lost an eye.

Planir smoothed his beard with lean fingers. 'Ingenious.' His tone fell far short of congratulation. 'So what have you learned of Corrain's purpose on his journey?'

Jilseth exchanged a glance with the others. 'Nothing as yet,' she admitted.

'Those are Soluran mages,' Nolyen ventured.

'Killing Mandarkin.' Planir leaned over the bowl, his sharp features hawk-like. 'Ever their favourite use for magic.'

Jilseth wondered at the faint contempt in his voice. 'They seem to have spells which I don't recall seeing in Hadrumal.'

'How do you know the dead are Mandarkin?' Tornauld demanded.

'I'm the Archmage. I know a great many things which I seldom have reason to share.' Planir looked up from the vision 'I take it the Mandarkin wizard escaped?'

'I confess that surprises me.' Tornauld sat back, folding his arms. 'After the Solurans' proficiency in the fight.'

'Did you assess his affinity?' Planir looked round the table. 'The Mandarkin mage's?'

'No. It never occurred to me.' As Tornauld apologised, the others shook their heads, sharing his chagrin.

Planir clicked his tongue, exasperated. 'We know precious little of Mandarkin magic.'

Jilseth could see the remote figures in the scrying spell

were hurrying to and fro, gesticulating. What were they doing now?

Planir ignored them. 'Soluran magic can be impressive, especially in combat. They certainly use a far greater range of quadrate spells to blend the four elements than we commonly do. But their elder wizards, the ones who rule their different Orders of magecraft, have nothing to teach their students to compare with the breadth of Hadrumal's knowledge.'

He gestured curtly at the scrying. 'They don't enjoy the peace that enables our learning to grow and flower with new understanding. Their focus is always on retaliating against Mandarkin spite, on defending against fresh assaults. They can work powerful spells with individual elements but they have no quintessential magic worth the name. Even their most skilful mages have no real experience of working with others in a nexus.'

He shook his head with regret. 'Soluran magecraft never allows for the unfettered exploration of affinity that's essential for the growth of a wizard's elemental understanding. Worse, each Order jealously guards its own archive instead of sharing discoveries and recording conclusions as we have done in our island's libraries for twenty generations and more. When a Soluran Order is lost, when a tower falls, too often all that hoarded knowledge is lost.'

'By your leave, Archmage,' Merenel observed, 'I don't imagine that's of much concern to Corrain.'

'It's clear enough what he seeks,' Tornauld agreed. 'Since Hadrumal's mages won't help him, he's gone in search of wizards for hire.'

'His Forest-born friend must have told him of Solura's mercenary mages.' Planir was more resigned than concerned. 'All the same, we had better have convincing proof to set before our own Council before we decide how to hobble his ambitions.'

He swept a hand across the bowl and the green-tinted water pulsed with a fleeting turquoise hue.

Tornauld exclaimed, astonished. 'Clairaudience through a scrying, Archmage?'

'Quite so.' Planir smiled as faint sounds rose from the surface of the water. 'Now, hush and let's listen.'

Jilseth watched the surface of the water shiver, casting the distant voices upwards.

How many mages could combine air and water magic like this? If those two elements weren't as antagonistic as air and earth, they didn't share the sympathy enjoyed by fire and air or earth and water. For an earthborn wizard to work such a spell so effortlessly? Jilseth hadn't the first notion how to go about it.

She couldn't imagine there was another mage in Hadrumal whose skills even approached the Archmage's, never mind rivalled Planir's proficiency. Not even amongst those worthy of consideration for the rank of master or mistress of the four elements.

He wore his favourite faded breeches and a loosely laced shirt. It was too hot to wear a jerkin today. Jilseth had always thought he wanted the newly arrived mageborn and lowly apprentice wizards to find him approachable.

Now she was seeing his preference for such humble attire in a new light. She suspected that the Archmage intended to have people underestimate him; most particularly the senior mageborn of Hadrumal as well as the princes and powers of the mainland, from the city states of Ensaimin to the Tormalin Imperial Court. How soon would they learn to regret that?

When Jilseth had gone straight to Planir, to admit her folly in Kevil, to explain how her magic scared the truth out of Lord Tallat at the cost of his humiliation, the Archmage hadn't chastised her.

On the contrary, he had said, in her position he'd have very likely turned Lord Tallat into stone. Such a statue set outside his manor gates would warn every baron in Caladhria not to take Hadrumal's name in vain.

Jilseth didn't think that Planir had been joking.

Tornauld leaned back in his chair, shaking his head. 'I can't make any sense of this.'

'They're concerned with treating their own wounded and reporting back across the river to their Elder and to Lord Pastiss.' Planir listened a little longer. 'Corrain, or rather, his companion's being told to shut up and wait till they're done or to start walking if that doesn't suit him.'

'I suppose that's too much to hope for,' Merenel said ruefully.

'Quite so,' Planir cracked his knuckles. 'Well, I don't suppose the Soluran wizards will keep them waiting long. They'll want to start hunting that Mandarkin mage. But we can make good use of even a brief delay. Nolyen, sustain the scrying and Tornauld, can you keep this clairaudience from failing?'

'I believe so, Archmage.' The burly mage braced himself for that challenge.

'Listen for any agreement between Corrain and the Solurans. They'll have to speak in some language which he can comprehend to do that.' The Archmage smiled briefly. 'Merenel, please convey my compliments to Hearth Master Kalion and ask if he will join us. Galen too, if he's with him.'

As Merenel went to stand outside the sitting room door, to bespeak Kalion through a fresh circle of flame, Planir contemplated the scrying bowl, the whispers rising like steam, incomprehensible.

'Kalion can tell you what our counterparts make of Corrain's request as they talk among themselves.' He looked up, his expression intense. 'Jilseth, teach this new dowsing spell to Galen and make sure that he can work it through a nexus with Ely, Canfor and Merenel, as well as the scrying that follows it.'

'Shouldn't I show you the spell first?' Then there could be no misunderstanding about who exactly had perfected this magic. Jilseth didn't trust Galen, or more likely Ely, not to try stealing some of their nexus's hard-won acclaim.

'No, I see what you've done well enough.' Planir's glance took in the four of them, the table, the bowl and the wizardry within it. 'I need to tell Herion, Rafrid and Sannin what's happening and I had better pay Troanna and Shannet a courtesy visit with the news.' He grimaced before looking at Jilseth once again. 'As soon as Galen grasps the working of this, you must go to Halferan.'

'Archmage?' She wasn't protesting. She needed to understand what he wanted of her.

'We can guess what Corrain's seeking.' He gestured at the scrying. 'We need to know if he's shared these ambitions with Lady Zurenne, with Lord Licanin or any of those other worthy nobles who came to solicit our help in the spring.'

'They didn't even know of the traps being laid for the corsairs.' Jilseth recalled the barons' bemusement in Kevil's marketplace.

'But they had taken Lord Tallat's nods and winks to mean they could expect help from Hadrumal,'

Planir reminded her, 'and his foolish lordship had been encouraged to such boasting by his captain's hints. The barons will have gone straight home to demand explanations from their captains and sergeants-at-arms. We've no idea what Corrain actually promised, to stir the Caladhrian troopers to such boldness.'

Planir shook his head, grim-faced. 'If Corrain is acting alone, thrusting a pole through the spokes of his cartwheels will be a simple affair. If word is spreading among Caladhria's barons that magical aid can be bought beyond the Great Forest, we'll have a very different tangle to bring before the Council of Hadrumal.'

Jilseth nodded slowly. 'But I won't be welcome in Halferan, any more than I was last time.'

Planir's sudden grin lightened the atmosphere of the whole room. 'Oh, Lady Zurenne will be pouring you iced wine and offering honey cakes once you tell her where that thieving steward, Starrid, is hiding.'

'Forgive me, Archmage.' Shock hollowed Jilseth's stomach. 'We haven't found him yet.'

To be accurate, they hadn't even been looking. Absorbed in the fascinations of quintessential magic, Jilseth hadn't given the scoundrel a second thought since her return to Hadrumal.

Planir waved her words away. 'You met the man, didn't you? You can scry for him from Halferan. He won't have gone so far away that you'll need the aid of a nexus; I'll wager good gold on that.

'Feel free to work your magic in Lady Zurenne's presence, or Lord Licanin's, come to that,' he added dryly, 'with as much garish magelight as a first year apprentice. Remind his lordship of the wizardry which he saw in Kevil. The time has come to curb this noble arrogance in Caladhria. We'll start by reminding them they must still deal with Hadrumal's Council, as they always have done, whatever bargain they might hope to broker with Solura's wizards.'

Jilseth swallowed her apprehension. 'I can certainly scry for Starrid from Hadrumal.' As long as some of his possessions were lying unnoticed in some corner. 'It may take some time for Lady Zurenne's troopers to reach him, once I know where he's skulking,' she pointed out. 'Perhaps longer to recover Halferan's coin, and Lady Zurenne will want the gold and silver safely back in her own strongroom before she reveals anything of Corrain's plans.'

'Bespeak me as soon as you find the rogue.' There was an ominous glint in Planir's eye. 'I'll deliver him to Halferan bound and gagged before any trooper's laced his boots. You may hang him by the seat of his breeches from the gatehouse gable to persuade him to spill his secrets.'

'What if he betrays Minelas for a wizard?' Jilseth realised she had no idea whether or not the treacherous steward had known his new master's true nature.

'Let him blab what he likes.' Now Planir smiled without a trace of humour. 'Let Caladhria's barons learn that they have very good cause to fear any mage not subject to Hadrumal's authority.'

'Archmage!' Tornauld was sitting at the table, keeping watch on their spell. 'The Soluran wizards have tended their wounded. They're summoning Corrain and his Forest companion.'

'Listen close, the three of you.' Planir gestured at Nolyen, who immediately leaned over the scrying bowl.

'Hearth Master Kalion's on his way.' Merenel hurried back from the doorway and took her seat.

As Jilseth hesitated, the Archmage ushered her towards the stairs. Halting on the threshold, his expression warmed.

'Before I forget, my congratulations to you all. These spells are a noteworthy achievement and promise new insights into our understanding of elemental essence and interaction. Be ready to demonstrate your working to the Council, as soon as we've dealt with this nuisance and can apply ourselves to the proper business of wizardry.'

'Naturally, Archmage.'

'We'll be honoured.'

Jilseth let Merenel and Nolyen speak for her. She had heard the door opening at the bottom of the tower's steps. Kalion's voice and Galen's floated up the stairwell, drowning out the murmurs from the scrying spell.

She had already found this a demanding day, even if success had gone a long way to assuage her weariness after working such intense magic. Now she had to do it all over again with the additional burden of showing Galen the innermost workings of her new spells.

Even if she had the magic to carry herself to Halferan today, Lady Zurenne would have to wait for tomorrow morning before Jilseth could find Starrid for her.

'Kalion, quietly, I beg you!' Planir's bellow reverberated down the stairs.

The Soluran mages' distant voices drifted through the spell behind them, challenging Corrain to explain himself.

— CHAPTER THIRTY-ONE —

CORRAIN WAS BREATHING as hard as a man fresh from battle. The sweat beading his forehead owed nothing to the warm day. Even offering these Solurans the briefest summary of Aldabreshin atrocities enraged him. The words had poured from him so fast that he could barely catch his breath.

He forced himself to stop, to allow for some response from the grey bearded mage who'd appeared behind them in the woods. The younger man who'd first been attacked in the clearing had come to summon them to explain themselves, now that the Soluran dead and injured were tended.

'We have no wizards willing to help us.' Corrain curbed an impulse to curse Archmage Planir to any god who might be listening. 'So we offer handsome rewards to any of Solura's mages brave—' he hastily checked himself. 'Any willing to use their skills to defend our innocent women and children against these shoeless barbarians.'

He forced a desperate smile, lest that stupid slip of the tongue had inadvertently insulted the Soluran wizards. They didn't look overly impressed; certainly not this older man with the lines of age and experience creasing his amiable face, sandy hair thinning to invisibility at his crown.

The younger mage was as yet largely untested, judging by his fresh complexion. Corrain would have called him little more than a boy. All the same, he had faced that Mandarkin onslaught without flinching, Corrain reminded himself, and wielded deadly magic without hesitation.

He couldn't guess at the woman wizard's age, not until she came closer. She was short in stature, solid in build, crop headed with her face scarred by childhood illness. Dressed like the men-at-arms in boots and breeches, a drab jerkin and cloak, she stood aloof from this conversation, scowling at the two Mandarkin captives.

One was the only survivor of the slaughter wrought by the burning blades. There could be no question that the younger man had kindled that spell and Corrain guessed that the older wizard had sought to stifle the Mandarkin mage. That enchanted wind sweeping up the soil had come from the same direction as he had.

The other prisoner was the one whose feet had been tangled in the ensorcelled grass. Corrain wondered who'd woven that spell. The woman? What else could she do? What else had she done? He had no clear idea which wizard might have worked those other magics to blind and silence the Mandarkin mage.

He looked at the two surviving henchmen. Like their dead comrades, both had been stripped naked. Kneeling on the grass, they cowered in abject terror if a Soluran swordsman so much as glanced in their direction.

The Soluran men-at-arms were busy dividing up anything of value found among the Mandarkin's possessions. Whatever they didn't want was casually slung into the fire kindled by the greybeard's magic.

They'd wasted no time heating water to wash the scrapes and gashes suffered by the two men-at-arms who'd survived the fight in the glade. Several of the grey-bearded mage's swordsmen had offered pungent salves to their comrades and herbs carefully tied in muslin were steeping in the hot water.

Corrain approved. Even if they weren't serious enough to be considered wounds, such injuries could fester nevertheless and cost a man a finger or a hand.

No one was offering succour to either Mandarkin captive, even though both men's oozing wounds were already attracting flies. The one who'd tried to cut his feet free had slashed right through his boots to the ankle bone beneath.

The woman wizard said something sardonic. Corrain looked at Kusint. 'Can you speak for me if they don't understand?'

'We understand you, man of the coast.' The greybeard's Tormalin was impeccable, his expression reserved. 'I have made several journeys to Col.'

'We have all mastered your Old Empire's tongue.' The younger man looked down his long nose at Corrain. 'For the purposes of scholarship.'

Maybe so, but the woman wizard spoke in scathing Soluran. She was examining some papers taken from one of the dead Mandarkin's gear.

'There are assuredly wizards in Col,' the greybeard observed, 'just as there are in Hadrumal. Why do you not seek help closer to home?'

'Have you ever visited Hadrumal?' Corrain asked, as casually as he could.

'No.' The greybeard was unconcerned. 'Our Order has ties to Col's university, so I travelled there to study in my youth.'

Corrain breathed a little more easily. 'Then you'll know Col for a peaceable city.' There would be the usual street brawls and guild skirmishes but the patchwork realm of Ensaimin hadn't seen marching armies in ten generations. 'Mages there have never been tested in warfare. We seek wizards with proven proficiency in battle to defeat these barbarians once and for all.'

He smiled, trying to mask the tension tight across his shoulders. Kusint had insisted that Soluran wizards weren't bound by the Archmage's edict. This conversation could become markedly more complicated if they knew of its existence.

The greybeard merely nodded, considering this. 'I see your reasoning.'

The younger mage looked askance at Corrain before addressing the older man. 'Orul? Why should we turn our backs on Mandarkin malice for people we do not even know?'

Did the elder mage outrank the younger man? Corrain had no idea. He could see the greybeard, Orul, had no answer for the younger wizard. He quickly offered one himself. If honour was no incentive, there was always coin. In the end, most things came down to coin.

'The gold and silver we offer could buy a great many books and scrolls from Col's printers and copy-houses, or pay for board and lodging to enable a long visit to their libraries, or to Vanam,' he added, recalling Ensaimin's other great centre of learning.

The woman wizard swiftly rebuked the fresh-faced wizard as she threw the Mandarkin captives' papers into the fire. Her spit of disgust followed them into the flames. Was that some comment on what she'd been reading or on his proposal?

Either way, Corrain chose not to let it pass. Even if she wouldn't talk to them, she'd clearly understood his words.

'Forgive me, my lady wizard. Have I offended you?'

She made him wait while she folded a vellum map back into precise folds.

'You could have lost us Espilan.' Her gesture indicated the younger mage. 'You assuredly cost us our prey.' Her speech was more formal, more old-fashioned than Orul's.

'This looks like a good haul to me.' Stung, Corrain nodded across the clearing. The Mandarkin dead lay where they'd been discarded. Six of the Solurans were digging what he presumed was a pit for their corpses. The fallen Solurans had both been decently shrouded and laid beneath a shady tree.

'These vermin?' The woman wizard glared. 'They know nothing. We wanted their master. Why else do you suppose Espilan was strolling in the sunshine like a cock bird flaunting his feathers? To lure him in! If you two skulking in the bushes had not delayed Orul, we would have caught him too.' She looked at the greybeard. 'You should have told your men to shoot them and been done with any doubt.'

'Selista!' The older wizard snapped angrily in Soluran. The language sounded ideally suited to argument, all harsh sounds and curt words.

Corrain sorely wanted to know what they were saying, but this was hardly an opportune time to ask Kusint.

Orul, the greybeard, broke off as loud rustling stirred the undergrowth. Every Soluran man-at-arms was instantly on his feet, bow or blade ready. Corrain turned, his hand on his sword hilt.

A cheery shout sailed through the greenery. Was that the Forest tongue? Kusint muttered an oath under his breath. 'It's Deor.'

Corrain saw that the Forest man was leading both their horses. Very well. They would deal with him in due course.

'What were the wizards saying?' he quickly asked Kusint while the Solurans were greeting the Forest man and asking him questions of their own. The woman wizard was unfolding that map to show something to Deor.

'The woman insists they cannot shirk their duties,' Kusint explained. 'She says they must pursue the Mandarkin mage at once, while he's weary with no swordsmen to back him.'

He nodded at Orul. 'He says they've time in hand for that and the two of them can manage one Mandarkin between them. The lad deserves a chance to travel and to study. I don't think their Order of Fornet has much coin for such things,' he added quietly.

Deor and the woman wizard, Selista, were approaching. The Forest man hummed a cheery tune under his breath.

A sneer curled Selista's lip. 'I have also travelled to Col. I know that southern mages revere their Archmage. Will he approve of our wizardry coming to Caladhria?'

'Naturally.' Corrain feigned all the confidence he could muster. 'He knows the Aldabreshin for the vermin they are.'

Deor said something to Selista and Kusint choked on an exclamation.

Selista looked at Corrain. 'You lie, man of the coast.' She spoke with absolute conviction.

'What—' Corrain knew he must look like he'd been slapped in the face. He scrambled to recover lost ground. 'No. The edict—'

'Some coast lord's decree means nothing.' Selista cut him off with a gesture. 'Deor says you lie. That's an end to it.'

'How can he say such a thing?' Corrain's outrage was barely blunted by the truth of the accusation. The Forest man's smirk infuriated him.

Deor addressed himself to Kusint, his words swift and fluid. Corrain was unnerved to see the Forest youth turn pale as milk, his freckles a vivid rash. Before he could speak, Deor explained.

'You know little of the Mountain Men, Caladhrian traveller, as you proved earlier. You do not know that they have magic of their own? Not wizardry.' He acknowledged Selista's skills with a self-effacing smile. 'This is a different art, drawing on the aether that links all living things.'

His tone hardened. 'The *sheltya* of the uplands share such enchantments with us in the Forest. My skills are humble indeed compared to theirs but I can hear untruth in a man's word, as plain as a cracked note from a flute.'

'Artifice, I believe you call it,' Selista added.

Corrain swallowed. Artifice. Aetheric magic. That's what Kusint had called it, when he'd explained how the Lescari rebels had outwitted their dukes.

Incredible though it sounded, Kusint had sworn those adept with this Artifice could send messages quick as thought to each other. The handful of Lescari exile rebels who'd studied the ancient aetheric lore at Vanam's university had travelled with different contingents of Captain General Evord's army and his allies inside Lescar. The dukes, their militias and mercenaries had been limited to communications relying on the speed of a flying dove or a galloping horse, so the rebels had secured a vital advantage.

Kusint had also said that this aetheric magic offered countless other enchantments. He'd mentioned these *sheltya,* who seemed to be something between priests and lawgivers among the Mountain Men, rumoured to have awesome powers enabling them to see right inside a malefactor's head. This was a cursed inconvenient time to discover that was so. Corrain could see the truth of it in Deor's smirk. He could even believe in some malign god's intervention. Had he insulted Talagrin so thoroughly?

'Be grateful that Deor heard the truth when you said you were no enemy to the Folk,' Selista continued, merciless. 'Else he'd have cut your throats with a bowstring before the next falsehood fell from your lips.'

'I considered doing that regardless.' Deor shrugged. 'But I was curious to hear Caladhrian spoken in these woods and to see that you were accompanied by a man of the Blood. Keep wandering,' he advised Kusint with ominous finality. 'These trees cannot shelter those who have other kin to call on, not this year.'

'You have your horses.' Selista jerked her head towards their steeds idly grazing on some grass beneath the trees. 'Be on your way, before we grow impatient with this delay.'

'Head west and you cannot miss the river,' Deor added.

'What rights can you claim over these woods?' Corrain demanded before rounding on Selista with a sneer to rival her own. 'What rights have you to say where we may travel?' He wasn't about to scurry off like some whipped stable boy. 'This isn't Solura.'

'No.' The wizard woman looked back at him, hard-eyed. 'So I need not answer to Lord Pastiss or to any Elder Mage of Fornet if I drown you where you stand.'

'Enough!'

Orul had come up, unnoticed. He cut a hand down between Corrain and Selista. If the gesture meant nothing to the Caladhrian, it did to the magewoman. She coloured and stepped back, muttering something mutinous under her breath.

Corrain held his ground as she stalked off, Deor at her side.

'Come.' Orul cupped Corrain's elbow with a firm hand and urged him towards their horses.

This time he didn't resist. But he wasn't about to give up. 'Forgive me, but the Archmage's edict doesn't bind Soluran mages.'

'What?' Orul paused, puzzled.

'Hadrumal's Archmage cannot forbid Soluran magic in Caladhria.' Corrain heard the desperation in his voice. He didn't care.

'I do not know what you mean. Hadrumal's customs are no concern of ours.'

It didn't take any Artifice to see that the greybeard was telling the truth.

'Mandarkin is our enemy and we must catch that wizard before he recovers his magic, if we can take him alive.' Orul looked at the Mandarkin corpses with regret.

'These men and others are making caches of food throughout the forest,' he explained earnestly. 'We fear they are preparing the way for an army to cross the mountains in the autumn, to attack us from the shelter of the forest throughout the winter.'

He stooped to scrape a few lines on the parched turf. 'Pastamar lies between the Mare's Tail and the Great River of the East. Our guess is that Mandarkin's tyrants seek to drive us out with fire and sword when the season is too harsh to sustain life without shelter and stores. Force enough Solurans back across to the westernmost bank in Usta and Wardor—'

He broke off to look at the Mandarkin captives. 'As well as pursuing that fugitive wizard, we must take those two to Deor's kinsman, whose greater Artifice can wrest the truth from them, whether or not they can be forced to speak willingly. The fallen cannot tell us what we need to know of their tyrant's plans.'

Corrain seized on that. 'There are mages in Hadrumal who can give the dead back their voices.'

That was no lie. The Archmage himself had said so and if Planir had been lying, Corrain was repeating what he'd heard in good faith. If Deor's ears were flapping to catch any falsehood, let him see if his Artifice could untangle that.

For the blink of an eye, Corrain thought that Orul was tempted. Then the Soluran mage shook his head. 'Hadrumal is too far away for any of us to reach with our skills and besides we would need the sanction of our Elders to seek such help. We cannot spend the time on such things. We must track down that Mandarkin before he can rest and recover his magic.'

Corrain's heart sank to his boots. A blind man could see that it was pointless to persist. They walked on to the horses in silence.

'Farewell. May we meet someday in better circumstances.' Orul's regret sounded genuine, though Corrain saw he had no real expectation of ever seeing them again.

He offered his hand with a heavy sigh. 'Good hunting.'

'Blessings on your kith and kin.' Orul was clearly troubled. 'I hope you find the aid you seek against these despoilers.'

If he thought the Caladhrians needed all the help they could get, why didn't he offer it? As the mage walked away, calling out to his swordsmen, Corrain began checking his horse's gear. He tugged every buckle and strap with barely restrained fury.

'Did that—' Did Deor's underhand Artifice mean he'd hear any insults tossed his way? 'Is anything gone from your saddlebags?' Corrain asked Kusint instead.

'Some food.' The Forest youth nodded towards Deor who was now examining the vellum which Selista had given him. 'That map will show him where to find the Mandarkin stores hidden in the forest.'

'Rewarding her ally and leaving her enemy hungry.' Corrain couldn't fault the bitch's tactics.

He watched her directing one of her swordsmen to bind the naked Mandarkin captives' hands behind their backs. Another man slipped a noose around each one's head, tugging on the end of the rope to tighten the knot just short of choking them.

'We have our coin.' Kusint gave a saddlebag a resolute slap. Metal chinked. 'And now we know for certain that the Archmage's edict is no hindrance. If we head back to the river we can pick up a road heading north for Resdonar.'

Corrain slid his stirrups down their leathers to hang against his horse's rough-haired side. He recalled that map which Orul had scratched on the turf. Resdonar was the province to the north of Pastamar. 'Any wizard there will be out hunting down Mandarkin just like these three.'

'Then we can take a ferry back across the Great River,' Kusint insisted. 'There will be wizardly orders in Wardor and Usta, far less hard-pressed.'

'How long will that take?' Corrain broke off as the Soluran men-at-arms gathered around the pit which they'd dug.

To his surprise and no little revulsion, he saw it wasn't intended for the Mandarkin dead, to keep their shades lingering in torment, prey to Poldrion's demons through the slow dissolution of their corpses by rot and worm.

They were laying their own shrouded comrades in the ground with the care of a mother laying her babe in a cradle. A single man wielded a short shovel, the dry soil pattering on the cloth like rain, while the others ringed the pit, heads bowed. Another swordsman stepped forward to chant with low-voiced fervour. Once again, Corrain wondered what gods the Solurans worshipped.

Such questions could wait. He turned to Kusint. 'We could be half a season on the road before we find a mage willing to set aside his own concerns for our gold. We don't have that time to waste. I thought we'd already be home by now.'

What had been happening back in Caladhria while he was away? Was this journey going to prove an utter fool's errand? These nagging fears sprang to the forefront of his mind as soon as he first stirred in the morning and kept him awake at night, long after he'd heard Kusint slip into sleep.

The only way to drive away such doubts was to look to their objective. Returning with magic to drive off the corsairs was the only way he could ever go home with his head held high. So he must find a wizard, and quickly.

'Then what do you propose?' Kusint demanded, needled.

'Hear me out.' Corrain laid a hand on the Forest youth's arm. 'We know there's another mage in these woods. We've seen his wizardry for ourselves. He's surely powerful enough to hole a corsair ship at the waterline. To kill the steersman and the whip master. But for the present, that mage has no one left to defend him. He'll have exhausted his wizardly strength. You heard what they said and I didn't see any sign of him using magic to flee. You'll be able to track him.'

Kusint stared at Corrain, wide-eyed. Finally he spoke, his voice thick with revulsion. 'The Mandarkin?'

'Listen.' Corrain gripped the youth's forearm more tightly. 'If we take him away from Solura, that's a favour we're doing them, aye and the Forest Folk. His magic won't be used against them in this war—'

Kusint wrenched his hand away. 'Would you pay an Aldabreshin corsair to drive off the slavers who raid Caladhria?' He ripped up his sleeve, baring his shackle galls and the scars of the burns he'd suffered in their escape. 'The villains who left you marked like this?'

'Yes.' Corrain spoke without hesitation. 'As long as I was convinced he could be bought and would stay bought. Now, as soon as they've moved off we can quarter this clearing for some hint as to which way the Mandarkin fled.'

He stole a glance at the Solurans. The men-at-arms were settling their weapons and armour comfortably for the march while the wizards stood with Deor. He now had hold of both rope halters, so they were doubtless discussing what to do with the captives.

'We can outstrip them on horseback if we can find the mage before they do.' Corrain gathered up his horse's reins. This beast was sturdy enough to bear a double load, for long enough to get them beyond Soluran bowshot anyway.

Could they outrun magic? That was an entirely different question. Perhaps they should hold off, if they couldn't find the Mandarkin without the Solurans knowing they had stolen their prey.

Could they rescue the man once those three mages had captured him? No. The Solurans would surely whisk him away, just as Planir and that lady wizard Jilseth had used their magic to vanish from Halferan.

They would take their captive to wherever Deor's kinsman with his eerie Artifice would be waiting to wrest the truth from the fugitive wizard. Would the Solurans test whatever words could be wrung from him with whips and hot irons? Corrain could offer the Mandarkin a far more pleasant future.

He turned back to Kusint. 'You said you wanted to help Halferan, to repay the barony for all the people's kindnesses. Have you forgotten that?'

'I have mistaken your measure entirely,' Kusint's green eyes were shadowed with disillusion, 'if you would make common cause with a Mandarkin murderer.'

'I seek magic to save Caladhrian lives,' Corrain retorted. 'You call that man a murderer? When those other mages choked those men to death with a cloud of soil and broke the very bones inside their legs? Let them answer to Saedrin, each man in turn. I won't pass judgement. Solura has no interest in our troubles so I have no interest in their quarrels.'

'Mandarkin raiders burned my mother's camp.' Kusint could barely contain his fury. 'That's how she was orphaned.'

'Haven't you travelled with me to save Caladhrian children from the same fate, at the hands of the corsairs?' Corrain challenged him.

'I will never agree to this!' Kusint's voice rose to an angry shout.

'Hush!' Alarmed, Corrain turned to see if the Solurans were paying heed to this quarrel. Instead he discovered that the two of them were entirely alone in the glade.

The mages and their men-at-arms had vanished into the woods, leaving only Mandarkin corpses littering the grassy lawn.

A few crows had already appeared. Corrain watched one hop forward to stab at a dead man's glazed eye with its vicious beak. How many Caladhrians had fallen while he was on this hunt? How many more would be abandoned to carrion eaters if the corsairs weren't stopped?

'I will not spend another season searching for some wizard who may not even be willing to leave his fireside,' he snarled at Kusint, 'when I can offer that mage those Solurans are hunting shelter from his enemies and coin besides, a thousand leagues beyond their reach.'

'Then you'll do it on your own.' Kusint sprang into his saddle and spurred his horse, heading westward towards the river.

Corrain was left standing there, wholly dumbfounded. His horse dropped its head to graze a little longer.

— CHAPTER THIRTY-TWO —

Halferan, Caladhria
9th of Aft-Summer

Jilseth watched Zurenne's maidservant set the broad washstand bowl on the withdrawing room's table. The girl had been swift to fetch it and the matching ewer from a bedchamber down the hall. She'd even brought a towel.

She wasn't bred to such service, if Jilseth was any judge, but she was quick-eyed, quick-witted and devoted to her new mistress.

The girl wasn't alone in that. Jilseth watched the manor's people going about their business, as she spent the afternoon kicking her heels on the bench beside the gatehouse. Zurenne had taken an unconscionable time to admit the magewoman to her presence.

The manor was far busier than Jilseth remembered it. Listening to passing conversations she had learned that most of those living in the barony's coastal villages had moved as far inland as they could. They were paying for their bed and board with friends and relatives with whatever food, goods and coin they'd brought with them, more than content to deny the corsairs such pickings.

Any distress at such upheaval seemed more than counterbalanced by the good cheer prompted by any mention of burning corsair galleys. Jilseth had heard such conversations time and again throughout the afternoon.

She also saw that even without the coin to buy them their festival feasting, the demesne folk looked to Lady Zurenne with loyalty and gratitude. She was far from the friendless widow whom Jilseth had first met in the spring.

That said, Lady Zurenne was still penniless. As Planir had foreseen, Hadrumal yielding to her demands and Jilseth offering to restore Halferan's fortunes was more than Zurenne could resist.

Jilseth only hoped that Starrid, or more likely Minelas before him, hadn't squandered the last of the barony's coin on liquor, whores and gambling.

'We need something that belonged to Starrid.' Jilseth wasn't going to attempt this scrying without something to anchor the spell.

Teaching the new searching and scrying spells to Galen and the nexus which Planir had appointed had taken until long after midnight. Time and again the magic had unravelled when Canfor sought to thread air through the three other blended elements. Jilseth had struggled to see how the white-haired wizard was going awry. Air was so antagonistic to her own elemental affinity with earth even when she wasn't tired. Arrogant as ever, admitting no lack in his own understanding, Canfor had been openly contemptuous of her deficiencies while visibly resenting her success in devising the wizardry in the first place.

Despite sleeping until noon in Hadrumal, Jilseth had needed to bathe and to breakfast before she was sufficiently rested to both translocate to Halferan and to make good on the promises which Planir's letter offered Lady Zurenne, guaranteed by his seal and signature.

Zurenne might have thought she was teaching the magewoman a lesson in humility, keeping her waiting like that. Jilseth had been glad of the respite, sitting on the bench in the shade, enjoying the summer afternoon.

'Raselle?' Zurenne looked to her maid. 'Go and see what Mistress Rauffe can find.'

The new steward's wife, Jilseth recalled. She poured water and set the ewer down on the table. Taking a seat she cupped the white bowl between her hands and looked into it.

What was Corrain doing today? They had learned nothing useful from finally finding his solitary lair in a leaf strewn hollow the night before. Even with the Greater Moon at full and the Lesser at half, barely enough light pierced the dense summer leaves to show them his drowsing, hobbled horse. Wielding magic powerful enough to see over a thousand leagues and the mighty wizards of Hadrumal were as dependent as some benighted peasant on the grudging illumination of the heavens.

They could see that Corrain was heading east. Galen had confidently stated that the Caladhrian must be coming home by land rather than sea. They had all seen the Soluran wizards rebuff him, although to Tornauld's severe embarrassment, the clairaudience spell which Planir had spun had unwound just as the Soluran magewoman confronted Corrain. Nevertheless, if they couldn't hear what caused that falling out between Corrain and his Forest companion, they saw that the Caladhrian was left without a guide. No wonder he wasn't retracing his steps to Solura. What could he hope to achieve there now?

Jilseth stirred the water with a thoughtful touch of mossy magic. She wasn't convinced that Corrain would give up so easily, if he'd gone all the way to Solura in his search for magical aid. She would have liked to know if Planir agreed. She would trust the Archmage's judgement over Galen's from solstice to equinox and back again, but he had been locked in private conversation with Kalion, Rafrid and Flood Mistress Troanna since first light.

Meanwhile, he had sent her here to learn everything she could of Corrain's plans. What might the volatile swordsman try next? Why would he head for Ensaimin? True, there were a great many wizards scattered among those independent fiefdoms and city-states. Lord Halferan had found one mage prepared to abandon his allegiance to the Archmage and Hadrumal. Had Corrain heard rumour of another such renegade? Would Lady Zurenne know?

'Can you find Corrain?'

Jilseth was so taken aback that she stared at the noblewoman. It was as if her own thoughts had prompted the question.

'Once you've found Starrid,' Zurenne added quickly. 'You must find him first and recover my daughters' inheritance. You must force him to hand back Halferan's coin, to the very last cut-piece.' The noblewoman peered into the water-filled bowl although there was nothing to be seen.

'Indeed.' Jilseth wondered at such vehemence, at odds with that earlier delay.

Had Zurenne been truly in two minds about accepting wizardly help or had that merely been a ploy, to show Jilseth and, through her, Planir, who was truly mistress here?

Of course, Zurenne wasn't Halfcran's mistress and they both knew it. Jilseth wondered where Lord Licanin was on the road journeying south from Ferl. He would be slowed by the entourage and baggage he had needed for the festival, to display his barony's peace and prosperity to his fellow lords. But he would send swift riders on ahead, carrying his letters in all directions.

Jilseth had seen such a horseman arrive not half a chime before she'd been finally been summoned from the bench beside the gatehouse. She could see a substantial pile of letters on a side table here in Lady Zurenne's sanctuary. It seemed several had been screwed up in a rage only to be salvaged from the log basket. The costly paper had resisted attempts to smooth out those creases.

'When I have found Starrid for you, I expect you to tell me what's going on here.' Jilseth pointed at the heap of correspondence. 'I want to know whatever you know of Corrain's alliances with the other coastal baronies' captains, of these attacks on the corsairs which their lords know nothing about.'

Zurenne shrugged. 'What little I know.'

'What of Corrain's journey to Solura?'

The noblewoman looked Jilseth in the eye, unblinking. 'I've no idea where he is or what he might be doing.'

Which was doubtless true, albeit very far from the whole truth. Jilseth would wager good coin on that.

She contemplated the water in the white basin and considered how she might shake the full story from Zurenne. Well, she could start with the gaudy magecraft that Planir had suggested, much as she disliked such theatrics, worthy of some apprentice too ill-disciplined or ineffectual to keep pace with more diligent pupils, turning instead to a life of playing the charlatan at the mainland's festival fairs.

'Shall I ring for a tisane tray?' Zurenne suggested.

'No, thank you.' Jilseth was content to sit and wait and see if silence provoked Zurenne into saying something unintentionally revealing. The tactic worked for Planir often enough.

Not this time. Not before quick feet sounded on the stairs from the great hall. Raselle returned, pink-faced.

'Forgive me, my lady.' She bobbed a second nervous curtsey at Jilseth. 'My lady wizard. Mistress Rauffe says that the men from the guard hall helped themselves to whatever Starrid left after they whipped him from the gate. When she cleared out the house, she slung the rest of his rubbish onto the midden beyond the walls.'

Zurenne turned back to Jilseth. 'Can you still work the spell?'

She had paled. There was more at stake here than she was admitting, that made it all the more important that Jilseth's spell didn't fail. Swift success would definitely put Zurenne in Jilseth's debt.

'If there's nothing of use where he lived, where did he work? Starrid must have kept your husband's ledgers and managed his correspondence.'

'Downstairs.' Zurenne was on her feet. 'In the muniment room.'

'Lord Licanin has the keys.' Raselle looked stricken.

'Not all of them.' Zurenne didn't reach for the household keys hanging from her chain girdle. Instead she slid a hand through the seam of her skirts into a hidden pocket. 'I'll go. Stay here.'

Jilseth smiled at Raselle. The girl bobbed another uncertain curtsey and busied herself with lighting the oil lamp, though it was hardly needed. The long summer evening was far from dusky.

Nevertheless Raselle trimmed the wick, fetched the spark maker and pressed the handles together, once, twice, a third time. Jilseth found the sound of toothed steel rasping on flint so grating that she almost snapped her fingers to light the lamp with a fiery cantrip. Then Raselle caught a spark with the woven tow.

'Where is my lady mother?' Ilysh's appearance in the doorway startled them both. They hadn't heard a whisper of her soft slippers on the hallway's polished floorboards.

When she'd finally been summoned, Jilseth had seen the girl at her lessons beside her sister at the long table on the great hall's dais. Their older maidservant had seemed more interested in her knitting than in their copybooks.

Now she saw Ilysh's gaze taking in the heap of letters, the bowl on the table and most particularly Jilseth's own presence. There was something deep in the girl's eyes. Defiance and some secret satisfaction, just like her mother.

Before Jilseth could think how she might tempt the girl into sharing confidences, they heard Zurenne returning. Ilysh vanished back down the hall. Jilseth heard a bedchamber door close a moment later.

Zurenne evidently suspected nothing as she returned to the withdrawing-room with assorted writing implements and accoutrements. She dumped them on the table, heedless of inky flakes soiling the embroidered linen.

Jilseth spoke before the maid could betray Ilysh's appearance. 'That pen-knife if you please.'

Zurenne picked up the hollow brass handle. 'Should I fix one of the blades?' Those would be stored within for shaping and trimming quills, to be poked through the screw cap and secured as it was tightened.

'That won't be necessary.' Jilseth dropped it into the water and faint threads of ink dissolved in an emerald flash.

She let the magelight brighten until green radiance coloured the whole ceiling with an unearthly hue. Emerald reflections flickered in Zurenne's eyes, though she maintained a fair pretence of composure. The maidservant was awestruck, her mouth slackly open.

Which would be more impressive? To draw out this display or to reveal Starrid in an instant? She could do either. Jilseth hid her own relief at finding the scoundrel so readily. That said, someone would need to identify the tavern where the villain was slumped over an outside table.

She passed a hand over the bowl, subduing the florid magelight. A vision floated on the water's surface. 'Do you know where this is?'

'Raselle?' Zurenne studied the scene within the bowl. 'Do you know of a tavern called The Four Songs?'

The tavern's painted sign depicted Trimon and Talagrin, Halcarion and Larasion. From the bulge in Talagrin's breeches and the revealing gowns of the opulently-bosomed goddesses, the upper rooms offered more than a bed for the night.

They saw Starrid spring up from his bench to approach a passing man. The erstwhile steward stretched out a grimy palm only to cower away as the man warned him off with a thorn cudgel.

'He's begging.' Zurenne's voice tightened with desperation. 'But if he hasn't got the coin, he must know where it's hidden. Raselle, fetch Captain Arigo. One of the troopers must know this place.'

Before the maid could obey, before Jilseth could tell them Planir would deliver Starrid bound and gagged, they heard a commotion in the courtyard below. Hooves stamped, harnesses rattled and voices shouted orders cutting across each other.

'Lord Licanin.' If Zurenne had been pale before, now she was ashen.

Ilysh reappeared in the doorway. 'Mama?' That single word held as much challenge as appeal. She saw the green radiance in the bowl of water and gasped. 'Have you—?'

'Go to your room,' Zurenne snapped. 'No. Fetch Neeny here.'

'If you want me to help, you have to explain,' Jilseth said swiftly. 'What have you done?'

Zurenne shook her head, her eloquent expression warning Raselle to stand mute.

Exasperated, Jilseth stifled the scrying magic, reducing the magelight to a pinprick in the depths of the bowl.

Ilysh barely managed to return with her sister ahead of Lord Licanin and a handful of his servants. Esnina rushed to hide her face in her mother's skirts. 'Mama!'

'Hush.' Zurenne silenced the child's sobs with a firm hand on her shoulder. 'My Lord Licanin.'

'Lady Zurenne.' Licanin threw himself into a chair, the dust of the road coating his boots and cloak. 'What has been going on here?' he growled.

Zurenne's eyes widened, all innocence. 'My lord '

'Don't waste my time.' He stabbed a finger towards the side table. 'You've had my letters. I want your answers, madam.'

Jilseth had thought he looked weary in Ferl. Now he looked exhausted. Lord or not, it had been an arduous journey for a man of his years.

'On whose authority has Captain Corrain made alliances with Halferan's neighbours? No, not alliances. Underhand pacts with their household troops without any lord's seal of approval,' the baron demanded with growing ire. 'Where is he? They told me at the gatehouse that he hasn't been here since the start of For-Summer!'

'We do not answer to you.'

'Lysha! Silence!'

Jilseth couldn't decide which shocked the gathering more; Ilysh's defiant words or seeing Zurenne so provoked that she actually raised a hand to her daughter. To no avail.

'I don't answer to you, mother,' Ilysh boldly declared. 'Only to my husband.'

'What?' Wrath propelled Licanin to his feet.

'Lysha?' Esnina looked up at her mother, no sign of tears on her red cheeks. As Zurenne stood obstinately silent, the little girl turned her head to gape at her sister. 'Lysha has a husband?'

Defiant, Ilysh blushed scarlet. 'Captain Corrain is now Lord of Halferan by right of marriage.'

'Marriage?' Licanin's bellow was loud enough to silence the noise in the courtyard below the window.

'We don't need you telling us what to do,' Ilysh shouted back. 'We won't need your coin once the lady wizard finds my father's fortune!'

The baron ignored her, narrowing his eyes at Raselle. At his gesture, a Licanin swordsman seized her arm. 'You, girl, what do you know?'

'Leave her alone.' Zurenne took a step forward, fending off Esnina's clinging hands.

'Well?' At Licanin's nod, the swordsman gave the maidservant a menacing shake.

'My lady Ilysh is truly married.' Raselle shot Zurenne a look of desperate appeal. 'In the shrine. I saw it.'

Licanin crossed the room with swift strides. He caught Ilysh by the chin and stared at her intently. Everyone saw the girl trembling, tears welling in her eyes. The baron released her with more gentleness than Jilseth expected.

'Wedded, I dare say, but not bedded.' He shook his head, somewhat calmer. 'You wouldn't let it go so far, my lady, whatever that man might offer you. I take it she was his price? For a few sunken galleys and some dead corsairs? You sell your daughter and her birthright cheaply, and to such a man.' His disgust was palpable.

'At least he was my choice,' Zurenne retorted. 'Who would you have handed me to, and my daughters, for the sake of Licanin's trade or to secure some favour among the parliament's cliques? At least Corrain is defending Halferan. He undertook to catch and kill the raiders instead of abandoning the coast to them!'

'I have abandoned nothing!' Her attack rekindled Licanin's anger. 'I have a grant of guardianship sealed by the barons' parliament. I will have this masquerade marriage set aside, and since this is how you safeguard your children, I'll see you set aside as well. They'll be raised in my own household—'

'You can do nothing until Equinox.' Zurenne defied him. 'Even then, don't wager that you'll succeed. Ilysh was married with every rite and legality well before any grant of guardianship. My lady Jilseth, you'll stand as my witness?'

As she held out a shaking hand, Lord Licanin rounded on Jilseth.

'You were privy to this marriage?' He was appalled. 'We have Hadrumal to thank for this outrage?'

'You do not,' she snapped, 'and I knew nothing of this till today.'

She wasn't convinced this was all that Zurenne was hiding. The noblewoman hadn't answered Licanin's question about Corrain's whereabouts.

'Then why are you here, madam mage?' Licanin gestured at the bowl on the table. 'To work more sorcery for the Archmage's ends?'

'No.' Jilseth dipped her hands in the water to wash them. Once she'd hidden the brass cylinder of the pen knife with an invisible touch of magic, she calmly rinsed her face. 'As I'm sure they can tell you at the gatehouse, I've not long arrived myself.' That was stretching the truth but patting her face dry with the towel hid her expression as well as muffling her words. 'The summer's heat on the road is punishing, isn't it?'

She would keep Zurenne's search for Starrid a secret, if only to drive the noblewoman deeper into her debt. But she could not let Lord Licanin's accusation go unchallenged. Any suspicion that Hadrumal had some underhand part in this scandalous marriage would run from barony to barony across Caladhria as quick as a rat chased by a cat.

'I can stand witness to today's events,' she said quickly as Licanin rounded on Zurenne, 'as my lady of Halferan doubtless meant, since I have no ties or obligations to this barony or any other. So I suggest we test these claims of a marriage.'

Perhaps hearing what had gone on would give her some inkling to Zurenne's motives. Before that, Jilseth urgently wanted some privacy, a candle stub and a spoon to bespeak Planir. To get those she must break the deadlock now paralysing the room.

An urgent voice called down the hallway from the door to the stairs. 'My lady Zurenne? My lord Licanin?'

'Captain Arigo?' The baron jerked his head at one of his men. 'Bring him here.'

'He knows nothing,' Zurenne said quickly. 'No one does, but those here in this room. I will see anyone spreading gossip flogged.' She warned Licanin's troopers with a ferocious glare.

Jilseth reckoned she had as much hope of silencing them as of serving soup in a basket.

'My lady. My lord.' The portly captain Arigo puffed as he entered the room. 'There's smoke on the wind.'

'How much? Where from?' Licanin hurried to the window.

Everyone looked worried. Jilseth understood their concern. At the height of summer, with the standing crops ripe in the fields, an unchecked blaze could leave ten dead of winter hunger for every victim of the actual flames. Not that Hadrumal's yeoman had to fear such disasters with mages on hand to stifle any spark.

'Let me help.' She didn't wait for an answer from Licanin or Zurenne. 'Open that casement,' she ordered the trooper standing closest.

He was the one holding Raselle in a painfully tight grip. As he released her, the maid fled to stand beside her mistress. The trooper forced the window open with a squeal of hinges.

'The wind's coming from the sea,' Arigo was explaining. 'Something's well alight towards the marshes.'

As the casement swung away from the mullion, it didn't take a wizard to smell the burning on the evening air. A broad swath of the westerly sky was feverish red and soiled with charcoal streaks.

'That's some blaze,' Licanin said uneasily.

Jilseth could taste the smoke. It was making her eyes water. She ignored such petty discomforts, concentrating with her wizardly senses instead. Air and earth might be opposed but fire and earth had no such quarrel. The burning carried on the breeze gave her the grasp she needed on the elusive element.

Jilseth closed her eyes, the better to follow the threads of the wind back to the marshes. Her magesight skipped along the fragments of ash carried aloft by the heat, each one with an elemental speck at its heart.

Whatever mages like Canfor or even Nolyen might claim for their own magic, every living thing was ultimately born of the earth, sharing its essence with the dazzle of diamonds and the humbleness of coal. Jilseth knew it was no coincidence that more Stone Masters and Mistresses had become Archmage of Hadrumal than wizards of any other affinity.

'The saltings dry out so at this season.' Arigo was wringing his hands. 'Only a spark and they'll be alight.'

'It'll burn itself out,' someone said, complacent, 'and the tides are springing high these next few days. That'll douse any embers.'

'Listen!' Jilseth's magic filled the room with noise, silencing them all.

She might have no hope of working clairaudience through water as Planir had but she could bend this ash-tainted breeze to the air-based spell readily enough.

The din that filled the room wasn't the commotion of distant peasants fighting to save a cornfield, nor even the lamentation of some villager losing a house to such cursed misfortune.

Wherever that fire was burning, dying men were spending their last breath on curses. Women wailed and begged before screams tore at their throats as viciously as their ravagers tore at their clothing. The uncomprehending bawling of terrified children was mercilessly cut short by the slick of unseen blades. Harsh laughter echoed through the horror.

'Stand aside!' Jilseth flung a skein of smoke at the mirror hung over the hearth. The image only lasted a heartbeat but that was sufficient to show a corsair raiding party laying waste to a hamlet. There could be no mistaking the Archipelagan's haphazard mix of finely wrought chainmail and crude leather armour, the men armed with curved swords.

'That's not the marshes,' Arigo quavered.

'Corrain said they come with the highest tides.' Zurenne murmured as the nightmare vision dissipated. 'That's how he knew when to find them in the creeks where they take on water.'

'How far inland are they?' Lord Licanin seized Jilseth's shoulder.

She shook him off. 'One moment.' As she took the measure of the spell, the gooseflesh that rose on her neck owed nothing to the breeze through the window. 'They're less than three leagues away.'

'Are they coming here?' Zurenne's voice rose in panic.

Lord Licanin jabbed a finger at Captain Arigo. 'Find me boys to ride the fastest horses in your stables. Not troopers. We'll need their swords. Lads who know the back roads to Karpis and Tallat. Make haste!'

Jilseth hurried to the table and scooped the penknife out of the water. Starrid could wait. She needed to scry for those corsairs to see which way they might be headed. But should she bespeak Planir now or later?

— CHAPTER THIRTY-THREE —

Halferan, Caladhria
10th of Aft-Summer

ZURENNE HAD THOUGHT the longest, most desperate night of her life had followed that dreadful day when she'd learned that her husband was dead. Huddled in her bedchamber's window seat, she watched the sky pale in the east while that evil red glowed undimmed in the west. She was too exhausted to decide if this was worse. All she knew was that this was different.

Before, she'd been trapped alone between disbelief and grief while stunned silence stifled the manor. Now she was assailed by noise and terror on all sides. The first of those fleeing the raiders had appeared while Licanin's men were hammering on doors around Halferan village to raise the alarm. That had broken up the arguments in the manor's courtyard as Arigo's men decided who should be riding inland, or north, or south, to spread word further afield.

The lady wizard's scrying had shown them this was no mere raid. A veritable army of corsairs was heading inland, burning and killing as they advanced.

Spurred to action by these panic-stricken arrivals, the Halferans had gone to recall the Licanin troopers from the village. They urged the demesne men to hurry to the farms where they laboured, to fetch hay carts and hurdles to block the roads, along with scythes, billhooks and pitchforks to make a stand along the hedgerows, to fend off attack through the fields.

Through the night, fleeing folk from the barony had arrived in successive waves of commotion. The demesne's defenders herded them towards the manor. Wagons had already been dragged into the courtyard, laden with sacks and barrels salvaged from the tithe barns that flanked the village beyond the brook. With the new arrivals bringing whatever they had snatched up before they ran, the compound was soon crammed to overflowing.

The men departed as swiftly as they arrived. With bread and beer thrust in their hands, they were immediately drafted to the outlying defences.

That left their women and children wailing and shrieking below Zurenne's windows from nightfall to first light. Their lamentations were only drowned out whenever urgent horses arrived or departed with the great gate slamming as they came and went.

Zurenne's head ached fit to split in two. Though she'd retired to her bedchamber, she'd abandoned any hope of sleep. She still wore the gown which she'd donned yesterday, when she'd thought her greatest challenge would be facing down Lord Licanin's displeasure.

The baron had written daily as he travelled from Ferl with that guardianship decree in his hand. Each letter had been more irate, commanding her to send her reply forthwith by his own messenger. Those bold young men had been forced to ride back empty handed. They could no more compel her to put pen to paper than Licanin's hectoring could.

Then Jilseth had arrived, offering that tantalising hope of recovering Halferan's gold and silver. With coin in the strong room, perhaps Zurenne would have been bold enough to defy Licanin. So much for that.

She heard a stealthy footfall outside her bedroom door. Raselle? Zurenne realised she was viciously thirsty, the jug of spring water by her bed long since emptied. She had no notion how long ago. No matter. Perhaps a tisane and some food would soothe her throbbing head.

The soft knock didn't come. Those careful steps retreated. Zurenne slid her feet to the floor. She stared disbelieving at the door before hurrying to pull it open. 'My lady wizard?'

Stood in the hallway, the wizard woman looked fit to drop, her eyes sunk in bruises of weariness. She spoke before Zurenne could ask what she wanted. 'We need message slips and cylinders.'

'For courier doves?' Zurenne rebuked herself. What else would they be for? 'Yes, I have some in my writing box.'

The night's incessant mumble from the Great Hall grew momentarily louder. Then someone shut the door below on those who'd arrived bruised or with broken bones, trampled in some rush of panic to escape the corsairs. Belated terror had struck down several greybeards and crones with apoplexy on the road while other families had arrived with invalids and ailing children already loaded onto handcarts.

Zurenne was stricken with guilt. She should go downstairs and make certain that her orders had been heeded. She'd decreed that suckling babes and their mothers couldn't be left to the chaos in the courtyard. They must have the dais while the rest of the hall was given over to the injured. The clutch of pregnant women was to be bedded down in the shrine. Drianon, Saedrin,

Ostrin and every other deity must surely pity those most vulnerable and innocent of all.

'What courier doves do you have in your lofts?' Lord Licanin appeared at the top of the stairs. 'What lords will they fly to?'

'No barony has seen fit to send doves here since the turn of For-Summer.' Zurenne rallied to accuse him. 'Any dealings they have with Halferan have surely been referred to you.'

Licanin waved her away, appealing instead to Jilseth. 'Can you—?'

She cut him short with a leaden shake of her head. 'I can only bespeak another wizard.'

'You've spoken to the Archmage?' Once again Zurenne could have slapped herself for a fool. Of course Jilseth would have done that. Then why was the lady wizard looking so apprehensive? 'Surely he is sending help?'

'Caladhria's concerns are none of wizardry's, as we have told you, first to last.' Jilseth looked at her, heavy-eyed. 'He tells me to use my judgement in accordance with Hadrumal's edicts.'

Licanin's disgust was as eloquent as it was inaudible. He strode past Zurenne to push the withdrawing room door wide. Jilseth snapped her fingers and a scatter of sparks shot through the air. Zurenne blinked as scarlet streaked across her vision to light the lamp and candles.

'You can tell us what we're facing?' Licanin demanded of Jilseth.

'Of course.' She flung out a hand and emerald magelight slopped over the rim of the basin left unheeded on the table.

Zurenne half expected the wizardry to stain the embroidered cloth. It merely faded to prosaic dampness.

Licanin hurried over to peer into the glowing bowl. Green magelight cast upwards to make an eerie mask of his drawn face. 'Saedrin save us.' His voice tightened with strain.

'What is it?' Zurenne took a step towards the table.

'See to your children, my lady,' Licanin snapped at her.

'They are safely abed.' As she'd opened the door to Jilseth, Zurenne had heard Neeny snoring, worn out by tantrums born of panic the previous evening.

Her indignation faltered as Licanin glowered. 'Lady Ilysh isn't. She's downstairs tending her wounded tenantry.' His sarcasm indicated he hadn't forgotten the wedded dignity her daughter had claimed. He shook his head. 'I wager she's ordered every linen closet and blanket chest emptied by now.'

'What?' Zurenne stared at him.

'Their grasp is closing around us.' Jilseth was studying the bowl intently.

'Show me.' Licanin tugged a carelessly folded map from the unbuttoned breast of his tunic. He spread it on the table; some draughtsman's painstaking work marred with smudged charcoal scrawls.

'They're here now, here and here.' As Jilseth touched the parchment, her fingertip left a precise brown dot.

'Can we hope to slow them there?' Licanin's dirty fingernail traced a short line. 'That's where our last riders are making for.'

'You sent riders to Karpis and Tallat last night. Have we had word of them sending help?' Zurenne swallowed cold apprehension. Those boys were no older than Lysha. Had they fallen prey to corsair swords as they raced to summon aid or to bring back its promise?

Neither Jilseth nor Licanin replied. They might as well not have heard her.

'I can give them pause for thought as soon there's light for me to see.' Jilseth studied the sky through the window. It was the colour of whey. 'As long as I can find a good vantage point.'

'A pause.' Lord Licanin looked grimmer, deep lines creasing his face. 'What can we do with that?'

Zurenne knew nothing of tactics or strategy. Warfare was men's affair, even if only in theory, pondered amid bottles of wine by recent generations in Caladhria, played out in the games of white raven that were considered so unsuitable for women.

Perhaps women didn't play white raven because their concerns were never so notional. The multifarious tasks of managing a household, of seeing all within it decently clothed and suitably fed, tending their ailments real and imagined; such duties demanded attention and action day in, day out, year round. When would a woman have time to squander saving a painted bird hidden amid wooden trees from a flock of equally imaginary predators?

Zurenne's lips pressed tight together. She wasn't going to humiliate herself by asking what the two of them planned. She would go and ask Lysha what she was playing at, she decided, resentful. She was lady of this manor, not her daughter.

Lord Licanin slapped the table. 'This tower's roof must be the highest point in the manor. My lady, the keys?'

Zurenne was meanly pleased to see his sudden gesture had startled Jilseth as much as her. Her hand went to the chain dangling from her girdle. 'Yes, I have the keys to the ladder.'

Licanin picked up his parchment, addressing Jilseth. 'I'll send you a runner. I need to know what you see and what you are doing, at the very least to warn the men.'

'If I may?' As Jilseth held out her hand to Zurenne, it shook with fatigue.

Zurenne closed her fist around the keys. 'I will come with you.' She challenged Licanin before he could object. 'I can carry messages back and forth. You can't spare a man who can hold a sword.'

He looked at her dubiously before finally nodding. 'Don't fall and break your neck.'

Before Zurenne could find a response, Jilseth was heading for the door. 'Let's not delay, my lady.'

'Indeed.' Zurenne shot Licanin a fulminating look as she swept out of the room.

By the time he caught up with them at the stairs, she was already drawing up the sides of her gown's skirt and petticoat. Tucking thick swags of cloth through her chain girdle left her feet unencumbered. Jilseth hitched up her own skirts as Lord Licanin hurried down to the hubbub below. Zurenne was callously amused to see him colouring with embarrassment at the sight of their stockings and garters.

She unlocked the door to the ladder leading upwards. Zurenne had always insisted on keeping this key. She hated to think what calamity might befall them if Lysha or Neeny found this door unsecured. Halferan had gently mocked her fears but she had insisted that some forgetful handyman might leave it so, his hands full of tools, his head full of whatever repairs needed doing to the broad strips of lead or the wood beneath their folded joints where some rain had seeped in.

A faint glow illuminated the darkness as Zurenne locked the door behind Jilseth. So this was another use for magelight.

'After you, my lady.'

'Thank you.' Zurenne started climbing, cautious in her soft leather shoes. Thankfully this fixed ladder had flat, wide rungs. She was soon reaching for the bolt securing the trapdoor that led to the roof. Flinging it open, she blinked in the strengthening daylight. As she climbed carefully out into the open, she smelled smoke ever more thickly on the gusting air.

The lead-covered roof was easy to cross, with only a shallow pitch to carry rainwater to the gutters and thence to the bird-faced spouts poking through the decorative parapet. As long as they took care not to trip over the leading's raised seams, they would not stumble.

Zurenne remembered Halferan bringing her up here on their very first day together at the manor, newly arrived as his bride. All that they could see was now theirs to share, he had told her fondly. As his father had bequeathed it to him, prosperous and peaceful, so they would see their son inherit. So much for those hopes.

'They're falling back across the demesne.' Jilseth had gone to the southward parapet.

Zurenne joined her to see a ragged line of men retreating across the pasture. The low sun smeared their shadows across the grass.

'The enemy?' She looked beyond that fragile cordon to see the horde already menacing the stragglers. The only reason that the corsairs hadn't already overwhelmed the Caladhrians was the raiders were pausing to set more fires along the hedgerows and in the carefully tended coppices.

'This burning is some new villainy.' Distraught, Zurenne contemplated the smouldering horizon. 'They used to leave what they couldn't carry away. Why wreak such destruction?'

'I can't say.' Jilseth stared intently at the closest thicket which was now blossoming with flames. 'But I can make them think twice about it.'

She raised a hand and Zurenne breathed blessedly fresh air. A breeze chilled the exposed backs of her knees and plucked at her looped skirts. All at once she saw corsairs come bursting out of the copse. Some collapsed after a few strides. One was caught in a lethal flare as the trees were instantly consumed by white-hot fire.

'I thought wizards were forbidden to kill.' Zurenne spoke aloud without realising.

'There's no edict against shifting a wind's direction.' Jilseth raised her other hand. 'Or to set it carrying smoke. They'll escape a choking if they run fast enough.'

Zurenne rejoiced at the coldness of the lady wizard's words. Only for a moment. While the corsairs had slowed, recoiling from the fires lashing them, the Halferans were flagging as they fought to give ground as slowly as possible.

When a fresh force of corsairs hacked their way through an unburned hedgerow, the Caladhrian line broke. The men fled, trampling haphazard tracks across the grass glistening with dew. The corsairs pursued them like lurchers after leverets.

'Licanin!' Jilseth leaned over the tower's parapet. Though she didn't raise her voice, Zurenne saw the baron look wildly around and then upwards, open-mouthed.

'Open the rear gate,' Jilseth urged, 'or your men will be cut to pieces.'

Zurenne saw Licanin hesitate. She grabbed Jilseth's arm, stricken. 'We cannot open that gate. If the corsairs see, if they force their way in, they'll be at the very steps of the hall!'

Where Lysha was striving to live up to her father's example. Once they had taken the great hall, they would storm the baronial tower where Neeny slept beneath this leaded roof. That was to say, Zurenne fervently hoped her younger daughter was still asleep. The last thing she needed was a hysterical child clinging to her skirts.

'They won't,' Jilseth said with compelling conviction before calling to Lord Licanin again. 'Send your men out to support them. I will do whatever I can.'

With the wind whispering around her, Zurenne couldn't hear what Licanin shouted below. Action all around him spoke louder than words. Troopers scrambled into their saddles and rode for the gatehouse. Men without mounts followed after as close as they could without risking a hoof in the face. The wagons barricading the archway were hastily hauled aside.

Anguished, Zurenne looked back to the routed defenders. Those coming to their aid must circle all the way around from the opposite side of the manor before they'd even see the foe. Even on horseback, she couldn't see how the men whom Licanin sent could possibly arrive in time to save anyone.

Jilseth muttered something and a shower of splinters exploded from the dark hollow in the enclosing wall that marked the rear gate.

'No!' Zurenne screamed, horrified.

Too late. The remaining Halferan guards, stiff-jointed, balding or grey, were running through the archway, drawn swords in hand. All that achieved, as far as Zurenne could tell, was to spur the raiders on. Even with the wind at her back, she could hear the barbarians' bloodthirsty howling.

The corsairs' baying was cut short. They stumbled and fell with the ground rippling beneath their feet like water. As Zurenne gasped, the grass split open. Archipelagans toppled into vast cracks yawning at their feet.

Jilseth hissed through her teeth. Drawing back from the parapet, she flexed her fingers. 'Closing the ground over their heads would doubtless break the edict.'

Zurenne wondered if Jilseth knew how savage her regret sounded. Unnerved, she turned her attention to the fleeing men. 'Saedrin save them,' she breathed.

Those gashes ripped through the turf had slowed pursuit, even if precious few corsairs were stopping to help their comrades. The Halferan guards were spread out in a half circle defending the gate, brandishing their weapons. As they gestured with frantic encouragement, the routed Caladhrians spent their remaining strength on running towards that flimsy offer of protection.

The mounted troopers rounded the curve of the wall and charged for the corsairs. Zurenne pressed her hands to her mouth, too appalled to even cry out. Those pitfalls would be the death of those horses if their riders couldn't pull up in time.

They didn't have to. A baulk of green turf, waist high to a man, reared up ahead of the galloping horses. Startled, men and mounts alike recoiled to mill around in confusion.

The corsairs recovered swiftest. Some were already scrambling up over the unforeseen rampart. Too late.

A solid line of horseflesh now defended the routed Caladhrians as they scrambled over the shattered remnants of the rear gate.

How was that to be closed now the gate itself lay in pieces? Zurenne looked at Jilseth. The lady wizard's attention was fixed on the dark archway. As soon as the last man was through, golden light filled the void. As the Caladhrians backed away, astonished, the mage-wrought radiance faded.

The wall was now a solid barrier of brick and plaster. If Zurenne hadn't known there'd once been a gateway, she would have believed it had never existed.

For a long moment, utter silence held the courtyard in thrall. Then she heard Licanin's voice as clear as if he stood beside them on the rooftop. 'Can you—?'

Zurenne saw him break off as the first of the horsemen came thundering back through the gatehouse. Women unencumbered by children hurried to shoo back inattentive youngsters in danger of being trampled unawares. Others ran to help hold the flat-eared horses snorting angrily at the crowd. The last stable boys had long since been sent out with the night's despatches. Maiden aunts and widows were already tending those wounded Caladhrians whom Jilseth's magic had saved from the corsair blades.

As the final trooper returned, the iron-bound wooden gates were slammed shut and barred, almost catching his horse's tail. The baron looked up and gestured, his question plain.

'I don't want to block our only escape.' Jilseth looked down at him. 'We cannot stay here much longer. I will do all I can to defend the walls and gates while you prepare the people to leave.'

'How—?'

As Licanin stared up, dumbfounded, Zurenne saw more corsairs storming across the fields. They were coming from all directions.

'How can we leave?' she shrieked at the lady wizard. 'We're surrounded.' That was no more than the simple, lethal truth. 'Where will we go?'

'North,' Jilseth said judiciously. 'The road to Karpis is largely free of corsairs as yet. There are too many raiders to the south and west of us and they're already roaming further inland. We must leave soon enough to stay ahead of their main force.'

'Heading for Karpis?' The thought of throwing herself on Lord Karpis's mercy made Zurenne want to vomit. She gritted her teeth. She would humble herself before him, if she must in such extremity, for the sake of her children and her household. Would that be enough? Zurenne wasn't the only one he had a grudge against.

'He will surely recognise you for the lady wizard who humiliated him. What if he bars his gates against us?'

'I will unbar them.' Jilseth promised with a wan smile. 'And invite him to balance any wish for revenge against the benefits of a wizardly ally in the current crisis. Then there's the prospect of explaining himself to Planir if I should be injured or killed.'

That should suffice. But now Zurenne was alarmed by more immediate concerns. The lady wizard was deathly pale. 'Did you get any sleep last night? When did you last eat or drink?'

'No, and honestly, I cannot recall eating anything since I arrived here.' As the wind tousled her hair, Jilseth dragged stray locks from her face with crooked fingers.

'Let me fetch you some food.' Zurenne knew without asking that she wouldn't persuade the lady wizard to leave the rooftop. Another realisation struck her as she hurried towards the open trapdoor. She looked back. 'You didn't need anyone up here to carry messages. Why let me come with you? Why have me stay?'

Jilseth shrugged wordlessly. Baffled, Zurenne climbed down the ladder as fast as she could. She fished the keys out of the fold of her skirt and, unlocking the door, found herself face to face with Raselle at the top of the stairs.

'My lady!' Scandalised, the maid dropped to her knees to tug Zurenne's skirts into more seemly order around her ankles.

'Where are my daughters?' Zurenne remembered who had been supposedly watching over their slumbers. 'Where is Jora?' she snapped.

'Below in the hall, with Lady Ilysh.' Raselle looked up, fearful. 'Jora's family came in from the village and her mother is ailing, my lady. I said I would watch over Esnina, since I would be here to serve you.' She choked on her final words.

Zurenne smoothed her skirts over her hips. 'Is Esnina awake?'

'Yes, my lady.' Raselle scrambled to her feet.

'I will sit with her while you fetch bread and wine, any fruit or cheese, whatever the kitchen can muster. The lady wizard needs breakfast.'

'Can she save us?' Tears stood in Raselle's eyes.

'I believe so.' Zurenne spoke with all the conviction she could muster. 'Hurry, please!'

As Raselle fled down the stairs, Zurenne locked the door to the roof ladder. If Jilseth needed to get down, she couldn't see that hampering her.

'Neeny?' She went quickly to the girl's bedchamber, uneasy. This silence was out of character. Zurenne would have expected to see her little daughter's curious face peering around the door as soon as she heard voices.

Esnina was in the window seat, hugging her knees with her bare feet drawn up under the hem of her nightgown. She didn't stir, simply looking at Zurenne with mute appeal.

'Sweetheart, it will be alright.' Zurenne rushed to wrap her arms around the trembling child. She tried to find some further reassurance. She couldn't, mortally afraid that whatever she said would be proven a lie.

Halferan had always insisted that he wouldn't lie to their children. If it was ever necessary to keep something from them, even to deceive them, he would rather keep silent and leave them guessing, even if that distressed them, rather than tell an outright falsehood.

Zurenne could only honour his memory with silence.

— CHAPTER THIRTY-FOUR —

The Great Forest
10th of Aft-Summer (Caladhrian Parliamentary Almanac)
12th of Lekinar (Soluran calendar)

CORRAIN WOKE WITH a start. Rubbing a hand over his face, bristles rasped beneath his grimy palm. Unwashed and stale-mouthed, he longed to go back to sleep. He was constantly fighting to stay awake now. These woods were shady by day and mild at night, tempting him everywhere with drifts of dry leaves softening sheltered, peaceful hollows.

No. He forced his eyes open again. The pale sky above meant that the sun was already rising. He must be up on his feet and more than that, he must be as alert as he ever had been, if he wanted to stay on that Mandarkin mage's trail. If he wanted to stay clear of the Soluran wizards and their cursed men-at-arms so diligently quartering these woods.

The Solurans themselves had only settled down for some respite in the very dead of night. Corrain had watched the three wizards huddle together, doubtless conniving at some magecraft. Their men-at-arms had shared the tasks of keeping watch and cooking simple food over a small, swiftly dug fire pit before wrapping themselves in their cloaks to sleep or stand sentry, turn by turn.

Corrain had withdrawn to prop himself between two young trees fighting to claim the same patch of open sky.

He had only managed a broken doze, stirring at every night-time noise in the woods. Was some Soluran seeking a nook for a piss about to stumble across him? Or was the entire contingent rousing at a wizard's command?

Knuckling his eyes hard enough to leave them stinging, he stood up as quietly as he could. A mouthful of water from the leather bottle at his hip was tepid and unrefreshing. His throat ached with fear as much as hunger. He could only hope that the Solurans were still camped in that glade. And that he hadn't misjudged how far away he needed to go, to balance the perils of being discovered against the risks of being left behind.

Something rustled above his head. He peered suspiciously upwards. Was Deor hunting him? Corrain hadn't seen hide nor hair of the Forest man over these past two days but he wouldn't wager a copper cut-piece on that evidence alone.

He only hoped that the Mandarkin mage was more valuable prey, especially if the Solurans were paying for Deor's woodcraft with the location of those cached stores. Corrain guessed that the sneaking redhead would value food ready for the taking above coin which his people would have to travel to spend on provisions. Or perhaps he'd found Corrain's horse and was already leagues away. That would be an unlooked-for stroke of luck.

He'd been forced to let the beast go, sparing a swift prayer to Talagrin that it wouldn't fall foul of some undeserved fate. Sneaking stealthily through the woods with the creature snuffling behind him was too ludicrous to contemplate. So he'd stripped off the gear that could snag on some branch and be the death of the hapless animal, slapped its rump and sent it on its way. If Talagrin were truly listening, maybe its hoof prints would persuade the searching Solurans that they were rid of him as well as Kusint.

Who would be here watching his back if only the fool had seen sense. Corrain's spark of anger faded as fast as it kindled. He'd misjudged the boy and that was that. He should have remembered that he only ever had himself to rely on. He was doing well enough so far. He'd kept pace with the hunters even if he'd yet to catch sight of the quarry they were both pursuing.

In this grey morning light, that was comfort as cold and unrewarding as the stringy dried meat in his saddlebag. Corrain grabbed a handful of strips and stifled a groan as he shouldered the heavy coin. Snatching mouthfuls of food here and there had done little to lighten his burden.

He chewed on beef strips pungent with herbs as he began walking warily through the woods. He searched out the waymarks he'd noted in the benevolent moonlight last night. A splintered snag there, a sapling strangled by honeysuckle on the far side of this deer track. He had to find those Solurans again, ideally before they broke camp or soon enough after to follow a clear trail. Just as long as they didn't catch sight of him first.

If they did, he didn't dare risk capture and have Deor's kinsman find his current plan among his thoughts. He would have to drop the money and run. Of course, that would leave him with nothing to induce the Mandarkin mage to help him, even if he managed to find the man. Corrain's shoulders sagged, and not merely from the encumbrance of the saddlebags.

What fool's errand was he pursuing? But what choice did he have? Beyond taking the money for his own and making a new life far away from Caladhria. Yes, he could do that. Until guilt drove him to cut his own throat.

Movement in the trees drove such treacherous thoughts clean out of his head. Corrain crouched low to avoid anyone's gaze scanning the woodland at man height. He glimpsed movement again, this time catching a glimpse of russet.

The youngest of the Soluran wizards had worn a cloak the colour of autumn leaves. Espilan, the wizard who'd been sent on ahead with a bare handful of guards to tempt the Mandarkin mage into murder. The Solurans surely couldn't think the Mandarkin was fool enough to fall for the same trick a second time?

There was no sign of the young wizard's escort. Corrain couldn't hear the most furtive footfall. More importantly, the woodland birds were singing their dawn songs without a care in the world.

If the Soluran wizard was out here alone, where could he be going? As Corrain rose to follow, the dead weight of the saddlebags nearly made his knees buckle. After swift, agonised deliberation, he dumped them in a hollow stump. He could come back to retrieve them later, when he had a better idea of what was afoot. Or he'd be dead and it wouldn't matter.

He slid his sword noiselessly from its sheath and crept through the trees. His eyes shifted constantly, watchful for any shimmer of Soluran hauberks amid the greenery, while striving to keep track of that russet cloak.

Now the Soluran wizard was slowing. Corrain fought an impulse to do the same. Caution was all very well but he had to see what the wizard was up to. Without the wizard seeing him.

He dropped low a second time as he saw Espilan staring straight in his direction. He breathed a little easier when Espilan's gaze slid downwards. The young wizard was looking into his cupped hands, where the merest shimmer of azure coloured the pallid dawn gloom.

This was interesting. From the shadow where he lurked, Corrain watched the Soluran through the lattice of twigs. Espilan's jaw was set, his eyes narrowed with determination. Corrain had seen that expression often enough in the guard barracks to recognise a young man out to prove himself.

He had set off without the rest of them, seeking the Mandarkin with his own magecraft. He was out to show that arrogant woman and the old man exactly what he was capable of.

Espilan looked away to the north. He headed off so quietly he must surely have muffled his boots with magic. Corrain followed as carefully as he could. He could only trust the faint breezes to cover any unavoidable noise.

Espilan went on, slowly, carefully, his direction unwavering. The sun rose higher, warming the day. Corrain soon emptied his leather water bottle and began keeping an eye open for a stream fit to drink from.

As they drew further and further away from that stump where he'd left the coin, he grew increasingly uneasy. There was no sign of the other Solurans. Perhaps the woman wizard and the old man mage were already on the Mandarkin's scent. They could catch him and Corrain wouldn't even know. Perhaps he should backtrack before he lost his waymarks entirely in this accursed impenetrable forest.

Blue light seared his vision. Birds burst from the bushes and trees. Corrain dropped to the ground, barely restraining his curses.

Hearing delighted laughter amid the frantic squawking putting more fowl to flight, he scrambled forward as fast as he could. The chaos subsided inconveniently soon. Corrain slowed to a snail's pace, wary of any brush of a leaf or crack of a twig beneath his hand or knee.

Espilan was intent on something on the forest floor. Flat on his belly and peering through the undergrowth, Corrain saw a writhing shadow caught amid coils of coruscating light. The struggling shape became clearer. Not because Espilan's magic was fading but rather the figure was growing more solid, more tangible.

Corrain recognised the Mandarkin now that whatever magecraft had rendered him invisible or insubstantial had been so violently stripped away.

The Soluran stooped over the captive wizard. His words might be unintelligible but his triumph was as plain as the daylight. Until Corrain's sword pommel hit the back of his head to send him sprawling unconscious into the leaf litter, the sapphire magelight snuffed.

Corrain wrenched at the reins coiled around his waist. He hadn't abandoned that horse without taking anything he might find a use for. Before the Soluran regained his senses, he must have him securely bound. These were not Hadrumal's wizards. He'd seen them kill without compunction.

He gagged the slack-limbed wizard with a sticky rag that had held rounds of dried apple. Once he had the reins buckled tight around Espilan's wrists and ankles, hands behind the wizard's back, he knotted the free ends together around a conveniently solid tree. The bleary-eyed Soluran was beginning to stir.

Corrain stepped back. 'Remember, I could have hit you hard enough to kill.'

He spoke slowly in formal Tormalin. For good measure, he turned his sword to show Espilan the heavy pommel before resting the blade on the wizard's shoulder, the edge pressing lightly against his neck.

'I don't wish to make an enemy of any Soluran,' Corrain told him. 'But I need a wizard to fight the corsairs. If you and your own won't help me, I must find a mage who can.'

Espilan's eyes blazed with contempt. Contempt and something else?

Where was the Mandarkin mage? Corrain looked back at the ground where Espilan's captive had lain only to see scuffed leaf mould. Before Corrain could wonder where the fugitive had gone, his feet were pulled out from under him.

He fell heavily. He would have thrust out a hand but his arms were pinioned to his sides. A searing coil of green steam dragged him along the ground, wrapping around him from head to toe and dazzling him to blindness. Corrain fought, bucking and twisting, to no avail. All that won him was deep gouges to his chin and forehead from stray twigs.

Another flash of emerald light hauled him upwards to slam against a tree trunk. Realising that his eyes hadn't been scalded into empty sockets was paltry relief. Corrain found a web of cold mossy tendrils swathed him, binding him to the tree. He was far more securely restrained than Espilan on the far side of this ragged glade.

He still had hold of his sword, though with it pressed tight to his leg, Corrain couldn't see how he was going to use it. As he flexed his shoulders to test these sorcerous bonds, the magic tightened to leave him gasping for breath. He heard the Mandarkin mage laughing with soft malice. He saw Espilan close his eyes and roll his head away, conveying his utter contempt without any need for words.

The Mandarkin mage hissed and the Soluran wizard was encased in mage-wrought ice. Vapour rose from the glittering jade mantle like a man's breath on a frosted day.

The Mandarkin stepped out from behind the tree where Corrain was bound. He looked the Caladhrian up and down. Hesitating before he spoke, he finally cocked his head towards the bound Soluran. 'You and he. Friend?'

If Corrain had never heard anything remotely like the man's guttural accent, he recognised the formal Tormalin that all these wizards seemed to know. Thank Trimon for that.

'No.' he said forcefully. Hadn't the mage seen him knock the Soluran senseless?

Before he could ask that, a shard of ice appeared in the Mandarkin mage's hand. He pressed the razor-sharp edge against the blood vessel pulsing in the side of Corrain's neck. Feeling the cold fire burning his skin, Corrain had no doubt that this magewrought blade could kill him as efficiently as any steel.

The Mandarkin mage raised sceptical eyebrows. 'True?'

'True.' Corrain put all the conviction he could muster into the word.

The Mandarkin stared up at him, deep in thought, the pressure from his icy blade unrelenting.

From a distance, Corrain had thought he was some youth like Espilan, yet to grow into his full height and strength. Close to, he realised the Mandarkin was older than he was himself by half a generation. The man was little more than skin and bone and he'd been hungry lifelong, Corrain guessed, to judge by his bowed legs and stunted frame.

His heavy leather tunic stank of sweat and he wore no linen beneath it to save his dirty skin from its chafing.

Corrain tried not to flinch away from his foul breath. The man couldn't have an unrotted tooth in his head.

Didn't wizards have spells to save them from a tooth-puller's pincers? He'd bet good coin that those in Hadrumal did. Mandarkin magic doubtless had other priorities. So did he. If this wasn't what he'd hoped for, at least he'd found what he'd been hunting.

Corrain looked into the Mandarkin mage's eyes, making sure his words were slow and clear. 'I will be your friend.'

He gasped as the emerald magic tightened further, crushing him against the rough bark.

The Mandarkin mage leaned close, his breath even more nauseating. 'Why?'

The cold from the ice shard was an excruciating itch. Corrain swallowed. 'I need a friend with magic.'

The Mandarkin mage's eyes narrowed, dark beneath brows and hair that might have been blonde if he'd ever fallen foul of some soap. 'Why?'

'I come from far away to the south.' Did the man understand? Corrain couldn't tell. He could only press on. 'We have enemies who attack us. We need magic to attack them.'

The Mandarkin was puzzled. 'You are friend or enemy to Solura?'

Corrain curbed an impulse to shake his head lest he cut his own throat on that cursed ice. 'Not friend, not enemy.' He tried to shrug but the magical webs held him tight. 'I care nothing for Solura. I fight for my own people—'

The Mandarkin was turning away. Whether or not he understood, he was losing interest in Corrain.

'I have gold,' Corrain shouted, 'and silver. And food,' he added as an afterthought.

The Mandarkin understood some of those words. A new light shone in his eyes, a light Corrain recognised from his years among troopers. Greed.

'Where?' The mage's gesture was clear enough. It was obvious that Corrain was carrying no more than his weapons and the clothes on his back.

'No.' With the ice blade clear of his neck, he could shake his head emphatically. 'I tell you and you kill me?' He forced a laugh. 'Then we are not friends.'

Whatever the Mandarkin mage might have said to that was lost as the skinny man spun around. Corrain saw that the ice encasing Espilan was melting faster than lard in a hot pan.

The Mandarkin snarled, raising his magewrought blade up high. The Soluran spat back through the muffling gag. In the next instant he was gone, leather bindings and all.

As Corrain instinctively surged forward, he felt the magic binding him to the tree weaken. Looking down he saw the mossy webs flicker and begin to fade.

The Mandarkin mage was looking this way and that, his lip curled in silent defiance. As he flourished his ice blade, Corrain saw the fear in his eyes. The man must be as worn out as everyone else by this relentless pursuit. No wonder his magic was failing him.

Espilan's escape could be the death of them both. Corrain didn't imagine old Orul or that hard-faced woman Selista would give him the benefit of any doubt. Not once Espilan explained how this Caladhrian had saved the Mandarkin mage from capture or death, whichever the young wizard intended.

With a convulsive effort, Corrain ripped himself free from the withering magic. The Mandarkin turned on him; his ice blade lengthening into a spear, Corrain brandished his broken manacle instead of his sword. When the Mandarkin had pressed that blade to his throat, he'd seen the distinctive scars of such shackles on the man's bony wrists.

'You want to be free? Come with me to my own people. So far away that no one will ever find you. Not those Solurans.'

He jerked his head towards the sun though in truth he'd no idea where Espilan might have fled. He shook the broken manacle again, this time to the north.

'Nor any man who would chain you. Earn gold and silver with your magic, keep it for yourself and enjoy the finest wine and food.'

Again, he wasn't at all sure the Mandarkin understood him. He broke off at the sound of booted feet trampling through the undergrowth. The Solurans didn't care who heard them coming now that Espilan had reported the Mandarkin's imminent exhaustion.

The ice blade crumbled away into milky steam. Corrain levelled his sword at the starveling mage.

'I am leaving,' he said with careful precision. 'If you will not help me, I will not help you.'

The Mandarkin mage grimaced and held out an empty hand, palm up and fingers spread. Corrain hesitated, unsure what to do. With a hiss of exasperation, the Mandarkin stepped forward and grabbed his wrist.

He leaned close to whisper. 'Show me gold. Then we go to your people.'

Corrain nearly ripped his hand free, no matter what that might cost him. As soon as the Mandarkin took hold, a crawling sensation began spreading up his arm. From there the vile prickling swept over his whole body.

Was he covered in spiders summoned to that magespun web? That revolting thought drove Corrain to the verge of panic. Looking down, he expected to see insects swarming over his hands, underneath his shirt and down the back of his neck—

Instead he could see his own boots through his arm. His body was no more than a rippling translucent outline. As he watched, his legs turned clear as glass, the twigs crushed beneath his feet clearly visible.

'Gold!' The Mandarkin mage jerked Corrain forward, unexpectedly strong fingers fastened on his insubstantial arm.

How could he be so solid and yet seemingly made of nothingness? Soluran shouts prompted a more pertinent thought. Espilan had already found the Mandarkin once despite this concealing magic. They had to get away as fast as they could.

Corrain pressed a finger to his lips, trusting that the sign for silence was common to people of any race. With the Mandarkin's hand clamped round his wrist, he swiftly retraced his steps.

Talagrin be thanked, the Solurans were a good way off. Better yet, they were heading towards the trees where Espilan had found his prey. That would only widen the distance between them as Corrain backtracked. Until one of those men-at-arms found a trail to follow. Unless these magics left some trace visible to other wizards.

Corrain glanced at the scrawny Mandarkin. Seeing the man's eyes were already glazed with effort, he decided against asking if the mage had any spell to cover their tracks. Better to find that hollow stump and prove his good faith. What might happen after that? Corrain couldn't begin to guess.

— CHAPTER THIRTY-FIVE —

RASELLE FINALLY RETURNED as Zurenne was beginning to worry that some misfortune had befallen her. Or Ilysh. Or that the kitchen had been so thoroughly emptied by all those needing food and drink that the maidservant had gone foraging in the guard hall or the steward's house in hopes of overlooked stores.

'There's fruit rolls, my lady, that Doratine put by for you,' Raselle said breathlessly, 'and cheese and cold bacon.' She clutched a makeshift bag knotted from kitchen muslin. 'And small beer.' Anxious, she offered a leather flagon with a matching cup for a top tied to the handle by plaited thong, such as a horseman might take on the road. 'Let me set breakfast for you here and I'll go aloft—'

'I'll go.' As Esnina whined and buried her face in her mother's lap, Zurenne resolutely removed the child's clinging hands from her waist. 'You must be good and brave, Neeny.'

She clenched her jaw against the tremor in her words as she raised the little girl's chin with a firm finger, to look deep in her eyes. 'I must help the lady wizard who's keeping us safe.' She had to put her trust in Jilseth. The only alternative was utter despair.

'While I do that, you must help Raselle to pack up our clothes and—' Words failed her.

What should they take or choose to abandon? What of her costly festival gowns? The heirloom Halferan silver and the rich hangings on these walls? The elegant furnishings of her withdrawing room and their bedchambers? Their precious clavichord brought here with so much care at such expense?

What of the barony's records and ledgers down in the muniment room? The archives of grants and strictures, the annals of tenants rewarded and punished? What of the statues in the manor's shrine, worthless in terms of coin but priceless for being so revered?

'Gather up our plainest, most hardwearing gowns and boots for travelling,' Zurenne resolutely ordered Raselle. 'My jewellery, my writing box and—' she looked distractedly around the room '—whatever you can find of most value to fill a single pair of saddlebags each. We'll decide what else to take when we know how we're to travel. Neeny, do as you are told!'

Zurenne forced herself up from the window seat, holding Esnina at arm's length. Raselle set the muslin bundle on the table and came to stop the child seizing hold of her mother once more. Esnina began to grizzle.

'Eat some bread.' Zurenne delved into the depths of the cloth and pulled out a hastily shaped plum roll. She left it on the table without looking at Esnina. If she did, she knew her courage would fail her.

Fumbling with her keys, she slipped the knotted muslin over one wrist. She held the leather flagon between her elbow and breast as she unlocked the door. Thankfully the square of pale blue sky up above offered sufficient illumination now that the magelight had gone.

Her haste nearly betrayed her as she climbed. Head-high up the ladder, she trod on the hem of her gown. Her foot slipped from the rung and if her toe hadn't caught the next by pure chance, she would have fallen all the way down to the unforgiving floor. As it was, small ale soaked the side of her gown, forced up out of the flagon as it was crushed between her body and the ladder.

Zurenne closed her eyes until her heart's pounding slowed and the stinging pain in her shin subsided. Since hitching up her skirts was impossible at this point, she climbed slowly and more carefully. Kicking her slippers forward made sure of no more missteps.

As her head emerged from the trapdoor, she saw no one by the southern parapet. Foolish as it was, Zurenne couldn't curb her alarm. However the rest might flee, a wizard could step a thousand leagues in an eye blink. She'd seen that for herself, when Planir had vanished from the dais. 'Jilseth?'

'Over here.' The magewoman stood in the opposite corner, looking down from the roof.

Zurenne paused to put down the muslin, freeing her hand from its loop and setting the flagon of ale carefully on the roof leading. Her gown smelled like a taproom floor but there was no hope for that. Once she was safely clear of the ladder, she found some plum bread for herself. For some reason, that near-mishap had provoked her own empty stomach to famished grumbles.

'Here.' She handed another sweetly fruited roll to Jilseth.

'Thank you.' The magewoman ate without looking at what she held, concentrating on the gatehouse.

All around the manor's walls, Zurenne could hear the corsairs howling, bestial and threatening. Their ranks were now thick enough for her to see the rearmost over the walls. They were wrestling with each other for a chance to get closer to victory and richer spoils than any village could offer.

Attackers clustered especially thickly around the gatehouse. Even several layers of iron-bound planking must be more vulnerable than a full armspan of mortared brick. How long before the raiders began battering down the gates?

Zurenne discovered the folly of a sharp intake of breath along with a mouthful of bread. She coughed until her eyes watered as she sought to clear her windpipe of crumbs.

Because the metal studding the inside of the gates was glowing more brightly than the rising sun. If the bracing on the far side was as hot, no wonder the raiders dared not approach. Wizardry. Zurenne could smell the smoke from the corsairs' fire-raising but the weather-aged oak of the gates was untouched by the scorching iron. 'I can't sustain this for much longer,' Jilseth said dispassionately through her mouthful.

'How will we get out?' Zurenne managed to reply calmly, more or less.

'That's a very good question,' Jilseth said with a cryptic smile.

Before Zurenne could ask what she meant, a surge of corsair yelling shook them both.

Zurenne swallowed with difficulty. 'Ladders.'

Crude affairs, lashed together from green wood and stolen rope, appeared at several points along the enclosing wall's tiled coping. More followed, taller, stronger, seized from barns by raiders taking the long view of their pillaging rather than revelling in wanton destruction.

The first corsairs appeared. A man reached for the ridged tile, preparing to swing his leg over, to sit astride the wall. He had a rope looped over one shoulder, ready to fix its grapnel and slide down inside the manor. More heads appeared, surely the vanguard of a swarm.

Down in the courtyard, Captain Arigo appeared with a motley assemblage of bowmen. He bellowed a command, his clenched fist slamming downwards. The flurry of arrows which resulted did little to deter the corsairs. A few disappeared, perhaps struck by a lucky shot or more likely betrayed by their own flinching. Most of the shafts went wildly astray, loosed by such panicked and inexpert hands.

Zurenne looked back to that first raider. She saw the tile crumble under his hands. He grabbed at another. It broke into shards that slashed his palms to the bone. His ladder shuddered. The top of the wall was rippling. Men began falling away all along the curve; their yells a sharp counterpoint to the unceasing menacing din.

What use was this magic? If the walls crumbled, they were lost! Before Zurenne could utter any such panicked reproach, she saw that she was underestimating Jilseth's abilities.

Once a ladder fell, the wall stilled. The tiles were remaking themselves with newly formed spikes to mock the corsairs beneath. Was that a note of uncertainty tainting their hateful roar?

'What else is there to eat?' Jilseth was walking towards the trap door with renewed energy in her stride.

'Meat and cheese.' As the lady wizard searched the muslin, Zurenne poured a cupful of the ale. She drank it down, grateful for the moisture if not for the taste.

'You must see to your children.' Jilseth ate quickly. 'Summon your carriage. Have Lord Licanin marshal everyone into a column no more than half the width of the road.' She reached for the ale flagon.

Zurenne ate the food left in the bundle, desperately protesting nevertheless. 'We'll be cut to pieces if we open the gates. We won't even get clear of the courtyard!'

'We won't risk it without Planir's assurance.' Abandoning the empty ale flagon, Jilseth began climbing down the ladder before Zurenne could ask what she meant by that.

Was this the courage of intoxication? Hardly. Small beer was brewed to refresh, not to intoxicate.

Zurenne took a moment to hitch up her skirts before following the lady wizard. Before she could catch up with Jilseth in the hallway below, Raselle appeared in the bedchamber doorway. The unmistakable sound of Esnina in a temper won out over everything else.

'Neeny!' Zurenne's irate shout startled the child to silence. Raselle stood stock still, wide-eyed.

'Go and find Ilysh,' Zurenne ordered her. 'Tell her I command her presence here at once. Tell her she will prove herself a grown lady of Halferan by doing her duty as her father would wish. Then make your way to the stables and see that our carriage is made ready for travel. Tell Master Rauffe to send up our small travelling chests, the ones that go inside the carriage. He is to pack the barony's most vital documents on the roof and rear stowage.'

What else had Jilseth told her to do? Zurenne couldn't remember and the lady wizard had already vanished into the withdrawing room. She hid her uncertainty behind swift words.

'Present my compliments to Lord Licanin and ask him to join myself and Lady Jilseth.' That would surely suffice.

'My lady.' Raselle bobbed a curtsey before running down the stairs.

'Esnina?' Zurenne walked swiftly into the bedchamber. She saw at once that Raselle had already made three heaps of dresses and shawls, one for each of them. Esnina was dressed for travel too. 'Fetch linen for us all, chemises and stockings.' She clapped her hands. 'Quickly!'

Before the little girl could think to argue, Zurenne hurried to the withdrawing room. What was Jilseth going to do to save them?

For all that she was alone in the room, the lady wizard was talking to a swirling circle of scarlet magic. She held a candle stub in front of a polished metal mirror.

'I believe so.' Jilseth didn't sound wholly certain.

As Zurenne pushed the door wider to enter, a veil of sparkling blue light swept across the threshold. Zurenne stepped back, startled. She realised she could no longer hear what Jilseth was saying. The magewoman was evidently speaking, her lips moving as her eyes darted from the spinning wizardry to Zurenne and back again. Then the door swung shut though Jilseth had made no gesture.

Zurenne could take a hint. She should also be indignant but in the midst of this crisis, she couldn't waste time and effort on inessentials.

Back in the girls' bedchamber, she was heartened to find Esnina doing as she had been told, as well as she could. 'Good girl.'

Zurenne thrust all thoughts of Jilseth and Planir resolutely from her mind. She must concentrate on salvaging what she could if her family must truly abandon Halferan. As soon as Jilseth left the withdrawing room, she could collect her writing box and letters. Meantime she could gather up her jewellery. She hurried to her own bedchamber.

'Mama?' Ilysh rushed in, her hair escaping from childish plaits and her gown smeared with blood and muck which Zurenne preferred not to contemplate. 'Raselle says we are to flee?' Her voice rose in disbelief verging on hysteria. 'But what about Captain Corrain?'

'Corrain?' Zurenne realised she hadn't given a thought to the trooper since Jilseth had first shown them the approaching corsairs. So much for his promises of bringing Soluran magic to their aid. After all that had been done and argued, it was the wizards of Hadrumal who were helping them, even if the Archmage's hand had been forced by Jilseth being trapped with them.

'We must look to our own resources,' Zurenne said firmly to her daughter. 'Captain Corrain isn't here and we've no time to waste.'

'But he promised.' Ilysh wailed, her cheeks reddening.

'So he did, but for all we know he could be dead.' Zurenne regretted her words as soon as she saw the desolation on Lysha's face. She tried to recover. 'There's no way to know, Lysha. We can hope not. But we cannot delay. Do you want him to come home and find us dead?'

Now Ilysh was weeping. Zurenne longed to fold her in her arms but knew she could not succumb. Time taken to comfort her daughter's distress could see them all lost. 'The lady wizard—'

'Madam mage?' Tear-stained, Ilysh ran out of the room, calling for Jilseth.

Zurenne heard the withdrawing room door open. As she went into the hallway, Jilseth was answering Ilysh. 'We have a plan and the Archmage's approval.'

'What is it?' Licanin was coming up the stairs. 'Why

did you summon me?' His voice was ragged with anxiety.

'Your men must get everyone ready to leave.' Jilseth repeated the instructions which Zurenne had forgotten.

'But the corsairs cannot get in as long as we don't open the gates.' Licanin sounded as petulant as Esnina.

'I can only ward them off for so long. My magic isn't limitless.' Jilseth's fatigue was apparent to them all.

Licanin stared at her, truculent. 'Then what—'

'Why can you not do as she asks?' Zurenne attacked him with the fury she couldn't direct at these foes besieging her home and threatening her children, causing her to be so harsh towards her daughters. 'She's proved herself time and again this past night and day. Why must you risk all our lives by arguing? This isn't some debate in your lordships' parliament or some wretched game of white raven!'

'The Archmage has promised us the shelter of a nexus weaving quintessential invisibility.' Jilseth's calmness drew the sting from Licanin's fury as he rounded on Zurenne. 'If we wait much longer, I cannot be certain that I'll have the strength to play my part.'

After a scowl that promised Zurenne a thorough scolding in due course, Licanin nodded. 'Very well,' he growled.

As if he had any more idea what a nexus might be than she did. If their situation wasn't so perilous, Zurenne could have laughed at the absurdity.

No matter. Licanin was already half way down the stairs. They could hear him shouting orders. His tone brooked no dispute or delay and Zurenne was honestly grateful for that. She doubted she could have commanded such immediate action without Jilseth backing her with magic as she had done against Lord Karpis.

How much magecraft did the lady wizard have in her? 'You must sit and rest while we make ready.' She urged Jilseth back into the withdrawing room. 'Girls, as quick as you like. Neeny, show Lysha what you're doing.'

To her relief, Zurenne heard Raselle and two other servants bringing their travelling coffers up the stairs. A glimpse through the window showed her their carriage with the horses being harnessed. She breathed a prayer of gratitude to whatever god had seen those beasts spared when every other mount had surely been pressed into battle.

Then she saw Master Rauffe gathering up the reins, his wife beside him on the driving seat. Doubtless she had him to thank. She could hardly blame him for hoping to save his neck along with hers. Or perhaps he was ready to risk himself saving her and her children? He wasn't Starrid, after all.

'My lady?' Raselle's hesitant appeal recalled Zurenne to her immediate tasks.

They were ready to depart sooner than she thought possible. Sending Raselle on ahead with the two girls, she ordered the lackeys to take the travelling chests down to the carriage.

Coming downstairs, Zurenne paused on the dais for one last look around the great hall. The vast building stood silent and emptied but for soiled linens, and whatever paltry treasures had been abandoned amid the crumpled blankets and scattered benches. She looked up at the hanging flags, the tangible history of Halferan, so far beyond reach, now far beyond saving.

'My lady?' Jora hovered by the outer door. 'May I go with my mother? It'll leave you more room in the carriage—'

'As you wish.' Zurenne was no longer interested in the woman's failings or excuses. Besides, she should be with her family in such desperate times. 'Are the sickest and most needy taken care of?'

'Yes, my lady,' Jora said with fervent relief.

'Very well.' Zurenne dismissed her and turned to enter the shrine through the door from the dais.

The pregnant women had already gone to whatever wagon had been found to carry them. Lamps improvised from saucers of oil with floating linen wicks flickered in front of every god and goddess. The statues looked down, their painted plaster faces unmoved.

Zurenne looked over at her husband's ashes, at his father's and mother's, their forebears behind them silently ranked in their funeral urns. Even the unceasing roar of the corsairs' attack seemed muted in here.

'I must see to the living.'

She didn't know whether she spoke to her dead husband or to any deity who might be sparing this little shrine some attention amidst the death and destruction sweeping along the coast.

'My lady Zurenne!'

That was Lord Licanin's shout outside in the courtyard, summoning her with as much restraint as he could manage in the face of so many onlookers.

With a pain that was nigh on physical, Zurenne tore herself away from the quiet sanctuary. Opening the shrine's door to the courtyard, the noise outside struck her with the force of a fist.

Raselle already had the girls in the carriage, their anxious faces at the window. Zurenne realised with a shock of shame that she hadn't asked after the maidservant's family. How distant was their farm?

Could the girl hope that her parents had already fled the raiders? Her brothers and sisters? How many did she have? Zurenne couldn't recall. Would some warning have reached them in time? Would Raselle have had any news from those arriving during the night?

Zurenne decided that asking would only add to the poor girl's distress. That gave her an excuse to stay silent, even as she silently berated herself for a coward. She would make amends to Raselle later, if they all lived to settle such debts. Now she must deal with more pressing matters. That much was no convenient lie.

Close by the carriage, Lord Licanin and his personal guard were on their horses. A double handful of Halferan troopers were saddling up to join him, as grey-haired as Captain Arigo or as beardless as young Reven, struggling to soothe his nervous chestnut colt.

The rest of the Halferan guard, who'd yielded their horses to the night's despatch riders, were joining the demesne's men who'd returned from the outer defences. Armed with tools and farm implements, those yeoman and labourers were determined to redeem themselves, marching on either side of the cowering column of women and children. Those on foot would leave ahead of Zurenne's carriage. Handcarts and the tithe barn wagons would follow, carrying those unable to walk. They would be guarded by the remaining Licanin horsemen.

Zurenne wondered how far they could possibly get. All the way to Karpis, or would they be cut to pieces before they had even passed the brook? That must surely depend on whatever this plan of the Archmage's might be.

— CHAPTER THIRTY-SIX —

'I MUST HAVE a clear view of the road ahead.' Jilseth stood on the cobbles, looking up at Master Rauffe and his wife.

Abruptly, Zurenne couldn't bear the thought of being shut away, unable to see whatever fate might befall them. 'Mistress Rauffe, please ride inside and help Raselle with the children.'

Mistress Rauffe opened her mouth, closed it again and climbed down from the broad seat at the front of the carriage. Jilseth climbed up and settled her skirts around her.

Zurenne held out her hand to Licanin. 'A blade, my lord, if you please. Lest the worst should befall us.' He had a dagger sheathed at his waist along with his sword and another in a scabbard fixed to his saddle.

He unhooked the latter and handed it over without a word. With a nod of acknowledgement, Zurenne climbed up to join Jilseth at the front of the carriage. Reven would have come to help her but she waved him away.

'Lord Licanin! The men must keep everyone tight together.' Jilseth gestured at the ragged column ahead.

'What happens now?' Zurenne asked as she hooked the scabbarded dagger onto her chain girdle.

'Since you're here, you can hold this.' The magewoman handed over a polished steel mirror which Zurenne belatedly realised was one of her own.

She fought to stop her hands shaking as she saw arcane scarlet magic swirling around the rim. It seemed she looked into some misty void of unimaginable depth. Yet she could see the sun's reflection on the mirror. If she touched it, what would she feel? Metal or emptiness? She dared not try.

'Jilseth? Wait for my word.'

Zurenne recognised the Archmage's voice, distant and tinny.

'What's happening?' she whispered.

'The nexus—' Jilseth paused. 'That's to say, four wizards of Hadrumal are working magic together to allow us to leave. They will create an illusion of Caladhrian cavalry come to relieve Halferan.'

'An illusion?' Zurenne couldn't help interrupting. What good was that?

Even though she managed not to ask the question, Jilseth answered. 'We need only to draw them away from the road that leads from the village to the gatehouse. Then the nexus will add an illusion of these defences holding while we are departing.'

'The corsairs won't see us?' Zurenne found this incredible. She would have disbelieved it outright, if not for the conviction in Jilseth's words. If not for the mirror shimmering with magic which she held in her hand.

'That's where I will do my part.' Unnerving intensity hardened Jilseth's hazel eyes. 'I must sustain a veil of air to hide us until we're well away.'

Could she truly do that? Zurenne longed to ask but dared not for fear of undermining the lady wizard's resolve.

'*Lady Zurenne?*'

Planir's voice startled her so thoroughly she dropped the mirror into her lap. Clawing it back before it slid away, she saw the Archmage's face framed in the crimson spell. He smiled at her.

'*Good day to you, my lady. Well, no, it's hardly a good day in any sense. But all being well, we'll see you and your people safely away from immediate harm.*'

Before, Zurenne had found the Archmage's self-assurance infuriating, along with his calm assumption of superiority. Now she clung to the hope which his confidence offered as surely as she gripped the mirror.

'Thank you.' What else was there to say?

'*Jilseth? Tell them to open the gates.*'

The magewoman passed the order on to Lord Licanin. He ordered one of his men to carry it forward before bowing to both Zurenne and Jilseth. 'My guard and I will bring up the rear, in case of attack. Reven, guard your lady with your life.'

'I will.' Taut with anxiety, the young trooper could barely bend his neck for a dutiful acknowledgement of his orders.

As the baron rode away towards the wagons, the Halferans guarding the gatehouse hauled the last of the barricades aside.

Zurenne could already hear a change in the roaring outside. A defiant note rose and yet it was fading at the same time. The corsairs closest to the gatehouse were indeed retreating. She could tell that without having to see.

How far away would they go? She stole a sideways glance at Jilseth, wondering if she dared ask. No, the magewoman's face was taut with concentration, her eyes looking inward.

A blue haze hovered around the men and women reluctantly shuffling towards the opening gates. It was somehow similar if not as bright as the magic which had shut Zurenne out of Jilseth and the Archmage's conversation. A shiver ran through the straggling line together with a rising murmur of unease.

'Stand!' From his place in their rearguard, Lord Licanin gave the order with absolute authority. 'The lady wizard's magecraft will protect us only provided we all stay within its bounds. As you hope to stand before Saedrin after a long and blessed life, you will do that, for your own sake and everyone else's. When you are instructed, you will walk forward and stay as silent as an untouched drum, if you hope to see this day's sunset!'

Did that mean the corsairs could hear them? Zurenne knew the well-tended hinges and the oiled locks would make little noise as the gate itself was opened but what of the heavy wooden bars dragged out of their sockets and brackets? What of the horses, the rumble of wheels from her carriage and the wagons, the crying children too young to understand why they must hush?

It was too late to ask such questions. Those gathered ahead were already moving. Master Rauffe looped the reins through his hands, encouraging the carriage horses with a subdued click of his tongue.

The day's heat had not yet begun to strengthen. Even so, Zurenne was sweating before the carriage reached the shadows of the gatehouse arch. She cupped her hands around the mirror, trying to save it from the trembling wracking her body. She looked down into the swirling fiery magic. Planir had gone, leaving only that shifting mist.

The carriage emerged into the sunlight outside the walls. Zurenne stared into the empty mirror, feeling hollow with dread. What would she see on either side of the road if she dared to look? Could she bear to go on without knowing, even if their brutal death was approaching?

Her head snapped up before she was aware of making a decision. The demesne folk trudged on ahead, pressing as close together as sheep terrorised by wolves. Only now the wolves had been scattered by their own fears.

The corsairs had abandoned the gatehouse and the road leading to it. Some were falling back around the curve of the manor's wall. Others were running across the pasture towards the abandoned village beyond the brook. The others were readying themselves to make a stand behind the scorched remnants of the hedgerows. Blades glinted evilly amid blackened stems threatening to lacerate any horse forced through the smouldering embers.

It was easy to see why they'd run. An array of armoured horsemen had emerged from the woodland beyond the junction marked by the barony's gibbet, where the highway divided to head northwards or inland. The sun burnished their breastplates and helmets, vivid with coloured plumes alongside snapping pennants fixed to upright lances. They rode forward, stirrup to stirrup, at a slow, inexorable pace that struck Zurenne as more threatening than any galloping charge.

She could have wept with relief. Before she could make a sound, Jilseth's hand clamped tight on her forearm.

'It's not real.' The magewoman spoke through clenched teeth. 'Your people cannot see it. They must not.'

Jilseth seemed to be appealing to someone else whom Zurenne could not see. Planir? She looked into the mirror but he was absent from the ruby magic.

It was soon clear to Zurenne that no one but herself and Jilseth could see this vision menacing the corsairs. Reven was riding beside them, one hand on his sword and the other gripping his saddle's pommel to stop himself turning to see if they were pursued.

Master Rauffe only had eyes for their horses, fretting with displeasure at these people walking in front of them. He soon had the team in hand and the beasts drew the carriage onwards more steadily.

Zurenne twisted to look backwards until the last of the tithe barn wagons left the gatehouse behind. No one closed the gates after them. She felt the weight of her own keys dangling on their chain bump against the bruise on her shin. She hadn't locked any doors. She hadn't thought to in her haste. Tears pricked her eyes at the thought of her home left open to thieves and despoilers.

What did that matter, set in the balance against the lives of her precious daughters and her husband's barony's people? She drew a deep breath. Thus far they were making their escape, their pace steadily increasing. The marching men were even having to curb those furthest ahead. Some were all too ready to break into headlong flight.

'They're not getting any closer.' Zurenne voiced a sudden realisation. The make-believe horsemen's slow progress was as much of an illusion as their existence.

'Who, my lady?' Master Rauffe looked this way and that, his face abject with fear.

'No one,' Jilseth snapped.

'*You can see the illusion because you're holding the mirror.*' Planir's voice spoke calmly in Zurenne's ear though his face was still absent from the vision. '*Your steward cannot.*'

Unsure what Master Rauffe would make of anything she said in reply, she simply nodded.

'*We don't want the corsairs to think the troopers are close enough to be a threat,*' the Archmage continued. '*If they attack and find they're fighting a delusion woven of sorcery, the entire spell will be broken.*'

Zurenne nodded again, less reassured. She could hear defiance swelling amid the corsairs' shouts. How long would they wait, trying to provoke these supposed Caladhrian defenders into joining battle? How soon before the raiders would simply surge forward to attack, driven on by their unceasing lust for slaughter and plunder?

'Are they getting over the walls?' Jilseth demanded.

Zurenne twisted and squinted. The raiders were hanging back from this side of the manor and the gatehouse but there was no way for her to tell what might be happening on the far side. 'I don't know.'

'The mirror,' Jilseth reminded her. Zurenne held it up at once, understanding the lady wizard had no time for courtesies.

'*No, they're not.*' Planir reassured them. '*Galen has picked up your spells around the compound.*'

Jilseth grunted by way of reply. 'I believe I will be forced to drop this veil once we reach the road through the woodland.'

'*You must maintain it until the last of the wagons has reached the tree line.*' The Archmage's face appeared in the mirror, merciless. '*Then we can weave an illusion behind you of defences across the highway.*'

'Very well,' said Jilseth doggedly.

How long would it take for them to reach that fragile hope of safety? The leafy green trees seemed to be getting no closer than the boldly deceptive troopers feigning that advance.

'Archmage!' Zurenne sat bold upright.

'*I see them.*' Planir's voice hardened. '*Ely?*'

A surge of voices from the mirror meant nothing to Zurenne. She stared aghast at the mob of corsairs who'd burst through the illusory ranks of horsemen. 'They don't see them?'

None of the corsairs had given the supposed troopers so much as a glance, let alone swung a weapon at them.

'Not coming from the other direction,' Jilseth said tightly. 'At least they can't see us either.'

Evidently. The newcomers were looking towards the manor house and their comrades clustered around it as if nothing lay between them on the highway. Some of the raiders broke into a run, gleefully calling in their unknown tongue. A share in such spoils was an alluring prospect however oddly the besiegers must be behaving to their unknowing eyes.

'What happens when they trip over us? Will the spell shielding us break too?' Zurenne gripped the mirror, demanding answers. The empty mist offered none.

A curious call, like that of a hunting horn but somehow not, was cut short. In that same instant, the blue magelight veiling them vanished. It flashed back into being in the next breath, even as Planir's angry voice rang out from the mirror.

'*We will silence them!*'

'I'm sorry!' Jilseth was more furious with herself than contrite.

Too late. The newcomers had glimpsed the Halferans cowering on the roadway.

Only for them all to disappear. The newly arrived corsairs halted, their confusion apparent even across such a distance. Zurenne cherished a frantic hope that the raiders might think better of approaching the site of such an unnatural apparition. Didn't these corsairs shun magic? Corrain had said so.

Those besieging corsairs had persisted with their attacks despite undoubted enchantments shaking them from the manor's walls. Zurenne discarded the captain and all his wisdom and broken promises.

It didn't matter. While the corsairs were halted by doubts, the Halferans had seen those supposed horsemen waiting to rescue them. Even as the magic enveloped them again, Zurenne saw the relief on their faces as they turned to embrace and cry out aloud with relief, tears streaking their cheeks with sunlight.

'Did you see?' Master Rauffe slapped the reins on the carriage horses' rumps. 'An army from Karpis!'

'No!' Jilseth reached for his hand. 'We cannot be scattered.'

Zurenne saw that some of the Halferan men guarding the column ahead had remembered Lord Licanin's warning that they must keep everyone within the blue haze of magic. How grotesque it was to see them raise blade and staff against their own women and children with threats of violence born of their own pitiful fear.

Too many of the guards did the opposite. Reaching for their loved ones' hands, they were running up the road. Some even discarded their weapons for the sake of catching children up into their arms, desperate to find safety amid the waiting horsemen.

'I cannot keep everyone hidden from view!' Jilseth's despair rippled through the thinning blue haze.

'My lady?' Master Rauffe gaped at the vista ahead. As he dropped his hands, the horses seized their opportunity to escape the commotion swelling behind them.

'Reven!' Zurenne saw the young trooper's horse leap forward.

The boy reined it back, not willingly. 'My lady!'

He pointed, protesting, at corsairs running down the road towards them. Too many of the Halferans had already outstripped whatever remained of Jilseth's magic. No raider would pass up such helpless prey.

'Tell Lord Licanin.' As the lad wrenched his horse's head round and spurred for the rearguard, Zurenne pressed herself into the seat with braced feet and clung desperately to the side rail with her free hand. 'Master Rauffe! Slow these horses!'

'My lady, I can't!' He was hauling on the reins but the team were united in their determination to flee.

'Are they coming up from the manor?' Jilseth demanded, intent on the scene ahead.

Once again, Zurenne couldn't tell who the wizard woman was asking. She answered for what little that was worth. 'I can't say.'

'*Galen!*' Planir's voice rose from the mirror. '*Let them into the manor.*'

Jilseth gasped as if she'd been doused with cold water.

Zurenne could only guess that was some consequence of the wizardry being worked around them.

'They can see the gates are open now. They can get over the walls. They're more interested in pillage than pursuit for now.'

For how long? Zurenne wished Planir hadn't undermined his encouragement with those last two words.

Could those original attackers possibly be delayed long enough for Licanin's men to cut down the raiders now holding the road ahead? Or could they simply force their way through? Some of the corsairs were spreading out into the pastures to cut down Halferans who'd abandoned the road in hopes of outstripping those blocking the way ahead.

Hooves pounded on the hard ground. Lord Licanin and his household guard appeared on either side of the coach. 'Take the whip to them!' he bellowed at Master Rauffe. 'There are fewer of these vermin ahead than behind. We'll trample them down and outstrip them!'

What of those left behind without horses or a seat in a wagon? Before Zurenne could protest, the baron spurred his mount onwards, his men pressing close. The remnants of Halferan's household troop followed, Captain Arigo leading them onward with hoarse yells of encouragement.

Jilseth said something which Zurenne didn't catch amid the noise. It sounded like an obscenity. Before Zurenne could speak, a more eerie magelight swirled around Licanin and his troopers. A cold grey radiance that none of them even seemed to notice.

'What was—' Before Zurenne could ask, she was horrified to see Jilseth slump on the seat, insensible.

The lady wizard fell heavily against Master Rauffe. His hands were full with managing the rebellious horses as the coach rocked and swayed, discarded possessions on the highway jolting their wheels. He threw Jilseth off with a heave of his elbow before he realised what he had done. She pitched forward, unable to save herself.

'Madam mage!' he cried, aghast.

Zurenne's choice was no choice at all. She had to let the enchanted mirror fall to grab hold of Jilseth's gown. Only her other hand on the seat's rail saved them both from a deadly tumble into the traces and chains and the horses' hooves pounding on either side of the carriage pole.

'My lady—' Master Rauffe thrust out a hand to help push Jilseth backwards. The carriage swayed alarmingly.

'See to your horses!' Zurenne managed to wrap her arm around the unconscious lady wizard's waist. As long as the carriage didn't overturn entirely, she and Jilseth were as safe as she could make them. Until the corsairs seized them.

She could only hope that Raselle and Mistress Rauffe between them were keeping Lysha and Neeny safe, tossed around inside the carriage.

The handle of the dagger which she'd demanded from Licanin dug into her side. She couldn't spare a hand for the weapon. Would she be able to get into the carriage if the corsairs forced them to a halt? If she did, what could she possibly hope to do to defend her daughters from enslavement or worse?

Her hand holding the seat rail ached. Every jolt threatened to tear her arm out of its socket. She could barely catch her breath. All she could do was watch Lord Licanin's men galloping ahead.

They had already forced a path through the terrified Halferans clogging the road. Now they spurred on to attack the corsairs, yelling obscenities with their swords raised high.

'Slow this carriage!' Zurenne yelled at Master Rauffe.

If he couldn't the horses would soon be trampling the closest Halferans. Master Rauffe's reply was lost in the commotion. She didn't ask again. Like the terror-stricken families huddled together on the highway, Zurenne couldn't drag her gaze from the skirmish unfolding ahead.

The numbers looked evenly matched. Wouldn't mounted men have a decisive edge? That was some truism of battle which she recalled her husband mentioning.

Perhaps not. One rider was already surrounded. Captain Arigo. Zurenne cried out with helpless anguish. His poor horse was falling victim to corsair blades slashing at its forelegs and hocks. The animal collapsed, its screams tearing the air. The portly guardsman, so long loyal to her and Halferan, vanished amid a murderous Archipelagan throng.

Reven spurred his colt's flanks bloody in a vain effort to save his captain. Heedless of his own safety, he set about the corsairs with crude sword strokes.

Zurenne gasped. Held aloft, all the Licanin and Halferan swords had shone bright silver in the sunlight. Now as their blades hacked downwards, inky darkness flowed along the steel.

Reven landed a glancing blow and the raider reeled away. Zurenne expected the barbarian to come back with a strike to be the death of the bold young trooper. Instead, the man stood frozen with shock. Even at this distance, Zurenne could see the lifeblood pouring from the Archipelagan's wound.

'Saedrin!' she gasped, disbelieving.

That slash on the corsair's chest was gaping ever wider. Inside a breath it was as broad as a man's hand, glistening scarlet splintered with bone. The deadly gash ripped upwards, snapping the man's collarbone so that his sword arm hung useless. Loops of bowel bulged through the blood cascading down his belly and thighs.

He threw back his head, screaming in unendurable agony. His shrieks ceased as he collapsed. As he toppled backwards, Zurenne saw he had been bodily torn apart. His corpse landed in the dust in two distinct halves.

She saw other raiders trying to flee and mostly failing. The slightest scratch from a Caladhrian weapon grew into a mortal wound before a man could take a handful of steps. The highway was a slaughterhouse of severed limbs and pools of blood.

'Come on!' Master Rauffe lashed the carriage horses into a gallop. He didn't give them a chance to shy away from the carnage. The frenzied animals plunged onwards, straining to escape the horrors littering the road.

The way ahead lay clear. Any raiders who hadn't suffered injury were scattering into the woods.

'Onward!' Lord Licanin appeared at Zurenne's side, his horse lathered with sweat and spattered with blood.

'Our people,' Zurenne screamed, encumbered with Jilseth limp in her swoon.

'They're following,' Licanin yelled before his horse outstripped the carriage.

With Master Rauffe's bellows urging the horses on, they soon caught up with the troopers whose swords glistened with that deadly darkness. Lord Licanin's guards clustered around him, grim-faced. The Halferans drew up around the carriage. Zurenne saw vomit on the shoulder of Reven's chestnut gelding. The boy looked at her, his face a mask of misery.

'We must find help!' Zurenne held Jilseth close as she shouted at what remained of her own household guard. 'For those on the road behind us! The faster we ride, the sooner we can send swords back to save them!'

The words rasped in her throat. Was there the remotest chance they would find anyone on the highway this side of Karpis Manor? Anyone other than murderous corsairs?

She fell silent as the men formed up to ride ahead of the carriage, a few falling back with Lord Licanin to guard the rear. Zurenne felt sick at the thought of those they had left behind to the raiders' brutalities. She could only cling on to the carriage's seat and save Jilseth from falling as they reached the debatable shelter of the woodlands.

This belt of woodland wasn't a broad one, only there to serve the closest farms. They soon sped through it, reaching open farmland once again. Spiralling smoke smudged the horizon on either side, towards the sea and inland.

Zurenne ignored such tokens of misery. She was scouring the clearer sky ahead for any plume of dust kicked up from the summer roads.

She would have signed away every plough length of Halferan land, poured every coin from the manor's strongroom's coffers into Lord Karpis's hands herself, in return for the sight of his liveried guards riding to their rescue.

— CHAPTER THIRTY-SEVEN —

The Great Forest
11th of Aft-Summer (Caladhrian Parliamentary Almanac)
13th of Lekinar (Soluran calendar)

CORRAIN HAD NO idea where he was. This cursed forest was full of different trees, each one shaped by chance and yet everything looked the same as far as he could see.

Where had this Mandarkin brought him? Corrain looked down at the sleeping mage lying beside the log where he sat. The scrawny man's head was pillowed on the saddlebags.

Corrain paused in his whittling to brush curls of green wood off his breeches. Testing his belt knife with his thumb, he continued. The blade would serve a little longer before he needed to fetch out his whetstone.

There'd been neither sight nor sound of anyone in this stretch of the woods; not since that startling moment the day before when a blast of white-hot light had swept them here.

So the coin from the hollow stump had bought that much magic from the Mandarkin, and Corrain ventured to hope, some trust. After all, the mage could have used such wizardry to abandon him and to steal the gold for good measure.

As they'd reached the hiding place, the mage had relaxed his hold on Corrain's hand. That eerie insubstantiality hiding them had yielded to the welcome sight of solid flesh and bone. Soluran pursuit was echoing through the trees as Corrain had unbuckled the saddle bags. The Mandarkin's eyes had gleamed as bright as the gold and everything had vanished in that furnace glow.

Corrain touched his cheek with tentative fingers. His face hadn't felt this sore since he'd been chained to his oar bench in the height of summer.

How skilled was this mage? Corrain hadn't seen the lady wizard Jilseth suffer any such scorching. He looked down at the sleeping Mandarkin. When would the skinny bastard wake up?

As soon as they'd arrived here, the starving man had ripped open the saddle bags, devouring whatever food he could find. Then he'd collapsed like a pole-axed sheep, unchewed meat still in his mouth. Corrain had noted that his last instinct had been to seize hold of the coin, both arms wrapped around the saddlebag as he slept.

He looked up at the sunny sky. Last night, between fitful snatches of sleep, he'd contemplated the lopsided Greater Moon. It was definitely waning from its full as the Lesser waxed fat past its half. Corrain laid his carving aside on the log and checked his count on his fingers. These last few days were blurring into each other almost as much as the trees were.

If he was correct, the most recent of the highest springing tides that the corsairs relied on would have come and gone two days ago. Had the Karpis and Tallat men succeeded in ambushing the raiding galleys? What of the three such tides before that? Had they shared their secret with the other barons' guards up and down the coast, as Corrain had urged?

Did he even need to come back with a wizard? Maybe the corsairs had been scared off, faced with resurgent, defiant mainlanders?

Maybe so and maybe next festival it would rain soup and hail sausages. Lack of sleep must be making him light headed. Lack of sleep and food. He wished he hadn't thought of soup and sausages. There couldn't be any such feast to be had inside a hundred leagues and what little food remained was pinned under the Mandarkin's vermin-ridden head.

Corrain took a drink from his leather bottle. Wherever this place was, there were signs that the Mandarkin and his men had spent time here before. A fire pit had been dug, lined with stones and later refilled, while close at hand a reassuringly swift and clear spring flowed along a pebble-strewn bed.

Was this place marked on the wizard woman's map? If so, the Solurans hadn't thought to come looking here. As soon as he woke at first light, Corrain had circled the campsite to make sure they were quite alone.

So far. He wanted to be away from here as fast as possible. Deor or some other Forest Folk might come scavenging around such a campsite.

The Mandarkin mage stirred. Not yet opening his eyes, he stretched his arms and legs and yawned.

'Good day to you.' Corrain poured water from his leather bottle into the crude cup he'd been shaping from a stubby branch snapped from a tree.

The mage looked at the cup with some surprise before taking it and drinking deep. Corrain hoped he'd take the thing as a gift, rather than the insult it implied. He wasn't letting that man's lips touch any bottle which he must drink from.

'Corrain. My name is Corrain.' He tapped his chest in case there was any confusion.

'Anskal. I am called—' The Mandarkin broke off to swill some water around his mouth before swallowing. 'Anskal.'

Briefly, Corrain wondered what he'd just decided against saying. No matter. Now the mage was rested, they had far more urgent business to address. He'd waited long enough to explain, silently rehearsing his words as he whittled.

'My home lies far away to the south,' he began.

'South is the home of dragons,' the Mandarkin said instantly. 'They are death to magekind.'

Both his eyes and his speech were far clearer today, as he declared that scrap of lore.

'I've never seen a dragon,' Corrain assured the scrawny man. 'They don't live in our lands or anywhere close.'

The Mandarkin pursed his chapped lips and then shrugged. 'Forgive me. Continue.'

'My home is attacked by men from the southern sea. We need a wizard to drive them away, to convince them never to return. They have no magic,' Corrain added. 'Not like the Solurans.'

Anskal cocked his head, curious. 'You have no wizards in your land?'

'Not ones who will fight.' Corrain did his best to contain his ire. He didn't want the Mandarkin to think his contempt for Planir and Hadrumal extended to all mages. 'They scry and—' What did wizards really do, when it came down to it? 'They help with other things.'

Anskal considered this. 'Your home, this is where you were born?'

'Yes.' Corrain nodded. 'I am Caladhrian and my lord—'

Anskal silenced him with an upraised finger and held out the cup. 'More water.' As Corrain obliged, he held out his empty hand. 'Your knife.'

Corrain managed to cover his hesitation by fumbling with a fold of his jerkin. Why would the mage try to stab him after they had shared a drink of water and their names? Anyway, if he tried, Corrain was confident that he could snap the little bastard's arm before he could do much damage. He unsheathed the blade which Fitrel had given him, Halferan forged steel.

'What—' He snatched back his hand.

Too late. Anskal had nicked his finger with the knife. Deft, the Mandarkin mage caught a smear of blood on the edge of the cup. He smiled at Corrain's startlement.

'As you grow, the land of your birth passes into your bone and blood.' He swirled the water around to sluice the blood from the rim and passed a hand over the cup. Magelight showed green between his dirty fingers.

As he looked into the spell, Anskal frowned. Corrain leaned forward to try to see the tiny vision.

'Your home has suffered,' Anskal warned.

'We must return as soon as we can.' Corrain set his jaw and looked away. It was better not to know for now. Or was it? What would his blood have shown Anskal of Halferan's coastal villages? Surely he couldn't mean the manor itself? 'What—?'

Too late. Anskal had emptied the cup onto the ground. He patted the saddlebag. 'I will help you for gold and for a life far from here.' His gesture took in the forest, Solura and Mandarkin beyond.

'We will give you all that you wish for and more besides.' Corrain nodded before pointing at the saddlebags himself. 'But we will need some coin for the journey.'

His thoughts were already racing ahead. Which way should they go from here? That depended on where Anskal had brought them. He wondered how close they were to the river and how much coin would it cost them to take a ship to the coast.

Curse that for a fool's notion. No Soluran vessel would give passage to a Mandarkin. They would have to head east. No one in Ensaimin would care who his travelling companion might be. East and then south. There must be some port on the Bay of Teshal where they could find safe passage to the Caladhrian coast. Any captain with a pennyweight of sense would welcome a wizard aboard if he was sailing to corsair-infested waters.

He had better find the map which Kusint had drawn him. Corrain grimaced. He hoped the fool youth hadn't fallen foul of those Solurans and their wizards, or that sneak Deor. Corrain didn't like to think of Kusint being questioned, even threatened with violence, for answers he couldn't possibly give.

But there was nothing he could do about that. Kusint had made his choice, just as Corrain had. Now the most important thing, the only important thing was getting home to make sure that wizardry drove off those accursed corsairs for good. Maybe the Mandarkin would be able to read the map and tell him where they were. He reached for the saddlebag.

'No coin.' Anskal looked up, a dark glint in his eye, and seized Corrain's bloody hand.

This time the white light didn't scorch him, though

being swept off his feet left him reeling like a drunkard. The sensation was akin to staggering across a ship's deck in the sort of storm that could break a ship in two. Or it would have been, if there had been anything beneath his boots. Thankfully the magic lasted barely a breath, even if that felt like half a life-time.

'Your sword!' Anskal shouted.

Corrain had reached for his blade as soon as he felt solid ground under his soles. As his vision cleared, he saw the white light shooting outwards to scour a wide circle of cobbles free of drifting ash. Acrid smoke stung Corrain's eyes. When he saw the scene before him, he would have wept regardless.

Halferan was burning. Not some coastal village but the manor itself. The gatehouse must have gone up first. It was a barely smouldering shell, a ruin of half-burned wood and smoke-stained brickwork.

Guard hall, stables and the steward's dwelling were still throwing off heat to challenge the summer sun even if few flames were visible. Greedy fires roared, full throated, in the great hall, flickering through the shattered and sooty windows. The roof beams were beginning to yield. As Corrain took in the nightmare, a rafter fell in with a crash of breaking tiles.

Raiders were searching the kitchen and the storehouses. Smashed doors and shutters hung askew on twisted hinges. Wasteful antics in the bake house and brewery had strewn malt and flour all around.

Their arrival may have taken the corsairs unawares but sword-wielding raiders were now running forward with murder in their eyes. Anskal grinned. A twist of azure magelight swept up mingled dust and debris to blind them.

As the Archipelagans retreated, coughing, their strangled yells of alarm brought others rushing from the unburned buildings. Anskal tossed up a handful of cerulean sparks. They drifted idly for a moment before darting straight for the foremost raiders. As one man dodged, the gleam shot into his ear. Two more swallowed the sparks as they yelled. The last dropped his weapon, clapping a hand to one eye.

They all collapsed, dead before they hit the cobbles. While their faces were contorted with pain, there wasn't a wound to be seen. The corsairs rushing to support their attack scrambled backwards, slipping and falling in their haste. An Aldabreshin shell-wrought horn sent a frantic alarm far beyond the walls.

Some stalwart had the presence of mind to find a short bow. He loosed a broad-bladed hunting arrow straight at Anskal. The Mandarkin's contemptuous gesture brushed the shaft aside a good plough length short. For good measure, he set the wood and feathers alight, their ashes scattered in the breeze before the steel head went winging straight back. It struck the would-be bowman between the eyes. He toppled backwards, screaming.

The terror on his enemies' faces was no comfort to Corrain. After half a season's journey, after all his ordeals, his lies and deceits, abandoning friends and allies because necessity outweighed everything else, after all that, he was too late.

The baronial tower's casements were swinging open. The rooms within had been looted. Whatever hadn't been stolen had doubtless been despoiled. He saw threads of smoke trailing from the ground floor windows. Had that fire had been deliberately set or were embers blowing in from the burning great hall? It made no difference. Once Lord Halferan's archive was burning, the insatiable blaze would consume Zurenne's elegant apartments above.

Unless magic could quench the fires. Corrain turned to beg for Anskal's help when he saw a man emerge from the kitchen door.

The cowering raiders looked to him for their lead. No wonder. Their captain's head nearly brushed the lintel and he was broad as well as tall, massively muscled. He wore a steel breastplate of mainland manufacture as well as black leather armour in the Aldabreshin style. Where the rest went close cropped or clean shaven, his long black wiry hair was swept back with some hard-set grease. His beard was tamed with plaited gold chains.

Amidst all the chaos, Corrain stood in a moment of clarity. Now he understood this destruction, the wanton devastation. This wasn't calculated depredation to leave farms and villages with just enough to tempt the survivors back to hope and replant, a cynical trick to fill corsair galleys a second time.

This was vengeance. This was a warning for any Caladhrian baron who dared to defy the Archipelagans. This showed them what to expect. Just as Lord Halferan had been murdered for refusing to give the corsairs his gold to save his people's skins, and for trying to find a wizard to defend them.

Corrain would have known the man with the chains in his beard in any guise from Tormalin to Solura. This was the corsair captain who had killed Lord Halferan. The man who had outbid him for Minelas's treacherous services.

Now he was here again, scant leagues from the marsh where he'd murdered the noble baron, where

Corrain had seen his comrades slaughtered or enslaved. He stood in the manor courtyard as arrogant as any trueborn lord of this beloved place. While Corrain had come too late to make good on any of his promises to Lady Zurenne and her daughters or to anyone else in the demesne.

All-consuming hatred overwhelmed Corrain's reason. 'Kill them!' he screamed at Anskal. 'Kill them all and burn their ship. Whatever gold they have stolen, you can keep it!'

He was running, sword swinging to cut down any corsairs who dared to stand in his way. That bastard with the chains in his beard had ducked back inside the kitchen. The shit-licking coward!

Before Corrain could reach the door, an icy blast of blue light swept over him. Seized with shivering so violent that he was forced to a halt, he could barely stay on his feet.

At least the magic knew him for Anskal's ally. Looking as insubstantial as gossamer, the wizardry slammed into the raiders, solid as a wall. It smashed them against the ravaged buildings. Men screamed as they fell to the cobbles, writhing with the agony of shattered bones. Some couldn't even do that, their backs broken like a stamped-on rat.

Laundry and bake house, brew house and kitchen, all loomed over the crippled men. With a slow rumble, the walls fell forward, crushing the corsairs' cries.

Some escaped the toppling buildings, blown off their feet by the magic to tumble down the paths that led to the storehouses beyond. A few were bold or desperate enough to scramble up and grope for broken tiles or shattered brick; anything they could hurl at the mage.

Anskal laughed aloud as these improvised missiles hurtled towards him. His gesture sent them back crackling with azure magelight. The rubble struck indiscriminately lethal blows, breaking noses and cracking skulls.

Corrain saw a handful of other raiders fleeing towards the far wall. Ropes hung from grapnels, showing how the scum had got inside the courtyard.

That first wave of magic had got there first. Corrain could see the sapphire haze shimmering above the tiled coping. He'd wager all the gold in the Halferan strongroom that no ordinary man could break through that.

He took a step, ready to run and nail the cowards to the bricks with his sword point. That same violent shivering stopped him and Anskal's magic flared bright all around.

'Hold fast,' the mage warned.

Corrain's protest died in his throat as he saw what was happening by the wall. Better to stay well clear of that deadly sorcery.

The corsairs had grabbed at the dangling ropes only to find the hemp doing Anskal's bidding. Coils twisted around their arms, hauling the raiders upwards. None were so foolish as to exult. There was no escape for them now.

Nooses looped around their necks, killing some men as swiftly and surely as any hangman. Others were flailing in vain with their limbs tugged out to full stretch. As the ropes pulled harder and harder, one by one their cries died and the ropes went limp.

Remembering the mage's weariness after the battle at the forest lawn, Corrain looked at Anskal. How much more magic did the Mandarkin have in him?

'Ware behind!' he yelled.

A trio of corsairs had appeared from the manor's shrine door. Each cupped something in a hand and Corrain smelled the pungent fumes of sticky fire.

Earthenware globes were already soaring through the air. Anskal contemplated them as if he had half a season to decide what to do.

'They're—'

Corrain had no time to explain as earthenware shattered in mid-air. He recoiled, though that would do no good if the clinging fire splashed him. He couldn't retreat or even dodge, held in place by Anskal's sorcery. Could the wizard's magic smother those vile flames before he was burned to death? Saedrin save them both.

The flaming gobbets never landed. Like the arrows and bricks, they flew straight back to the men who'd thrown them. In the blink of an eye the men were shrouded in flames that flashed from yellow to wizardly scarlet. In the next breath, the magefire vanished to leave only a smudge of pale ash on the cobbles.

'You wanted them all killed.' Anskal rubbed his hands together and for the first time he took a step away from the saddlebags. 'I believe I have fulfilled our bargain.'

There could be no doubt of that. Corsairs lay dead wherever Corrain looked. With barely one brick left on top of another around the manor courtyard and the great hall a roaring inferno, there was nowhere left for them to hide.

Anskal looked expectantly at Corrain and the magic that held him yielded. Corrain swayed. He hadn't realised how hard he'd been pressing against those invisible bonds. He took a step to be sure of his balance.

'My thanks.' That hardly seemed adequate acknowledgement of the mayhem Anskal had wrought.

The wizard was already searching the pockets of the closest corpse. He looked at Corrain, his eyes hardening ominously. 'You promised me gold. This man carries none.'

It would, Corrain realised, be a grievous mistake to let Anskal suspect that he'd been cheated. He pointed at the burning tower.

'The strong room is below ground, underneath there. What coin is there, it's yours. If the raiders have already taken it, we'll find their ship and take it back.'

'Very well.' Anskal didn't look entirely pleased with that prospect.

He gestured and the tower's swinging windows vanished in a shower of glass and wooden splinters. As the smoke cleared, Corrain saw the fire had been blown out as well. Even the blaze in the great hall had been blasted into oblivion.

'Show me,' Anskal commanded him.

'Wait.' Corrain couldn't bring himself to see who might lie dead in the baronial quarters.

Who else had died beneath these broken buildings? What of the village beyond the brook? He walked towards the gatehouse to get a clearer view.

He had told himself to expect it. The reality still hit him like a fist in the gut. Halferan village had been reduced to a wasteland of burned and ransacked buildings.

What had happened to Hosh's mother? The unbidden thought choked Corrain. Had Abiath burned alive in her little thatched cottage or had her throat been cut by a corsair sword? What about old Fitrel?

As he turned away, heartsick, he saw that wasn't nearly the worst of it. The road leading north from the gatehouse was strewn with discarded possessions. Further on, up towards the trees, the corpses of horses lay swollen with rot in the summer's heat. Wagons, abandoned askew in panic, blocked the highway completely.

The thought of what lay among them was unbearable. The bodies would be unrecognisable after they had lain in the sun like this, gnawed by foxes at night and pecked by crows in the day.

Had they had any warning that the corsairs were coming to kill them? Could Zurenne have ever been persuaded to leave Halferan? Even if she had, could she have escaped the raiders? From the carnage on the high road, it was clear that whoever had tried to flee had left it far too late. And she would have been the last to flee. So Corrain's quest for vengeance wasn't nearly done. Slowly, fury began to burn through his despair.

Anskal grabbed his arm. 'There is no gold and little silver.'

Corrain hadn't realised how long he'd stood there, as devastated as the scene before him. He saw that the Mandarkin had used his magic to rip up the cobbles beside the baronial tower. A gaping hole in the ground made a mockery of the strong room's iron-barred stairs and bolted door.

'Where have they taken the coin?' Anskal shook his arm.

Corrain began walking towards the ruins of the kitchen. 'That man,' he said slowly. 'The one with the gold chains in his beard. He was their leader.' He was walking faster. 'If your magic can learn where he's been in the past few days, you can find his ship. Your coin will be on it.'

If it wasn't, Corrain didn't care. He turned to grip Anskal's narrow shoulders.

'After that, I will help you find his anchorage in the southern seas. He has allies there who've preyed on this coast for years. Kill them and you'll have more treasure than you could ever wish for.'

These corsairs had destroyed his life and now they had destroyed his home. He would see their cursed haven obliterated. He would see every last galley sunk to the sea floor and that blind bastard's trireme splintered to kindling.

He let Anskal go and hurried onwards. Corrain tore at the splintered laths and crumbled plaster of the ruined kitchen, heedless of broken brick ripping at his fingers. 'Once we find his body, your magic can find his home.'

He wasn't going to let Halferan's destruction stand as a monument to the corsairs' dominance. He would cut off that murderer's head and stick it on a pole by the ruined gatehouse. Then he would take Anskal to the anchorage and stick the blind corsair's head on the stern post of his burning trireme. Let the Archipelagans read an omen in that.

'I can do this,' Anskal chided.

Corrain found himself picked up and set down ten strides from the ruined building. Debris flew in all directions, bodies tossed this way and that, limp as rag dolls. None of them the one that they sought.

Anskal narrowed his eyes. 'You said they had no magic.'

'Where is he?' Corrain didn't understand. Where was the black-bearded corsair's body? The magic had cleared the wreckage of roof and walls down to the kitchen's tiled floor. 'He must have escaped through the back.'

'Perhaps,' Anskal said thoughtfully.

'If not, he's somewhere in there.' Corrain waved at the looted storehouses and the corpses dangling on the wall beyond. 'Or strung up yonder.'

He was not going to be denied his revenge, even on a dead man.

— CHAPTER THIRTY-EIGHT —

'WELL.' PLANIR LEANED back in his chair. 'What do you suppose the Council will make of that?'

'They can be thankful we're the only witnesses.' Troanna's tone implied that this was hardly comfort.

'So that is Mandarkin magic.' Kalion was peering into the broad silver bowl. Intrigued, he looked across at Rafrid. 'I take it his affinity is with the air?'

'That's his principle element.' Rafrid's thick brows knotted. 'I suspect he has a double affinity, given the speed of his instincts with water magic. Flood Mistress?'

Troanna nodded. 'I believe we'll find that's so.'

Jilseth looked covertly around the room. Did anyone else find this scene incongruous? The four most powerful wizards in Hadrumal had woven their magic together in this scrying nexus but no outsider would know them for what they were. Only Kalion in his scarlet silken robes looked like some balladeer's notion of a wizard. Planir wore his usual threadbare breeches and a ragged shirt while Rafrid could have been any workaday merchant strolling along Hadrumal's high road with his tunic unbuttoned in the heat.

'As to what the Council makes of this,' Troanna continued, looking more severe than ever, 'that will very much depend on what this pestilential pair do next.'

'What are the other corsairs doing?' Rafrid asked. 'Those horns will have carried the alarm some distance.'

'Let's follow their calls and see.' Troanna didn't need to reach for the scrying bowl for the emerald magic to flicker beneath her gaze.

'They're all running,' Rafrid said with amusement. 'Like rats who've heard a hunting dog. I believe they'll be rowing away before the noon chimes sound.'

'That makes sense.' Kalion contemplated the bowl. 'They know there are wizards on the mainland, even if they don't know what we may—' he looked sourly at Planir '—or may not do to defend the innocent.'

'If that particular signal is a specific warning of wizardry being used against them,' Rafrid mused, 'we could send the coastal winds to mimic those horns whenever a corsair galley approaches the coast. That could well deter them.'

'The sight of their own galleys burned to the waterline hasn't put them off landing again,' Troanna pointed out.

The Flood Mistress had been summoned from her garden, so Jilseth judged from the soil staining her fingers and the sackcloth apron protecting her plain green gown. She looked as dumpy and unremarkable as any other woman in her middle years, twice married, twice widowed and many times a mother.

Was it true, Jilseth wondered, that a woman lost a tooth for every child? If so the gaps in Troanna's teeth would give a tally of her children, but that answer would be a long time coming, given how seldom the Flood Mistress smiled.

Jilseth closed her eyes. Her wits were wandering again. How long before this giddiness subsided?

She felt a hand on her knee and opened her eyes to see Nolyen regarding her with concern. 'Are you alright?'

Though he kept his voice to a murmur, Canfor shot them both a penetrating look from the far side of the room. Jilseth managed a serene smile. Let him make what he liked of that.

'Do you need some water, or some wine?' Sannin leaned forward. She was sitting on the far side of Merenel, who sat subdued beside Jilseth.

Who was the curly-haired magewoman more in awe of in this gathering? Sannin or Troanna? Jilseth couldn't decide. But she mustn't let these idle thoughts distract her.

'No, thank you, madam mage.' She forced a smile.

Curse them for their concern, well-meant though it was. Now everyone was looking at her; the pre-eminent mages seated round the table and everyone else in the chairs that loosely ringed the room. Tornauld sat on the far side of Nolyen with Herion at his other elbow. Galen and Ely sat opposite, flanking Canfor beside the Archmage's white raven table.

For the first time that she could remember, the door to this sitting room in Planir's tower was not merely closed, it was locked. The first nexus spell that the Archmage and the Masters and Mistress of Element had worked had been an impenetrable defence against scrying.

Then they'd used her shale magic to follow Corrain through the Forest and to find him in Halferan when the Mandarkin mage had translocated them both there. She felt a glow of pride at that.

'Jilseth!'

She sat up straight. 'Flood Mistress.' Not that Jilseth wanted to answer questions from anyone but Planir. Not until she felt a good deal more sure of herself.

'Are you recovered?' Troanna's manner was so stern

that it was hard to tell if she enquired out of genuine concern or mere courtesy.

'I am recovering,' Jilseth answered carefully.

Not nearly fast enough for her peace of mind. If she was asked to work any magic or, worse, to join in a nexus, her weakness would be mercilessly apparent.

Rafrid turned in his seat. 'This is the first time your magic's outstripped your endurance?'

'It is, Cloud Master.' Jilseth couldn't help a blush of embarrassment. Arrogant apprentices usually suffered such humiliations, and were the butt of jokes for half a season.

'An unpleasant experience. I remember it well.' Rafrid's sympathetic smile offered her some comfort. 'Don't fret. Your strength will soon return.'

'We can hope so. Not everyone is so fortunate.' Troanna stripped such reassurance away.

Kalion drummed his fat fingers on the table. 'It won't be long before we get word from the Caladhrians. We should consider our response.'

'Do you imagine they'll be indignant that we plucked one of our own out of mortal danger,' Planir asked pointedly, 'while we left Halferan's mundane populace to the corsairs' mercies?'

'There are limits to what even this nexus can do,' Kalion snapped.

'Quite so,' Planir shot back, 'as I have long pointed out.'

'Enough!' Troanna spoke before the fuming Hearth Master could reply. 'You two can debate the wisdom of meddling on the mainland at the next Council meeting.' Her relentless gaze returned to Jilseth. 'Where you will have a great many questions to answer, madam mage.'

'Flood Mistress.' Jilseth braced herself. At least this unexpected gathering gave her a chance to test some arguments in her own defence. She only wished she could think of more.

'That last spell which was your final undoing, that was blackblade?' Troanna was hardly asking a question. Everyone in the room knew the answer.

'It was,' Jilseth said steadily.

Troanna shot a warning glance at Ely as the slender magewoman whispered to Galen. Ely froze.

'How did you learn such a working and when?'

Jilseth hadn't expected that. 'I— that's to say—'

'I taught it to her,' Planir said coolly. 'In case of direst need, and that situation on the Halferan road surely qualified.'

'The highest level of quadrate magic. Not easy in such circumstances.' Rafrid turned to smile at Jilseth again. 'Well done.'

Troanna ignored them both. 'Your magic killed. What have you to say to that?'

Jilseth could see Canfor's face hardening on the far side of the room. He didn't like to see the Cloud Master praise any mage of different discipline.

'Well?' Troanna demanded.

Jilseth thrust the distraction aside. 'I used my magic in my own defence as we have always been told is permitted.'

As Planir had insisted when he'd explained the deadly sorcery, his silence spell thrusting Zurenne away from the withdrawing room so that no one might overhear, in Hadrumal or Halferan. Why had he done that, if he truly had no qualms about Jilseth using such lethal magic?

Troanna shook her head. 'You could have saved your own neck by translocating away.'

'I wasn't sure I had the strength or focus to achieve a translocation.' That was the honest truth, much as Jilseth hated to admit it.

Troanna continued as if she hadn't spoken. 'Instead you gave those Caladhrian swordsmen a magical means to kill. What will that mean for Hadrumal's reputation on the mainland?'

'It should enhance it,' Kalion growled, 'and not before time.'

Jilseth wasn't sure if the Hearth Master was defending her or not, given his scathing look at Planir.

'You think we should arm all the Caladhrians thus?' the Archmage challenged him.

'I think we have reached the point where doing nothing no longer remains an option,' Kalion replied angrily.

'By your leave?' Troanna scowled at the two men. 'Jilseth?'

She had no choice but to answer the Flood Mistress. All she could think of was another question. Didn't that mean she'd already lost the argument? She pressed on.

'What of Hadrumal's reputation, if I had used my magic to flee and left Lady Zurenne and her daughters to be slaughtered?'

Too late, Jilseth realised she was echoing Planir. That didn't endear her to Kalion, judging by his expression.

Troanna raised her eyebrows. 'You would rather we had left you there?'

'Not at all.' Jilseth managed not to point out that she'd scarcely had a choice in the matter. She had been senseless at the time.

'If the barons of Caladhria's parliament challenge our actions in rescuing Jilseth, we can point out that she left the Halferans much better equipped to defend themselves,'

Rafrid observed. 'With the blackblade bespelling their weapons.'

'What of this? What if that?' The Archmage snapped his fingers and a stone appeared from nowhere to fall into the scrying bowl. 'You understand ripples, Troanna. They proceed in predictable patterns only until something else interrupts them. It's not fair to demand answers of Jilseth when none of us knows what will happen next.'

'To be precise, until we know what this Mandarkin mage will do next.' Rafrid nodded agreement. 'Which will interest the Council far more than any mainlander baron's outrage.'

'Shannet will tell you to kill him and be done with it. I'm forced to say I must agree.' Even so, Troanna couldn't hide her dislike of the frail old magewoman. 'Your rights and duties as Archmage extend over all those using wizardry in Caladhria or any other land once part of the Old Tormalin Empire.'

Kalion nodded. 'The Solurans cannot dispute it. Archmage Trydek secured that agreement from every Soluran Order.'

'I cannot share your confidence, and I have easily as many acquaintances across Soluran wizardry,' retorted Planir. 'Half of the Orders listed in Trydek's Decree have vanished into the mists of time, to be replaced by another score or more since. None of their Elders have signed any such agreement or even know of Trydek's Decree, as likely as not.'

Rafrid nodded. 'They'll acknowledge Hadrumal's authority over our own mageborn. There can be no argument there. But do you think any Order will stand idly by and let us discipline one of their own?'

'I cannot think of anything that will unite Soluran

wizardry faster,' Planir said flatly, 'and the last thing we want to see is an Archmage in Solith with a tower overlooking the Lake of Kings.'

Despite her persistent light-headedness, even Jilseth could see that Planir's words were weighted with particular meaning for the Element Masters and Mistress. It was some consolation to see that Canfor, Ely and Galen had no more idea than she did why that was so significant. Nor yet Tornauld and Nolyen, Herion, Sannin or Merenel.

Rafrid was looking beyond the table to those other seated wizards. 'Do we want any Soluran Elder to assume that he has similarly free rein over Hadrumal's mages, if one of us strays within reach?'

Planir shook his head. 'I would be failing in my duty as Archmage if I allowed such a precedent to stand.'

Kalion waved an irritated hand. 'This mage is of Mandarkin. The Solurans will be delighted to see him dead. We all know that.'

'Do we know what Mandarkin wizardry's enmity might mean for Hadrumal?' Rafrid answered his own question. 'No, we don't, Hearth Master, and I for one would like to know a good deal more about these distant mages before we risk that roll of the runes.'

Kalion would have replied but Rafrid silenced him with a curt shake of his head. 'I don't want to hear only from our Soluran friends. With all goodwill, they cannot be impartial. Hatred for Mandarkin is bred in Soluran bone.'

Troanna wasn't listening. She snapped her fingers and the scrying bowl glowed green. 'These mages of The Order of Fornet. They were pursuing this Mandarkin. Shall we give them leave to hunt in our dominion? Then we won't encroach on Soluran sensibilities.'

'Letting them do our dirty work for us?' Planir grinned before looking more serious. 'That is an option we'd do well to consider.'

'There'll be those on the Council who'll object,' Rafrid warned him.

For the first time, Kalion agreed with the Cloud Master. 'Those who've got wind of his magic. There's a good deal there that we've not seen before.'

'Very good, Hearth Master,' Planir approved.

'What?' Kalion looked bewildered.

Planir raised a quizzical eyebrow. 'Those who've got wind of an air mage's magic?'

'This is hardly the time for levity,' Troanna said testily, 'and a weak joke is hardly improved by having to explain it.'

As far as Jilseth could see, Kalion hadn't even realised he'd made a jest. He smiled belatedly, unconvincing.

'I must confess,' Rafrid admitted, 'I'm curious to know how that Mandarkin scryed for the Caladhrian's home by using his blood.'

'And how he tied that into translocating them both straight there,' Planir was equally frank in his curiosity. 'There was earth magic in that working, I'm sure of it.'

'It certainly wasn't pure fire.' Kalion was drumming his fingers again.

Jilseth was seized by a longing for the Soluran spell that snapped bones. Just the tiniest fracture in one of the Hearth Master's fingers would stop his cursed tapping.

She folded her own hands in her lap and looked down. When this abominable exhaustion passed, she really hoped she would feel less bad-tempered.

'I wonder who'll be the first in the Council,' Rafrid speculated, 'to suggest we offer the Mandarkin sanctuary.'

Jilseth reckoned Canfor was ready to oblige well before the Council met. He was looking at the scrying bowl with an avid expression somewhere between desire and impatience.

To be fair, he wasn't the only one. She looked at the mages sitting respectfully silent around the four at the table. It would be no challenge to find a nexus in this room who'd haul the Mandarkin straight here, whether or not he wanted to come.

'To learn all we can of his lore? Isn't that one of our foremost duties to our office?' With a rueful shake of her head, Troanna noticed, for the first time apparently, that she was still wearing her gardening apron. She stripped it off and bundled it in her lap, muttering under her breath.

'What will the Soluran Orders make of that?' Rafrid threw the question out not expecting an answer.

Kalion smacked his hands down on the table. 'What are we going to do?'

'Why do we have to do anything?' Planir's reply was as immediate as it was predictable.

Rafrid barely managed to interrupt the wrathful Hearth Master. 'The Aldabreshin may yet solve our problems for us.'

'What?' That distracted Kalion from his perpetual argument with Planir.

Rafrid nodded at the scrying bowl. 'That Mandarkin mage has just slaughtered an entire corsair band. As we know full well, the Archipelagans consider the only good wizard is a dead wizard, and preferably skinned alive for good measure. You don't think they'll pursue him?'

'Who's to tell them what occurred?' Kalion wasn't challenging Rafrid. He looked thoughtful.

'There's every chance some stray raider was lurking in that village,' Rafrid pointed out. 'He'll be running for the shore like a fox with his tail on fire.'

'So unless he has the wits of an addled egg, this wizard will take himself back to Mandarkin and that will be an end to it.' Planir didn't sound too hopeful.

Nor did Rafrid. 'Only if someone warns him about the Aldabreshin and their flensing knives.'

'Then they have to catch him,' Troanna said drily, 'without another boatload of men dying.'

'He won't be in any hurry to leave.' Kalion shook his head emphatically. 'Not when the Caladhrian barons' parliament will offer him wealth beyond imagining to sink every raiding galley plaguing their coast.' He glared at Planir. 'Which is why, Archmage, doing nothing no longer remains an option.'

His assertion hung in the air.

'That is a distinct possibility,' Planir acknowledged. 'Do you think they will summon a special sitting of the parliament?'

'Have they done that inside a generation?' Rafrid frowned.

'Of course they will.' Kalion had no doubt of it. 'With nearly eighty days before the Autumn Equinox? Not even the most hidebound lord will protest when they learn a mage is on hand here and now to save the year's harvests and to put an end to this corsair menace for good.'

For the first time, Planir looked at Jilseth. He smiled. 'It seems you have further business with Lady Zurenne and Halferan's concerns.' He glanced around the table. 'I cannot think of a better way to learn what the Caladhrian parliament intends, and to discover what this infuriatingly persistent Captain Corrain has promised his new ally.'

'True enough.' Kalion said grudgingly.

'Once we have some idea what they're planning, your baronial contacts will be invaluable,' Planir assured him.

'Never mind the Caladhrian parliament,' Rafrid said dubiously. 'You'll have to persuade the Widow Halferan of our goodwill, after our nexus rescued Jilseth and left her all alone on the road.'

'Her men fought safely through to Karpis.' Troanna was strikingly unsympathetic.

Jilseth would have expected more compassion of a mother, and Troanna was a grandmother to boot.

But the Flood Mistress was first and foremost a mage. It was never wise to assume that a wizard would react as some mundane man or woman might.

A thought hovered on the edge of her exhausted mind. How much more foolish it might be to assume they could guess the Mandarkin's future course. They knew nothing of the man himself and precious little of his deadly magecraft, or the harsh land that had spawned it.

The Archmage had an answer for Rafrid. 'We can start by making good on our promise to Lady Zurenne, to find her errant erstwhile steward.'

Jilseth had no idea what Planir was talking about. Then she remembered. Starrid. She'd promised to find him for Zurenne and recover whatever he'd stolen. Was that only a few days ago? It seemed like half a year.

She wouldn't be doing that any time soon, not unless her magic returned to some approximation of her usual strength. Jilseth's chin lifted defiantly against the nagging fear that it never would. A fear she couldn't admit to anyone, not even Planir.

— CHAPTER THIRTY-NINE —

Siprel Inlet, Caladhria
12th of Aft-Summer

'YOU CANNOT KILL everyone.' Corrain grabbed Anskal's bony shoulder. 'You must not destroy the ship, not before we have seen who is captive below decks or chained to the oars.'

Not that Lady Zurenne would be shackled on the rowing benches, nor her daughters. But Corrain clung to that last fragile hope; they might be here with other newly enslaved innocents in the galley's hold.

He hadn't found their bodies when he'd steeled himself to search those abandoned wagons on the road leading away from the manor, demanding that one concession from Anskal before agreeing to tell him what he knew of the raiders' vessels and who might be aboard. The Mandarkin mage had been very eager to find the black-bearded corsair's galley and whatever treasure it might hold.

Once Anskal had asked his questions, blood from one of those killed in Halferan had been enough to bring them here. Corrain was surprised to see that the black-bearded corsair had brought his galley to anchor in this inlet. The bastard must have seen those two half-submerged blackened hulks, as his rowers rounded that bend.

Doubtless he'd been too arrogant to imagine such a fate could ever befall him. More fool him, Corrain

543

thought, though the notion brought him no great comfort.

Nor was it much consolation to see how well the men of Tallat and Myrist had done, to send so many of the raiders to Saedrin to answer for their crimes. Bodies jostled in the water. The retreating tide was forcing them ever closer together in the shrinking stream. Laggard corpses were stranded, one by one.

Marsh kites weren't letting this windfall go to waste. From their vantage point behind one of the ubiquitous salt-thorn thickets, Corrain watched the brindled birds feed. They must have come from leagues around. Lesser scavengers could only wheel overhead, calling plaintively.

Where the reeds met the mud, silver lizards darted out to snatch mouthfuls from some rotting corsair already washed back and forth by successive tides. When the waters returned, the crabs would come scuttling to claim their share. Not too swiftly, Corrain hoped. These scum deserved a generation of torment at the claws of Poldrion's demons. A Soluran generation; thirty three years compared to the Tormalin twenty five.

'I cannot burn this one?' Anskal gestured at the galley riding at anchor close by the burned-out wrecks.

'Not till we know there are no innocents aboard.' Corrain repeated. 'Not before we've found your coin,' he added quickly.

That gave Anskal pause for thought. The mage stared at the galley, eyes narrowing.

Had Captain Mersed burned those captured ships deliberately? Corrain was sure he'd warned him against leaving such alarming evidence to warn off other corsairs who might fall into their hands. Had the young

Tallat captain ignored him? Or had some sticky fire got away from the raiders when they tried to hurl it at their attackers?

On one ship, perhaps, but to burn both so thoroughly? Corrain could always go to Tallat and ask. Then he would be taken straight to the baron, who would ask him all manner of questions, and Corrain would have to admit to his abject failure to make good on the boasts he'd made before so many witnesses, before he'd sailed north from this very inlet.

Anskal nodded. 'I have it.'

Before Corrain could ask what he meant, three horizontal shafts of lighting sliced across the inlet. Each one skewered a man standing on the stern platform beside the ladders grounded on the mud. Ripping straight through each man's chest, the lacerating brightness leaped onwards to the closest corsair. As those men died, the lightning bolts sprang on to kill the next and the next after that.

Before Corrain could shake off the tormenting recollection of Minelas murdering Captain Gefren and his comrades in these very marshes, the galley was rid of all the armed and armoured Aldabreshi. Their gaping wounds smoking, they sprawled dead and blackened from the stern platform all along the central walkway to the prow and its upthrust post.

'Now we find the gold,' Anskal gloated. Corrain followed him across the sodden earth and up the galley's stern ladders. 'Where?' Anskal demanded.

Silent, Corrain kicked a lightning-scarred corpse aside and hauled up the stern hatch. 'Down here.'

He went first, ignoring the mage's annoyance. If there were any Halferan women and children below, Corrain would see them brought up into the sunlight without any delay.

But no such good fortune offset all the calamities he had returned to thus far. The holds were empty of people. Instead, coin coffers were stacked waist high and topped with baskets filled with platters and cutlery, candlesticks and any other fine wares a household might boast of, wrought from silver or pewter. The black-bearded bastard and his gang had been plundering the Caladhrian coast far and wide.

Corrain opened the topmost of a slew of leather bags bundled together in sacking. He saw tangled gold and the glitter of gems; jewellery from the humblest ring cut from a dead woman's hand to necklaces once gracing the neck of a fine merchant's wife. Corrain threw the bag away. The thought of finding some festival gift that Lord Halferan had given Zurenne wasn't to be borne.

'Ah, I see.' Anskal pushed past him.

Sick at heart, Corrain turned back to climb the ladder, ignoring the Mandarkin's thanks. Setting his jaw, he walked down the centre of the galley, searching the benches on either side for any face that he might recognise among the terrified, cowering slaves. Fitrel hadn't been among the corpses on the road, nor yet Reven or fat old Captain Arigo.

But as Corrain looked with growing desperation, he saw the slaves chained to these oars were men as ragged and filthy as he had been, all bearing the old scars of long-standing captivity.

Anskal emerged from the galley's stern hatch. 'I find more silver and copper than gold.' He didn't sound too displeased.

'There will be plenty of gold in their anchorage.' Corrain brushed aside an irritating tangle of hair. The chain dangling from his manacle caught a knotted lock teased by the wind.

As he ripped it free, heedless of the stinging, he recalled that brash vow which he'd thrown at Talagrin's feet. Was that why Zurenne and her daughters had died? To punish him for all the insults he'd hurled?

Had Corrain's impiety been the death of Hosh as well, getting the fool boy killed for the sake of his escape with Kusint? Where was the Forest youth now? Had he made his way safely back to his own people in Solura or had some hostile Forest Folk waylaid him to steal the food and coin he carried?

Anskal was looking at the chained slaves. 'What of these?'

Was that compassion in the Mandarkin's voice? Numb with exhaustion, physical and mental, sickened by his failure to find any survivors from Halferan, Corrain couldn't find it in his heart to care. 'Do as you think best.'

Anskal shrugged and raised a hand. The slaves began to scream and weep, utterly terrified whether they were Archipelagan or mainland born. Some were trying to hide beneath their benches as if padded goat-hide could possibly save them from lethal wizardry.

The sharp crack of splitting metal echoed around the inlet. The slaves' yelps were cut short as they realised they weren't being harmed. As the first few sprang to their feet, Corrain realised that Anskal's magic had merely shattered their fetters, freeing their feet.

The closest to hand looked at the Mandarkin, wonder on their faces. Some of them clasped beseeching hands, not that Corrain or Anskal could understand their desperate pleading.

Anskal pointed at the stern ladders. As soon as they realised that they weren't to be killed, the rowers began to run.

Corrain stood aside, letting them flee. They'd soon lose themselves in the marshes. If they survived the quicksands and plunge pools, they could take their chances on the highways and byways. The mainland-born or those who spoke some Tormalin would probably meet with mercy. If the rest were slain out of hand for their dusky skin and incomprehensible tongue, that was surely a tragedy, but Corrain couldn't grieve for them. Not when he was already beset by so much heartbreak.

As Anskal came to stand beside him, Corrain realised some goodwife's cherished perfume was trying and largely failing to mask the reek of his unwashed body. The Mandarkin had also shed his rancid leathers for an Aldabreshin tunic, bright as a bankfisher's wing, and scarlet trews. The shore breeze tugged at the hem of a grey brocade cloak doubtless stolen from some village headman's festival clothes press.

Anskal was looking north and south as the anchored galley swayed at the whim of wind and water. 'There will be more ships along the coast.'

He had an inconvenient memory for anything Corrain said, whatever his lack of fluency in Tormalin.

'Perhaps but the highest tide was two, three days ago. They'll most likely have ridden the ebb out to sea yesterday or the day before.'

'This is the sea?' Anskal looked around the inlet. 'I had thought it would be bigger,' he commented, mystified.

'You've never seen the sea?' Corrain realised that was hardly a surprise, if Mandarkin was a country of cold mountains and northern deserts. No wonder talk of springing tides and ebbs would mean nothing to the mage.

'The sea is out there.' He pointed. 'Salt water, open water, from horizon to horizon. Can you catch ships so far from land that you cannot even see it? If you can, what will you do with your loot?'

He gestured at the thicket of salthorn where they'd been hiding. Anskal would know he was pointing to the dark scar beside the tangled stems. As soon as they had arrived, the mage's sorcery had summoned up his booty from Halferan so he could cache it like a squirrel hiding nuts for the winter. Or a Mandarkin scouting party preparing the way for an invading army.

Corrain shook his wrist to slide the manacle round and tucked the chain back up his sleeve. If nothing else remained, there was still vengeance.

'Go to their anchorage now and you'll take them all by surprise; those at anchor and those sailing home. You can have all their treasure.'

Anskal shook his head. 'We will see what remains on this shore.'

He snapped his fingers and a gout of water surged up from the inlet, sparkling in the sunlight. At Anskal's nod it fell into a waiting bucket. The Mandarkin gestured at the rowers' benches. Scraps of goat hide and matted tufts of cotton tore themselves free. At the sweep of his hand, they plunged into the bucket. The water shimmered and glimpses of mud, reeds and surging foam visions rippled across the surface, too fast for Corrain to see.

Anskal shrugged. 'As you say. No ships except burned like those.' He nodded at the blackened hulks.

'So will you take us to their haven?' More corsair dead was welcome news but Corrain wouldn't be satisfied until he saw the Aldabreshin anchorage choked with wrecked ships and every driftwood hut and oiled wood house razed to its black stone foundations.

That would be his oath fulfilled. Then he'd get rid of the shackle and shave his head, and after that? Once again, Corrain found he just couldn't care.

Anskal was walking the length of the galley to the prow platform. He laid a hand on the upcurved timbers but whatever he found didn't satisfy him. Scowling ferociously, he returned to the stern. Pushing past Corrain, he wrapped his bony hands around the steering oar.

His expression changed. Coming quickly to plunge his hand into the bucket, he studied the water intently. When Corrain tried to see what the sorcery showed, Anskal moved to block his view. He looked up; his eyes veiled, and said something harsh in his own tongue.

'You don't go without me!' Corrain reached to grab hold of the Mandarkin's cloak. Would that be enough to share in the spell?

Blinding oblivion enveloped him with that dizzying uncertainty over which way might be up or down. As the heat of the wizardry became the oppressive humidity of the Archipelago, Corrain smelled the unmistakeable stench of the anchorage. The white magelight faded to leave him blinking in the harsh sun. He had forgotten how bright Aldabreshin skies could be.

He breathed a little easier when he realised they stood on the headland on the southern side of the haven. They were well away from the main encampment and a good distance beyond the pens where slaves were held for the Archipelagan traders.

That relief was short lived. Corrain swallowed a shocked gasp when he saw how many ships lay at anchor. Not merely a flotilla of unknown galleys but a whole handful of triremes besides. The settlement had swollen grotesquely with these newcomers. With every scrap of greenery stripped from the shore, the ugliness of those makeshift huts was clear.

Corrain searched desperately for the *Reef Eagle's* pennant. The galley was nowhere to be seen. Perhaps the vessel was safely away on some trading voyage. Unless it had already fallen victim to Caladhrian vengeance.

Had Hosh been slaughtered out of hand with the rest of the *Reef Eagle's* slaves by some uncaring Tallat or Myrist sword? Then he was dead in Caladhria and that was some consolation. If he wasn't decently burned, perhaps he'd have his mother for company amid Poldrion's demons. Corrain hadn't found Abiath's body on the Halferan road but how could a frail widow woman hope to escape the corsairs?

Corrain's eyes stung. The breeze must be carrying more dust than usual with everything so dry.

'Who rules this place?' Anskal's eyes were darting everywhere.

'The master of that boat.' Corrain pointed without hesitation to the blind corsair's trireme.

Anskal flexed his bony fingers, his expression more feral than Corrain had yet seen it.

Scarlet flames sprang up all along the trireme's side rails. Not spreading like a normal blaze, nor even with the insidious speed of sticky fire. In that single instant, the entire boat was ablaze.

The sight didn't warm Corrain as much as it might have, even as the wind carried frantic yells across the haven.

'You must burn them all.' He pointed again and again. 'Every vessel with three banks of oars. Those belong to the worst thieves and murderers. Kill them first. Then sink the rest.'

Anskal didn't answer. He strode forward to the water's edge and knelt in the lapping wavelets, spreading both hands in the water. Magelight glowed murky green in the depths.

Corrain looked apprehensively at the settlement. The distant figures were running back and forth, not knowing what to do in the face of this unexpected, unprecedented attack. That would change in a heartbeat, if they realised where the wizardry stemmed from. Would Anskal's magic betray their presence all the way out here on the headland?

He gripped his sword hilt. Would the overseer, Ducah, lead the charge? It would almost be worth it, to see that brute's face again, for him to see Corrain with a blade in his hand. To know who had brought this unstoppable death and destruction to the raiders' liar. For Corrain to kill him.

Looking across the anchorage, Corrain saw that the blind corsair's trireme was wholly ablaze. The last few of those trapped aboard were jumping frantically through the flames in hopes of reaching the water.

No one ashore could have the slightest doubt that magic was attacking them. Each leaping figure, slave or corsair, was seized by a twisting tongue of crimson flame. They writhed in mid-air, arms and legs flailing, screaming in agony. The wind carried the sickly scent of burning flesh along with their cries.

What was the Mandarkin mage doing now? That emerald glow in the depths was fading rather than strengthening.

'They're leaving!' Corrain jabbed an urgent finger at the galleys all swarming with activity.

Anchors were hauled from the seabed or abandoned as overseers cut their ropes. Slaves were lashed to their benches, some flourishing oar blades, others already churning the water. Corrain winced. Though he couldn't see the blood running down the slaves' flogged backs, his own scars throbbed in sympathy.

'They're leaving! Can't you see?'

The galleys closest to the mouth of the haven were making ready to abandon those vessels hampered by the need to manoeuvre around their comrades.

The kneeling Mandarkin wasn't listening. Corrain reached for Anskal's shoulder. A massive blow to the chest knocked him off his feet. He lay flat on his back, more stunned with surprise than winded.

'They do not leave,' Anskal said, conversationally. 'I do not permit it.'

Uneasy, Corrain got slowly to his feet.

Anskal was telling the truth. Those galleys heading for open water were making no headway at all. Their way was blocked by a swelling wave taller than Halferan's baronial tower. Green as glass, its upper edge broke into an endless curl of foam without ever sweeping towards the shore.

Anskal grunted with satisfaction and turned his attention to the long low houses standing on their black rock steps. 'Where does he dwell, this ruler?'

As long as the bastard died, that was what mattered, Corrain told himself. 'The second one, over there.'

A thunderclap shook the anchorage. Out of the clear blue sky, a shaft of lightning skewered the building. Every shutter and door flew outward; splinters as long as a man's arm scything through the settlement's panicked denizens. Those who escaped death or injury fled in all directions.

The building's walls collapsed inwards. Cerulean magic crackled through the great cloud of dust. Tendrils darted outwards, dappled grey and cobalt. They seized those fleeing by the ankles. The only ones to escape the sorcerous bonds were those who flung themselves down in utter surrender, to lie prostrate or curled up like a child trying to deny some nightmare.

Those who struggled were swiftly punished. Each magic tendril cracked like a whip, snapping them up and down. Corrain winced, remembering how Ducah had once done the same to a snake. Thankfully at this distance he couldn't see if anyone's head had come off like the serpent's had.

'There are innocents there,' he protested.

Anskal shrugged. 'They must learn.'

'Learn what?' Corrain's unease was growing.

Anskal stood up, shaking glittering green drops from his hand. The impossible wave holding back the ships didn't falter.

'That I rule here now.'

'What?' Corrain's hand went to his sword hilt.

A crack of blue light sent a shock of pain searing up his arm. He didn't need to draw the hilt to know the blade was shattered into uselessness. He couldn't have done so anyway. He couldn't have closed his numbed fingers if his life depended on it.

Anskal was smiling cheerily. 'You promised me gold and jewels and all my wants met. I see I can have that here and slaves of my own to serve me. I will be a good master,' he promised. 'They will not raid your shores again, not while I rule.'

'This wasn't what we agreed.' Corrain wondered if he could reach across for his belt knife without Anskal noticing. Perhaps if the Mandarkin turned his back. Could Corrain throw the narrow blade hard enough and true with his off hand to do more than wound the mage?

Was taking that chance worth the certainty that he'd be dead before he drew his next breath? Worse, Corrain was forced to conclude, the knife would surely shatter or melt or vanish in a puff of smoke before it even grazed the Mandarkin.

Was there a wizard breathing who wasn't treacherous scum? Was there any other way he could kill the double-crossing swine? Corrain didn't care if he died doing it, as long as he succeeded.

'Among my masters, an agreement no longer stands if one finds that the other has lied.' Anskal might have been having an amiable conversation over a flagon of ale in a tavern.

'I haven't lied.' The denial was out before Corrain could be quite sure. He had been guilty of so much deceit over these past seasons.

Anskal's face hardened. 'You said they had no magic.'

'What?' This accusation made no sense. 'These people abominate wizards. They will kill you as soon as they can.' The warning was out before he thought better of it.

Anskal shrugged. 'So you say. Why should I believe you?'

Corrain shut his mouth and looked away. He'd never thought this day would come, but now he hoped that Ducah had survived. Saedrin send the brute the right stars to slit the Mandarkin's throat. This very night, for preference.

Sooner or later Anskal would have to sleep to regain the strength to work his astonishing magic. Corrain had seen that for himself.

'What are you going to do with me?' He couldn't help his voice thickening with hatred. 'Am I your slave now too?'

Anskal looked genuinely surprised. 'I owe you my life. I do not forget my debts.'

'Then what?' Corrain's gorge rose at the prospect of being kept here as the mage's lackey.

Though if he was, he could search for Hosh—

That feeblest of consolations was ripped away. The wizard's magic wrapped him in white light and Corrain's hands and face were burning. Was that some punishment from Anskal or a warning?

He'd barely had time to ask himself that question when his feet thudded onto the ground. As the fiery light faded, the full agony of his blistered skin was nothing to the anguish that seized him.

Anskal had sent him back to Halferan.

— CHAPTER FORTY —

Halferan Manor, Caladhria
24th of Aft-Summer

THE CARRIAGE HALTED with a jerk. Zurenne looked across to Ilysh and Esnina sitting close together on the opposite seat, Lysha's protective arm around her sister.

'Whatever we see, however bad it may be, we will not give Lord Karpis the satisfaction of seeing us distressed.'

She kept her voice low lest someone overhear beyond the carriage's thin wooden door. They owed Lord Karpis that courtesy, for his hospitality these past dozen days.

For his wife's sake anyway. Kindly and practical, Lady Diress had seen them bathed, clothed and comforted without any word of enquiry or reproach over whatever had been said and done during these past few seasons.

She'd even come from her own chamber one night, with soothing tisanes and aromatic candles when Neeny's nightmares had overwhelmed Zurenne's efforts to calm her.

'Yes, Mama.' Ilysh managed a fleeting smile and laid her free hand over Esnina's tight-laced fingers.

The little girl sat silent as she did so often now, eyes huge in her pinched face.

'Where will we go, my lady, after—' Raselle's question faded away.

The nearer they had drawn to Halferan, the more Zurenne had wondered if the maid would shuffle up on the seat they shared, to press close to her for comfort, as Esnina had done to Ilysh.

She held out her hand and gave the maid's fingers an encouraging squeeze. 'The hunting lodge at Taw Ricks, remember?'

As reports had come in through these past ten days from the Halferan survivors and Lord Licanin's men, they had learned that the corsairs had overlooked that most easterly of the barony's residences. Lord Karpis's scouts had confirmed this too. There was nothing which Zurenne could say to stop them riding wherever they liked now, under the pretence of lending a hand with this essential survey of Halferan's suffering.

That said, she was grateful for his armed guards bolstering Licanin's ranks on this journey today, even at the price of having both those noble lords riding alongside her carriage. Even if those scouting parties were reporting no sign of corsairs or their ships, there were persistent rumours of vagabond bandits lurking in the marshes.

Zurenne knew she must be grateful lifelong for the Karpis troopers who'd charged down the highway during her family's escape, driving off the pursuing corsairs before their headlong flight had taken them more than a league from Halferan.

Several stable lads had got through with word of their plight and Baron Karpis, or rather, his captains, hadn't hesitated to saddle up and ride out. They had arrived just as Zurenne had given up hope, after Jilseth had vanished so shockingly.

'Taw Ricks.' Raselle's forced smile was wholly unconvincing. 'Of course, my lady.'

Zurenne didn't blame the maid for such a lack of enthusiasm. She had only ever visited the cramped and aging building at the turn of Aft-Summer to For-Autumn, to celebrate the rites honouring Talagrin and to acknowledge the tithes paid by the local villages. Her husband had been far too willing to overlook its inconveniences on his more frequent visits with horses, hounds and guests to share in the thrill of the chase.

She blinked away the faint threat of tears. 'We will soon see the lodge refurbished. Mistress Rauffe and Jora and the others will have already made a start.'

Hopefully. If being set this task for the living could drag their grieving thoughts from all those who had died in their nightmare flight from the manor, Jora's mother and father among them.

Zurenne fought to stop her hand shaking as she reached for the carriage door handle. All those murdered here and out on the road had been decently burned. Licanin's men had promised her that. There would be no dead faces to reproach her. They would only appear in her nightly dreams.

'My lady.' The door opened and Master Rauffe pulled down the folding step.

Lord Licanin offered his hand to help her down. 'Zurenne.' Then he stood in front of the door to bar Ilysh's way. 'The children must wait in the carriage,' he said sternly.

'Mama?' Ilysh looked past him.

Zurenne lifted her chin. 'My daughter is Lady of Halferan in her husband's absence. She should see what's become of her inheritance.'

Everyone heard the contempt in Lord Karpis's wordless exclamation, unconvincingly turned into a cough.

Licanin shot him an impenetrable look before narrowing his eyes at Zurenne. 'That will be for the parliament to discuss, if Captain Corrain fails to return before the Equinox. In the meantime, you will ruin her future prospects if you allow this scandal to spread.'

All the same, he stepped aside and allowed the girls to leave the coach. Raselle followed close behind.

Zurenne saw Ilysh's face harden, refusing to yield to whatever emotions she felt. She heard a murmur stir the Halferan guards and could readily guess at its meaning. The girl had seldom looked more like her father.

Esnina was too young for such fortitude. Her little face crumpled as she looked around. Raselle hurried forward to gather her into her arms, muffling the child's wailing in her embrace.

Up on his horse, Lord Karpis coughed again. 'There is nothing to be gained by picking over this rubble. Get into your carriage, my lady, and you should make Taw Lodge by nightfall.' He recalled his own troopers to their well-drilled ranks with a gesture of his riding crop.

'Lady Ilysh.' Zurenne held out her hand, seeing that her daughter's hard-won poise was in dire peril. 'Let us pay our respects at our shrine. Raselle, please sit with Esnina in the carriage.'

Zurenne's first glimpse of the courtyard had shown her those accounts of utter devastation had told no more, or perhaps, rather less, than the brutal truth. Only the shrine still had its roof. What devastation lay beyond its closed door remained to be seen.

Would the shrine ledgers be there? Zurenne could have slapped herself for a fool. Why hadn't she thought to grab those before their headlong flight? She had to have some written proof of Ilysh's clandestine marriage, if she were to stand the faintest chance of persuading the barons' parliament that Lord Licanin's grant of guardianship should be considered afresh.

Did she even have until Equinox? From what Lady Diress had said, a great many barons were calling for an extraordinary summons of the parliament, despite the coastal lords' reports of the galleys burned by their valorous captains and the daily reassurance from scouting parties that no more corsair ships had been seen on any horizon. Just these past few days, so Lady Diress had said, Baron Karpis had received letters from merchants in Pinerin and Claithe, claiming that the raiders had abandoned the sea lanes running along the Caladhrian coast between Col and Relshaz.

Zurenne stole a glance over her shoulder at Lord Karpis. If Licanin's grant was challenged, whenever the parliament assembled, he wouldn't hesitate to propose himself as Halferan's most logical guardian. For all her kindnesses, Lady Diress had behaved as if that question were settled by the mere fact of Zurenne's arrival beneath their roof.

Ilysh's hand gripped her fingers painfully hard as they approached the shrine's closed door. Zurenne opened it awkwardly with her off-hand. She wasn't about to shake Lysha loose.

'Oh, Mama!' Ilysh's voice broke on a sob of distress.

The shrine hadn't burned like the great hall, though the inner door was grievously charred around the edges. But some great shock had jarred the gods and goddesses from their plinths. Statues had toppled this way and that, their heads, arms and feet lying broken on the floor.

Not all the funeral urns had fallen from their shelves but most of those to survive unbroken had fallen over, their covers lost. Their contents had poured unhindered down to mingle with the haphazard fragments scattered over the cracked tiles. The draft from the doorway stirred the drifts of ash, filling the shrine with a pale haze.

Zurenne cleared her throat. 'Your father has long since passed safely to the Otherworld. That's what matters most. We will see this shrine resanctified. Let's make that vow together, in his name.'

Now she did take her hand from Ilysh's, trying not to wince as fragments of plaster and gritty ash crunched under her sturdy shoes. What remnant of her husband was she trampling underfoot?

She took the soiled linen cloth from the shrine table. Drianon be thanked, the box holding the shrine ledgers was underneath. The lock had been forced but when Zurenne lifted the lid, she saw the leather-bound books were intact.

'Call Master Rauffe,' she said to Ilysh. 'That needs to go in the carriage. This can stand as token of our vow.' She walked swiftly to the door and knotted the linen through the ring of the handle.

'Yes, Mama.' Ilysh turned on the threshold. As she did, she gasped.

'What is it?' Zurenne hurried to join her.

A column of sapphire light shone in the centre of the courtyard, as tall as a man and seemingly no thicker than a single hair.

Standing behind her daughter, she wrapped the girl protectively in her arms. As Ilysh looked up, Zurenne realised her child was taller than she was now.

'Mama? Is that magic?'

Curiosity distracted Ilysh from her distress. Zurenne could even see Esnina peering open-mouthed from the carriage window.

Before Zurenne could reply, several figures stepped through the azure magelight, one after another. She recognised Jilseth at once and one of the other two. The unassuming, bearded young man with an unfortunately weak chin was unknown to her but the curly haired girl with Tormalin features had appeared in Zurenne's bedchamber in Karpis Manor, barely a chime after their chaotic arrival.

Merenel, that was her name. She had assured Zurenne that Jilseth was safe in Hadrumal. Zurenne had wanted to scream at the lady wizard. Why had she and her innocent children not been rescued? She had restrained herself. What was done was done.

Besides, Halferan owed Hadrumal a debt of gratitude for that uncanny darkness sliding up and down the troopers' swords, making the merest touch of a blade so deadly. Despite all those who had died on the road, the survivors would never have escaped without it.

'My—' Zurenne released Ilysh from her embrace and led the girl forward to curtsey at her side. She addressed herself to Jilseth with a determinedly courteous smile. 'Madam mage.'

It was plain the lady wizard had suffered in her own way. Her face was drawn and sallow, the whites of her eyes unhealthily clouded.

'Lady Zurenne.' Jilseth took a step forward from her companions. The shaft of blue behind her flickered. 'Lady Ilysh.' She inclined her head respectfully to the girl. 'I am so sorry for your distress, your own and the barony's.'

Zurenne heard Lord Karpis hurriedly stifle that false cough as Jilseth looked affronted at his mockery. For a fleeting moment, she savoured the thought of his humiliation at a wizard's hand again. No, they had far more important concerns.

'Might I hope for some assistance from Hadrumal as we rebuild? She gestured at the ruination. 'Labouring by hand, we'll be lucky to clear the ground before For-Winter.'

There could surely be no argument. Wizards had helped with raising half the great halls in Caladhria, if baronial lore was to be believed.

'By all means.' Jilseth smiled. 'We can also offer you far more immediate and practical help.'

She turned to that searing blue light and another figure stepped through it. He was an older and far more robustly built man. He had to be. He carried a bound and gagged figure slung over one shoulder.

'He tried to make a fight of it.' The newcomer dumped his burden on the dusty cobbles.

As the man found his footing, Zurenne belatedly recognised him. So did a great many others, judging by the astonished whispers hissing around the courtyard.

'Master Starrid.' Zurenne let everyone see her contempt.

The unassuming young man stepped forward. 'We have also recovered the coin which this scoundrel stole from Halferan, as well as the revenues embezzled by the thief and deceiver Minelas.'

The young wizard's words were pure Caladhrian and of the noblest blood besides. That prompted more whispers among the dumbfounded troopers.

'Baron Licanin. Baron Karpis.' He bowed to the lords in turn, unabashed at being the focus of such shameless curiosity.

Zurenne honestly wondered if Karpis was about to fall victim to apoplexy. His complexion was the colour of the crumbling bricks heaped on all sides.

Licanin was swifter to recover. 'You have me at a disadvantage, my lord?'

'Master Nolyen of Hadrumal, these days.' He smiled. 'I imagine you've met my father Baron Pardal at some parliament or other.'

Was that somewhere up near Duryea? Zurenne hastily gathered her wits. While Master Nolyen had been talking, the heavy-set wizard's gestures had summoned successive iron-bound coffers to make an impressive stack in the courtyard.

'We will stow your funds wherever you want, my lady Zurenne. Or keep the coin safe in our own vaults, to be brought forth as and when you need it.' Quizzical, the older mage contemplated the gaping hole by the baronial tower. 'You seem to have the most remarkable rats if they can dig holes like that.'

The roar of laughter that swept the courtyard was out of all proportion to the joke, prompted far more by relief and unlooked-for hope.

Zurenne allowed the merriment to run its course before she replied. 'My thanks, Master—?'

'Tornauld,' he supplied, in an accent straight from Ensaimin's markets.

'Master Tornauld. We will let you know.' After smiling at Ilysh, Zurenne looked boldly at Karpis. Let him mock now if he dared.

'What do you want to do with this offal?' Tornauld shoved Starrid's shoulder, sending the erstwhile steward stumbling forward.

Close-linked manacles secured his hands behind his

back. He showed no sign of mistreatment; his clothes were clean and tidy, quite unlike his appearance in Jilseth's scrying.

Nevertheless Zurenne wondered what magecraft had been wrought around him or on him. His eyes bulged, white-rimmed, above the clean and efficient linen gag. She was glad of that. She had no interest in anything he might say.

Once she had wanted him hanged, she recalled distantly, with him knowing she was there to witness it. Not anymore. Not after all that she had endured. What was to be gained by another death, even the loss of a life as utterly worthless as this one?

She even felt a pang of compassion. Starrid was staring at the ruins of his former dwelling. Behind the gag, his face twisted with grief.

'Why?' Zurenne realised this was the only thing she wanted from the wretch. 'Why did you betray my husband's memory?'

The linen unknotted itself from Starrid's mouth, prompting a shiver around the courtyard. He looked blankly at Zurenne. 'I never betrayed my lord. But when Master Minelas came and Lord Halferan was dead?' Some colour returned to his pale cheeks. 'Why shouldn't I take some recompense? I had worked hard and done my best and my only reward was always being told I was never good enough.'

Now, absurdly, he was growing angry with her, even as he stood there in chains with the threat of wizardry hovering over him.

'I never betrayed my lord but he made a laughing stock of me.' Starrid spat out a linen thread. 'He should have whipped that Corrain from these gates for making me a cuckold. Not just dropped him down to ride as a trooper, all winks and enjoying his favour just the same at every season's turn.'

'You had wronged your wife first.' Zurenne remembered Halferan's anger. 'Everyone saw her bruises.'

Starrid stared at her, uncomprehending. 'Why shouldn't I do as I saw fit inside my own doors? She belonged to me. She was nothing—'

Zurenne couldn't tell which of the mages promptly gagged Starrid with the linen again. She was merely grateful.

Could it really be that simple? This stupid, selfish man had taken out his petty resentments on her and her daughters, for the sake of whatever wrongs which he imagined he had endured at her dead husband's decree?

Zurenne found that profoundly depressing, even amid the ruins of her home. Then she realised that particular rune definitely showed two faces. This knowledge was unexpectedly liberating. She had no faults to answer for here. She owed nothing more to this mean-spirited sneak-thief. She could spend her energies on those who deserved it, freely and guiltless.

'As long as he quits the bounds of Halferan, I have no interest in punishing him further.' She dismissed Starrid with a gesture of absolute finality. 'If he sets foot in the barony again, then his life is forfeit and any man who takes it may claim his reward from me.'

The murmur which that provoked among the troopers satisfied Zurenne that her words would soon spread far and wide.

'He is not welcome in Karpis,' the baron said swiftly. 'Any man seeing him should whip him on his way.'

'And in Licanin.' The grey-haired lord's expression led Zurenne to suspect similar decrees would follow the length and breadth of the realm once the Caladhrian parliament next met.

Old Fitrel stepped forward, unconsciously squaring his shoulders as he addressed the wizard Tornauld. 'By your leave, master mage? The keys?'

Tornauld grinned and the shackles simply dropped from Starrid's hands. Zurenne could swear she heard him whimper even through the linen gag.

'You can be on your way,' Fitrel said with relish. Seizing Starrid by the elbow, he propelled him towards the village road and the highway beyond.

Acknowledging Karpis and Licanin with a brief nod, Jilseth came over to Zurenne and Ilysh. 'We'll leave you to set about your business.' She handed them each a silver necklace. A triangular sigil of their birth runes hung from the fine chain. 'Hold the pendant tight and say my name. Then I'll know you wish to speak to me.'

'My thanks.' Zurenne could say nothing else, given that she would have to take up the merchant wizard's offer to keep Halferan's wealth in Hadrumal.

She looked at the coffers of coin and wondered exactly how much gold and silver they held. There did seem to be rather more of them than she recalled in Halferan's strong rooms. Were the wizards paying her recompense for Minelas's crimes? If so that was all well and good. They should help with more than merely the practicalities of clearing up this devastation.

She caught sight of Baron Karpis, thin-lipped with dissatisfaction. Let him try claiming dominion over Halferan, Zurenne thought with rising courage, when she had the means to summon advocates like that noble Caladhrian wizard so readily to hand.

'My lady! My lady!' Fitrel came running back through the roughly cleared wreckage of the gatehouse. 'My lady! It's the captain! It's Captain Corrain!'

— CHAPTER FORTY-ONE —

Halferan Manor, Caladhria
24th of Aft-Summer

CORRAIN VERY NEARLY turned tail and ran. The shock
of seeing Starrid shoved out into the road was only
surpassed by his disbelief at hearing Fitrel shouting as
he ran back inside the walls. Then he heard what the old
man was bellowing.

He was calling out to their lady. Zurenne was alive?
Corrain's unwilling feet forced him closer. He saw the
assembled men and horses, the Halferan coach in the
desolation of the courtyard.

Then he saw the wizards. The lady wizard Jilseth and
three more besides. Corrain stumbled to a halt, transfixed
by the shimmer of magelight. He couldn't go on. He
couldn't retreat. He could only stare at the unearthly
radiance. He didn't even glance at Starrid when the man
staggered past, fleeing towards the high road leading to
the woods and beyond.

'Corrain? Lad? Where have you been?' Fitrel was at
his side, all anxious solicitude. 'Poldrion forgive me, but
we'd given you up for dead. Again!' The old man tried
for a grin to make a joke of his words.

Corrain couldn't manage a hint of a smile, nor any
attempt at reply. What a fool he'd been, to come back. He
should have foreseen the possibility of finding someone,
if only a stray tenant salvaging bricks for rebuilding.

He hadn't really thought where his feet were taking him. What did it matter? Not a jot, once he'd walked out to Siprel Inlet and discovered that greedy Mandarkin, Anskal, had already used his magic to collect the treasure he'd cached in the mud. Corrain couldn't even reclaim that fragment of his honour. He had hoped to share out the coin somehow, to salve Halferan's hurts in their dead lord and lady's names.

He should have kept on walking northward, to Ensaimin and beyond until oblivion claimed him in some distant wilderness. What a fool he had been. If he had never come back, if no one had seen him, they could have believed him safely dead. There was no hope for that now.

But Corrain couldn't find it in him to resist as Fitrel led him inside the ruined manor. Incredibly, he saw Lady Zurenne and Lady Ilysh standing hand in hand close to the shrine door. He blinked, unable to believe the sight before him.

'My husband!' The girl's triumphant cry rang back from the manor's enclosing wall.

Amid the stir around the courtyard which that claim caused, Corrain only had eyes for Zurenne. He walked slowly towards her. This felt like a dream. Surely he would wake to find himself cold and stiff in the marshes. Unless everything dissolved into the nightmares that pursued him as relentlessly as Poldrion's demons, when he finally sank into exhaustion every second or third night.

'Where have you been?' Zurenne looked at him, mystified. 'What have you done?'

The words came unbidden. 'My best. My oath.'

Shocked to hear himself speaking, Corrain clamped his jaw shut. This wasn't a dream. He wasn't about to admit to all that he had done this summer.

Not in front of a gaggle of mages studying him with keen interest. If the lady wizard Jilseth looked fit to drop, those other three looked as sharp as freshly honed blades.

Corrain's wits felt as dull as a jug handle. How utterly deluded he had been, to ever imagine he could outwit a wizard.

'Where is your companion?' Zurenne looked to see if anyone followed him. 'Kusint?'

'Gone back to his own folk, my lady.' Corrain managed to force out that half-truth. Could he tell Zurenne the whole of it, once they were alone? He quailed at the thought of her disappointment and of her contempt when she learned what depths he finally had stooped to.

Lord Licanin stepped forward, his gaze penetrating. Corrain hadn't even registered his presence. 'What of— your ambitious plans when you took that galley northwards? To save us all from the corsairs?'

Licanin knew, Corrain realised. He knew that Corrain had promised to bring back a Soluran wizard, believing that Hadrumal's mages were no more use than a broken reed.

Corrain saw Zurenne colour as she looked apprehensively at Licanin. The grey-haired baron didn't see. He was looking covertly at Lord Karpis. Karpis looked merely bewildered by this turn of events.

Those wizards flanking Jilseth were regarding him with close interest. What did they know? Corrain had no notion, and why were they standing beside a whole stack of strong boxes? That was a puzzle and a half. Were they buying Lady Zurenne's silence about all Hadrumal's offences against her with the coin to rebuild Halferan?

Corrain cudgelled his sluggish wits. If Karpis didn't know of Corrain's boastful intention to find a wizard and bring back salvation, then he must not betray Zurenne's agreement to that foolhardy endeavour.

'I did what I could, my lady.' He stared into her eyes, hoping she would read something of his efforts into those lame words.

'You told my captains how the corsairs ride the tides. You told them where to trap them.' Lord Karpis spurred his horse forward. 'That's all well and good and we have chased them off for now, but the sailing season is far from over. What have you to say to that?'

Corrain could hear the fear in the man's voice. Much as he would have liked to leave him prey to doubt, he saw the same dread in Ilysh's eyes.

He managed a faint smile for the girl. 'They won't be back.' Anskal had promised him that much and the Mandarkin mage did owe him his life, never mind any gratitude for the gold he'd won.

'How can you be certain?' demanded Zurenne.

Corrain choked on the prospect of admitting what he'd done. Besides, with any luck, Anskal was already dead. He groped for another half-truth.

'The rainstorms that come up from the south will reach their islands any day now, and besides—' he broke off as Ilysh's gasp of relief pierced him to the heart.

'Thank you.' The girl held out her hands.

She looked so like his dead lord that he couldn't bear it. Corrain sank to his knees. His legs could no longer support him. He pressed Ilysh's soft hands to his forehead and wept.

— CHAPTER FORTY-TWO —

'Is HE A broken man?' Planir's query wasn't without compassion.

'That remains to be seen. He is mightily humbled.' Jilseth was waiting for the Archmage to ask if she were a broken wizard. Not that he'd ever be so tactless, but she was increasingly convinced that was the essence of her situation.

Planir leaned back in his comfortable chair. They were in the Archmage's private sitting room. Jilseth had no doubt that any rumours about the two of them spending time behind closed doors now would have nothing to do with him tumbling her.

She'd put her money on Ely if anyone was taking bets on who exactly had betrayed her current distress to the fascinated gossips of Hadrumal's wine shops.

'There's no rumour in Caladhria of any magic being used against the corsairs.' Elbows on the chair's arms, Planir steepled his fingers. 'Rafrid, Tornauld and Canfor haven't heard so much as a whisper, not even in Halferan.'

'Corrain hasn't even told Lady Zurenne or her daughter what he did. He says he went to Solura but claims that he couldn't find a wizard to help him.'

The pendants were enabling Jilseth to listen to every conversation which Zurenne or Ilysh might have. So far she had heard a mind-numbing quantity of tedious irrelevance about the defects of the Taw Ricks hunting lodge and infuriating indecision about precisely how the ruins of Halferan manor should be made good again.

Jilseth wasn't about to protest to the Archmage. For now, this was all she was good for. Until her magic returned to its former strength, unless her magic returned in any significant measure, she was reliant on her nexus support to work the most trivial wizardry.

Even her own element seemed to have failed her. Before, she would have revelled in unravelling the earth-wrought spells which Planir had crafted into those silver pendants. Now she had no more hope of doing that than Canfor.

'If we do hear any such rumour, we'll have to deny that Hadrumal was involved,' Planir smiled with bleak humour, 'naturally in such a way to make everyone think entirely the opposite. As many problems as that might cause for us, with everyone from the Emperor of Tormalin down, it will probably be preferable to the mainland powers and princes knowing the truth.'

'There are those who know the truth.' Jilseth was troubled by that. 'The Forest lad who was travelling with Corrain, and those Soluran wizards. They must suspect that he's responsible for the corsairs disappearing from Caladhrian waters so completely and unexpectedly. At worst, they will have been scrying after him and seen what he's accomplished in the Archipelago,' she concluded with disgust.

'I am beginning to suspect the worst,' Planir admitted. 'Neither Hearth Master Kalion nor I can get any of the Elders of Fornet to agree to us paying a visit, even before we tell them what we would like to discuss. Not that we would have very much to discuss. I imagine they will see anything short of us ousting this Mandarkin wizard as a direct insult.

Jilseth nodded. 'The last Soluran alchemists left on this morning's tide, taking ship for Col.'

They had been unhelpfully vague about exactly how and when they had been summoned home.

'Which means we're waiting for the Elders of the Soluran Orders to make the next move.' Planir's eyes strayed to the white raven game table over by the window. 'Or their king.'

'Unless the Mandarkin acts first.' Jilseth readied herself to stand up. She was still so unutterably weary that even such commonplace actions took their toll.

'A moment longer of your time, if I may.' Planir was looking at the mantel shelf over the hearth. 'You say that Lady Zurenne ordered that all the funeral ash from the shrine be swept into one reliquary. I've been thinking I could devise some magecraft to separate those remains, so that she might set an urn in her shrine for Lord Halferan once again. Do you think she would welcome such an offer?'

Jilseth could see that Planir was looking at Larissa's funeral urn and remembering his own dead lover. She told herself that he didn't intend any cruelty, reminding her that her most prized talent, her necromancy, was as lost as the rest of her magic.

'I believe she would, Archmage.' Jilseth allowed herself a small glow of triumph. If she couldn't control her magic, she could still control her voice.

Planir remained lost in thought, his brow creased. 'I think I will bespeak Usara and Shivalan.'

That startled Jilseth out of her own preoccupations. 'In Suthyfer?' What could anyone in those remote islands have to offer? Halfway across the ocean on the far side of distant Tormalin, they were stepping stones to those wild lands which the Emperor was so keen to see colonised in order to enrich his people.

'There are precious few wizards of Hadrumal with any direct experience of using their magic in battle.' Planir sat up straight. 'Even fewer who survived the experience,' he added bitterly.

'Those who drove off the Elietimm?' Jilseth had wondered if she'd ever hear that story but that wasn't her most immediate concern. 'You really think we will have to fight this Mandarkin mage ourselves? To placate the Solurans? Is it so vital to mollify them?'

For a sickening instant, she felt relieved. As long as her magic hadn't returned, she wouldn't be one of those wizards called upon to attack the Mandarkin mage. She wouldn't have to risk the humiliation of being found wanting.

Or run the risk of succeeding and having to live with the knowledge that her magic had wrought more death, as it had on the road from Halferan. No, Jilseth thought savagely. Not even that was worth the price of living the rest of her life without wizardry.

'The Solurans aren't my concern. Not yet. But this Mandarkin is bound to make trouble sooner or later. Once he's grown tired of indulging himself with whatever he's found on that island, he will need to release those corsairs he's got penned up, to find him more food and wine or whatever other entertainments he fancies.'

Planir shook his head, his exasperation coloured with grudging respect. 'I don't hold out much hope of us getting wind of his plans in advance, not given how effectively he can hide himself from even a nexus scrying as well as from all those Aldabreshin who'd love to sneak up and cut his throat in his sleep.'

Troanna, Ely and Nolyen were taking that as a personal insult. Jilseth could have been amused if it hadn't been so serious.

'It must be a perilous life,' she observed, 'to be a wizard where he comes from.'

Planir nodded. 'I'll ask Usara to pass my compliments to Aritane and see what she can tell us of Mandarkin.'

'Aritane?' The name meant nothing to Jilseth.

'The *sheltya* woman?' Planir raised his brows in surprise when Jilseth shook her head none the wiser.

'They're akin to priests among the Mountain Men, as well as law makers and enforcers of those laws through their unparalled command of Artifice,' the Archmage explained. 'We offered this woman Aritane sanctuary in Suthyfer after she had offended against her own people's strictures on using aetheric magic for personal gain.'

He waved a hand. 'In truth, the whole affair was considerably more complicated and so we were glad to offer Aritane a refuge, for the sake of her knowledge of *sheltya* Artifice which she could share with Lady Guinalle and the other adepts in Suthyfer.'

Because the proper study of mages is magic, and as Jilseth was realising, this Archmage saw no reason to limit his studies to elemental wizardry.

She nodded. 'I remember.' Or more accurately, now she knew enough to go and ask the rest of her nexus what they knew of this woman and her history. She was puzzled nevertheless.

'Do the Mountain Men have much to do with the Mandarkin?'

'More than anyone further south,' Planir said frankly, 'and I would like to hear other opinions to set in the balance against Soluran hatreds.'

As he broke off, Jilseth was sure he'd been about to say something further.

'The islands of the Archipelago are far closer than those of Suthyfer,' she observed. 'You don't think that the Aldabreshi will move against the Mandarkin mage themselves?'

'Let us hope so,' Planir said frankly. 'If I knew of a way to encourage that, without seeing my own hide nailed to a gatepost, I'd be sailing from domain to domain myself and offering a reward. Though that doesn't address the problem of how anyone gets a knife into the Mandarkin's throat while he weaves such complex spells of protection all around himself.'

'Merenel said—' Jilseth hesitated. 'I believe Hearth Master Kalion is trying to devise some way of unravelling another wizard's magic through a nexus scrying.'

She wasn't telling tales like Ely. Kalion wouldn't be working on something so outrageous without Planir's full knowledge and consent. Jilseth wanted to see if Planir shared her own misgivings at the thought of such a thing.

Instead, he grinned. 'The Emperor of Tormalin told me some seasons ago, how the challenges of all this exploration over the ocean is driving advancements in metalworking, in shipbuilding, in almost any craft you can name, clear across the realms that once made up the Old Empire. Do you suppose he imagines the same will be true of wizardry, if this Mandarkin mage does decide to challenge us?'

'So you think he will?' Jilseth asked, uneasy.

'We may hope not, but we'll plan for every eventuality.' Planir regarded her over his steepled fingers once again, his grey eyes opaque. 'Since, as I think we'll discover all too soon, this business is very far from over.'

— CHAPTER FORTY-THREE —

As Hosh picked his way through the ironwood stumps, he realised that an Archipelagan was coming towards him. Not heading for the bloodstained circle of stones where so many of the terrified corsairs were seeking omens amid all this unforeseen calamity. The man was heading directly towards Hosh, his expression intense.

'You there, broken-face slave,' the stranger rasped, one hand on the hilt of his curved sword. 'Stand!'

What else could he do? Hosh stood motionless. As he waited he wondered who this man might be, other than a raider from one of the galleys trapped in the anchorage by that impossible wave.

Hosh thought that the wave was beautiful. Not only because it was keeping all the corsairs penned up and unable to rob helpless Caladhrians. Where it caught the sunlight, it shone like the emerald necklace which he'd once seen Lady Zurenne wear, a festival gift from Lord Halferan.

The ever-changing foam at the top reminded him of the pearl studded bracelet which his long dead father had given his beloved mother on their wedding day. Marsh pearls of course, small and irregularly shaped. Nothing like the smooth and lustrous pearls from the southern reaches of the Archipelago. Like the one the raider who was approaching him was wearing on a chain threaded through one ear.

'What do you want with him?'

That was Ducah's bellow, hostile as ever. Where was the brute? What had Hosh done to enrage him? Nothing that he could think of but that made no real difference if Ducah had chosen his victim for the day.

Then Hosh realised with a shudder of relief that Ducah wasn't hailing him. The brute was striding towards the strange corsair; a copper-skinned Aldabreshin with angular scars gouged into each arm.

'You have some quarrel with the *Reef Eagle*?' Ducah's sword was already drawn.

Once again, that was no surprise. Hosh had lost count of how many men he'd seen Ducah kill.

The scarred man sneered. 'My master's business is no concern of—'

Ducah swung a lethal blow at his head. The scarred man recoiled, snatching for his own hilt. Ripping his blade free of its scabbard, he blocked Ducah's stroke, just barely. That did him no good.

For such a massively muscled man, Ducah was both light on his feet and deft with his hands. He turned his rebounding sword with an agile twist of his wrist. The blade swept back in low to bite into the scarred man's thigh.

The newcomer staggered backwards, his riposte robbed of its strength. Ducah swatted his curved sword aside before thrusting his blade deep into the scarred man's belly.

'No!' As he gasped with futile denial, the unknown Aldabreshin let his sword fall unheeded. Sinking to his knees, staring down in disbelief, he clutched at Ducah's blade in some last desperate impulse to deny his own fate.

The brute ripped his sword away, slicing one of the dying man's fingers clean off. That wasn't an end to it. Ducah drove the tip of his blade into the hollow of the raider's throat. The dead man's eyes bulged, blood gushing from his mouth. He choked voicelessly, his windpipe severed.

Ducah wrenched his sword free one last time to hack the dead slave's head from his shoulders. It bounced past Hosh before the rest of his corpse toppled forward to hit the ground beside him.

Hosh had already dropped to his own knees. Now he pressed his forehead to the sandy soil. There was no point in saying anything. If Ducah had decided to kill him, then he was already dead.

Ducah grunted with satisfaction and edged the point of his sword under Hosh's sparsely bearded chin. 'Who is your master?'

Hosh had to raise his head or have his throat cut. Ducah's relentless blade forced him upwards until he was sat back on his ankles.

'I serve Nifai who serves Serdi who is master of the *Reef Eagle* and thus is my master.' Hosh contemplated Ducah's bloody sword and sincerely hoped that somewhere in there he'd offered the reply which the bare-chested brute was seeking.

He had noticed Ducah and the wily overseer standing with their heads close together for a good long while the previous evening.

Ducah grunted again. 'Come with me.'

Hosh walked helplessly after him. They headed for

the *Reef Eagle* pavilion. That was unexpected. All these houses and the driftwood hovels between them had been abandoned for fear of the apparently all-powerful wizard. No one wanted to suffer the same fate as Grewa's household.

Today, Hosh noted, the sparkling veil of wizardry hung around the *Red Heron's* pavilion. The wizard was moving from dwelling to dwelling as the fancy took him. The only constant was that shimmering mist that no Aldabreshin arrow, spear, or sticky-fire pot had been able to penetrate.

Ducah led Hosh around to the back and the kitchen steps. Nifai was sitting on the lowest black stone stair. He looked up sharply as Ducah explained the blood on his sword and trews. The overseer looked at Hosh.

'What were you doing wandering so close to the sorcery?' he demanded.

Hosh wasn't about to explain he'd come to enjoy the sight of the magical wave. 'I was looking for omens across the water,' he mumbled. That was surely a valid excuse, with everyone else on the island frantically searching for guidance.

'No,' Nifai said emphatically. 'You will stay within sight of me or Ducah at all times. Do you understand?'

'I do.' Hosh ducked his head and wondered what this was all about.

Apart from the wizard's arrival, obviously. That had thrown the whole anchorage into uproar.

Nifai leaned forward. 'What do you know of this mainlander magic?'

Hosh could see the dread in his eyes as well as Nifai's undoubted intelligence questing this way and that for some advantage over the rest in this fearsomely uncertain situation.

'I know some stories of wizards.' With this near-hysterical horror of magic swirling around the anchorage, Hosh wasn't about to admit to anything more than that. Contamination was a word he'd heard on all sides. Some of those who'd survived the destruction of Grewa's pavilion had already been killed out of hand, for fear of some taint of sorcery clinging to them.

Besides, what he'd said was mostly true. Hosh had only heard tell of magecraft until that appalling day when Lord Halferan was murdered. He looked out to sea. That impossible wave didn't look quite as beautiful as it had before.

'You will tell us all that you know,' Ducah growled.

'Of course.' Hosh wasn't about to argue. Not when he could see that apprehension was making the bare-chested raider more prone to violence than ever.

Nifai studied Hosh before speaking further. 'This mainlander will surely ask to speak to those of us he has trapped here, sooner or later. You speak his tongue. You will speak for us, for the *Reef Eagle*.'

'Of course.' He was hardly going to refuse.

Nifai stood up. 'Very well. Now stay here.'

With a nod, he walked a short way off with Ducah. Hosh heard a snatch of their low-voiced conversation. They would learn all they could of mainlander magic from Hosh. Then they would send him to talk to the wizard, if no summons came before the Amethyst moved into the arc of Death. Hosh was already tainted with sorcery, what with being mainlander born, but since he was mainlander born, there was no risk of the contamination spreading to either of them.

If it turned out that the wizard killed Hosh, that would be a loss but there must be other slaves who spoke the mainlander tongue. In the meantime they could keep him safe by the pavilion, well away from anyone else who might want to kill him or worse, make use of his mainlander knowledge for themselves.

Hosh made sure his expression stayed suitably hangdog. That was surely appropriate after being told to stay here like some errant hound.

Inside, he was exulting. He wanted to know everything this wizard could tell him. How many galleys had he sunk? Surely the summer's losses were now all explained. Hosh particularly looked forward to hearing how the corsair with the gold chains in his beard had died.

Always assuming he could find some way to get through that silvery mist. There was every chance he'd end up approaching it with the point of Ducah's sword in his back, Hosh didn't doubt the bare-chested raider would cut his throat if he tried to retreat instead of facing the magic.

He turned at the sound of footsteps up at the top of the stone stair. It was Imais. Hosh was astonished to see her here when everyone else had run away as far as they could on this little island.

Then he saw she was carrying that tall glass jar with a spray of canthira leaves tied inside it. Once again, that made sense for the Aldabreshi. The Canthira Tree stars had risen on the eastern horizon two nights ago.

Imais took a cloth bag out of a pocket in her loose cotton trews. Hosh saw it buck and squirm. A mouse to go in the jar. He sensed rather than saw the malevolent brown scuttle of the scorpion beneath the leaves.

'Is that the same mouse?'

'Same?' Imais looked at him, curious.

'The mouse you put in the jar with the vizail blossom. What happened to it?' Hosh found he desperately wanted to know.

Imais smiled. 'Mouse lived. Scorpion died. A very good omen for you. So Nifai asks me to see what happens under these stars.'

Hosh's face must have shown his sudden distress.

'Different mouse,' she assured him. 'I loosed the other.'

Hosh nodded mutely. He didn't trust himself to speak, not with Ducah and Nifai within earshot. He couldn't watch Imais drop the newly caught mouse into the perilous jar. He walked towards the corner of the building instead, gazing across at the *Red Heron* pavilion.

Who was going to live longer, he wondered. Him or that mouse?

ACKNOWLEDGEMENTS

This past year has seen the unexpected death of my father in law, Ernie. A man of many talents, he lived life to the full, through eighty one years that took him from a farm labourer's cottage in rural Oxfordshire to travels all over the world as a professional motorsport and commercial photographer. In retirement, he was as active as ever, with a busy social life and always involved in the local community. He was also a key part of the support network that's enabled me to write these books.

My thanks to all the family members and friends who've supported us through this bereavement. This book wouldn't have been written without you.

My thanks to Jon, David, Jenni and Ben at Solaris, for their understanding and sympathy and for making sure I had the leeway to make this a book we can all be proud of.

More than ever, I'm grateful for the camaraderie of my fellow writers, for my wonderfully keen fans and for all those SF&Fantasy enthusiasts I meet at conventions and other events.